Praise for *A Wedding in Springtime*

"This clever combination of wit, romance, and suspense strikes all the right notes... This entertaining novel is a diamond of the first order."

—*Booklist* Starred Review

"Engaging subplots involving unforgettable supporting characters make this one a must-read."

—*Publishers Weekly* Starred Review

"Forester promises her fans a warm, humorous jaunt through Regency England—and she delivers with a cast of engaging characters and delightful intrigue."

—*RT Book Reviews*, 4 Stars

"Amanda Forester gives us likable characters, snappy dialogue, and sweet, sweet romance."

—*Drey's Library*

"A delightful, fun, sweet, all-around fabulous read."

—*Book Savvy Babes*

"Full of humor, mystery, intrigue with a good dose of romance... you won't want to miss this entertaining and captivating tale. This is historical romance at its finest."

—*Harlequin Junkie*

Also by Amanda Forester

The Highlander's Sword

The Highlander's Heart

True Highland Spirit

The Highland Bride's Choice (novella)

A Wedding in Springtime

A MIDSUMMER BRIDE

Amanda Forester

sourcebooks
casablanca

Published by Sourcebooks Casablanca, an imprint of Sourcebooks, Inc.
P. O. Box 4410, Naperville, Illinois 60567-4410
(630) 961-3900
Fax: (630) 961-2168
www.sourcebooks.com

Printed and bound in the United States of America.
VP 10 9 8 7 6 5 4 3 2 1

To my family and friends, who accept me as I am.
And to Ed, who makes me believe I'm even better.

Prologue

Off the New England coast, 1810

THE SHIP WAS GOING DOWN. AND SINCE SHE WAS ON said doomed vessel, the situation was most inconvenient.

The ship's normal sway across the water ceased and it began to list to the port side. Harriet and Nellie had taken refuge in their cabin when the enemy frigate began to fire. Now the shouts and shots and clangs of battle raged on the main deck above them.

Harriet held tight to the bunk, trying to steady her balance and her nerves. Her father was a renowned American sea captain and had once told her he laughed in the face of battle. Harriet was a long way from laughing, but she was determined to keep a level head.

"I am sure it will be well," soothed Harriet, trying to think of something comforting to say to her long-time maid, Nellie. Neither lady believed it.

"Trouble, the both of you," muttered Nellie. "You're just like your mother, you are."

"You cannot possibly blame this on me," defended Harriet. "All I wanted to do was go to New York to meet my parents. I have no idea where that English frigate came from."

All became deadly quiet and the ship's list became more pronounced. Harriet's pulse raced. She had been on ships all her life, though never in a sea battle, and this movement of the ship was unknown to her. It scared her in a way that sickened her stomach. The only thing between them and the ice-cold waters of the Atlantic Ocean was heading to the bottom of the sea. If they didn't want to go with it, they needed to get out of their cabin and abandon ship.

"We must get on deck," said Harriet with what she hoped was calming cheerfulness.

"No! We'll be killed," gasped Nellie.

"Sounds like the battle is over. Hopefully we will find our dear Captain Wentworth has repelled these English scum. But either way, we need to get to the decks." And find a lifeboat. She spared Nellie that last concern, the poor woman was terrified enough as it was. Truth be told, so was she.

Harriet scanned the cabin. To her dismay, much of her equipment had been thrown to the floor in the battle. Many of the glass vessels had shattered, but some items were salvageable. The ship listed further to port side, sending more books toppling off the shelves.

"If we are going to leave, we should do it." Nellie was right of course, but Harriet could not leave her work behind.

"Let me just grab a few things." Harriet scooped up a copper alembic, her mortar and pestle, several metal vessels, and a small box furnace and placed them in a blanket from her bunk, tying them up to form a carry pouch.

Clutching her precious equipment, Harriet led Nellie through the narrow passageway, which proved difficult. Furniture and stores and belongings had been thrown about, and they were forced to crawl over the debris and up the steep narrow stairs to find the main deck. Harriet had to use some muscle to clear enough of a path, but the thought of being trapped on a sinking ship was more than enough motivation to get her in the mood for a bit of exertion.

After some struggle, she reached daylight and slowly peeked out of the hatch. The main deck of their merchant brig was unrecognizable. The main mast had been struck and hung down at an odd angle; the canvas sails and rigging now littered the deck. The English warship was lashed to the side of their vessel. Much to Harriet's distress, English sailors had taken command of their ship and were forcing the American sailors into a line.

This was supposed to be a quick sail from Boston to New York, where she would join her parents. How could it go so wrong? And why would an English ship attack them?

Captain Wentworth saw them and gave a quick shake of the head. He did not wish them to be seen. Harriet moved back into the shadows, out of view.

"This is an outrage," Captain Wentworth shouted, a bright-red patch growing on the outer thigh of his white pantaloons. "By what right do you attack this merchant vessel? We are an American ship!"

"You are harboring deserters from His Majesty's

Royal Navy," said an English officer. He wore a blue coat with one gold epaulet on his right shoulder, which Harriet guessed marked him as the captain. Though why he would attack an American vessel so close to their own shores was unknown to her.

"These men are all American citizens," said Captain Wentworth.

"These men are all able-bodied sailors and are needed for service. Congratulations, men, you have hereby volunteered for service in His Majesty's Royal Navy."

"This is outrageous!" bellowed Captain Wentworth. "You cannot press these men into service."

"I get paid by the head, my dear captain," said the English captain. "So yes, I can and will press these men into service. All except these two." He pointed at two sailors. "These two I know have served in the navy before and have deserted their post. They shall be hanged from the yardarm as traitors."

"No!" Harriet dropped her bag and charged on deck before she could consider the advisability of her actions. She knew these sailors and could not stand by and allow them to die. "These men are American citizens. Jimmy and Pat may have served in your navy in the past, but they are Americans now. You have no right to enter judgment against them. Besides, Patrick is not even English. He's Irish!"

"Good afternoon." The English captain took off his hat with a swoop and gave her a bow. "How lovely of you to join us. Unfortunately for your case, the Royal Navy does not recognize American citizenship, let alone see that as a justification for shirking military service. And frankly I could not care less whether this man is Irish or not. Discipline must be maintained."

"You cannot attack and board an American vessel and press her sailors into service. You cannot possibly do that. You are nothing but a pirate!" Harriet was outraged. Utterly. She glanced at Captain Wentworth and saw fear in his eyes.

Only then did she recognize her own predicament was dire. Traveling with Captain Wentworth, a long-time friend of the family, should have ensured a safe passage from Boston to New York, safer even than an overland journey. Harriet was accustomed to traveling by sea, but there was another, uglier side of sailing from which she had always been protected.

She had stumbled upon it now.

"Piracy is a serious charge. Fortunately, I am only following orders." The English captain gave her an unholy smile, cracking his weathered face. "I believe introductions are in order. I am Captain Beake, and who might you be?"

"This is Miss Harriet Redgrave, daughter of Captain Redgrave and Lady Beatrice." Captain Wentworth spoke with authority.

It had been a long time since anyone had called her mother by her title. In America, Harriet's mother was simply Mrs. Redgrave, and by all accounts happy to be so. In England, she was the daughter of an earl, a man she fled when she was just seventeen years old.

"Lady Beatrice?" Captain Beake's tone was doubting, mocking even.

Harriet had never touted her aristocratic pedigree, she never had cause to want to be anything other than her father's daughter. But now it was important to more than just herself to gain a modicum of respect from the English captain.

"I am the daughter of Captain Redgrave and the granddaughter of the Earl of Langley." Harriet squared her shoulders and met the English captain's eye, daring him to doubt her.

"Are you now?" The English captain scratched his chin. "Perhaps I should return you to your grandfather. He must be concerned for your welfare."

"I am sure he would reward you for delivering her to him unhurt." Captain Wentworth emphasized the last word.

Harriet shook her head, but Wentworth glared at her, his lips a thin line. He directed his gaze at the broken mast, the ominous black clouds, and then the ocean. His message was clear. The ship was going down and the weather was coming up.

"Captain Beake," Harriet said with what she hoped was authority. "I will accept your generous hospitality to be restored to my grandfather on one condition. You will not harm Jimmy and Pat." Harriet gave him the look she saw her mother wear only in times of great annoyance or peril. Her father called it the "societal setdown" and said it was a look perfected in the cradles of all aristocratic tots. Harriet hoped she could mimic her mother well enough to make up for her otherwise unconventional upbringing.

"I don't know why you should be in the position to make orders," grumbled Beake, but with a quick nod, the two sailors were released. "I shall leave them to deal with the weather. Honestly, a quick death may be preferable to drowning, but I am always at the service of a lady."

"Remember, no harm must come to her, or Lord Langley will hunt you down and have you and every man of your crew tortured unto death," warned Captain Wentworth.

Harriet made no comment to this patent untruth. In the twenty-three years she had been alive, she had never heard from her grandfather. The only thing she knew was that after her mother eloped with her father, Lord Langley had disinherited his daughter and refused to have any contact with them since.

The rest of the scene played out like a dream. Her trunks and Nellie's smaller bag were brought on board the English vessel, along with most of the American crew. Harriet did feel a little safer to be surrounded by men she knew, for while they were a little rough at times, they could be trusted. Jimmy, Pat, and the American officers, including Captain Wentworth, were left behind on the sinking ship.

"Be safe!" she called to the men.

"We shall make it back to land and alert your parents," said Wentworth, as bold a liar as he was a captain.

She stood at the stern and watched the American brig sink beneath the waves as she sailed away. She prayed for the safety of each man, many of whom she had known her entire life. The sun set over the place of her birth and she watched the land grow farther and farther away until the horizon was covered by black storm clouds.

When there was nothing left to be seen, she staggered through the driving rain to the bow and glared in the general direction of their destination. England. The land her mother had fled. How would her grandfather react when she arrived?

It was only darkness ahead.

One

"So we have a deal?" Duncan Maclachlan, Earl of Thornton, handed a quill pen to Lord Langley, trying not to let his enthusiasm show. Being a generally reserved man, it was not a difficult task to accomplish.

"Yes, we do." Lord Langley dipped his pen in the ink and signed his name to the contract. "I look forward to working with you in the future."

"As do I." Thornton breathed deep. This transaction was definitely going to help his situation. The financial crisis was becoming dire. "Have ye plans to leave London for yer country house?"

"Yes, yes, I suppose I should." The elderly Lord Langley leaned back in his chair, his bulk making the chair squeak in protest. "I do not wish to travel, but staying in London for the summer, that would be even worse. And yourself? Do you have plans for the summer?"

"House party."

Lord Langley grimaced. "Not for me. Too much bother. All those children running about."

"Children?"

"Such as yourself. Those young bucks can be irritating beyond words, and the young ladies are far worse."

Thornton smiled. "Then I fear ye would despise my summer plans. The Duke of Marchford asked me to host a house party at Thornton Hall in Scotland."

"All the way to Scotland? No, too far, odd notion."

"He is my friend and I am always pleased to be in his service."

"Had to, eh? Him being a duke and all. But who will travel all that way?"

"He is a duke…"

"Ah yes, and in want of a wife." Langley shook his head. "The hills will be crawling with young ladies come to take their shot at the biggest prize in all of Britton. Oh, I don't envy the young, no I surely do not."

"Youth is a crime age will correct in time."

"And what of yourself? You also are of unmarried status and in possession of a title. You best take care of your own neck, lest you find it in the matrimonial noose as well."

Thornton only smiled. He could not even begin to think of matrimony until he had resolved his financial difficulties.

"You best be double cautious if Marchford's grandmother will be attending." Langley got a wistful look in his blue eyes. "The Dowager Duchess of Marchford is a woman you would do best not to cross. I've heard she has contacts with a matchmaker."

"I've heard the same."

"I fear you may be in someone's sights."

Thornton merely shook his head. As an impoverished

Scottish earl, he was not at liberty to take a wife. Ironic in a way, since he was not opposed to the institution of marriage as his friends proclaimed to be. Yet unlike them, he found conversing with the female of the species challenging, which was just as well, since his restricted pocketbook forbade ladies of any variety.

A banging on the front door could be heard all the way in the library and interrupted the conversation. The butler arrived shortly after to inform his lordship that a Captain Beake and a young lady had arrived to beg an audience with him. No card was presented.

"What? Never heard of him. Send him on his way," demanded the earl.

"Very good, sir. I only bring it to your attention because the lady claims to be a relation of yours."

"Got all the relations I need. Don't need any more poor relations crawling out of the woodwork trying to get their fingers on my money."

The butler paused and cleared his throat. "The young lady claims to be the daughter of Lady Beatrice."

Silence fell heavy on the room. Lady Beatrice was Lord Langley's only child. At the age of seventeen, in a scandal still discussed by society matrons with malicious enjoyment, Lady Beatrice had run away with a sea captain—an *American* sea captain—never to be seen again.

Naturally, everyone assumed Lady Beatrice was mad, for what young woman of sane mind would elope with an American sea captain? Poor Lord Langley tried to hush up the scandal by saying he had her confined to an asylum, but everyone knew the truth.

"These imposters." Lord Langley sat down hard on his chair. "Every once in a while I have someone pretending to be Beatrice come 'round the house trying to steal money from me. Someday they will murder me in my bed."

"I will send them away, my lord," said the butler.

"No," Langley sighed. "Curiosity and hope are the bane of men. Send them in."

"Shall I stay to ensure yer safety?" asked Thornton, a trifle curious himself.

"Yes, that would be appreciated. Thieves, naught but thieves. Stay and be a witness to my demise."

"Try to keep yerself from murderers at least until our transactions are completed," commented Thornton with a touch of humor to lighten the moment.

"All heart you are," muttered the old man, but the edges of his mouth turned up.

The butler escorted in two persons of dubious quality. The first was a man whose life was etched in the lines on his face. His tanned features revealed him to be a man of action; his eyes squinted, as if still staring into the sun. His blue coat marked him as a sea captain, and he looked every bit of his occupation.

The second person was a lady in a simple muslin dress, wool coat, and pelisse that had seen better days. Under a ragged bonnet, her auburn hair was pulled back in an efficient manner and her most striking feature was her height, about the same as her male companion's.

"Captain Beake and Miss Harriet Redgrave," intoned the butler, as if apologizing for their presence in the room.

"What do you want?" snapped the Lord Langley. "You'll get no money from me."

The sea captain appeared slightly taken aback by

this pronouncement. "This lady, Miss Redgrave, presented herself to me as your granddaughter, the daughter of Lady Beatrice."

"I told you, Captain Beake, that I have never met my grandfather. He would not know me," said the lady with an unruffled calm that was intriguing, considering her situation.

"Ah, but what grandfather would not know his own flesh and blood? Why, you are the smitten image of him." Captain Beake attempted to make his case.

"I do not believe the correct turn of phrase is 'smitten' image, Captain Beake." Miss Redgrave glanced away with such disdain that Thornton immediately saw the likeness between her and Lord Langley. Could it be true?

Lord Langley's eyes opened wider and he stared at Miss Redgrave for a long moment. "Where are you from, Miss Redgrave?"

"America. Boston. This gentleman, and I use the word loosely, attacked my ship, pressed innocent Americans into service to the British Crown, and abducted me here. My only aim is to return to America on the next ship home. My parents will be frantic with worry."

"Ah yes, what bonds there are between parent and child, and even greater bonds between a man and his only grandchild." Captain Beake gave the room an oily smile. "So much so, I'm sure we can negotiate the price of reward for returning the little miss to you unhurt and unmolested."

Lord Langley's eyes narrowed. He stepped toward his desk and put his hand on the box of dueling pistols.

"You can have no business with me, Captain. I will bid you a good day."

"Ah, but perhaps I did not make myself clear." Captain Beake tugged at his blue coat as if he was about to make a speech. "I protected this young maiden on the voyage. On this ship there are many men, no? I made sure to protect her innocence."

The innocent Miss Redgrave snorted. "Protect me? You kidnapped me!"

"Good day, Captain," growled Lord Langley, his eyes ablaze, his hand gripping the box. "A good day to both of you."

"The least you can do is compensate me for the burned timber!" demanded Captain Beake. "This chit almost set the ship ablaze what with her mad experiments. Odd goings on, if you ask me. Had to lock her trunks in the hold to protect us all."

"The voyage was very long," defended Miss Redgrave. "You cannot expect me to abandon my experiments just because you got the notion to sink my ship. Besides, the fire was mostly contained by the time you found it."

Thornton had no idea what to make of this interchange, and for a moment, it appeared neither did Lord Langley, who merely stared at the two persons before him.

Seizing the opportunity, Captain Beake once again pressed his case. "You see, she admits she started the fire. Some compensation must be in order—"

"Out!" thundered Langley. "If you kidnapped this young woman on the high seas, I most certainly hope she caused you as much trouble as possible. A good day to you, sir!"

"Do a good deed, see how you are rewarded," grumbled Captain Beake as he shuffled out of the room.

His movements were followed by two sets of cold eyes, so similar that Thornton glanced back and forth between Miss Redgrave and Lord Langley to confirm what he was witnessing. The appearance of a grandchild to the Earl of Langley.

"You can go too, you imposter." Lord Langley leveled his disdain at Miss Redgrave. "How dare you play on the sympathies of an old man?"

"Sympathies?" Miss Redgrave countered. "I have not heard my mother ever mention you in the same breath as the word 'sympathy.'"

"Do not talk about the Lady Beatrice as if you were worthy to lick her boots. You are naught but a scheming female, trying to weasel away my money. I have met some conniving females trying to walk away with a portion of my blunt, but you want to be recognized as my heir and steal it all!"

Miss Redgrave's green eyes flashed. "I have no interest in your wealth. I have no need for your precious money. I know you have had no contact with our family for many years, but I thought you might at least have some consideration for your own flesh and blood."

Langley stood with his hand still on the box of pistols, so Thornton did not quit the room, though now he was not sure whom he was there to protect.

"You'll never get ahold of my money! You have no proof you are my granddaughter!" charged Langley.

Miss Redgrave's mouth formed a thin line. "Could

you ask the butler to bring in my trunks and ask my maid to step in?"

Thornton wondered what Langley would do, but the request was granted. "Curiosity," muttered Langley under his breath.

Silence fell while they waited for whatever entertainment Miss Redgrave might be able to produce, giving Thornton an opportunity to study her. At first he assessed whether he thought her capable of posing any threat, but he rejected the notion. She stood with her back to the door, not in a defensible position, which would have been instinctive for a would-be marauder.

Miss Redgrave was certainly tall, and with her serviceable wool coat and tanned face, her appearance gave the impression she was more interested in practicality than beauty. Yet he had to admire her pluck. Despite her position, she stood up to both a captain in the Royal Navy and a peer of the realm without flinching, a feat most men could not boast. She radiated an outward calm, yet he could see her white knuckles where she clenched her hands, betraying her nerves.

Despite his role as protector to Lord Langley, Thornton felt a sudden urge to reassure her. If she had truly been abducted all the way from America, she must have had a most difficult voyage.

Two trunks were brought into the study, one so heavy it required two footmen to carry it. Lord Langley allowed this, most likely out of curiosity about what she could produce. Thornton also suspected the man feared he was in the presence of his errant daughter's child.

"I do not know who you are, sir," Miss Redgrave addressed Thornton in a brisk businesslike manner, "but I have something of a sensitive manner to show his lordship."

"Of course," said Thornton, as disappointed as the ejected staff to not see what she had in her trunks. "I shall bid ye farewell."

"Stay," commanded Lord Langley. "What if there is something in the trunk to hurt me?"

Thornton felt it time to introduce himself. "I am the Earl of Thornton, at yer service, Miss Redgrave."

"A Scotsman, are you?" Her tone was approving, not like most who could barely hide their disappointment once they discovered Thornton's earldom was located in wild Scotland.

"Aye."

"You are a friend to my grandfather?" Her tone indicated a clear disapproval.

"Business partner," he explained, surprising himself with how quickly he abandoned Lord Langley to his fate in order to win her approval.

She smiled at him and her face came alive. Without warning, his solid, methodical heart skipped a beat.

Two

HARRIET REDGRAVE HELD HER HANDS TOGETHER SO NO one would notice how they were shaking. She had feared her meeting with Lord Langley would not go well, but somehow she had harbored hope that she would find him kind and understanding. Unfortunately, she now understood why her mother had taken flight.

They waited in silence, her grandfather in mute disapproval, his friend, or guard or business partner, standing by his side. If there were a prize for tall, dark, and brooding, Lord Thornton would win it. With his short black hair and gray eyes he made for an imposing figure. What he was thinking she could only guess, but she feared not much escaped his gaze. She clasped her hands together harder. She would not show weakness.

Nellie Bowler entered and made a polite curtsy to the esteemed personages assembled in the room.

"Nellie!" exclaimed Lord Langley. "Is it you?"

"Yes, Your Grace, it is I," said Nellie.

"But how… how is this possible?" Langley stuttered.

"I went with my mistress," said Nellie simply.

"You went with Beatrice? You went *with* her?" Langley's tone rose higher. "All this time I thought you ran off in shame, and now I learn that you helped my own daughter, my only daughter elope. With an American! How dare you ever show your face here again?"

"I am here with Lady Beatrice's daughter." Nellie's tone was even, but her voice was an octave higher than usual and Harriet could tell she was rattled.

"The point of Nellie being here is not so you can chastise her, since she is so far out of your employment as to be irrelevant, but to demonstrate to you who I am," said Harriet, hoping to turn Lord Langley's fire away from her maid.

Bushy eyebrows clamped down over Langley's eyes. His mouth formed a firm line. "Even if you have Nellie here, why should I believe a word either of you say? How do I know you both did not concoct this story to cheat me out of my money?"

"For the last time, I do not wish for your money." Harriet shook her head as if reprimanding an errant child. She went to one of the trunks, unlocked it with a key from her reticule, and pulled out a smaller case. She opened the case with a separate key, producing a leather pouch. She thrust the pouch at Langley. "Open it!" she demanded.

Lord Langley did so cautiously, as if the contents might jump out at him, but suddenly he became quite interested and pulled out a handful of gold coins, inspecting them in the light.

"My name is Harriet Redgrave." Now that she had his attention that fact bore repeating. "My mother is

Lady Beatrice, my father is Captain Redgrave. The sea has been good to my father; he has taken many a ship, many an English ship, during the war for independence. I have no need of your money, Lord Langley. I have quite enough to carry on my own."

"Your father would let you carry a fortune in gold unprotected?" asked Langley.

"No! I was not unprotected. I was being escorted by a dear family friend, Captain Wentworth, to meet my parents in New York. They initially had planned a short visit, but my father was recently offered a position with the United States government. Since they would be living in New York for a while, I went to join them and I packed everything I would need, including my laboratory equipment and some funds from the family vault."

"Laboratory equipment?" Thornton asked with a raised brow. It gave her a strange tingle, the Scottish lilt to his voice. She wished he would talk more just to hear it.

"I am an amateur scientist in the new field of chemistry," explained Harriet. "Though my visit to London is unplanned, I do hope I can meet some of the scientists that heretofore I have only read about in their published papers." This pronouncement was met with silence, as it usually was. Harriet sighed. Her scientific interests were generally met with blank looks. She had hoped perhaps it would be different in a more elite set in London. It was not.

"I cannot see this as anything more than a wild tale. I will grant that you have imagination, but nothing more will you win from me." Langley folded his arms across his chest.

"I would be willing to sign papers relinquishing any claim on your inheritance immediately," declared Harriet. "Besides, would not my older brother be heir, not me?"

"Beatrice has a son?" Langley asked Nellie.

"Four of them, all strapping lads, and of course Harriet here," replied Nellie.

"Five?" Langley sat down hard in his desk chair, as if overwhelmed by the weight of the circumstances before him. He shook his head, as if fighting off belief. "No, no, I will not be fooled."

"If I may suggest," Lord Thornton said in his rich, earthy tone. "Miss Redgrave, do you have any items from Lady Beatrice? Any letters? Something that connects you to her?"

Harriet opened her other trunk to retrieve her mother's last letter to her. She had read the happy missive several times during her voyage to England, hearing her mother's cheerful voice and wanting to believe someday they would be reunited.

"This letter is from my mother." She handed it to Lord Thornton. She was glad he was here since he seemed to be an impartial judge in the situation. Despite having just met the man, she felt he was someone she could trust.

Thornton opened it and Langley stood to read the letter beside him.

"It is signed 'Your Affectionate Mother,'" accused Langley. "It could be from anyone."

"Is this your daughter's handwriting?" asked Thornton. "Do you have any old letters from her?"

Lord Langley stilled and his head bowed, as if he had been caught committing a crime. He sighed and went to a wall of books. He pulled out what looked to be some large volumes but actually was a false front. From behind it, he pulled out a locked trunk and placed it on his desk. Everyone in the room stepped closer, wondering what was in it.

Langley took a key attached by a small chain to his watch fob and unlocked the trunk. He looked up at Harriet for a moment, opening his mouth as if to speak, but closed it again and shook his head. He opened the trunk and stepped back, allowing the others to see what was inside.

"Unopened letters?" Thornton peered inside.

"Unopened letters from my mother!" Harriet grabbed a handful and shoved it at her grandfather. "Did you never even read her letters?"

"As long as the letters kept coming, I knew Beatrice was alive," Langley said weakly as he lowered himself into his desk chair.

"You never wrote her one letter and yet all these years she continued to write to you," Harriet said in a soft voice. "What a good daughter she is to you."

Langley took out his handkerchief to wipe his eyes and blow his nose.

"May we open one of the letters to compare the writing?" asked Thornton, getting back to the business at hand.

Langley nodded and Thornton opened the most recent letter. He spread out the two letters side by side on the desk.

"The writing looks the same to my eye," stated Thornton.

Langley took a deep breath and nodded.

"What are these boxes?" Harriet pointed to the small packages stacked neatly in the trunk to the side of the letters.

"I never opened them," said Langley in a small voice.

"Perhaps it is time," suggested Thornton gently.

Langley nodded and opened one of the packages. It was a small miniature in a gold frame, featuring a drawing of a young man.

"Why that is Matthew, my oldest brother," declared Harriet.

The next three packages produced miniatures of her other brothers, Mark, Luke, and John. "My mother was influenced by biblical names," explained Harriet. "I do not know where 'Harriet' came from."

Langley opened the last package with shaking hands. He looked carefully at the miniature then clasped it to his chest.

"Is it me?" asked Harriet softly.

Lord Langley nodded. "Harriet was the name of my mother."

❧

After a heart-wrenching acceptance between Lord Langley and his long-lost granddaughter, Thornton felt it was long past time for him to remove himself from the scene. Harriet's maid also indicated she should present herself to the servants hall, and everyone walked out into the entryway. Lord Langley excused himself for a moment to find the housekeeper to arrange a bedchamber for Miss Redgrave and Nellie followed him, leaving Thornton momentarily alone in the entryway with Miss Redgrave.

These were moments he dreaded. Alone with a young lady. Particularly after the emotional exchange he just witnessed, the usual topics of banal conversation seemed even more awkward. Weather? No. Refreshments? No. Politics? Definitely not. General compliment on appearance?

Thornton searched her person, looking for an easy target for a compliment but came up short. He was far from being a connoisseur of fashion, but even he could tell there was nothing remarkable about her coat or bonnet. Yet she had just been through an ordeal and the silence was growing. Something needed to be said.

"It must be nice to be so verra tall," he blurted. Tall? Had he just commented on her height? It would have been better to say nothing.

Instead of being offended, she gave him a slow smile. "Yes, I am tall. Most people pretend not to notice. My father and brothers are even taller than I, so I do not feel so out of place." Much to his surprise she walked closer and stood next to him shoulder to shoulder. "You are even taller than I."

"Aye." His heart raced. She was very close. It was actually nice for once to have a lady be more at eye level. He was taller than most men and towered over the women of his acquaintance, but here was a lady he could talk to without feeling freakishly large.

"It is nice to find a man with height to him. It reminds me of my family." There was a sadness about her mouth when she spoke.

"You must miss them," he said.

"Very much." She blinked as if fighting back a tear. Thornton was touched. Unlike most societal ladies who presented an air of poised disinterestedness, Miss Redgrave's emotions were apparent and raw. It gave him courage to speak from his heart as well. "Ye have been verra brave to face such adversity, not to mention standing yer ground against Lord Langley."

Miss Redgrave's shoulders relaxed as if freed from burden and she graced him with another smile. "Thank you. You are very kind. I am fortunate that you were here tonight. I doubt my grandfather would have listened to me had you not been the voice of reason." She reached out and shook his hand. "Thank you."

Thornton was surprised by the gesture and feel of her bare skin against his own. Her hand was surprisingly delicate and cold.

"Yer hand is so cold," he said in a voice so low it was almost a whisper. Instinctively he enclosed her hand in both of his to warm her.

"I was more nervous than I should like to admit," she said in a soft voice.

"Here we are now, everything is ready," bellowed Lord Langley, entering with the housekeeper following behind.

Thornton dropped Miss Redgrave's hand and jumped back as if he had been caught molesting her.

Miss Redgrave dropped him a curtsy and followed the housekeeper up the stairs to her bedchamber.

"Thank you for keeping her company for a few minutes," said Langley with a smile. Thornton was relieved Langley had either not seen the handshake or was not concerned by it.

"I am pleased ye have been reunited with yer family," said Thornton politely.

"Can't lose her too," mumbled Langley, glancing around to make sure Miss Redgrave was no longer within sight. "No, I shall learn from past mistakes."

"Past mistakes?" echoed Thornton.

"Beatrice. Should have married her off as soon as it was legal. A wedding would have kept her close to home."

"I am no' sure marriage—"

"Marriage!" interrupted Langley. "That is what we need."

"Whose marriage?" Thornton was lost.

"Harriet's marriage of course."

"Did she not say she would return on the next ship to America?"

"Need to act fast, good thinking." Langley rubbed his hands together. "What about your house party, my lad? Might be just the thing to find her a husband."

"Ye be welcome if ye wish, but—"

"Good, good. I have a chance to redeem my reputation here. I shall have her married to a lord at the very least, or a duke, or maybe even a prince." Langley looked him up and down like he was choosing a horse at Tattersall's. "Even a Scottish earl might do," he muttered.

Thornton edged toward the door. "I shall bid ye a good night."

Langley cast him a conspiratorial grin. "I will see the girl married respectably this time. And you're going to help me do it!"

Three

HARRIET AWOKE IN A STRANGE, ORNATELY DECORATED bedroom, and it took several moments to remember where she was. It all came back in a tumbled heap. She had been accepted by Lord Langley, introduced to the servants, given a hastily prepared welcome dinner, at which she sat at the far end of a long table from her grandfather. They ate in silence with no less than four footmen in attendance. At the end of that odd charade, she had been given her mother's old bedroom, where she took her first opportunity to write a letter to her parents, and gratefully fell asleep.

Despite everything that had happened, many of her thoughts circled around one man, and it was not her elderly grandfather. Lord Thornton factored prominently in her thoughts and even her dreams. She had never before been so afflicted, and was not sure what to name this growing interest in a man she had only just met.

True, Lord Thornton was a handsome man, and true he had been kind to her. Perhaps it was simply finding a friend in a strange land that had her so captivated. That must be it. Yet she found herself anxious to meet her "friend" once more.

"I see you are awake." Nellie bustled into the room with a wide smile. "Well now, such doings I don't know what to make of it. They gave me my old room, can you imagine? Haven't slept in that bed since I was a young girl."

A bit bemused by her maid, Harriet accepted the offered dressing gown. Nellie had been working for the family since before she was born. She knew Nellie had come over from England with her mother, but honestly she had never given it much thought. Everything in London was new to Harriet, but to Nellie it was coming home.

"I suppose we should make our way to the docks and book passage home," said Harriet without much enthusiasm. She was accustomed to sailing short trips with her father, but the passage across the Atlantic was not something she relished repeating. And yet, there was only one way home.

Nellie scrunched up her nose. "His lordship will send a man down to do that for you. If you don't mind me saying, things are different here in London. Ladies do not visit the docks. Ever." Nellie was firm on this.

"I suppose that would be best," conceded Harriet. "It would allow me time to visit some of the museums I have only read about. Can you imagine? Right now, I am within a short walk of the National Gallery and the British Museum!"

Once again Nellie shook her head. "Ladies do not scamper about London on foot. Ever."

"Perhaps I could borrow one of his lordship's horses?"

"Gads, child, no! If you must visit a place, you will ride in a carriage. And you really ought to have a man escort you. I can go with you if there is none other. Or perhaps me and one of the footmen." Nellie looked up at the ceiling, thinking aloud.

"Do you think one of the footmen would be interested in visiting the museum?"

"Interested? No, of course not. But propriety must be observed. You are the granddaughter of an earl and you are in London."

Harriet sighed. She hardly knew herself anymore. "Fine, whatever you think is best." It wasn't that she objected to propriety; she simply couldn't spare a moment to think about it. As long as she got to visit the British Museum, the entire staff could tag along for all she cared. Might even be educational for them.

"Good!" Nellie smiled at her like she was an obedient child. "Now I've been through your gowns, and I think the white with the blue sash would be perfect, though now that you are in London, you should consider visiting a modiste to get some frocks in the latest fashion. And your bonnets have been ripped to shreds from all that wind."

"Whatever for?" asked Harriet. "I reserved some frocks and bonnets from the rigors of the wind on decks. They should do. Besides, we will not be here more than a few weeks before we can find passage on a ship back to America."

Nellie's face fell and she busied herself with Harriet's wardrobe. "I have been thinking. As far as I know, my parents are still alive. And I haven't seen my brothers and sisters in over thirty years."

"Oh." Harriet suddenly saw her maid in a new

light. Nellie had always been there and Harriet had simply accepted her presence in their lives as if she belonged to their family. But she didn't. She belonged to another family, one she had left so many years ago.

"Come here, poppet," said Nellie and sat on the foot of the bed. Harriet joined her like they used to when she was young and Nellie was bandaging a scraped knee or a cut finger. With four elder brothers, Harriet had always been an active child.

"I have not set foot in this house since the night we ran away," began Nellie. "Being here brings it all back. Your mother was seventeen and I was nineteen. It seems so young now, but we thought ourselves very mature. Lord Langley was pressing Beatrice to marry a Lord Ashcroft—very old and very rich. Beatrice refused and they had a terrible row, which ended with him saying he would lock her away for madness and her saying she wished he was dead. Oh yes, the servants heard it all!"

"Sounds very dramatic." Harriet had difficulty seeing her calm, poised mother in this explosive light.

"It was! I caught her sneaking out of the house and she declared she was running away with an American sea captain. Well, I thought she might really be mad! Oh, I tried to talk her out of it, I don't mind saying. I didn't know your father as I do now or I wouldn't have wasted my breath. But in the end, she was resolute and I had a choice to make. I could alert her father, I could go back to bed and pretend I saw nothing, or I could go with her and make sure she was looked after."

"You chose to take care of my mum."

"Yes. Though I had no idea I would stay away so long."

Harriet had a pang of guilt for never once considering what a sacrifice Nellie had made to stay true to
her mother. "Of course you would like to visit your
family," said Harriet. "How silly of me not to think of
it. I think of you as so much a part of my family that I
forgot you had one of your own."

"Truth is…" Nellie shifted a bit and took a deep
breath. "Truth is, I was happy in America and had not
thought to leave it, but now that I'm here, I would
like to go home."

"Oh. I see." All the air in Harriet's lungs suddenly
deflated. "You want to stay here."

"Yes, dear, I do." Nellie patted her hand in an
apologetic manner. "But of course I will stay with
you until you are ready to sail and we shall find you
a nice lady's maid to travel with you. I'm sure your
grandfather will likely send an escort with you too."

"Yes, yes, that would be fine." Harriet's mind
whirled. In all her visions of the future, Nellie had always
been by her side, the way she always was. And now she
would be alone. It was not fine. Not at all. And yet…

"You should go visit your family now," blurted
Harriet before she lost her courage. "You must wish
to see them."

"I confess I do, but I would not leave you unprotected."

"I have my grandfather now, such as he is, and I
believe you have done enough to protect the ladies of
this family. It is high time you take care of yourself."
Harriet felt a rush of pride for having voiced what she
knew to be right, followed by despair when Nellie
happily accepted her offer and began to pack her bag.

Harriet plastered a smile on her face as she hugged

her maid, her friend and surrogate mother, good-bye. She snuck one of her leather pouches of gold into the maid's bag when Nellie was not attending and packed her off in a hack for the ride across town to where Nellie's relatives lived.

Harriet waved and smiled and was immensely pleased that the tears did not begin to fall until the carriage was well out of sight. She turned to go back in the house. Now that there was no one to witness her tears, she decided it was time for a good cry.

She had not gone more than a few steps before she was thwarted in her plan, met in the entryway by her grandfather, dressed in his hat and coat.

"Good, you are dressed." Langley gave her a curt nod of approval. "They are bringing around the carriage. I have asked the maids to pack your trunks. Do you need to take all of them?"

"Whatever do you mean? Where are you going?" Once again Harriet's world was shifting sidewise.

"The house party. Lord Thornton has invited us to attend." The earl smiled hopefully.

"I am sorry, I fear you have misunderstood." Harriet smiled, though she would have rather pushed past him to have a moment of privacy. "I am not here for a house party. I only wished to meet you and have a roof over my head until we, or rather *I*, could book safe passage back to America."

"Yes, well, I sent a man 'round to procure you tickets, and the first ship available leaves in one month." He pursed his lips together as if soured by the enormity of the lie he just told.

"I cannot believe that one month is the soonest option."

Langley's eyes grew soft and pleading. "Harriet, I know I have no right to ask, since I have not been able to be present in your life—"

"Chosen not to be present in my life," interrupted Harriet.

"Yes. Quite. But the thing is, I would like to make up for lost time. A visit to the Scottish Highlands would be rather nice and we could get to know each other better."

"Scottish Highlands?" Harriet did not wish to admit it, but her interest was piqued. She had always wanted to see that part of the world, almost as much as she wished to see the British Museum.

"Yes, so beautiful this time of year."

"Lord Thornton invited us?"

"Yes, he was quite insistent we attend." Her grandfather's eyes gleamed, though whether with familial happiness or malicious scheming, she did not know him well enough to tell.

"He wished us to attend?" she asked. Did Thornton want them to come to Scotland? Later she would conclude her decision was the result of a lack of sleep and overwrought nerves, but at the moment an image of a tall, brooding Thornton beckoning her to the Highlands became a powerful incentive. Besides, she should at least spend a little time with her grandfather.

"Very well then, I accept. But I must insist we visit the British Museum before we leave town."

"But we haven't the time—"

"Or I will not go."

Lord Langley gave her a tight smile. "I'll take you there now, on our way out of town!"

Four

PENELOPE ROSE ACCEPTED A CUP OF TEA FROM THE Dowager Duchess of Marchford. As the companion to the elderly duchess, it was expected that Penelope would join the duchess for tea while she entertained visitors. This afternoon, the Duke of Marchford and his friend Lord Thornton joined them.

"Tea, dear?" The duchess offered a cup to her grandson, the current Duke of Marchford. He accepted with stoic silence that bordered on sullen. Not that Penelope could blame him, since the dowager had just informed him she had invited several more families to his house party.

"Lord Thornton, would you care for some cake?" The dowager offered a delicious morsel to his lordship and he accepted. As a close friend to Marchford, he was not an uncommon visitor at Marchford House. He was also accustomed to the legendary disagreements between the elderly duchess and her grandson, and had learned to eat his cake quietly and let the combatants battle it out. Penelope also accepted some cake, and much like Thornton, she waited to see the show.

"Of course, it would have been nicer and a good deal easier if you had chosen to hold your house party at our own country seat and not Thornton Hall of all places," said the dowager.

"I wished to spend a few weeks in the peace of the country, away from society," complained Marchford. "Thornton has been gracious enough to allow me to host my little gathering at his country seat in Scotland. I intended to invite a few friends to go hunting, not host the house party of the summer."

The dowager smiled slowly. "Yes, it has become one of the most sought after invitations."

"The whole *point* of the excursion into Scotland was to *avoid* society." Marchford was clearly nettled.

"Bah!" The dowager waved a hand at him. "You are a duke. You are unmarried. Society would follow you to Botany Bay."

The butler entered the morning room and announced a visitor, which was enough for Marchford and Thornton to stand in a calculated retreat.

"Whoever it is, I absolutely forbid you to invite them to the house party," demanded Marchford.

"The visitor is Lord Langley," said the butler.

The dowager gave an arch look. "Lord Langley? What on earth is he doing here? Never fear, he will not receive an invitation from me."

"Actually," said Thornton in an apologetic tone, "I have already invited him."

"*Et tu, Brute?*" Marchford groaned and the men left the morning room.

Lord Langley was ushered in and sat opposite the dowager. "Good afternoon." He was a well-dressed

gentleman, somewhat portly around the middle, but
with an active face, silver-streaked black hair, and
sharp, blue eyes.

"Good afternoon," said the dowager. After an
uncomfortable pause, she added, "Tea?"

"Yes, please," said Langley. "I would like it with—"

"I know how you like your tea," interrupted the
dowager. "Sugar, no milk."

"Yes," said Langley accepting the cup. "You have
a good memory."

"You will find I have a good memory for many
things," said the dowager with a malicious purr in
her tone.

Lord Langley wiped his brow and shifted uncom-
fortably in his seat. What exactly the nature of the
bad blood between the dowager and Langley was,
Penelope did not dare ask. They were contemporaries
and had known each other a good deal longer than
Penelope had been alive.

"Your Grace," began Langley.

"No, please, you must call me Antonia, the way
you always did when we were children." The duchess
again smiled. It was the kind of smile a mouse might
see right before being devoured by a cat.

Penelope tried to keep a smile from her own face.
Whatever Langley had done to irritate the dowager,
she was giving no quarter today.

Langley sighed—or perhaps it was more of a groan.
"Antonia, I have come because I would like to know
your contact for this matchmaker the whole *ton* is
talking about."

"I am so sorry, but Madam X is very reclusive.

I could not possibly reveal her identity," said the duchess with a bite to her tone. "Besides, are you not too old to be wanting to find a new wife?"

"What? Oh, no, it is not for me," assured Langley. "It is for… that is to say… the truth of the matter is that it is for my granddaughter." His voice trailed off such that he ended in a whisper.

The dowager raised an eyebrow. "I was not aware you were blessed with grandchildren."

Langley shook his head. "Neither was I."

"So your granddaughter has returned," said the dowager with a sip of tea. "You must have been quite surprised to see her. And so remarkable since your daughter has been living in a sanitorium for the past four decades."

"My daughter was married to a Captain Redgrave, as you well know," said Langley in a low voice.

"How interesting for you, to have such connections."

Lord Langley put his teacup down on the saucer with a loud clank. He glared at the dowager, who smiled sweetly in return. "I see I have come on a fool's errand." He set down his teacup on the table and stood.

"You were right about the fool part," said the dowager, all pretense of pleasant conversation drained from her face.

"Will you never let go of the past? It has been over fifty years."

"Leave it to you to be so precise with your times. What a shame it was not a characteristic you held earlier in your career."

"Why are you so quick to bring up things of the past? Why hold on to such trivial matters?"

"Trivial? Trivial?" The dowager rose along with her voice. "You call leaving me at the altar on the morning of our wedding a trivial matter?"

In the silence that followed, Penelope tried not to gape. The dowager had been engaged to Lord Langley? Well now, this was definitely an interesting morning.

Lord Langley dropped his gaze. "I wrote you a note telling you why I could not go through with the marriage. My parents did not approve of the union. They threatened to cut me off."

"Coward," accused Antonia, regaining her seat. "I did not receive the letter until after I returned from the church—after I had waited for you for three hours. Do you have any idea how humiliating…" The dowager coughed, took a deep breath, and regained her composure with a sip of tea.

Lord Langley sat with a thud and stared at his teacup. "I thought there was nothing else I could do."

"Nothing else? You cannot possibly suggest that leaving me standing at the altar for public ridicule was the only way you could have handled the situation."

Lord Langley's face turned red. "What will it take for you to forget what is past, what I cannot change?"

Antonia stilled. "Would you have changed it?"

Lord Langley paused and took a deep breath. "I cannot tell you how I have regretted my actions."

"I never even received an apology," stated the dowager.

"Then let me ask your forgiveness now." Lord Langley's voice was strained.

A slow smile crept onto the dowager's face. "Lord Langley does not make an apology easily," she explained to Penelope.

"Are you going to forgive him?" asked Penelope.

Antonia sipped her tea and ignored the question. "What help do you need, Lord Langley?"

"My granddaughter, Harriet Redgrave, has arrived from America, though she wishes to return and soon. I need her to stay. I also fear there may be unpleasant talk about her, considering how her mother…"

"Eloped with an American sea captain," supplied the dowager.

"Yes, you are correct." Lord Langley sounded like someone was choking him. "If Harriet could secure an eligible offer soon, it could stave off unpleasant rumors and malicious talk."

"So you wish her to make an advantageous match."

"Not just any match; I need her married off to a man within my social standing. I need to show that she is every bit the granddaughter of an earl. There can be no scandal, no whispers of her being anything less than a Langley."

"You wish her to marry a member of the aristocracy."

"I want a title for her!"

Antonia graced him with a cunning smile. "I shall speak with Madame X. Naturally, additional funds are required for a marriage to quality."

Langley waved his hand. "It is of no consequence, but Harriet must be wed soon. She talks of returning to America. I cannot allow it. I cannot."

"If anyone can assist you, it would be Madame X," said the dowager.

"I certainly hope my trust is not misplaced. We have but one month, and that only because I lied and said there was no earlier ship. She must be made to stay. I will not, cannot, lose her again."

Penelope exchanged a look with the dowager. Lord Langley had clearly never recovered from losing his daughter.

"We will contact Madame X," said Penelope, "but we cannot force Miss Redgrave to wed against her will if she wishes to return to her family…"

"I am her family now," interrupted Langley. "I was foolish once and lost my daughter. I have another chance. I will not lose her too! Whatever it takes, whatever it costs, I will see Harriet wed within a month's time!"

❧

Harriet was impressed. "This is the place?" she asked to confirm.

"Yes, miss. This is Marchford House," said Lord Langley's footman. The same footman who had to beg her to leave the British Museum, pleading that if he did not bring her to Marchford House within the hour as commanded, he would be given the sack. Harriet was reluctant to leave, but not heartless, so here she was.

Marchford House was built on a large scale, though not ostentatious, which made it that much more impressive. The Duke of Marchford was quality, there could be no doubt.

"Well, I suppose I should go in and find my grand-father. I hope they know where he is; otherwise, it could take some time," said Harriet gazing up at the imposing structure.

"There is His Grace, the Duke of Marchford, now, miss," said the footman, indicating two gentlemen leaving the house. One was a handsome man in an exquisitely tailored royal-blue superfine coat, buff breeches, and well-polished Hessians. Beside him was the Earl of Thornton, more soberly attired in olive green.

"Hello!" called Harriet running up to the men. She was more excited than she wanted to admit to see Lord Thornton again. "Good day, Lord Thornton, I did not expect to see you here. I am just coming to meet my grandfather."

"Good day to ye, Miss Redgrave," said Thornton with a polite bow. "I believe Lord Langley is in the morning room with the duchess and Miss Rose."

"Thank you, I'm glad someone could give me directions; otherwise, I might get hopelessly lost in this big house." She smiled at the men, who appeared slightly taken aback by her statement. Thinking she must have said something wrong, she changed the subject. "I am glad for your invitation to visit the Highlands. I have always wanted to see that part of the world."

"I am glad ye will be able to attend," said Thornton, though he exchanged a glance with his friend that suggested otherwise. "Please allow me to present my friend, the Duke of Marchford. This is Miss Redgrave, granddaughter to Lord Langley."

The duke's eyebrows raised skyward. "Lord Langley's granddaughter? It is a pleasure to meet you, Miss Redgrave."

"You are no doubt surprised—grandfather was too last night," said Harriet. "He did not know I even existed until I arrived, probably because my mum ran off to America with a sea captain."

The duke made a slight choking sound but recovered himself quickly. "Yes, quite. You will certainly be interesting company for our little house party."

"Interesting?" asked Harriet. The way he said the word did not sound positive.

"Ye'll be our only American," supplied Thornton.

"Oh, yes, of course," said Harriet. "I'm glad to hear the house party will be small. I do enjoy more casual gatherings."

"I could not agree more, but I fear we are both bound for disappointment," said Marchford. "Good day, Miss Redgrave."

The men bowed and Harriet turned to walk up the steps into the house.

"I am glad ye will be joining us, Miss Redgrave," called Thornton, turning back to her. He gave her a small smile. "I do hope the Highlands live up to yer expectations."

"I'm sure they will," said Harriet, comforted that her invitation had been confirmed, "especially if I have you to guide me." Her heart beat faster at the thought.

"The pleasure will be mine." Thornton bowed again and turned back to his friend.

Harriet smiled all the way up the stairs and into the grand entryway. If the outside of Marchford House was impressive, the inside was astonishing. Although Harriet considered herself more of a scientist, she had an avid interest in antiquities, and Marchford House was full of them. As the butler led her to the morning room, she could not help but stop and appreciate the prominently displayed Renaissance artwork.

"Miss Harriet Redgrave," intoned the butler as she was introduced to the morning room.

"She must not know," said Langley in a harsh whisper, which Harriet guessed she was not meant to overhear. Her grandfather stood, a tight smile on his lips. "Antonia, please allow me to present my granddaughter, Miss Redgrave. Harriet, this is Her Grace, the Duchess of Marchford."

Harriet came forward and gave her nicest curtsy to the duchess. The duchess gave her a sweeping look, which made Harriet wonder if she had passed inspection. From the narrowing of the duchess's sharp, blue eyes, she guessed not. The duchess was an older lady, with perfectly white, impeccably coiffed hair in a distinguished style that befitted her age. Her gown was of shimmering emerald and everything about her from her gold-handled cane to her jeweled slippers looked expensive.

"It is a pleasure to meet you, Miss Redgrave," said the duchess with perfect diction. "I understand you are lately from America."

"Yes. I left Boston for New York, but my ship was seized and sunk by the British Navy, and I was brought here. I had honestly never thought to visit England, but now that I am here, I am enjoying the museums. They are quite fine in my estimation."

"Well," said the duchess with that startled look Harriet was growing accustomed to seeing on people's faces. "Please do have a seat, and allow me to introduce my companion, Miss Penelope Rose."

"Hello!" said Harriet.

Penelope blinked. "Hello to you as well." Penelope was a young woman, perhaps in her mid-twenties, as Harriet was herself. In keeping with the occupation of a companion, Penelope was dressed sensibly, a drab comparison to her rich surroundings. Her brown hair was pulled back in a simple knot and everything about her spoke of efficiency and quiet confidence.

"I am glad you are enjoying your visit to London, Miss Redgrave," said Penelope.

"Oh my stars!" exclaimed Harriet jumping to her feet, causing the duchess to clank down her teacup in surprise. "Is that a Titian on the wall? You have some amazing artwork!"

"Yes, yes, indeed," said Lord Langley hastily. "Harriet, my dear, Her Grace has kindly offered to sponsor your presentation into society. But let us away. We will see you ladies at the house party. I wish you all a safe journey. Come along, Harriet."

~⁂~

Penelope watched with some interest as Langley hustled Harriet out the door.

"Well, Madame X?" asked Antonia, meeting her gaze. "Are you ready for a matchmaking challenge?"

Penelope gave her a half smile to show she was not a coward. "I imagine you should double whatever you were intending to charge Lord Langley for our services."

"Done!" The duchess was not one to turn away income. Her grandson, the current Duke of Marchford, had cut off the majority of her funds in an attempt to force her to move to the dowager house in the country. The dowager, however, had taken matters into her own hands and went into business with Penelope as matchmakers to the *haut ton* under the pseudonym "Madame X."

"It will be a challenge," admitted Penelope. "I may be forced to take up strong drink before the end of the house party."

"I feel inclined to have a strong drink now," declared the duchess. "But when we find a titled husband for the likes of Harriet Redgrave, not only will our financial worries be solved, but the reputation of Madame X as the best matchmaker in the country will be sealed!"

Five

"YE'RE A MARKED MAN," THE EARL OF THORNTON commented as he watched a never-ending stream of carriages pull into the drive of Thornton Hall.

"You are also a bachelor, my friend," said the Duke of Marchford, leaning on the tower parapet beside him. "Perhaps they come for you."

Thornton raised an eyebrow. "Ye may say it as oft as ye wish, but it still winna make it true. The maidens come for ye, the young men come for the maidens, and the parents come to ensure their favored child does not leave here without marriage papers being signed. London's elite did not travel all the way to savage Scotland to have their daughters be mistress of this crumbling tower."

"Thornton Hall is hardly crumbling," objected the duke. He could hardly deny anything else.

Thornton Hall was situated in the heart of the Scottish Highlands. If one wished for a distant retreat, one could not ask for a location more remote unless one traveled to the Isle of Skye. Originally built in the sixteenth century, Thornton Hall was the ancestral home of the Maclachlan clan and had endured many improvements and expansions by subsequent lords of Thornton. The hall embraced Gothic architecture and had two requisite towers and several smaller turrets. On the rocky hills above, Thornton Hall even boasted its own ruins, the remains of Maclachlan Castle.

The grounds, at least what could be seen of them from the road, were all meticulously groomed, and the entryway, main parlors, dining rooms, and ballroom were all well appointed. Whether the upkeep of the home and grounds extended beyond what was immediately obvious was the matter of some debate.

"Everything did look verra nice when we arrived today," said Thornton in an ominous tone. "I fear my mother has once again seen fit to replace the drapes and the upholstery. At great expense no doubt." Despite his difficult financial situation, his mother spent money, or rather purchased things in his name, with such alarming frequency that some of the local shopkeepers had gone so far as to hint at not providing any more goods until his debts were paid.

"Lady Thornton should be pleased to serve as hostess for this house party," commented Marchford.

"Pleased? She is beyond pleased. She is ecstatic—an emotion I fear also came with a pressing need for a new wardrobe!"

Marchford winced. "Sorry, old man. I will not have you incur any other expense for this house party, you understand. I have invited these guests and the entirety of the cost shall be mine."

"Nay, I canna…"

"I am quite resolved on this matter. I will be forced

to meet you at dawn if you continue to oppose me on this."

Thornton lifted his hands in surrender. "Fine. But only because I concede ye are a better shot." Unfortunately, Thornton could ill afford to feed all these guests without his friend's help, as well they both knew.

Thornton leaned his arms against the cool stones of the parapets and enjoyed the brisk breeze. "O' course ye are welcome at Thornton at any time, but why not hold this party at yer own estate? And it's no use telling me about the variety of hunting for a gaming party, I canna believe it."

Marchford sighed. "The war with Napoleon goes poorly. Many now fear the emperor has his eyes set on the British Isles. The house party was intended to bring together some of our previous and current military leaders to plan the next offensive and the defense of our homeland. I wished to hold these meetings as far from London as possible to keep these plans from falling into enemy hands. London is hardly safe."

Thornton nodded in understanding. Marchford had recently returned from three years in Spain working for the Foreign Office and had gained a reputation for flushing out spies both abroad and at home. "I thought we caught the spy who had infiltrated society."

"We caught one, but I am relatively confident spies remain at large in London society."

Thornton shrugged. "I dinna doubt it, with what Napoleon is paying for information."

Marchford frowned. "How would you know what traitors are being paid?"

"I've heard rumors, my friend. Do ye doubt even me?"

Marchford sighed and rubbed his forehead with his hand. "This is a nasty business. Makes me daft with suspicion."

"I am sorry to hear yer mental state is failing."

Marchford cast his friend an imperious look just as a large boom rocked the house and gave the tower a quivering jolt. Both men grabbed on to the battlements to keep from falling.

"What was that?" asked Marchford.

Thornton was too busy running down the stairs to answer. Following the smoke, they ran to where the sound had originated. A bedroom door burst open and more acrid smoke billowed out. A young woman staggered from the room, coughing hard and coated in soot.

Thornton caught the young lady in his arms, who appeared unsteady on her feet. He quickly scooped her up in his arms and carried her down the stairs and out through a side door so she could breathe the fresh air.

"Stop!" The lady tried to say more but began coughing again. "I can manage."

Thornton placed her down on the stone step and rubbed her back to try to help her breathe. "Dinna fear, just take several deep breaths."

The lady did as requested and, after several deep breaths with her head down, looked up at him with a rueful smile.

"Miss Redgrave!" A jolt of something flashed through him. What had happened here? Was she all right?

"I am sorry to cause such trouble," she said, trying to smooth back tendrils of her auburn hair that had escaped her bun. "Especially since you were so kind as to invite us."

"Are ye hurt?"

"No, I am fine." She smiled, her teeth white in contrast to her soot-covered face.

"I do apologize. I canna understand what has caused this. If ye will be well, I need to return to discern what has happened."

"Oh, I can tell you that. It is my fault entirely. I have been traveling so long I simply could not wait to begin my next experiment as soon as we reached the house."

"Experiment?" asked Thornton.

"I dabble in chemistry."

"Chemistry?"

"Yes, I do apologize, but I was slightly careless with my mixing, and I had a tiny little explosion."

"Explosion?" Thornton realized he was copying her like a parrot, but given her extraordinary tale, he could not find sensible speech.

"Do not worry. There's no damage, or at least I think I kept it to a minimum. I've had many much larger explosions at home."

And now Thornton could think of nothing to say. He often lacked conversation with ladies, but this was worse than usual. He sat beside her mute on the step. An awkward silence engulfed them.

Harriet pressed her lips together in a manner that hardly improved her appearance. Her face and hands were dirty and her frock appeared to have been torn in the explosion.

At length, Harriet spoke again. "I don't think we

ever properly met each other. I mean I know your title, but what is your name?"

Thornton opened his mouth but no speech emerged, his mind spinning at this unconventional female. What kind of an introduction was this? "I am Duncan Maclachlan, Earl of Thornton, at yer service."

"Harriet." She held out her soot-covered hand.

He smiled in spite of himself. He took her hand in his and they shook hands then held on for a moment longer. "Yer hands are not cold this time."

"Chemicals. Explosions. Keeps them warm." Her eyes were a bright green.

"Might I suggest a fireplace? Or would that be too conventional for an American such as yerself?"

"I shall try to amend my ways. For you. Since you saved me." She gave him a slow smile.

Perhaps it was some of those chemicals wearing off on him, but he was suddenly flushed with heat as well. Being cast in the role of hero was new to him. Whenever adventure struck, it was always his friends for whom the ladies swooned, while he was the sensible one who picked up the pieces and took care of the details. Yet in Harriet's eyes, he saw himself a different man.

"It was my pleasure." Never had he spoken those words with more truth.

"I suppose I should go help clean the mess." She stood up and wiped the soot off her hands and onto her skirts.

Thornton stood and gave a polite bow. She returned it with a smile.

"Thank you for your help, Lord Duncan… I mean Lord Thornton." She looked away.

Thornton could not tell exactly beneath the soot, but he suspected she was blushing. "I am at yer disposal if ever any o' yer plans go awry."

Harriet turned back with a broad smile. "I fear that would keep you busy day and night. And now that I think of it, I am mostly confident the fire has been put out of the drapes, but I should go confirm." She whirled and disappeared back into the house.

Thornton found he needed to take a few deep breaths himself before returning to the house. She was so unlike any other female he had ever met he became utterly perplexed and simply ended up being himself. Imagine a lass who dabbled in chemistry. Tiny little explosion? Not when his mother found out. He hustled back into the house. It seemed his self-assigned role as Miss Redgrave's protector might prove to be an extensive occupation indeed.

❧

Harriet Redgrave rushed back into the house away from her rescuer. The main entryway was filled with confused guests all talking at once about what had happened. She avoided the crowd and ran up the side staircase Lord Thornton had carried her down. *Carried*. Yes, she had actually been carried, by a man who picked her up like she was a wisp, which she knew full well was hardly the case.

Her heart was beating fast before she had even taken one step. She had done many things in her life, but never had she been swooped up by a man and rescued. Not that she needed rescuing... much... but it was an interesting sensation. As a devoted scientist she should look into this intriguing reaction.

As an unmarried female, she should leave it be.

She feared she had made a mess of things with Lord Thornton. Every word from her mouth made the man appear more perplexed. It was a situation most girls dream of, being carried out of a burning building by a tall, dark, handsome man, who was an earl no less. Any other girl would have known how to handle the situation. Any other girl would have flirted, whatever that might be, and would have secured his undying affection before teatime. But of course, any other girl would not have set her room on fire within two hours of her arrival.

Harriet hustled to her room with the intent of hiding as much of the evidence as possible. Voices sliced down the hallway from her room. Unhappy, raised voices. She paused outside her door, out of sight. It had been her considerable experience that after a slight incident, people often needed a little time to settle their sensitivities before talking to her.

"Where is Lord Langley? Should he not take things in hand?" demanded an angry male voice Harriet recognized as the Duke of Marchford.

"Lord Langley took ill on the journey here," said Penelope Rose. "Nothing dire I believe, but he has been confined to his bed until he has recovered, so we will be taking over as chaperones and introducing Miss Redgrave into society."

"Why, Grandmother?" asked the duke, his voice low and deep almost like a growl. "Why would you offer to sponsor an American, an American who apparently likes to engage in the wanton destruction of property, at my house party?"

"I grant you Harriet Redgrave is a trifle eccentric," hedged the Dowager Duchess of Marchford.

"Eccentric?" interrupted the duke. "Eccentric is what you called Uncle Melvin when he took to wearing paper hats and digging holes in the garden wearing nothing but his stockings and bedroom slippers. This is… I'm not sure what. Just look at this mess of bottles and powders and things. I am afraid to touch it lest I blow out the whole wall."

"Every lady should have a hobby," said Penelope. "Miss Redgrave told me she enjoys chemistry. Apparently, there was a minor incident."

"Minor? The drapes are still smoldering. Lady Thornton is going to be quite displeased."

Harriet leaned against the wall with a sigh. The Earl of Thornton was married. Naturally, why wouldn't he be? Why should it matter to her in the slightest?

"Lady Thornton is displeased with everything, so it will be no great change to her temperament," muttered the dowager.

"Grandmother, I want to know what you are about. Why take an interest in chaperoning an American chit with a penchant for blowing things up?"

"Lord Langley asked if I might sponsor her," explained the dowager.

"The Lord Langley you have frequently referred to as an odious man who had as much compassion as a rabid fox caught in its burrow?" Marchford's voice was without humor. "Miss Rose, kindly tell me what this is about."

A pause silenced the room and Harriet held her breath. If the duchess was not friends with her grandfather, then why had she offered to chaperone?

"Miss Redgrave is in need of our help. We are helping," said Penelope.

"What kind of help?" asked Marchford suspiciously. "Grandmother, I have heard rumors that you have a contact with a matchmaker. Please don't tell me you are mixed up in this."

"Your wish is granted. I shall not speak of it."

Harriet bit her lip. So this is why her grandfather arranged for her to attend this house party. He wanted her to get married. She turned away and found Thornton standing a few paces behind her. What must he think of her?

He walked closer and leaned down to whisper to her. "I do believe I prefer chemistry to paper hats."

She smiled at his kind words, especially since she expected, and probably deserved, censure.

He offered her his arm and they walked into the room together. Perhaps it was her own imagination, but she could feel the heat from his body. Harriet experienced an unfamiliar feeling of acceptance and something else she had more difficulty naming. It was not usual for a man to offer friendship, particularly right after she had experienced a little "incident."

"Good news," Thornton announced to all in the room. "Miss Redgrave is unhurt."

Nobody seemed particularly relieved at his pronouncement. Harriet did a quick survey of the damage to the room. It was still smoky, but it had escaped major damage. The drapes were singed at the bottom, but perhaps no one would notice.

"What is this?" A woman dressed in a fine silk gown and a scarlet brocade turban entered the room and surveyed it with horror. The lady was older than Thornton but still retained much of her beauty, though her appearance would have improved without the pinch between her eyebrows. "What has happened? Have the chimneys caught fire? Did that maid leave a candle unattended?"

"Nay, it was an accident," soothed Thornton. "No harm done." Except the singed drapes, but the less said about that the better. "Mother, may I present Miss Harriet Redgrave. Miss Redgrave, my mother, Lady Thornton."

Lady Thornton was his mother, not his wife. And somehow, in spite of everything, it made Harriet smile. "It is a pleasure to meet you." She extended a hand, but Lady Thornton appeared stunned, as if Harriet had offered her a snake, so she let her hand drop.

"Miss Redgrave is the granddaughter of Lord Langley," explained Thornton.

"I thought Lord Langley's only child was in a sanatorium," said Lady Thornton bluntly.

"Worse than that," said Harriet cheerfully. "She ran away with an American. I have only recently returned for a visit."

Lady Thornton's jaw dropped, but whatever she was going to say was averted by Thornton.

"I am glad ye are here, Mother, the guests downstairs are in desperate need of yer attention," said Thornton, neatly ushering his mother out of the room.

"It is a pity we could not get out of that invitation,"

said Lady Thornton from the hallway when they were almost out of hearing. "Well, I suppose we cannot avoid the acquaintance now, but I do wish you would try to limit her exposure to our other guests. Her type can be so lowering."

Harriet gulped air and glanced nervously at Miss Rose and the dowager, but they were too busy avoiding her eye to notice. The Duke of Marchford was inspecting the drapes.

"She is our guest, Mother," said Thornton in a low voice.

"'Tis a shame," continued Lady Thornton. "I can hardly abide the chit being here. Her mother was fit for Bedlam; I recall the story now. Ran off with some American sea captain. Should have been locked in an asylum if you ask me. Lord Langley probably would have done so, had he been able to get to her. Goodness only knows what is wrong with the grand-daughter. A danger to everyone in the house. I dinna suppose ye could ask her to leave?" Lady Thornton's voice trailed off.

Harriet had not been here more than a few hours and now she was going to need to leave. But go where? It had taken several days from London to get here.

No one spoke. The dowager cleared her throat but looked away. Penelope smoothed her skirts in a casual manner, as if by ignoring the awkwardness it would go away.

"I do believe it is time for tea," said Penelope.

"Perhaps I should stay here and clean up a bit," said Harriet.

The Duke of Marchford exchanged looks with the dowager and then Penelope. "Not at all," he said with a sigh. "You have been invited by Lord Thornton; therefore, you are my guest as well. Would you do me the honor of accompanying me to tea?" The duke offered his arm and Harriet accepted.

So far she had caused an explosion, set her room on fire, been rescued by an earl, and was going to tea on the arm of a duke. All things considered, it had been an eventful beginning to her trip to the Highlands. But the real danger was about to begin—she was about to be introduced to society.

Six

THORNTON CONTINUED TO GUIDE HIS MOTHER AWAY from Miss Redgrave until he had escorted her all the way back to her dressing room, which he noticed she had redecorated. Again.

"Miss Redgrave is our guest, and whether or not her father was an American is hardly relevant to our being polite," he gently chastised.

His mother whipped her head toward him at his rebuke. "I am trying to help you. This is your chance to find the right lady to wed. I know several young ladies of position and wealth will be at this house party. We need to find one who has both, you know. It will do us no good for you to marry for connections alone; we need a sizable dowry." She spoke in the clipped tone of London society it had taken several highly paid linguists to perfect. She might have started her life as the rich daughter of a Scottish merchant, but her aspirations were much higher.

"I shall not marry for money, Mother." Thornton stated the cold fact while staring at her, willing her to accept it this time.

His mother's jaw tightened and her nostrils flared. "You cannot mean that! We must have funds. We must."

The desperation in her voice stilled him. "What do ye owe now?"

Lady Thornton turned away. "'Tis not my fault. My luck was going so well I could not lose."

"Gambling again? What did ye lose this time?"

"Thornton Hall," her voice cracked.

His heart stilled. "What do ye mean? How could ye lose the estate?"

Lady Thornton spun to him, her eyes flashing. "I needed funds for some investments and a little pocket money for some fun, so I put the estate as collateral."

"Ye did what?!" Thornton began to pace. "Mother, we are in a precarious financial situation as it is. I have told ye so, many, many times. How could ye?"

"I was assured it was a secure investment, a safe bet! I was trying to win back some money for you, dear."

"I have told ye, asked ye, pleaded wi' ye, not to invest wi'out checking wi' me first."

"Well, it's done. No use wasting your tears over it."

"Fact is, ye bet the estate and ye lost. Ye lost everything."

Lady Thornton's lips formed a thin line. "So what if I did? This old hall would have been sold off years ago had not I married your father and saved it. It was my money that saved this estate, mine. That is why my father saw to it I was given full control over the estate, and if I want to bet against it or sell it off, I can."

"If it is yer goal to ruin me, then ye have done yer job verra well." A cold, hard fear seeped into his bones.

"Ruin you? Nay, how can you say that? I only want what's best for you. Now, don't fret now. I have a plan. There are some very rich ladies, English ladies, that would make fine brides. We have until the end of the month before…."

"Before what?"

"Before we will be forced to move and the lot will be sold." Lady Thornton turned away and spoke in an airy voice, as if it was no great consequence to lose the estate that housed generations of Thornton lords. "But it need not come to that. If you follow my advice, you can be wed before the house party is through, and all will be well again."

Thornton shook his head. "I will not marry for money. Not even to save the estate."

"Duncan! Do you understand we will be forced out?"

"Then ye best get packing." Thornton turned and left before what he truly wanted to say could escape his lips. All his work, all his efforts to pull them out of debt, it had all been for naught.

❦

Despite the clear advantages to having Harriet introduced to society on the arm of the Duke of Marchford, Penelope felt obligated to suggest that Miss Redgrave wash her face and change her gown first, and then meet the guests in the tearoom. They wished Harriet to be accepted in society, and it would not do to send her down looking like a chimney sweep.

Penelope and the dowager retreated across the hall to their rooms to give Harriet privacy to change.

"That could have gone better," grumbled the dowager, reclining into a chair.

"Lord Langley forgot to mention her interesting... hobbies," commented Penelope.

"Alchemy is not a hobby; it is a liability. Now I understand why he would offer such a large sum to Madame X to have Harriet credibly married off, and to a titled gentleman no less."

"It will be a challenge to have her accepted in society," admitted Penelope. "It is a shame so many followed the duke this far north."

The dowager gave her a wry smile. "Perhaps someday you will have children of your own and understand a mother's drive to see her daughters wed. The Duke of Marchford is on the open market. Madame X has been inundated by requests to have their daughter connected to him."

Penelope gave a surreptitious eye roll. "Does he suspect?"

"Suspect us to be Madame X? I am not sure. He knows we are somehow involved, and he knows I came into a bit of financial independence a few months ago after our last success."

Penelope smiled. It had been nothing short of a family coup to secure the funds which allowed them to remain in London, rather than be sent off to the dowager house as Marchford had planned. "At least we can have no financial worries anymore."

"I would not take that bet," the dowager shook her head. "The new carriage alone was quite dear."

"And unnecessary," muttered Penelope.

"What? And travel all this way without fresh springs? It would have been the death of me."

"We should still have much remaining. Madame X's last success should have set us up for life."

"For life? Wherever do you get such notions? I am a good deal more expensive."

"But I am not," said Penelope simply. She did not like the way the dowager avoided her eye.

"Let us go and check on Miss Redgrave," said the dowager, changing the subject in a manner Penelope found suspicious. "It is time for her debut in the tearoom."

They found Harriet scrubbed clean and dressed in something resembling a passable day gown. Her gowns were well made and of quality material, yet were not of the latest fashion to be found in London. Penelope supposed that could only be expected since Miss Redgrave was a new arrival from America.

As they all walked down to join the others for tea, Penelope was struck by how Harriet reminded her of a rambunctious puppy, making happy comments, wide-eyed and eager to explore something new. The impression left Penelope interested in becoming better friends with the guileless Harriet Redgrave, yet she dreaded the reaction of some society mavens who were sticklers for etiquette.

Outside the parlor door, they met Lord Thornton, who had a fierce look about him.

"Lord Thornton?" asked Penelope. "Is there something the matter?"

"Nay, all is well," he said in a tone that suggested otherwise. "Yer Grace, may I escort ye in?" he asked the duchess, as was proper.

"I prefer Miss Rose's arm today, but perhaps you could be of use to Miss Redgrave."

"I would be honored." Thornton gave a quick bow and offered his arm to Miss Redgrave.

"Thank you, Lord Thornton," said Harriet. "I shall feel so much safer with you by my side."

"Are ye ready to face the societal lions?" asked Thornton, a smile creeping onto his face.

"As long as you are here to make sure I am not eaten alive."

Penelope and the dowager held back a moment, allowing Harriet to make her entrance. It was good for her to enter on the arm of Lord Thornton, showing all those within where he thought her place to be. Within the parlor was a veritable army of London's societal elite.

"Oh no!" whispered Penelope. "The Comtesse de Marseille is present. She will ruin Harriet before supper."

"Thornton has her in hand," whispered the dowager in response. "He is reserved but not cruel and the only one of my grandson's acquaintances I credit as capable of intelligent thought. Let us see what he does."

Thornton paused for a moment, surveying the scene, then directed Harriet to the comtesse. Though Penelope could not hear the interaction, she noted that Harriet made a passable curtsy and she was introduced.

"Now that witch cannot deny Harriet her acquaintance. Nicely done, lad," commented the dowager in an undertone.

"It will not stop her mouth," muttered Penelope.

"Only the grave could do that," said the dowager. "Look, now he's taking her on to Sir Antony."

They watched as Lord Thornton introduced Harriet to several notable personages in the room, keeping the conversations quite brief, and then left her with Lady Devine, known for her kind character and enjoyment of any individual she would classify as an "original."

Thornton retreated past them to attend to his other duties as the host. The dowager rapped her cane on the floor to get his attention over the din of the crowd. He stopped before them with a solemn bow.

"Well played, my lad," the dowager praised. "I appreciate your efforts for our little prodigy."

"I am, as always, in yer service, Yer Grace." His attention was diverted by his mother, in monstrous ostrich plumes, entering the parlor. "I wish ye both a good afternoon." Thornton bowed and disappeared into the crowd in the opposite direction of his parent.

"He is even more glum than usual," noted Penelope.

"He has been beggared by his mother's extravagance and now will have to face the necessity of marrying into money before his creditors take the shirt off his back," said the dowager.

"You think Lady Thornton has matrimonial plans for him?"

"Yes, of course, I would be shocked if she did not. Note all these unmarried ladies. Their parents may have brought them for Marchford, but once he is claimed, a Scottish lord will have to do."

❧

Harriet did not care if she was accepted in society, yet she did not wish to become a pariah either. She was relieved to face the gauntlet with Lord Thornton by her side. She knew he was someone she could trust. Whatever else he might be, he was a friend when she needed one.

The room was a minefield. One wrong step, one wrong word, and her debut into society would be ruined forever. Many pairs of eyes were leveled at her—so many that she almost felt the need to do something extraordinary to amuse them all. Of course, if she randomly broke into song, she might find herself locked in the attic for the duration of the house party. She was, after all, the daughter of a madwoman who ran away with an American.

After a kind conversation with Lady Devine, Harriet felt confident enough to accept a small biscuit and look to find friends of her own. In one group of seats, several young women were engaged in conversation.

"Hello," said Harriet, boldly sitting in an open chair.

The girls all stared at her then turned their heads to a pretty creature in a white muslin day dress, with a smart ivy-green spencer. Her features were striking, with gleaming black hair, gray eyes, and rose lips. Her pale skin appeared never to have seen the sun. To Harriet, she looked like someone who needed a romp in the sunshine and a good beefsteak to feed the blood.

"Good afternoon," said the girl, her voice even. "Have you come from India?"

"N-no," said Harriet, slightly taken aback from the question. "I am recently from America."

"Oh, I see. I have heard about you." One side of her mouth slid up into a half smile, though not a particularly nice one. "I only thought you were an Indian because your skin is so very brown."

"I do enjoy being outdoors, and of course, during the crossing on board one is always out in the sunshine as often as one can be."

"How odd you do not have bonnets in America," said the girl with a smirk. Her friends began to giggle, some hiding their faces behind their fans. Harriet tried to ignore them.

"I am happy to meet some young people my own age," said Harriet. "I am Harriet Redgrave. It's nice to make your acquaintance." She stuck out her hand, determined to be friendly.

"Oh my! Is this how Americans introduce themselves? Shall I try it, ladies? Hello. My name is Priscilla Crawley. Nice to make your acquaintance." Priscilla mimicked Harriet's voice and actions to more giggles from her friends.

"Thank you so much for making me feel welcome," said Harriet without trying to hide the sarcasm and removed herself from their presence. She only made it five steps before she heard the girls break into raucous laughter. So much for trying to make friends.

From her vantage point at the tea table, Harriet watched as Lord Thornton and his mother approached Miss Crawley, and introductions were made. Priscilla smiled divinely and Thornton bowed in return. She said something, leaning close to him, and he smiled.

Harriet reached for a second biscuit only to be intercepted by the dowager duchess and Penelope. They could not have come too soon.

Seven

HARRIET REDGRAVE SPENT A TEDIOUS AFTERNOON IN the company of the dowager and Miss Rose. She had hardly had a sip of tea and had only eaten one small biscuit before the two women whisked her back to their room with whispered warnings of the irreparable damage to her reputation the eating of more than one biscuit could produce.

The remainder of the afternoon was spent getting a lesson in etiquette. The dowager helped at first, but soon claimed a headache and lay down on the daybed, leaving Harriet in the kind and capable hands of Penelope. Harriet preferred Penelope, as she was gentler and more patient. Yet Penelope was also blunt in her critique, and after several hours of having her manners under review, Harriet wished Penelope would be less honest.

"I have been walking since the age of one and in the twenty-two years that have followed I was not aware I was doing it wrong." Harriet sank into a chair.

Penelope followed her lead and sat on the settee, her posture rigid and correct. "I acknowledge my suggestions may seem petty, but so is society I fear. I wish for you to avoid malicious gossip."

"No chance of that, is there? I mean even if my manners were impeccable, I would still be the daughter of Lady Beatrice, Lord Langley's insane daughter. Why is it so difficult to believe my mother left because she fell in love?"

"People assume one is mad if they make a choice different from what society generally condones. Running away to America does seem rather…" Penelope searched for a word. "Unusual."

"Perhaps it is, but my mother has been quite happy. My father was successful at sea, and I have lacked for nothing, though we do not hold to as strict an adherence to etiquette as does London society."

"It sounds like you have enjoyed your life in America."

"I have and I do. I plan to return next month. I can only imagine how my parents must be worried. I sent them word as soon as I arrived, but of course it takes a while for mail to cross the Atlantic."

"So you plan to return to America?" asked Penelope.

"Yes, which leads me to another question." Harriet decided to ask Penelope directly. "Did my grandfather arrange with you to find me a husband?"

Penelope paused for a moment, searching her with discerning eyes. Harriet did not look away. She wanted the truth.

"Yes," said Penelope at length. "That is, he arranged with us to contact Madame X, a known matchmaker to London society, to arrange a marriage for you with a titled gentleman."

"Titled?" Harriet slouched back further in her chair.

"So now I am to be pawned off on not just a gentleman but one with a title as well. He is only doing this to restore his reputation since my mother left."

"Yes, I think he did mention something of that nature."

"Well I don't care a scrap for it. I have no intention of being married off so that my grandfather can restore some sense of injured pride. Please relate my feelings to this Madame X and let her know her services are quite unnecessary."

Far from being offended or shocked, Penelope accepted her words with composure. "I shall relay your sentiment."

"It won't stop them, will it? Perhaps I should remain in my room for the remainder of the party. I should hate to get compromised or trapped into marriage."

"Rest assured Madame X does not employ such trickery. You are safe from her, at least. If you do not care for the man she chooses for you, you can always refuse."

"Yes, well, I suppose you are right. I do fear my dowry may pose a temptation that will lead people to doing something rash."

"Your dowry?"

"Yes, fifty thousand pounds is a considerable amount."

"I should say it is!" declared the dowager, suddenly sitting upright.

"Yes. My mother put away money in some London bank and over time it added up. She told me she wanted me to have the option of joining London society someday if I wished it, but of course I had not thought to ever do so."

Harriet rose and walked to the window. She did not care to discuss her dowry. She had already run into problems with men who would not scruple to do anything to get their hands on the capital. "I would prefer the size of the dowry not to become known."

"Yes, yes, of course I understand your sentiments. Madame Leclair?" The dowager called her lady's maid, who emerged from a side room. "Did you hear about Miss Redgrave's dowry? I hope you know what to do with that information."

"*Oui*, Your Grace."

"Please go downstairs and ask if our trunks have arrived," said the dowager, whose wardrobe and sundry traveling accoutrements required a separate coach.

"Plagued by fortune hunters?" Penelope crossed the room to the window and they sat in the window box.

"Yes, you understand."

"Not from personal experience. I did not become the companion to the Duchess of Marchford due to my great fortune."

"You became my companion because you have more sense than anyone else in my acquaintance," declared the dowager, closing her eyes once more.

Penelope smiled and glanced at a clock. "You should go and dress for dinner. I do hope our trunks arrive in time or we shall be forced to eat in our rooms. I fear I have not yet gone over the table expectations. Did your mother instruct you?"

"Of course she did." Harriet tried to keep the bite out of her tone in wanting to defend her mother. Truth was her mother had allowed Harriet to experience an unconventional childhood and had many times told Harriet she wanted to give her the freedom she had never experienced.

"Good. If you are confused by anything, just look over to me. I bribed the butler to have you seated across from me."

"You did what?"

"It was easy, the staff are months behind in their wages. Easy to bribe."

Harriet viewed Penelope from an entirely new perspective. Penelope Rose was a resourceful creature, and one she was glad to have on her side.

❧

"Finally!" breathed the Dowager Duchess of Marchford. "I thought we would not see our trunks before dinner."

"Just in time," commented Penelope, as she directed the footmen who were bringing up the numerous trunks the dowager felt necessary for a short venture into the Highlands. Madame Leclair swept majestically through the room and began unpacking the duchess's trunks, putting away the gowns, hats, capes, shawls, shoes, bonnets, and other essential items.

"I shall leave you to dress." Penelope took her trunk into her adjacent room, a room most likely designed to house a lady's maid or a companion of a wealthier, more important person. That is what she was. A paid companion. No shame in it, of course, but it was no great honor either.

Things would change when she started to draw income on the capital they made through their clandestine business as matchmakers. As a single woman, she would still not be allowed to live alone, perish the thought. But at least she could live with some independence.

Penelope opened her trunk and saw at once that it was not hers. The gowns inside were fine and definitely unfamiliar. She carried the trunk back into the dowager's room and handed it to Madame Leclair. "I believe I took one of the dowager's trunks instead of my own. Have you seen mine?"

"That is your trunk, mademoiselle," said Madame Leclair.

"I thought it looked like mine, but when I opened it, none of my clothes were inside. I believe this must belong to the dowager."

The dowager yawned audibly in a manner Penelope had never seen before. If Penelope didn't know different, she would say the dowager was pretending to be tired to get rid of her.

"This is your trunk, mademoiselle," repeated Madame Leclair.

"But it is full of—" Penelope stopped short when she noted a pointed look pass between the dowager and Madame Leclair. "What is this? What have you two done?"

"We have a lovely surprise for you," said the dowager, a sugary sweet smile on her face. "We replaced your wardrobe."

"What do you mean?" asked Penelope.

"Your gowns needed updating. If you are to accompany me as my companion, I expect someone with a little more sense of style."

"My gowns were perfectly serviceable." Penelope rifled through her trunk to find layer after layer of unknown clothing. "Where are my gowns?"

"The maids—" began the dowager.

"You gave my gowns to the maids?" gasped Penelope.

"I tried, but they would not have them," said Madame Leclair.

"What was wrong with them?" demanded Penelope.

"Wrong, *oui*, very wrong," said Leclair with a dismissive wave of her hand. "Gave them to the poorhouse, poor souls."

"You gave them to…" Penelope spun around and stared at the dowager. "You gave all my clothes to the poor?"

"Of course not. I could hardly give away what you were wearing. But I did replace what I could. At least take a look at the gowns."

Penelope took out a blue damask, a golden silk, and something of pink that was so light and airy she thought it must have been spun of clouds. They were beautiful, all of them, and it gave her a lump in her throat. What was she going to do with these clothes? She could hardly wear them.

"Do you not adore them?" asked the dowager.

"These are all ball gowns. None of them are practical."

"I should hope I did not buy you anything practical. But here, you have not opened your other trunk."

"I do not have another trunk."

"*Oui, mademoiselle*, this is for you," said Leclair with a wink and opened a second trunk, larger than the first. In this trunk Penelope found a scarlet riding habit, several morning dresses, and others.

"I cannot believe you did all this."

"But there is more!" Leclair brought out bandboxes of hats, bonnets, and another smaller trunk just of slippers and boots.

"I do not know what to say," mumbled Penelope. "This must have been very dear. How can I pay you back?"

The dowager coughed slightly and asked Madame Leclair if she would run down to the kitchen to ask if they would bring up tea. Leclair gave a pinched look of injured pride—she was a French lady's maid, not a common messenger—but she complied.

"I shall pay for that," mumbled the dowager.

"Your Grace, I appreciate this, but I cannot possibly accept such extravagant gifts," said Penelope, holding herself straight and tall. "I should be much more comfortable in my own clothes."

"Yes, about the money. I decided you needed a new wardrobe so I…" The dowager turned away and took a deep breath. "So I used the funds we acquired from our success as Madame X."

"You used our funds?" Penelope swallowed hard a lump of foreboding. "Please tell me you did not use *my* funds."

"I thought it appropriate since it was to benefit you."

"You spent my money?" cried Penelope. Those funds were going to provide her an independence so she would not have to be anyone's companion. "I asked you to have your solicitor invest the money."

The dowager turned to Penelope, her bright-blue eyes blazing. "And I have invested the money. I have invested it in you. There is no reason why you should be so shabbily dressed."

"Those were my funds. You had no right!"

"If I am going to be seen with you, I should be able to demand a style of dress that is appropriate."

"But these gowns are not appropriate. They will

make me look like I am putting myself forward. People will talk."

"People may notice you, which is a good thing. You are a young lady. Why should you be attired in clothes best suited for a woman twice your age? You are much too young to be dressed as a matron. Where did you get your clothes? They are dreadful."

"They were my mother's!" cried Penelope.

"Aha! My point is made. Why would you wear such gowns? I have seen your sisters. They do not languish in such unattractive attire."

Penelope sighed and paced the room. "When my sisters and I first came to London, we were sponsored by our aunt, but we had very little to buy new clothes. It seemed more important for my two elder sisters to have the appropriate adornment to put themselves into society where they could meet husbands. After a few years, my elder sisters were married and it was time for my younger sisters to come out into society. Of course they needed new gowns and such."

"Now that all four of your sisters are married, when does it become your turn?" asked the dowager with a pointed look.

"I do not wish for a turn. I do not wish to be dressed in such finery."

"You dress like an unemployed governess so that no one will notice you. These plain gowns of yours are like a shield."

"And what is wrong with that?" demanded Penelope. She had been unfavorably compared to her beautiful blonde sisters her whole life. As the only brunette of the family, and a rather plain one at that,

Penelope had learned early not to compete in the same games as her sisters.

"You have given up on yourself. You consider yourself a spinster."

"I *am* a spinster."

"You are still in your twenties. Perhaps you never found a husband because you never even looked for one. You were too busy finding husbands for your sisters and hiding beneath frilly lace caps."

Penelope unconsciously felt her head to ensure her lace cap was in place. "Are you more concerned with my wardrobe, my marital status, or keeping me dependent on you by robbing me of the living which would have given me my independence?"

"What a thing to say!"

"You just wish to keep me because I am the only companion who has stayed with you for more than a week!" accused Penelope, and at once she was shocked by her own words.

"And you are just angry because I am forcing you to join society, instead of hiding behind plain muslin gowns and sensible shoes."

Madame Leclair cleared her throat. "Your tea, Your Grace, it will be brought up shortly. Miss Rose, this is for you." The French maid handed Penelope a sealed missive. "With your permission I shall retire to the servants' hall for tea."

"Yes, yes." The dowager gave her a wave. When the maid was gone, the dowager gave Penelope a critical glare. "It is time you stopped making matches for everyone else. It is time for you to seek your own husband."

Eight

HARRIET DECIDED TO CHECK ON HER GRANDFATHER before dressing for dinner. He may have been a relation she only met recently, and he may have been conspiring against her to try to get her married, but he was still family.

She walked upstairs to another wing of bedrooms for the gentlemen and found her grandfather asleep. She sat beside him for a while, watching. His breathing was congested, but steady and even. A quick hand to his forehead assured her that he was not febrile.

She had wanted to talk to him about calling off the matchmaker, but she would not wake him for anything. Sleeping and ill, he did not look the formidable foe he had appeared when they first met. The years of his life lined his face and it suddenly became important that he make a full recovery, if only so they could argue over his intrusion into her life.

She tucked the blanket around him. Despite the difficult circumstances that brought her to the British Isles, she was glad to have met her grandfather, and she acknowledged that his interest in a matchmaker most likely came from concern for her well-being. Perhaps she should be touched that he wished her to stay on this side of the Atlantic.

"You do better at winning arguments when you are not conscious," she whispered to her grandfather. "Good night."

In the hallway, she encountered a group of gentlemen who were returning to dress for dinner. She had met them earlier at tea, where none had shown the slightest interest in making her acquaintance. She moved past them but was recognized.

"I say, Miss Redgrave, is it?" said one handsome gentleman. "I met you briefly but we had not a chance to talk. I hope we can remedy that at dinner."

"Oh yes," said another man. "I also would enjoy becoming better acquainted."

"That would be nice." Harriet was a bit confused but flattered. Perhaps she had misjudged society. Perhaps they were not as unfriendly as they initially appeared.

"Do you play cards, Miss Redgrave?" asked another man. Several men interjected their opinions on which card game was the most enjoyable to play with young ladies, but while they were talking, Harriet could overhear another conversation.

A man further down the hall asked another in a low tone, "What is this sudden fascination with the American?"

"She's dowered at fifty thousand pounds," answered another man. "Just had it from my valet. It's all the talk in the servant's hall."

They were after her money. Her fortune, not a sudden impulse toward friendliness, was behind these overtures. "Thank you, gentlemen," said Harriet firmly. "I shall not keep you."

She strode off in a determined manner, not caring where she went, as long as it was away from those men. She wandered about and found herself back on the main floor. She needed to clear her head and calm down a bit before meeting whatever new maid had been assigned to her, and who was probably gossiping about her fortune at this moment. If only she could focus on her experiments and leave all this nonsense behind.

Harriet passed an open door and could see bookcases in the gloom. Perhaps a quick visit to the library would be helpful. It would be empty at this time of day since most people would be dressing.

She whisked into the library, shutting the door behind her. The room was mostly dark, lit only by a single candle, and thankfully no one appeared to be inside. She leaned her head back against the door, closed her eyes, and took in a deep breath. She loved the smell of books.

"Good evening."

Harriet jumped with a small shriek and put one hand on her heart and the other on the doorknob. She could make a quick escape if she had to. "Who's there?"

"Sorry if I gave ye a fright." Lord Thornton stepped out of the shadows toward the light of a single candle. "I stepped into the library to collect some papers from my desk." He held up a stack of letters.

Harriet sighed in relief. "I am sorry to invade your privacy. I had no idea there was anyone here."

"Are ye lost?"

"No, I simply needed to escape for a moment."

Thornton frowned. "Is someone bothering ye, Miss Redgrave?"

"Yes! Lots of someones." Harriet walked further into the room and sank onto a leather couch.

"Can I be of assistance? I am most willing to be at yer service, as I offered earlier." Thornton sat beside her but at a respectable distance. "Who has disturbed ye?"

"Men!"

Thornton leaned back, his eyebrows raised. "All of us?"

"Well, not all at once perhaps, but men in general have been a pox to me."

"I deeply regret being a pox to anyone. Please tell me what injury ye have to report so I may appropriately apologize for the misdeeds of my brethren."

Harriet smiled. The Scotsman before her was apparently made of sterner stuff than most Londoners she had met, given that he received her unusual proclamation without censure. "First of all, my grandfather has hired a matchmaker to tie me down and hitch me up to some gentleman with a title."

"Anyone in particular?"

"No, just a man with a title. Doesn't matter if he is eighty years old or lives on a diet of whiskey and beer. If he has a title, I'm up for bids."

The corner of Lord Thornton's mouth twitched up. "If I meet any elderly drunken lechers with a title, I shall let ye know."

"Much appreciated." She kept her tone flat but could not keep from smiling.

"But of what else have ye to accuse the entire population of men?"

Harriet paused. The room was dark and Thornton was more understanding than most. She had felt quite alone after Nellie left. She missed having a person with whom to share her secrets. Thornton was listening. And here in the dark, she was tempted to tell him everything.

"Do you know how difficult it is to be dreadfully rich?" The words were from her lips before she realized just how much she sounded like a spoiled petulant child.

"Nay, I have not had that curse."

"I am sorry, I must sound horrid. The trouble comes from people wanting to make that money their own. If I wed, my husband will instantly become a rich man, and I will lose any scrap of independence. He gets the gold, and I get a tyrant. For every decision in life, I would have to look to him."

"So ye have no interest in marrying."

"None whatsoever. I cannot see how it does a woman any good."

Thornton thought a moment. "Children?"

"I suppose that is the only thing a woman cannot do without some assistance from a man. Though I find it quite inequitable that women are required to do the lion's share of the work."

"Verra true, I fear."

"Yes, yes, it is. And these men, they are worse than vultures. At least a vulture waits for its prey to die first. These men are actively trying to hasten my demise."

"I am not sure I follow."

"Men will stop at nothing to gain my hand or,

more importantly, my money in marriage. I have been hounded by men who lack any sort of moral compass who have tried to compromise me into forcing a wedding."

"Ah, the old 'compromise the heiress so she'll be forced to marry me' trick." Thornton shrugged but his eyes gleamed. "Standard procedure for a gentleman down on his luck."

"It becomes tedious to always have men flattering me to my face but insulting me behind my back. They come on sweet as sugar trying to get me to run away with them. I've even had a few who tried to kidnap me."

"Abduction?"

"I awoke once in the middle of the night to see two men climbing in my window. I screamed and they grabbed me."

Thornton frowned, the amused glint in his eye gone. "That is going too far. What did ye do?"

"I fought them until my father burst in. My father made his fortune as a privateer you know, so he is handy in a fight."

"Good to know." The smile returned to Thornton's eye.

"But what of you? I confess I know little of social conventions, but are you not 'on the market' so to speak?"

Thornton laughed. "I suppose, but I am not at liberty to take a wife at this moment, although my mother may feel differently on that score."

"But why are you avoiding matrimony?"

"I imagine I shall fall into wedded bliss at some

point, but unlike yer false suitors, I coud'na feel comfortable marrying a lass for financial gain."

"Then you are a different sort of man than I have met before."

"I am pleased to hear it."

"But why? Forgive me, I know I'm blunt, but why not marry an heiress? I have it on good authority that it is the fond practice of many a gentleman who has run afoul of his vowels."

Thornton's eyebrows raised. "Afoul of his vowels?"

Harriet winced. "Sorry. IOUs. I've been told not to speak such. My father was a sea captain, you understand. He would take me with him on board when the ship was docked. I grew up playing on the decks. It was fun, but I fear I picked up some language that is rather colorful."

"Yer secret is safe. As for me, my family's debts are mine to pay. I will never marry a heiress because neither of us would ever know whether I had wed for affection or for more material gains. It does not seem like a strong foundation for a lifetime together."

Harriet was impressed. "I wholeheartedly agree. I wish more men were like you."

Lord Thornton's silver eyes danced in the candlelight. He was made from sturdy stock with black hair, square shoulders, and solid features. His nose, brow, and jawline were not prominent but definitely masculine. His features were not extraordinary, and while he might recede into the background around the current dandies who dressed with more flash, in the candlelight, she was struck by the fact that he was a handsome man.

A man with whom she was sitting in a near dark room, alone. Which, despite being raised in an unconventional household in many ways, she knew not even her father would approve. *Especially* not her father.

Her heart skittered a bit faster and she was suddenly very aware just how little space separated them. They were together on the same couch. She could lean forward and touch him.

Touch him. She swallowed on a dry throat. What was wrong with her?

"Good thing you have sworn off marrying an heiress." Harriet giggled in a nervous fashion she found irritating in other people.

"Avoid them at all costs. I should fear for myself now, except that ye have sworn off marriage in general, so I have nothing to fear." His tone made the statement almost a question. His eyes met hers for too long. "I should escort ye back." He stood.

"Yes!" Harriet jumped up too. "No! I shall walk myself back, no need to trouble yourself."

"If ye have any difficulty, know that I can be called upon to assist. Day or night," he added in a way that made her heart pound.

"Yes, well I shall give that some thought." Probably more than she should. She backed away from him like he was a dangerous beast. "Good evening then." She tripped over a side table, which went down with a bang. She almost went down too but caught herself and quickly righted the table.

Harriet looked up slowly. "If you ever think of this conversation, can you forget that part?"

A slow smile spread on his face. "Never happened. Ye are grace itself."

Harriet stifled a laugh. "Don't stretch the truth too far. Your imagination will rebel against the patently absurd."

"Good eve, Grace."

"Good eve, my lord."

Nine

I T   W A S   N O T   E V E R Y   D A Y   P E N E L O P E   R E C E I V E D   A
summons from a duke to have a clandestine meeting.
But that was exactly what the Duke of Marchford
had done. The short note said to meet him in the
blue parlor before dinner. The blue parlor, which
was used exclusively for breakfasts, would be isolated
at this time of the evening. Nothing could be
clearer. The Duke of Marchford wanted to speak to
her alone.

She had to dress, naturally. Her options were
limited. Nothing the dowager had packed for her
seemed appropriate. The gowns were all things other
people would wear, gowns her sisters would wear. She
sat heavily on the bed with a sudden realization. The
dowager, wrong as she was, was actually right.

Penelope had given up. Why should her sisters,
some older, some younger, all wear gowns of the latest
fashion while she was relegated to their rejects and
more sensible, unattractive options?

When had she given up on marriage for herself? Was
it her first season? Was it even before that time? Her

sisters, whose welfare had consumed her, were now all married and well cared for. So when was it time for Penelope to take a chance on the marriage mart?

She wished to say never. It was easier not to. Easier not to care. Easier to remain in her old clothes. Easier to remain...

Invisible.

She turned the word around in her mind. Obscurity was exactly what she wanted. She wanted to remain invisible. People who could not be seen could not be criticized. They could not fail, for they never tried. They could never lose, for they never played the game. They were safe. And they were cowards.

Penelope Rose was many things but never a coward. She went back to her closet and picked not the dress she wished to wear, but a gown one of her younger sisters would choose. She picked the gown of the most gossamer fabric over a silk underdress that was so light it practically floated off the ground. Most shocking of all was its color. Pink. A soft rose pink with a deeper rose-colored ribbon to form a high waistline, and a low-cut neckline revealing more of her bosom than had ever before seen the light of day.

She called for a maid to help with the enclosures, which were in the back and impossible to do herself unless she had detachable arms. To her surprise, Madame Leclair came herself. She helped Penelope into her gown as if being dressed by the duchess's own lady's maid was commonplace.

"You will allow me to fix your hair," said Leclair.

It was not a request. Conscious of the honor being bestowed upon her, Penelope could only agree and watch in horror as Madame stuck the curling iron into the fire.

"Do not concern yourself. I have not ever left a permanent scar."

It was reassurance—or possibly a warning not to move about or complain. When Leclair was done, Penelope stared back at the image in the glass, unsure who the woman was. She was unrecognizable to herself. Her plain brown hair looked anything but ordinary, piled high and falling down in ringlets, framing her face and cascading down her back. In her hair were little jeweled pins, which picked up the light and sparkled.

The dress clung to her in places no other dress had ever clung. The underdress was a darker rose with soft pink gauze over it. The gown hugged her body and caressed her curves. Madame had insisted on a different corset than she was accustomed to wearing. This one lifted parts of her to new heights, such that her cleavage blossomed out of the gown in a suggestive manner. The effect was soft and sensual and, dare she say it? Arousing.

"I cannot be seen looking like this," she muttered.

"Of course you can," came the dowager's voice from behind her.

Penelope turned to the dowager, who was smiling at her. "This gown is not proper."

"Hang proper. You look lovely. Wear it while you can, my dear. Your breasts won't always cooperate so nicely."

Penelope could not help but put a hand over her chest. "Your Grace! I fear you have only confirmed my fear that this is not a gown that should ever see the light of day."

"I agree with you. What you are wearing is an

evening gown. Most definitely a gown for the night. Now you need only one thing to complete your look." The dowager opened a blue velvet box and showed the contents to Penelope.

"Your pearls?" asked Penelope.

"They were my mother's. Come, let me see them. I did not work tirelessly at choosing these gowns for you so you could go to dinner half-dressed." The dowager put the pearls around Penelope's neck. In the mirror, the girl before Penelope smiled and sparkled. She was beautiful. And beautiful was not something she had ever felt before.

"What do you think?" whispered the dowager as if afraid she might break the spell by speaking too loudly.

Penelope turned the elder woman and gave her an uncharacteristic hug. "Thank you," breathed Penelope. "You were right. I was hiding behind my practical clothes."

"Ugly clothes," muttered Madame.

"As I was saying, I would never have thought to change my wardrobe, and while it may be some time getting accustomed to this new look, I do think it is time to be brave."

"Good for you." The dowager nodded approvingly. "May this be the beginning of a fashionable change for you. Especially if you would like to accompany me to the opera."

It was time. Time to step up to the challenge of being present in society. She would be invisible no longer. And in this dress, she was sure to be noticed.

And the first person who was going to notice her was the Duke of Marchford.

Penelope's new clothes, or perhaps her new corset, made her walk differently. She always held herself with good posture, that part was nothing new, but her clinging dress made it impossible to take long steps, so she was forced to take shorter ones, and somehow everything moved and flowed a little more. Her hips rocked, her bosom jiggled—it was all quite disconcerting. She hoped she could get to the drawing room before he arrived so she could sit somewhere in the shadows, preventing him from having the dubious honor of watching her try to slink into the room.

She was not so lucky. The Duke of Marchford rose somberly from his chair when she entered. Even when he stood at his full height, his eyebrows continued to rise. He noticed. She swallowed compulsively. Now she had to attempt to walk toward him. In full view. With him watching. Brilliant.

She was Penelope Rose. She was not a coward. Her chin rose and she took a bold step forward. Unfortunately, a little too bold; trying to take too long a step, she caught her foot on her gown. She tripped and staggered forward, right into the arms of the Duke of Marchford.

"I am so sorry," she said, pushing him away even before she had found her footing.

"Good heavens, Miss Rose," said Marchford, easily setting her upright. "What happened to you?"

"Your grandmother happened to me," lamented Penelope. "She has tossed away all my clothes, everything I had packed for myself, and left me with two trunks full of the most fashionable, most impractical gowns you could ever imagine."

"Sounds devious enough to be my grandmother," said Marchford warily. "I suppose I should apologize for her interference in your affairs, but I do believe you knew what you were getting yourself into."

"I hardly knew it would come to this." Penelope motioned down her body.

Marchford's eyes trailed down her length, from her curled hair to her slippered toe. "One thing I will say for Grandmamma, she does know her fashion."

Penelope met his eyes. "A compliment?"

"Simply a fact. You would look lovely if you could keep your feet beneath you."

"Thank you," muttered Penelope and found a chair so as not to risk falling over. Leave it to Marchford to deliver a compliment with enough of a sting to leave one feeling wounded. "You called me here for a reason?"

"Did I?" Marchford started as if she had shaken him awake. "Oh yes, quite. We had an arrangement in London, one that I would like to continue."

Penelope felt her cheeks begin to burn. The way he said "arrangement" brought to mind something entirely different than the facts would allow. She cleared her throat and tried to get herself under better regulation. It must be the dress making her stupid. "What would you have me do?"

"Do?" Marchford's gaze seemed to be getting distracted. He was now addressing himself to her bosom. "Yes, quite what I would like you to do." His eyes flicked up to her face and then gravitated back down again.

"Do you like your grandmother's necklace with the

gown?" asked Penelope, confused as to what would be so fascinating as to draw his gaze.

"What?" He looked up at her as if surprised to see her attached to the body at which he was staring.

"The pearls."

"What pearls?"

"The pearls I'm wearing. The ones you are staring at."

"Oh!" He turned away and picked up some papers on the side table. "Yes, pearls. Very good. So Grandmother didn't allow you anything sensible to wear. Too bad. Too bad."

"So what was it you wished to say to me?"

"I would like you to continue to keep your eyes and ears open for me." Marchford was now addressing his papers. "I need to know as much as I can about what is happening in this house. There is a strong likelihood that spies have attempted to infiltrate society to the extent that they may be present at this house party. If you notice anything out of the ordinary or unusual, I would appreciate it if you would inform me immediately."

"I shall do my utmost, although as I have said before, I shall not reveal the secrets, plots, or plans of your grandmother. As her companion, it would be unseemly."

"Yes, yes, of course. Since we are staying at Thornton Hall, I should like to arrange a time and place to meet regularly for you to give reports. Would this place and time be acceptable to you?"

"Yes, that would be fine."

"Thank you, Miss Rose." Again, the duke did not look up at Penelope.

"Is something the matter, Your Grace?"

Marchford looked her straight in the eye. "I would suggest a shawl for dinner unless you would like to see a riot erupt over who gets to take you in."

Penelope gave a tentative smile. "You are jesting with me."

"A shawl, Miss Rose. Please favor me and find a shawl."

Penelope was halfway back to her room before she realized the duke had paid her a compliment.

Ten

HARRIET SAT IN A CHAIR, A FAKE SMILE PLASTERED across her face. Surrounding her were attentive gentlemen, undoubtedly lacking funds, who were practically salivating at the thought of fifty thousand pounds.

"Would you care for refreshments?"

"I just brought her a cup."

"Would you like to dance?"

"They are not playing any music."

"How about a private game of cards?"

"Would you like to take a stroll in the garden?"

"She's not going anywhere with you!"

"Thank you, gentlemen!" declared Harriet, rising to her feet and causing a near riot as the men who were seated jumped up, generally in the way of those who were standing. "I do need to excuse myself."

"I shall be pleased to escort you anywhere to the ends of the earth," declared one potential swain.

"That is very kind, but since my destination is the ladies' retiring room, I doubt your presence would be appreciated by the other guests." Harriet headed for the door, walking as calmly and sedately as a woman running for her life could do.

On the way, she saw the dowager, who gave her a knowing smile. Harriet resisted the urge to confront the elderly lady. She supposed by publicizing her dowry, the Duchess of Marchford was trying to help, but she would appreciate it much more if the duchess would stop helping.

Miss Priscilla Crawley was leaving the ladies' retiring room when Harriet approached. Harriet was not particularly happy to see her, but to be fair, Miss Crawley looked utterly ravishing in a cream gown with a burgundy sash just below her ample bosom.

"Miss Redgrave! What a shame your trunks did not arrive in time for you to dress for dinner tonight." Priscilla gave her a sad puppy face that Harriet supposed was mock sympathy.

Instinctively, Harriet glanced down at her white muslin gown with six inches of lace around the hem. It was one of her best, and until this moment, she had thought it very nice. "You look lovely tonight, Miss Crawley," said Harriet, clinging to the high road.

Priscilla cast her a haughty look as if Harriet had said something insulting.

"Good evening, Miss Redgrave," said a voice behind her with a strong French accent.

Harriet turned and gave a curtsy to the Comtesse de Marseille. "Good evening."

"How clever of you to circulate the amount of your dowry," said the comtesse with an arch look. "Now you shall never want for company. Desperate men may be induced to marry *anyone* for that prize."

Harriet ignored the giggles behind her from Priscilla and her friends. She tried to think of how to respond to such thinly veiled insults, but the comtesse merely sailed away with the snickering girls in her wake.

Harriet attempted to take refuge in the ladies' retiring room, but she found the gossip within even more venomous. Harriet returned to the drawing room with slow feet but painted on a smile and, with a deep breath, joined the fray, determined to do her best.

～⌘～

When the men rejoined the ladies after dinner, Thornton had found himself engaged in the process of watching the tall, lithe Miss Redgrave rather than doing what he ought. As a result, he noted that Miss Redgrave lacked the cool air of social sophistication expected in society. Instead, she was open, frank, and friendly.

Word had spread regarding her dowry and she did not lack for company. Although she smiled, the emotion did not reach her eyes. She may have won male attention, but she did not appear pleased.

Thornton had a mind to rescue Miss Redgrave from what appeared to be some rather forward would-be suitors. Unfortunately, his mother interrupted his plans by bringing Miss Crawley to him again. Miss Crawley was a lovely girl—cool and reserved, every-thing Harriet was not.

Despite Miss Crawley's practiced aloof manner and bored demeanor, which marked her a lady of good breeding, he could not help but be amused by Harriet, who told one of her suitors she liked to climb up into the rigging of her father's clipper ship. At his aghast face, she amended that she always wore pantaloons instead of skirts on board ship. When the poor man started to cough, she slapped him so hard on the back that he fell to the floor.

The company stopped and took notice of Miss Redgrave hoisting the terrified man back onto his feet. They began to titter and Thornton turned and laughed into his sleeve.

"What an awkward girl," commented Miss Crawley with disdain. "But what can you expect from the daughter of a madwoman. I am sorry you could not refuse to allow her admittance to the house."

"Wouldn't have refused her even if it was possible," said Thornton. "Would ye care for some refreshment?"

The lady accepted and Thornton made his escape, asking a footman to bring out more wine. It was fortunate Marchford had brought supplies, for Thornton's wine cellar would never have served so many for long.

Thornton made his way casually to the throng of gentlemen around Miss Redgrave. They came in every age, rank, and societal standing, but were united in their mutual need for an influx of assets. Fifty thousand pounds was a fortune. It was certainly enough to save Thornton Hall, and save himself and his mother a good deal of trouble and embarrassment. But it was not a basis for a marriage, as his mother had amply shown him.

Miss Redgrave caught his eye when he drew near. Lord Punthorpe was in the midst of telling her the full extent of his pampered pedigree. It was a long-winded recitation, and since he had only just made it to the reign of Queen Elizabeth, Thornton had to be impressed by the man's recall of his family tree. The look in Miss Redgrave's eye was one of a lass begging for mercy, and he could not call himself a gentleman without responding to her call for help.

"Excuse me," Thornton interrupted. "Forgive me, Miss Redgrave, but Lord Langley is awake and asking for ye."

"Oh!" said Harriet, jumping out of her chair in a manner more like a happy puppy than a lady of refinement. "I shall go at once!"

"I shall escort you!" claimed one man.

"No, I claim that honor," said another.

"Nay, ye must stay and enjoy yerselves," said Thornton and held out his arm to Harriet. "I shall see to her safety."

As soon as they were outside the drawing room and beyond hearing, Harriet breathed an audible sigh.

"The evening was wearing on ye?" asked Thornton.

"Horribly. I enjoyed it more when I was being ignored."

"No chance o' that now."

"Which will make for a very long house party. I'm only glad my grandfather woke up to call for me."

"I confess," said Thornton, escorting her up the stairs, "that I have misled ye. I dinna ken whether yer grandfather is asleep or not."

"What do you mean?"

"I spoke a wee fib to get ye out o' the room."

"Ah! You have saved me! Thank you!" She gave him a hug which surprised him so much he instantly wanted more. This time her smile lit up her face.

"I am glad my dishonesty meets with yer approval," said Thornton with an uncharacteristic chuckle.

"It does when it gets me out of a fix." Her eyes were gleaming. "Thank you."

"Ye are most welcome, Miss Redgrave."

They stopped at the hallway leading to where the young ladies and their requisite chaperones were staying. It would be unseemly for Thornton to go further. Harriet smiled up at him, almost at eye level. It was nice to look into a lady's eyes, not down at the top of her head.

"Thank you again," said Harriet. "You are definitely getting into the habit of rescuing me."

"All part of the Highland hospitality service." Thornton leaned a shoulder on the wall. It was a more casual posture than he had ever taken with a member of the opposite sex, but she was so friendly, so apparently immune to societal constraints that it put him at ease.

Harriet raised one eyebrow. "And what, pray tell, is part of the Highland hospitality service?"

"Nothing out o' the ordinary," Thornton created. "Rescuing from explosions, protection from fortune hunters, and relief from dull conversation."

Harriet's green eyes danced in the candlelight. "This is a standard practice for you?"

"The standard *American* package." Thornton could not say it without a smile.

"Ah! It all becomes clear!" Miss Redgrave laughed and stepped closer. "And what do I owe you for this generous protection?"

"Nay, no cost, naturally, to my guests."

"So you protect against explosions, fortune hunters, and poor conversation. What about malicious gossip?"

"Och, lass, the *ton* lives on gossip and wine. To stem that tide will cost ye extra." Thornton leaned forward.

"Name your price," demanded Harriet with a smile just for him.

A kiss.

Thornton coughed and straightened himself. He was careening toward dangerous territory. He should not be talking to her alone anyway. He had the uncommon feeling of being at ease with her, no small feat considering his experience to date with members of the fairer sex.

"I should return to the other guests," said Thornton, recognizing it was an abrupt change of topic, but fearing the repercussions should he allow himself to continue the conversation.

Miss Redgrave blinked and stepped back. "Yes, yes, of course. I should not keep you." She turned and disappeared down the hall.

Thornton returned slowly to the drawing room, aware that he had handled things poorly. His mother was right about one thing. Miss Harriet Redgrave was dangerous.

Eleven

"YES, LORD THORNTON!" MARCHFORD CALLED FROM across the room when Thornton reentered the drawing room. Marchford was surrounded by a bevy of females of every size, shape, and age. He did not look happy about it. He walked over to Thornton with a trail of admirers in his wake. "What do you need?"

Thornton was too good a friend to expose the man's ruse, so he held his tongue until Marchford was close enough to whisper. "Am I in need of something?"

"Yes," said Marchford in a booming voice. "Yes, of course I can assist you. Forgive me, ladies, duty calls."

Marchford led the way out of the drawing room and Thornton followed him all the way upstairs to a little-used salon. There, Marchford sank into a leather chair and put his hand over his eyes.

"Too much feminine society?" asked Thornton.

"When I walked into the parlor, I swear I heard someone call, 'release the hounds!'"

Thornton smiled and sat across from him. "I seem to be in great demand tonight to protect people from unwanted suitors. Only one way to stop it."

Marchford gave him his full attention. "Which is?"

"Announce yer engagement."

"Not you too. I am tired beyond words of matrimony. Besides, it is hindering my ability to search for foreign agents."

"Are ye certain there is a spy in our midst?"

"I can be certain of nothing. I do know that a spy would not wish to miss such an assembly of London's elite. I have gathered men to discuss plans for the war, but so many more people managed to acquire an invitation that I think it quite probable that a spy has weaseled his way in as well."

"How are ye going to flush out this spy of yers?"

Marchford sighed again. "Have not quite figured that out yet. I hope an opportunity will present itself."

"Good luck, my friend. After yer success in catching spies, would ye no' think any agent working for the emperor would be wary of ye?"

"Perhaps."

"Likely they would also carry a grudge. Ye may be a target as well if ye get in their way." Thornton was ever wary.

Marchford shrugged. "I would rather they come after me than another. If there is someone in society taking orders from Napoleon, no one is safe until that person is found."

"I am at yer service as always. I am surprised to say this, but I miss having Grant around. He was not particularly useful in a crisis, but at least I knew what side he was on."

"He was invited but is apparently still on his honeymoon," said Marchford in a baffled tone.

"Still? Long time, is it not? Ye would think he would grow tired of having naught but his new wife for company."

"True. Perhaps there is something to marriage we bachelors are missing."

The men pondered the question for a moment then laughed and shook their heads. After a glass of something and more talk of how to catch an enemy agent, they found the hour had grown late, so the two friends made their way to their respective bedrooms on the upper floor of the manor house. Marchford stopped and pointed without a word at his bedroom door. It was ajar.

"Did ye leave yer door open?" whispered Thornton.

Marchford shook his head and pulled a small pistol from his waistcoat. Silently, Thornton shuttered the light on his lantern and Marchford softly opened the door further.

The men listened at the door for any sound. Thornton scanned the gloom, trying to spot anything that might be dangerous. He heard nothing. At the signal from Marchford, he unshuttered the lantern, casting the room in its light.

"Marchford? Is that you, honey?" a woman's voice came from behind the bed curtains.

Thornton glanced at Marchford, but he shrugged his shoulders and shook his head. The voice was unknown to him and he was not expecting company.

The men scanned the room, but finding nothing else out of place, they surrounded the bed. Thornton put the lantern down on the table and prepared for a fight. He had made it his practice to avoid fights when possible. Despite being a peace-loving fellow, he was, after all, a Highlander by birth, and if there was going to be a fight in his castle, he was going to be a part of it.

Thornton and Marchford threw back the curtains simultaneously, charging forward. The woman shrieked when Marchford threw back the covers to expose his attacker. What he discovered was a naked lady.

Recognizing that this was not an ambush, Thornton turned his back to her. "Good evening, Lady Stinton."

"I do apologize for any misunderstanding. I believe this is your wrap," said Marchford.

The young widow sputtered in a manner Thornton feared would lead to tears. A fair fight, or even an unfair one, he could handle. A woman in tears was beyond his expertise. "A thousand pardons," he soothed. "We were under the impression this was the room of the Duke of Marchford. We in no way meant to intrude on yer privacy."

"I do apologize for this dreadful misunderstanding," added Marchford, walking away and quickly repocketing the gun.

Thornton followed Marchford out of the room, and they stood in the hall inspecting the ceiling and pretending not to notice the outraged young lady leave the room in search of her own quarters.

"Thank you, my friend," said Marchford. "I am not sure what she was after, but I appreciate your help in avoiding entanglements."

"I think we both know what she was after," said Thornton with a sidewise glance.

"Lord Thornton." The butler came into view,

carrying a candle of his own. "Ye have another visitor and he is demanding to speak with the Duke of Marchford tonight!"

❧

Marchford and Thornton entered a small parlor to determine who had so demanded an audience with His Grace the duke. The man inspected his timepiece as they entered, as if they had kept him waiting.

"Mr. Neville," said Marchford. "Has the Foreign Office sent you all this way from London?"

"Yes. I arrived as quickly as I could. I need to speak to you immediately. Alone," he added with a severe glare at Thornton. The man was small of stature but not in confidence.

"Lord Thornton, I believe you are acquainted with Mr. Neville from the Foreign Office," said Marchford, ignoring Neville's demands.

"Aye, o' course," said Thornton. "Ye shot that traitor Blakely before he could kill Grant. I shall never forget yer assistance in protecting our friends."

"My service is to the Crown, not to you nor any of your friends. Now I wish to speak to His Grace alone," persisted Neville.

"I am feeling generally unappreciated, so I will bid ye a good night," said Thornton with a bow and a slight smile at Marchford. The duke and Neville had crossed paths before.

"Tell the footman to bring some warm punch," commented Marchford in a lazy tone. "I am certain Mr. Neville's nerves could use soothing after his long journey. And if his don't, mine certainly will need reviving after hearing all of what Mr. Neville has to say."

When they were alone, Neville demanded to be apprised as to the current situation. "I knew I needed to come to Thornton Hall when I heard you were planning this gathering. I need a report of your dealings here. Have you noted anything suspicious?"

"Most of the guests have only arrived today. I am probably behind schedule, but alas no spies were revealed before dinner."

"You must do all you can to discover these traitors. And of course, I noted that several military generals and admirals were among your guest list. Pray tell me, for what purpose are they here?"

"Mr. Neville," said Marchford, with a calculated change of subject, "how unconventional of you to arrive uninvited. I must have been away from London too long. I am not familiar with these new casual customs."

Mr. Neville glowered. It was a look Marchford was accustomed to, so he paid it no heed. "I am not here for a social visit," growled Neville. "I'm here to help you catch the traitor who may be in your midst. Also, the Foreign Office needs to be aware of any high-level meetings so they can be kept secret and safe."

"I was not aware you were so concerned with my safety."

"Your safety?" scoffed Neville. "It is the safety and security of any plans developed that is my concern. Where will these plans be kept? How will these plans be transferred? The risk of spies and traitors is everywhere. Napoleon has already conquered most of Europe. Would you see him on the British throne as well?"

Marchford began to search the room for refreshment. The butler was taking too long with the punch. Surely Thornton would have a bottle of whiskey stashed somewhere. "Mr. Neville, you need to put your vivid imagination to better use. Have you considered the occupation of writing novels?"

Mr. Neville ignored this. "If you are using or developing any sensitive information, I demand to hold this information for safekeeping."

Marchford was saved from an immediate reply by the arrival of the punch bowl. He took over mixing the contents and Neville was blissfully quiet.

"You need not concern yourself. I will ensure its safety," said Marchford.

Mr. Neville puffed himself up to his full, albeit diminutive, height. "As an agent of the Foreign Office I demand—"

"Rum punch, old man?" Marchford handed the man a cup of punch. "I do not wish to fall prey to the sin of pride, but I have been told my punch is beyond the common fare."

"Your Grace." Neville took an obliging sip of the offered cup of punch. "I need to take control of… my word, this is good." He took another sip of punch. And another.

"Let me refill your cup." Marchford gave the government agent another hearty helping and watched with amusement as Mr. Neville drank it down. "It has been a long journey for you."

"Yes." Mr. Neville relaxed back into his chair. "Very long. The roads toward the end were especially bad."

"You need to put new springs on your coach. Makes a world of difference."

"I am only a representative of the Crown. I traveled most of this way by post."

"No! My dear man, let me refill your cup." Marchford poured out another cup and smiled as the agent sank further into the pillows of the chair. "You must be so very tired."

Neville obligingly yawned. "Yes, it has been a long several days. I am quite weary of the road."

"Then you must stay and rest before you return to London. Do not worry yourself about anything. I shall let the housekeeper know to turn down an extra bed for you." And with that, Marchford made his escape.

Twelve

"'TIS TIME." TAM MET HIM AT THE GATE, LANTERN IN hand, and Thornton followed the older stable master into the castle.

Thornton had risen even earlier than usual in the predawn morning, hoping this might be the day the mare would foal. "How are things progressing?" This foal had every chance of being a fine racehorse, perhaps his best, and he needed things to go smoothly. Not only did his financial survival depend on it, but these horses were his passion.

Tam shook his gray head. "Water broke but she's agitated something fierce, up and down."

Thornton stepped quickly to the mare's stall. She lay on the clean straw and groaned. He patted the chestnut mare gently. "How long has she been pushing?"

Tam hung the lantern on a hook on the stable. "Too long, my lord. Dinna like it."

Thornton quickly stripped off his jacket and cravat and rolled up his sleeves. "Let's get her up, see if repositioning helps."

"Aye." Tam helped Thornton encourage the mare

to her feet, even as she whinnied in protest. She pawed the ground and her nostrils flared with her short breaths.

"There ye go, my dear," crooned Thornton to the mare. "It will be all right."

The mare turned around and lay down again. With a groan, two hooves emerged. The horse grunted and strained, but no further progress was made.

"The foal is breech." Thornton knew he had to act fast. If the foal was not born soon, it could die.

"Too long. Most likely stillborn," said Tam in his blunt manner.

Thornton ignored him and stripped off his shirt. Things were going to get messy. "Ye can do this," he said to the mare in a soothing voice. "Yer bairn will be a great one." He wrapped a cloth around the slick legs of the foal and pulled down to help with the birth. Reaching in, he rotated the foal. Then he pulled on the legs of the foal as the mare pushed with a contraction. With effort, the hocks were delivered, followed by the hips.

"Hardest part is done. Just a little more." Thornton spoke softly to the mare. He was sweating with the exertion. This baby must live. He pulled hard, and with a grunt from the mare, the foal was delivered.

"No' breathing," said Tam grimly.

"Come on, breathe!" Thornton grabbed the cloth and vigorously rubbed the colt. "There's a good lad, breathe now." He paused to feel for any signs of life.

"Stillborn," muttered Tam.

"Nay, wait." Thornton rubbed the colt more, his

heart sinking. He paused and finally felt what he was waiting for.

"He breathes!" Thornton took a deep breath himself, relief flooding through him. "Och, he's a bonnie lad." To be frank, the wet colt just born may not have appeared to his best advantage, but Thornton smiled at the black colt with true affection.

He was going to be a fine one. The colt briefly raised his head and Thornton gently scratched behind his ear. The colt would fetch a big price if Thornton could be induced to sell. His horses were like family and he was extremely particular about who received one of his prized ones.

"Big one, he is," said Tam, more interested now the colt lived.

"Aye, little wonder she had difficulty wi' him. I shall name him Lazarus, because he came back from the brink of death and hopefully will help us to do the same." Thornton stood and felt the need for soap and water.

Two stable lads sauntered in through the side door to begin their workday and were immediately entranced by the new colt. The mare stood and everything appeared to be progressing well.

"Stay wi' them and let me know if there are any problems," said Thornton. He grabbed a jar of soap and strode out of the main keep to wash. The colt lived. It was going to be a beautiful day.

❦

The air was fresh and the hour was early. Harriet Redgrave climbed over rocks and up grassy hills to the ruins of a castle above. She was following a track of hoof prints to try to catch sight of some local deer. Being raised close to the edge of the great American wilderness, she was accustomed to tracking potential dinner items with her brothers. This morning was strictly sightseeing. The sun was just peeking over the horizon, casting the landscape in the orange hue of sunrise.

It was a glorious morning. The air was crisp, but the sun was warm with the promise of a clear day. It was considerably better than London, where she feared her lungs would burst from the smoke and general haze settled permanently over the city. Not to mention the smell. With so many people living in one place, the odor of waste of all sorts offended her nostrils. How anybody could become accustomed to such conditions was beyond her.

Harriet was a country girl, raised on the coast of Massachusetts. The wilds of the Highlands were different from anything she had ever seen—surely she did not have ancient ruined castles tucked away in the hills around her house. But still, the Highlands reminded her of home, fresh and clean, and verdant in multiple shades of green. Of all the places she had traveled since arriving on these shores, the Highlands were the one place she would miss once she finally left.

Harriet stepped over rocks and scampered ever higher, until the rocks were boulders and she was more climbing than walking. Above her the ruins of a castle soared. The castle had two towers on either side of a five-story square keep. The wall around it had been breached, and she climbed over it at a low place and wandered around the castle itself.

It was awe-inspiring. She had seen drawings of castles in books but was unprepared for just how large a structure the castle actually was. What must it be like to live in such a place?

Harriet walked along the wall of the main keep and trailed her fingers along the edge of the stones, smooth and cool to the touch. How much had these stones seen? She walked around to find a door. It was clear from her rambles she had approached the castle from the back and was now walking around to the front.

The front of the castle had a sturdy oak door that looked oddly newer than the stones around it. Newer and locked. Frustrated, she put her hands on her hips and stepped back, looking for another way to get in.

"Hey there, lassie!"

Harriet whirled around and faced an elderly farmer, approaching her with a pitchfork in hand.

"Ye're no' to be trespassing. Move out wi' ye!"

Harriet folded her arms across her chest. "I am a guest of Lord Thornton. Who are you and why are you threatening an unarmed young lady?"

The man stopped short, removed his cap, rubbed his gray hair, then put the cap back on. "I'm Tam, I am. And I dinna threaten anyone, miss. I just lead them back to their rightful place. Like sheep."

"You think I'm a sheep?"

"Aye. Nay. Aw, have pity, lassie. I'm supposed to keep people away. Can ye go away now?"

"As you wish," said Harriet to be obliging. The man had a pitchfork after all.

"Thornton Hall is that way." He jerked a thumb over his shoulder, and Harriet could see the manor house in the valley below. She had indeed come up the long way.

Harriet began to stroll toward the castle gate in the direction of Thornton Hall, but as soon as Tam had disappeared around one side of the castle, she hustled around to the other side. It was not every day she had a chance to explore a real castle!

She rounded the corner and stopped short, utterly dumbfounded at the sight before her. It was Thornton, drawing up water to wash in the well. And other than boots and breeches he was… *naked*.

Thornton used jar soap and scrubbed his hands, arms, and chest. Harriet could only watch in awe as his muscles rippled under his skin. Living with four brothers, she had on occasion seen a shirtless man, but never had she been so afflicted. She knew she should back away, since he had not yet seen her, but she could not move.

The water glistened off his skin in the golden light of dawn. She was seized with an overwhelming urge to touch him. Instead of backing away, Harriet took several steps closer. Thornton turned and dropped the bucket.

"Miss Harriet!"

"Lord Duncan." It was not quite his name, but it was the best she could do.

Silence fell over them. Thornton was dripping wet, clean, and to Harriet's eye, the most beautiful half-naked Highlander she had ever seen. Of course he was the *only* half-naked Highlander she had ever seen.

"I was… that is to say… I was not expecting anyone to be awake so early." Thornton was indeed surprised.

She knew she should leave, but her feet remained planted to the ground. "I am an early riser." It was spoken apologetically, but she was not at all sorry to witness the sight before her.

"I should dress. 'Tis unseemly. My clothes, they are near. Dinna move. Stay there." He gave the order and she was more than willing to comply. "I shall be back directly." He practically ran around to the back of the castle.

Harriet took a deep breath of the cool morning air. They certainly knew how to grow them in the Highlands. She shook her head at herself. What was this sudden interest in a man? Her passion had always been her work. No man had ever elicited such a reaction. It was almost chemical in nature. Her heart was pounding, her cheeks were flushed, and she was sweating even in the brisk morning.

Very unnatural.

To calm herself back into good regulation she focused on reviewing the elements. All forty-six of them. Science was so very reassuring (usually), predictable (generally), and safe (occasionally). Men were... here her mental faculties met their limit. She had no idea what men were except that they were not reassuring, predictable, or safe.

If she had any sense she would leave, but Thornton had asked her to stay, and not even wild horses could drag her away.

"Miss Redgrave."

Harriet turned and smiled at Thornton, who emerged from the back side of the castle and strode to her. He was wearing work clothes: a dark-blue coat, buckskin breeches, and Hessian boots. He looked every bit the lord of the manor. She ignored her desire to see him again unclothed.

"Good morn to you, Lord Thornton. I see you have located your shirt."

"I do apologize for my appearance earlier. I had no expectation any of the guests would be awake or present at the castle."

"No, it is I who should apologize. I am clearly where I should not be. A man already attempted to run me off with a pitchfork. I am in the wrong. This is your home, you should feel free to do as you please." *And if you want to run about half-naked, I invite you to do so.*

"I was just washing this morning. I sometimes come up to the castle to make some repairs and I try to keep my clothes clean so…" Thornton was a terrible liar. "Aye then, verra well. Nice weather we shall have today."

Harriet desperately wanted to ask him more about why he was undressed but refrained. The voices of Penelope and the duchess and her own mother urging her to show a little more decorum prevented her from asking impertinent questions. But she wanted to, make no mistake.

"I have never seen a castle before. I fear my curiosity got the best of me."

"What? Are there no castles in America? Nay, I suppose not," Thornton answered his own question. "Well then, allow me to show ye about."

Harriet hoped he would open the main door to the keep, but instead he offered his arm for a tour of the castle grounds. She took his arm and a tingle of excitement ran down her spine. She must be more interested in castles than she realized.

"The castle was built over a thousand years ago," commented Thornton. "It was inhabited until lightning struck the north tower, causing it to crumble and catch fire. The Lady Thornton o' the day demanded her lord rebuild a more modern manor home, which ye see below."

"It is quite an impressive home, bigger even than the castle perhaps."

"It is bigger than the castle. Though it would be better if it had been built on a more modest scale."

"Why do you say that?"

"Maintenance and upkeep of such a large structure, even a more modern one, is quite dear."

"You call that modern? A building more than thirty years old in America is considered rather ancient."

"I suppose it is all point of view."

"May we go inside? I would love to see it!" Harriet could not help but ask. They were passing by the front door. The locked front door.

"Nay, the castle ruins are not sound and I do not wish anyone to be hurt."

"Is that why you have Tam to scare folks away?"

"I certainly hope he did not scare ye. Tam is here to make sure the young bucks do not go climbing up towers and falling to their death. Bad form to let yer guests be killed."

"And that is why the front door is locked?" asked Harriet.

"Aye, 'tis safer this way."

"And why does Tam carry a pitchfork?"

Thornton was silent a moment, though his face revealed nothing. Finally, he shrugged. "Highlanders," he offered as an explanation.

Harriet shook her head. "Keep your secrets then."

"Ye are a clever lady, Miss Redgrave."

"Should I apologize? I have been informed that being clever is not considered a good attribute if one is a female."

Thornton smiled. "It is a compliment from me. I enjoy our conversations. I never ken what ye will say next."

The warmth of his approval cheered her. She looked out over the lush, green valley, dotted with fluffy white sheep. When had she ever been given a true compliment from a man? Not counting her own family, possibly never. "It is beautiful here. Since arriving in London, I had only one goal, to return home as soon as possible, after visiting the museums of course. One does not get the opportunity to study the exhibits at the British Museum every day. But here I could relax happily for a long time."

"Truly?" Thornton regarded her with some surprise. "Most ladies who visit, my mother included, can only think of how soon they can return to London."

"How very strange. The air is much cleaner here."

Thornton smiled. "So it is."

Harriet smiled in return, and they continued their walk around the castle.

"Here is the cistern gate and a path down to the river that feeds the loch below," said Thornton.

"It is lovely." The babbling of the river was comforting to her. Thornton put a booted foot on a large rock and leaned an elbow on his knee, gazing down on the sunlight glittering on the loch below.

"How have ye survived yer first evening at Thornton Hall?" he asked.

Harriet shrugged. "I wish the amount of my dowry had not been made known. I fear now I am being courted by men looking for a way to pay their creditors and the ladies have yet another reason to dislike me."

Thornton frowned. "I canna abide ye feeling uncomfortable."

"I am the daughter of a madwoman, or so they say. Naturally they assume I would be touched in the head myself. They know I was the cause of the incident yesterday and now they fear I might burn the house down while they sleep." Harriet turned away. For some reason, that hurt worse than others. She was accustomed to being thought odd, but she did not relish being considered dangerous.

"I know it was an accident, Miss Redgrave. It could happen to…" Thornton paused, amending himself. "Accidents do happen."

"Yes, but it could not happen to anyone because no one else would be mixing chemicals in their room. It is only that I find chemistry so interesting. I cannot understand why everyone else does not share my interest. Perhaps I am touched."

"Ye are an original. And that is a good thing."

"So is not burning down the house," muttered Harriet. "At home, my father built me a laboratory in one of the outbuildings. I thought he was being kind, but perhaps he was trying to save the house."

"That puts me in mind…" Thornton held out his arm. "Come, let me show ye something."

Harriet put her hand on his sleeve and again experienced a strange tingling. She allowed him to lead her around to the back of the castle, her heart twittering in an odd manner.

"What do you think of this?" Thornton stopped in front of a stone structure. "It is the old bakery for the castle. It is made entirely of stone except for the roof. O' course, there is no glass in the windows, so there is a bit of a breeze."

"It is very nice." Harriet was not at all clear why he would point out this nondescript structure for her notice.

"Mayhap this might be a place for ye to practice yer experiments in peace."

Harriet clapped her hands and ran in to inspect the building. It was rustic and dirty, but with a little work it would be perfect. She turned back to him, her eyes meeting his. "Thank you."

Harriet experienced a rush of something warm and sweet. No one save her own parents (and they only reluctantly) encouraged her work as an amateur chemist. He was thinking of her and allowing her to pursue what even she had to acknowledge was an odd hobby in a female. "Thank you so much. This will be perfect. Having a fresh breeze will be lovely. I always open all the windows when I do experiments anyway." It was a good way to let the smoke disperse. "How can I ever repay your kindness?" She walked up and took his hands in hers.

"No need, no need." He squeezed her hands and

looked away, flustered. "Thinking o' the house. Dinna care to have Thornton Hall burned to the ground."

"You are a very nice man," said Harriet, stepping back. "But do not fear, I shall keep the secret between us."

"Appreciate it." Thornton gave her a slow smile that made her toes curl. "Would ye like some help wi' yer things?"

"You cannot wait to have my experiments out of your house?" Harriet teased. "Very well, I know where I stand in your estimation."

"I hold ye in high enough regard to respect yer work"—Thornton offered her his arm—"and wish it far from my draperies."

"Fair enough!"

They walked back down to Thornton Hall via the direct route of a dirt path and stone staircase. Along the way, Thornton proved an able guide, naming mountains, trees, and plants. Within the house, Harriet packed her things into a trunk and, not wanting to set the servants to gossip, Thornton himself shouldered the trunk and marched it out a back way. They knew that meeting in the morning, particularly with Thornton in a state of undress, would be looked upon with censure, so they chose to keep their own company and avoid criticism.

"You cannot possibly carry that heavy trunk on your shoulder all the way up to the castle," said Harriet.

Thornton merely grunted and continued his trek. Going up was slower than coming down, but Thornton made steady progress. Harriet was impressed; she knew just how heavy that trunk was.

He was breathing hard by the time they reached the castle gates but waved off all offers of help. Finally reaching the old stone bakery, he set the trunk down with a groan.

"Are you all right?" asked Harriet.

"Aye. And I thought the caber toss was difficult. I think I will add this event to the games this year." He leaned against the wall and rubbed his shoulder.

"I cannot believe you carried that heavy trunk all the way up, but I thank you." Harriet was impressed and had a sudden compulsion to help him rub away the tension in his shoulder. She stepped forward and put her hand up to his shoulder but lost her nerve. She patted his shoulder in a friendly manner instead. "I hope you will recover."

His eyes locked with hers. He drew her in without a word.

"I should get back to the hall," he said, but the fire in his eyes was saying something else.

"Yes, of course."

"I will tell Tam to look after ye. Let him know if ye be needing anything."

"Thank you," said Harriet again, acutely aware of his closeness and how no one else was present. She leaned toward him; she couldn't help it.

He took her hand and kissed it, burning the mark of his lips on the back on her hand as if she had been branded.

"Good day," he whispered, bowed, and was gone.

Thirteen

"Did any of those young bucks chasing after Harriet last night have a title?" the dowager duchess asked Penelope as Madame Leclair attended her hair.

"Two of them did; most did not," replied Pen. "I don't understand why you spread the rumor regarding her dowry. Now she is surrounded by fortune hunters."

"Spread a rumor? Me?" Antonia was aghast. "I did nothing of the sort, but it is a good thing somebody did; otherwise, Miss Redgrave would be quite ignored."

"Better ignored than pursued for all the wrong reasons."

"Psshaw! Wherever do you come up with such notions? If Harriet is treated like a social outcast at her first social foray, she may never be accepted in society. Trust me. She needs something to make her acceptable."

"I think she is fine the way she is," said Penelope, defending her new friend with more loyalty than truth.

The dowager shook her head. "We will need to work on that gel's comportment. I think it best if we recommend she not speak at all."

"I doubt it would work. Besides, she declares herself uninterested in finding a husband."

"Nonsense. How old is the gel? Twenty-three? Of course she is interested in finding a husband. What woman who finds herself unwed at the age of twenty-three doesn't want to marry?"

"I am twenty-six."

The dowager waved her hand dismissively. "Exactly my point. You should be looking for a husband as well."

"I did wear your gown at dinner, but it all came to naught."

"That is because you wore that huge shawl over yourself. You were completely covered. I have no idea why, for you looked very well."

"I looked ridiculous." Penelope did not add that Marchford himself had recommended that she cover herself. She still wasn't sure if it was a compliment or censure. "I do wish you had not thrown away my regular gowns."

"I wish you had never had them to begin with. You look very well this morning in the white morning dress and the light-blue spencer. Quite sharp."

"The white is too bright," complained Penelope.

"That is what *white* is supposed to look like," countered the duchess. "Your morning gowns had all faded to gray."

"I still do not see how changing my wardrobe is going to find a husband."

"It certainly cannot overcome that sour attitude." The dowager looked over a box of jewels and selected one for morning wear. "But if you never marry, it is of no great consequence. You are my companion after all, and now you look respectable enough to be seen in public with me."

There are times in the life of a companion when one is required to bite one's tongue. Penelope found this was one of those moments. "What is our plan for Harriet?" she asked, turning the subject.

"What we need is a titled gentleman, not too high in the instep, so as to make Harriet palatable, or perhaps one whose financial woes have made him desperate. Where is the book?"

Penelope reached for her annotated copy of Debrett's *Peerage of England,* which was useful as a veritable shopping list for eligible men. She and her sisters had made notes as to the marital availability, financial status, and moral character of as many bachelors as they could. The book had come in handy when finding husbands for her sisters and was now used to find husbands for the clientele of Madame X. The only thing it had not been able to do was find a husband for Penelope herself.

"Take a look over these pages and find some potential candidates," said the dowager. "There may be a few more people arriving today or even tomorrow. It is a long journey after all. We can only hope someone gets greedy for her dowry."

"Should we not also take into consideration her feelings?"

"Naturally. Think how horrid she would feel if we could not find her a husband. Every girl wishes to be married, Penelope."

Penelope gave the dowager a weak smile and went

through the side door to her conjoined room. She closed the door and reclined on her bed, the copy of Debrett's beside her. Every lady in her twenties wanted to be married. Perhaps that much was true.

But every lady in her twenties would not actually get married. That much was also true.

～∽～

Harriet stayed at the castle until the sun rose clear and bright over the surrounding hills. The guests would be waking soon and she needed to return to the house. She was not particularly looking forward to the day, since she was scheduled for more "lessons" with Penelope and the duchess.

Her feet moved slowly down the hall to the room of the Duchess of Marchford. She could not quite decide how she felt about these lessons. She wanted to be accepted by the people in her grandfather's world and perhaps even wanted to understand her mother a bit more. Despite this, she was having difficulty caring for all the precise rules of the *ton*.

"I have requested a table service be brought up to our sitting room," said Penelope, gesturing at the small table. "Now remember at table to always begin with the outside and work your way in when picking up the silver."

Harriet sat at the requested meal, trying unsuccessfully to attend to what Penelope was saying. What difference could it possibly make which utensil she grabbed? Any one of them could be used to hoist the food to her mouth. Was that not the purpose of silverware to begin with?

Why would people care about such trivialities while there was a whole world around them waiting to be explored? The natural world had always fascinated her. So many questions of how and why captivated her attention. But instead of working on her next experiment, she was spending hours learning how to address a viscount and when to wear gloves.

"Miss Redgrave?" Penelope's voice sliced through her reverie. "Are you attending?"

"Yes, yes, quite."

"Then why did you select a dessert spoon for the soup?"

"Oh, sorry. Is this one correct?" Harry made a random selection of another utensil.

"That is a fork," said Penelope.

"Sorry, I suppose I have let my mind go wandering." Penelope smiled. "It must be a lot to take in all at once."

"Actually, my mother has devoted hours to try to teach me how to behave like a lady. I fear I have no memory for such things, and my father always supported me in getting out of comportment lessons and other things he thought were absurd." Harriet sighed and slouched in her chair.

"Sit up straight, gel!" demanded the dowager without ever looking up from her book.

"Yes, Your Grace," answered Harriet, straightening her shoulders.

"It does not appear that you are enjoying your lessons, Miss Redgrave," commented Penelope.

"Please do call me Harriet. I appreciate the time you are both giving me, but sometimes do you not feel that all these trivial rules are irrelevant compared to other studies, Miss Rose?"

"And you must call me Penelope. What other studies?"

"I would much rather spend my time reading about the building blocks of our world than learning how to sit properly or walk properly or breathe properly. What possible difference can it make? Why must there be a right and wrong way to sit, stand, walk, and talk?"

Penelope smiled. "It is the nature of society I suppose. Once it is learned, it becomes second nature."

"But I do not care for these things."

"Are all Americans as focused on academic pursuits as you are?" Penelope gave up on the table setting and invited Harriet to sit next to her on the window bench. Sunlight filtered through the draperies.

Harriet flung open the drapes and smiled at the burst of light. "No. None. Do not think I represent American ladies, for it is not the case. I am an unusual creature even in Massachusetts; in England, I am nothing short of an oddity." Harriet sat on the window seat and leaned against the wall.

A slow smile graced Penelope's face and she also leaned back. "You might be surprised to learn what is beneath the surface of many ladies. The only difference is they hide it better."

"I do not wish to hide myself away and become just like every other young miss who seems to be judged only by her external appearance, not the contents of her head."

"You are very right. But perhaps the two do not have to be mutually exclusive. Might it be possible to act with a touch more decorum and still pursue your scientific interests?"

Harriet chewed on her lip, realized what she was doing, stopped, and gave Penelope a shrug. "I suppose you are right. My mother would agree with you, and even my father, truth be told. I will try to improve myself."

"I will as well," said Penelope. "You have inspired me to attend to the discipline of reading. Let us work a while longer and then break to engage in the development of our minds."

Harriet smiled. "Thank you, Penelope. I am so glad you are here to help. It is difficult to be taken away from one's family without any friends to rely on."

"I should hope you would think of me as a friend," said Penelope. She lowered her voice and glanced over to where the dowager was taking a nap while pretending to read. "I also enjoy finding a friend at these gatherings."

"Do you not have friends of your own at these occasions?"

It was Penelope's turn to shrug. "The dowager prefers an older crowd, so I generally end up with the matrons."

"What do people do here for amusement?"

"The men will do some hunting; that is the supposed intent of this house party."

"Supposed?" asked Harriet.

"Marchford chose this remote location to be able to hold some private meetings with some of the military elite. Since it is all supposedly casual, their families were invited. It soon became the most coveted invitation in town, particularly for any family with a daughter of marriageable age, for who would not wish to bag a duke? The duchess added to the guest list considerably with her list of marital prospects for her grandson. He might wish to do some work at this gathering, but he is in the minority, poor man."

Harriet could not begin to think of the Duke of Marchford as a "poor man" since he always seemed very much in control of his surroundings. Of course, no one could quite control the dowager duchess. "Tell me more about these meetings. They sound intriguing."

"That is all I know. There are current and retired admirals and generals on the guest list, but I do not know more about it."

"Admirals you say?" Harriet glanced up at the ceiling, turning the possibilities in her mind. "That puts me in mind of an idea."

Penelope frowned. "Am I going to like this idea?"

Harriet smiled. "Probably not."

Fourteen

OVERALL, IT HAD BEEN A SUCCESSFUL MORNING WITH the military leaders. Marchford had carefully selected men of understanding and vision to review their current military operations and make recommendations for future strategy. Marchford considered waking Mr. Neville to let him sit in but decided to let the man sleep.

There was also considerable distrust between the Foreign Office and the military leaders. The Foreign Office feared rogue commanders might surrender to Napoleon or, worse, join his ranks. They pushed for more control. On the other hand, the admirals and generals were convinced that recent security breaches could be laid at the doorstep of the Foreign Office and, as a result, did not wish to have their battle plans revealed in detail to those who might share them with enemy agents.

Marchford was distressed at the depth of distrust. Napoleon did not need to set foot on English soil to cause turmoil, discord, and confusion; the English top officials were already doing it to themselves. Without trust, they might as well concede defeat.

This is where Marchford hoped to play a role. He was a spy hunter. If he could ferret out the cause of the leaks, he could restore trust, and hopefully the two sides would begin to work together again.

The meeting had gone well, if tentatively. Everyone was on edge. Everyone needed to be reassured that the people with whom they spoke were trustworthy, and no one showed all their cards. Napoleon's armies seemed unstoppable, having conquered much of Europe. It was clear now that his sights were set on England. He was coming, that much was clear. But when? And where? And what could they do to stop him?

After a brief respite for some refreshment, the men gathered once more in one of the castle's more opulent drawing rooms. Marchford scanned the room with satisfaction. The generals and admirals were seated around the table in a sober style which befitted the occasion. Together they were going to plot a way to end this war and bring an end to the threat Napoleon posed.

Marchford was certain that, with some directed effort, they could devise a plan to end the turmoil and strife that had plagued him for most of his adult life. He wanted to see an end to the war in his lifetime, not have it drag on like previous conflicts between the two countries.

Marchford stood to address the prestigious men assembled before him. He had carefully prepared his next statements to focus their attention on the issue at hand and avoid any strife between the factions. It was a delicate situation, one that needed to be handled with precise diplomatic care.

"My esteemed guests—" began Marchford.

"Aha!" Miss Redgrave burst into the room followed by two rather irate footmen. "I knew you would be meeting today and I have something to say!"

"Miss Redgrave! This is a private affair, please leave immediately," demanded Marchford.

"Forgive me, but I have important business to discuss."

"Get my grandmother and Miss Rose," said Marchford in an undertone to one of the footmen.

"Several months ago I was sailing to New York and my ship was attacked without provocation by a ship of the Royal Navy," began Miss Redgrave.

"Get Thornton too," said Marchford in a low voice to the other footman.

"Our ship was fatally damaged. Once our captain conceded defeat, the English boarded our vessel and proceeded to press our sailors, most of them Americans, into service of the Royal Navy. Now I ask you, does this seem right?" asked Harriet.

"I do apologize for this interruption," said Marchford. "We shall continue presently."

"We are American citizens! By what right do you attack our vessels?" demanded Harriet.

"Miss Redgrave, please cease this instant," said Marchford in a low voice that everyone obeyed.

"I do thank you for this opportunity; it will not take long." Miss Redgrave turned to him with a wide smile—one that said she had no intention of listening to anything or anyone besides her own agenda. Short of physically removing her, which was something he knew would only add to the spectacle, Marchford was at a loss as to what to do.

"You must know that outrage in America is growing," continued Miss Redgrave. "The populace will not tolerate this continued aggression. You must act now to stop it!"

"Miss Rose!" Marchford waved Penelope into the room. "Would you not like to take Miss Redgrave to your salon?" He had to do something to get rid of this travesty called Harriet Redgrave.

"Hello, Penelope," said Harriet. "I was just addressing our esteemed guests to discuss the very real danger of attacking American ships and pressing her sailors into service. The American people will not stand for this forever. Eventually, the Americans will rise up again to throw off the fetters that bind them. In this era of crisis and uncertainty, you can ill afford to wage wars with both France and America."

"Miss Rose—do something!" hissed Marchford.

"Yes, of course," said Penelope. She walked to the middle of the room next to Harriet. "I believe Miss Redgrave has a point, one that you all would do well to listen to."

"Miss Rose," groaned Marchford.

"Is something the matter?" asked Thornton, also entering the room.

Harriet shocked the room by actually standing on a chair. "Gentleman, please, I ask you to consider the problem of British war ships attacking American vessels for the purpose of abducting their crew for your war effort. The only reason I stand before you today is because I also was abducted off of a sinking vessel and taken against my will to England. This practice must stop. Heed my warning!"

"Thornton?" Marchford was desperate to stop this tirade.

Thornton strode into the room, his serious eyes piercing. "Miss Redgrave." He bowed before her and offered his arm. She took it and stepped off the chair.

"Have you come to escort me out of the room?" she asked.

"Aye."

"You think I am wrong?"

"Nay. I ken ye have the right of it," answered Thornton. "Good day, gentlemen. We will leave ye to yer deliberations."

Marchford shook his head and looked to the heavens.

❧

Harriet kept her hand on Thornton's sleeve and walked out of the room with her head held high. He had said she was right. He had defended her in front of Marchford and all the old generals.

"Thank you for your support!" gushed Harriet when they were safely in the hall.

"I merely spoke the truth," replied Thornton.

Harriet noted the looks on the faces of Penelope and the Duchess of Marchford and realized she was not safe quite yet.

"Foolish gel, I'm ashamed of you," declared the dowager. "Whatever gave you the idea of breaking into one of Marchford's meetings?"

"I need to do what I can for the American sailors who are being pressed into service," Harriet defended her actions. "They are seizing ships and forcing the sailors to serve in their navy. It is slavery!"

"You simply cannot address a room full of people to whom you have not been introduced."

"They know me now. I doubt they will ever forget my name."

The dowager threw up her hands and turned her back on her.

"While I appreciate the passion you feel for your cause, you must understand you are ignoring protocol, bucking tradition, and defying conventions," said Penelope.

"And this is bad?" asked Harriet.

"Only an American could ask such a question," said Thornton, but he smiled when he said it. "Perhaps ye would enjoy a walk through the gardens."

Penelope nodded her approval. "There are others in the garden so you will not be alone, but please do not leave the garden." She hustled off to find the dowager, who had left in disgust.

Thornton led Harriet out a back door to the gardens behind the house, which opened up into the wilderness of the Highlands. Unlike the front of the estate, which was meticulously maintained, the back of the house was less carefully kept. Harriet instantly decided she liked it better.

"I know breaking into the meeting was unusual—" began Harriet.

Thornton made what might be considered a snort and raised an eyebrow at her.

"Yes, yes, fine, it was very unusual," conceded Harriet. "But it was the only way I knew to address the council. I fear war between our countries."

Thornton led her down an open path with low

hedges, past a fountain, long since turned green with age and neglect. He turned past a higher hedge until they were no longer visible from the house. Here, he motioned toward a bench and they both sat down.

"I do thank you for getting me out," said Harriet softly. "Once I was in, I figured they would have to cart me off."

"I appreciate ye not requiring me to carry ye."

Instantly, she regretted her hasty surrender. She could have left in his arms. "Perhaps another time," she murmured. The emotions and odd feelings she had experienced with this man earlier flooded back. She struggled to keep her mind focused on her mission. "Do you think they will listen? Do you think they will heed my advice?"

Thornton shifted slightly on the stone bench. "Yer approach did guarantee that they heard ye, but perhaps did not win them over to yer cause."

Harriet's shoulders sagged. "I suppose you are right. It's only that if our two countries go to war, my father and brothers will be called to fight. I do not wish to see them in harm's way."

"Yer sentiment is perfectly understandable. I will say I find it outrageous that yer ship should be attacked and ye brought here against yer will. I am impressed ye held yerself wi' such poise."

"Thank you." Something within her melted, and she realized how angry she had been. "Thank you," she repeated. "I think I needed to hear someone acknowledge that it was an injustice."

"It was. I would be quite angry."

"Yes! I have been furious, but I didn't know quite

what to call the emotion. How is it that you can identify quite quickly the nature of the problem when no one else seems to be able to?"

Thornton shrugged. "I'm not English, for a start."

Harriet gave him a wide smile. "That's right! You are a Scot."

"Worse yet, a Highlander."

"Not half as bad as an American."

Thornton smiled and spoke with his soft Highland lilt. "Verra true."

"We should band together. It is not so bad being an outsider if you can do it together. The outsiders looking in on God's chosen."

Thornton cocked his head a bit in thought. "I dinna believe that the Lord reserves his love more for some than for others. Are we all not his children? The good Lord must appreciate differences. Look at the variety o' plants and animals. He made them all and called it good. Why would he make only one type of person?"

"You sound like my mum. I thought she was attempting to save my feelings when it became plain that I was a bit different from all the other girls."

"Different? How so?" His eyes, black and deep, met hers.

"Thank you for pretending not to notice, but I recognize I am awkward in society. First, I am ridiculously tall for a girl. Second, I have a passion for science and chemistry which is unusual in the extreme. I have always been different." Harriet looked away. It was a sensitive subject.

"Just as yer Creator made ye to be," said Thornton softly.

Harriet looked up slowly and once again became caught in his gaze. "Thank you," she whispered. He seemed to understand what she needed to hear. She leaned closer on the bench.

Voices coming nearer distracted her. On the other side of the hedge, young ladies giggled at their own jokes.

Thornton leaned close to her ear, sending shivers down her spine. "And I think ye are the perfect height."

He was gone before the young ladies rounded the hedge and found Harriet sitting demurely on a bench with a radiant smile on her face.

Fifteen

"Miss Rose." The Duke of Marchford said her name with definite disdain.

"Yes, Your Grace?" answered Penelope as she entered the blue room to have her meeting with Marchford. She was dreading it. She knew there would be comment regarding the behavior of a certain American; it was inevitable.

"About Miss Redgrave." The duke rose and directed Penelope to take a seat. "Today Miss Redgrave accosted every man present without respect for rank, age, or title. She pursues questionable if not destructive hobbies, and is unabashedly American. Why, Miss Rose, why is my grandmother sponsoring her presentation into society?"

"She was asked to do so by Lord Langley."

Marchford began to pace, his hands clasped behind him. "Your reasoning is not sound. There are few in this world whom my grandmother holds in less regard than Lord Langley."

"I learned that fact myself," said Penelope, "You should have seen them sparring in the parlor."

"Miss Rose, I must know what this is about."

"I fear I am not at liberty to say, but I invite you to speak with your grandmother. I cannot be her companion if she knows I would betray her confidence."

"I thought we had an arrangement, Miss Rose." The duke's words were low and soft and for some reason resonated within her.

"Our agreement was that I would keep you informed of anything that might assist you in apprehending spies, traitors, and enemies to the Crown. I never agreed to tell you what schemes your grandmother was plotting."

"Can you tell me if one of her schemes is to embarrass me before all the military leaders of our time?"

"I believe this is an incidental occurrence," answered Penelope. "But since we are exchanging information, can you tell me what happened between Lord Langley and the duchess?"

The duke sat across from her, looking every bit the man for the title in an impeccably tailored coat of royal blue and a cravat so white it gleamed. "My grandmother was not born into the aristocracy. In truth, she was born the daughter of a respectable gentleman of moderate income and what might be considered modest connections. She hit London by storm and with naught but her wit and her charm was soon accepted into some of the most elite circles in Town. Lord Langley fell in love with her and made a rash offer, but his parents did not approve. In the end it was all handled very badly and my grandmother was left on her wedding day with a broken engagement and, if the rumors are true, a broken heart."

"This is all very romantic, but how did she end up marrying a duke?"

"Apparently, my grandfather had been a friend to Langley, disagreed with his treatment of her, and made an offer on principle."

"That is quite remarkable." Penelope paused, considering this bit of news. She had always assumed Antonia's marriage had been arranged. It also explained why the duchess had so little money of her own and needed to pursue the career of matchmaking to maintain her living without being banished to the dower house. "I suppose that explains why she is not of a romantic nature, since her own attempt at love went so terribly wrong."

"Yes, which is why I am at a loss to explain why she is helping the granddaughter of a man she loathes. Come now, Miss Rose, I shared information with you; it is time you did the same."

Penelope sighed. She had a feeling he already knew or suspected their involvement with the infamous Madame X. "Lord Langley is anxious to have his granddaughter respectably wed. The dowager knows how to contact Madame X, and so she did."

"A matchmaker," he spoke the word low, like a curse.

"Yes, a matchmaker. I understand you do not have positive associations with the word."

"Why would you suppose that? Just because my arranged marriage resulted in a supposed alliance with a lady already married."

"It was unfortunate Lady Louisa decided to wed another." Penelope kept a straight face, although now she could hardly think back on the event without laughing.

"And not tell me about it," growled Marchford.

"It was revealed before the engagement ball."

"The *day of* the engagement ball." Marchford paused a moment. "I just realized I have more in common with my grandmother than I realized."

"So what are your plans for matrimony now? You know you are a hunted man."

"Yes. Quite. I would not doubt that matchmaker of yours has been hired to trap me into matrimony."

Penelope smiled and said nothing of the plots the dowager was fostering to get Marchford wed to her choice. "You will get no rest until you have wed."

"Perhaps I should enlist the help of a matchmaker." Marchford spoke in jest, but then his eyes turned serious. "Why not? You are right: I will get no rest until I am engaged."

"Engaged, wed, with an heir bouncing on one knee," said Penelope lightly.

"True. I cannot be bothered with trying to find a bride. I am currently occupied with important matters of state. What I need is someone to analyze the candidates and find a likely few. I will make the final choice, and the engagement will be announced. Yes, this will be perfect. I would like you to arrange a meeting for me with Madame X."

Penelope coughed compulsively. He could not possibly have asked for that. "I cannot."

"Why not? You are helping Lord Langley."

"Madame X is very exclusive."

"She would take the case of an American but not me? Odd sort of exclusivity."

"I meant to say she is reclusive. She will not meet with anyone."

"But she meets with you and my grandmother. Tell me the truth, have you met the woman?"

"Yes," squeaked Penelope, for it was the truth.

"Then she will arrange things through you?"

"Yes, but—"

"Good, you will tell her what I am interested in and you will arrange it with her."

"Her services are quite dear." Penelope was desperate to evade him.

"She may send me the bill and it will be paid." Marchford waved a hand as if he could not be bothered with trivial details. "Now then, take some notes on what I would like in a bride." He pointed to a writing desk.

Unable to think of a plausible reason to recuse herself, Penelope moved to the desk and took a piece of paper. Marchford waited for her to dip the quill in the inkwell before he began. "First, she needs to be sensible and not too young. I cannot have some giggling miss twenty years my junior."

"Then she would only be eight years old."

"Quite so. Unseemly."

"And illegal."

"She needs to be well-read and accomplished. She needs to be able to run my household with efficiency. And most important, she needs to be able to hold her own against my grandmother. Someone who can treat Grandmother with respect, but also be her own person."

"And what of appearance?" Penelope's voice was raw. This is where she was passed over every time. Men might say they wanted a sensible wife but would then make an offer to the prettiest face in the room.

The duke looked up to the ceiling as if picturing his perfect bride. "I am not in need of anyone with striking looks, for I have found the women with the most beauty are often the least confident and most needing of reassurance. Also, I would dislike having to constantly defend my territory. No, give me a woman of quiet beauty and inner confidence."

Penelope could not think of what to say. Could he really mean this?

"Did you get all that?" asked Marchford after a long pause.

"Oh! Yes, quite. And what of fortune? Family connections?"

Marchford shrugged. "I have no need for an heiress. Give me someone from a respectable family. I do not wish for in-laws who will cause problems or be looking to be bailed out of a fix." Marchford frowned. "I have enough interference from my grandmother as it is; perhaps it would be best if my future wife is an orphan."

"Anything else of importance?"

"Let me think. She must be sensible, intelligent, self-confident, and able to work with my grandmother. I am not sure where you can find such a saint, so wish Madame X good luck."

Penelope reviewed the list. It could not be. Had he truly just described her? "I shall do my best."

"Good! I look forward to reviewing a list of candidates."

Marry me.

"Yes, of course." Penelope banished traitorous thoughts. A peer of the realm, particularly a duke, did not marry a little nobody companion. She was a sensible girl and it was time to get her errant imagination under better regulation.

"I will see you at dinner," Marchford turned back to his newspaper as if nothing unusual had occurred.

She was dismissed.

As Penelope was walking out, Mr. Neville walked past and spied Marchford.

"Your Grace!" Mr. Neville called and entered the room uninvited, closing the door behind him.

Marchford regarded him with annoyance. One of the reasons he had called these meetings to take place in the Highlands was to avoid such persons as Mr. Neville. He had thought Scotland too far for Neville to travel. He had underestimated the man's resolve.

"I understand you had meetings today. Meetings to which I was not invited," accused Neville.

"Yes, you are correct," said Marchford mildly.

"But... but... I have come all this way to participate in these meetings," sputtered Neville. "I must know that things are being conducted in a secure manner. I need the names of the attendees, careful notes must be taken and kept secure. I must review any documents or plans that may be developed as a result of said meetings."

"I understand your concern." Marchford turned back to his newspaper. Maybe if he ignored the man Neville would disappear.

"Marchford!" demanded Neville.

Marchford looked over his paper at him. "I did not realize we were on such familiar terms."

"Your Grace," Neville ground out. "I demand you include me tomorrow!"

"I fear that is not possible." Marchford held up his

hand to quiet any rebuke. "You must understand the level of distrust between the generals and the Foreign Office is deep. If you were to come, others would leave. Let me work with them first, then we can discuss any plans that evolve."

"Well, I suppose that will have to do." Neville appeared slightly mollified. "I only want what is best for England."

"God save the King."

"Crazy man that he is," muttered Neville as he left.

⁓

"Are you feeling better?" Harriet asked her grandfather. She was followed into the room by Penelope and the dowager duchess, who surprised her by expressing an interest in visiting Lord Langley.

"All this fresh country air. Bad for the lungs," complained Langley from his sickbed. He was marginally improved, but the process was slow.

"What you need is company," advised the dowager. "Miss Redgrave, perhaps you should stay with your grandfather tonight. I shall arrange for your meals to be brought here."

"No," croaked Langley on a hoarse throat. "I want her downstairs, meeting gentlemen."

"She has introduced herself to enough gentlemen today," retorted the duchess.

At Langley's confused face Penelope said, "Today Miss Redgrave presented herself at Marchford's meeting with the military leaders and informed them of the injustice of capturing American vessels to press men into service."

Langley was quiet a moment. "Bet Marchford was riled up. Well, can't say I approve, but that's the Langley spirit in you!"

"Incorrigible, the both of you," declared the dowager. "The point is Miss Redgrave has made a serious social error. She may be ostracized from society no matter how great her dowry. Fortunately for you, I have circulated a rumor that she has contracted the same illness as you and her actions today were the result of delirium and high fever."

"So I must stay here with my grandfather?" asked Harriet.

"Yes, until this crisis is averted."

Harriet smiled. It was the best news she had heard all day.

"I'm sorry, dear," said Langley. "Perhaps we should do as they suggest."

"I do not mind a bit," said Harriet. "I would quite enjoy staying here. Let us bring over a table, Grandfather. Do you play cards?" A happy vision of domestic tranquility danced before her eyes.

"Too bad we don't have four people for a set," said Langley, giving the dowager a hopeful look.

"Oh, fine then," the dowager snapped. "Penelope bring over two more chairs, Lord Langley wants to play whist."

Lord Langley graced his former fiancée with a wide smile. And a sneeze.

Sixteen

THORNTON STEPPED LIGHTLY UP THE CRUMBLED STAIRS to the ruined castle above Thornton Hall. A light shone from the windows of one of the outbuildings. It was five in the morning. No staff was supposed to be there. No houseguest would be awake for another four hours. Miss Redgrave had unfortunately taken ill. Whoever was there could only mean trouble.

Thornton was a peace-loving man by nature but a Highlander by blood, a fact made plain by the claymore sword he swung over his shoulder. Marchford may have preferred a brace of pistols—he was English like that—but nothing beat the sheer intimidation factor of a sword almost as long as he was tall.

He slowed a bit as he approached the castle. The sky had shed the inky blackness of a cloudy night to the cool gray of predawn. Morning came early to the Highlands in the summer. The fog settled itself comfortably around the castle and the candle through the window shone in an orange halo through the mist. Silently, Thornton approached the outbuilding, the old kitchen of the ruined castle. Straining against the muffling effect of fog, he froze, trying to place the faint sound emanating from the building. It was... humming.

Edging up to the building, he peeked inside and, through the illumination of several candles, saw the odd laboratory of Miss Redgrave. The room was even more filled than when he had seen it last. Bottles, boxes, books, and papers lay about in a haphazard manner. Small piles of rocks and metals and heaps of powders were lined up on an old table on one side of the room. Many tiny, oddly shaped bottles with cork stoppers were scattered across another table on the opposite side. A small fire was burning in a metal dish, with a bottle propped over it, held up by a strange metal contraption. What kind of lass was Harriet to have such an unusual interest?

Suddenly, Harriet's face appeared in the open window, inches away from his own. He pulled back instinctively and lost his balance, setting him down hard.

"Hello! Oh, I say, I am sorry. Did I startle you?" Harriet added further insult to his humiliation by hopping through the open window like a gazelle and offering a hand to help him up.

"I am fine, thank ye. Nay, I dinna need help to stand."

"Are you hurt?" she asked.

"I am fine!" he answered more harshly than he intended. "What are ye doing here? I thought ye were ill."

She smiled at him, and he suddenly realized she was in a rather natural state. Her auburn hair was down and framed her face with gentle curves. Her hair was surprisingly thick and long, much different than the sensible knot she typically wore. She wore a long wool coat, but peeking from underneath he could swear she wore nothing but her chemise. Unlike her sensible dress during the day, this Harriet Redgrave was a wild thing, at home with the fey creatures of the Scottish Highlands.

"The duchess started a rumor I was febrile to explain my behavior yesterday. I feel fine but I could not sleep. I am doing some testing and I could not wait any longer to find the results." She clapped her hands together and her green eyes shone with an ethereal glow in the mist. "Besides, it is almost dawn. I am shocked at how society feels the need to sleep away half the morning."

He had felt the same way many times, having an innate affinity for the morning his friends did not share. "I am glad to hear ye are well, but it is still dark and ye shoud'na be here alone." The thought of any harm coming to his Harriet made his stomach roll—though when she had become "his" Harriet, he could not say.

Harriet shrugged. "You are right, I suppose. But have you ever had something you were so passionate about you could not wait to get back to it? Like an excellent book or Christmas morning or returning home after a long absence?"

Thornton hesitated, considering the question. He liked books, but not to the point where passion came into play, Christmas had been largely banned by his grandmother, who feared it would spoil him to be given any presents, and the only thing he felt in returning home was dread. "What has captured your passions, Miss Redgrave?"

She gave him another smile. "Come and see."

He followed her into the old kitchen, thankful she chose the door this time instead of the window. She described her experiments with a rousing passion. She picked up odd-shaped bottles and pointed to powders. She explained her equipment with odd names like *alembics*, *curcubite*, and *pelican*. He had difficulty following her narrative, but he had no trouble appreciating the fire in her eyes when she spoke.

"Interesting," he said, knowing it was insufficient for the excitement with which she described her work.

Harriet sighed. "I think 'interesting' must mean something different than I thought, because every time I hear it, I know the person does not wish to talk any more about my experiments." She turned back to stirring something in a metal tin.

"It must be lonely to have a passion for something so few people share." He loved his horses, but it was a passion shared by many. He was not alone in it as she was.

She stopped what she was doing and looked up at him, her eyes searching his. "It can be lonely. There are not many who share a fascination with chemistry, and fewer still with whom I can discuss it."

"And here, ye have no one at all."

Harriet returned her focus to the fire in the tin plate. "Yes, you are right." Her voice was soft.

He cursed himself for making her sad and attempted to remedy the situation. "Chemistry is an unusual hobby. How did ye start?"

The change of subjects earned him a smile. "My father's brother was fascinated by it. He refused to go into the navy as expected and instead charted his own course. Most of the family tried to pretend he no longer existed, but he was always welcome at our house. He had a way of making children laugh, and he showed me all his chemistry experiments. My father kept the boys away from the potential evil influence of science. I suppose he thought it could do me no harm. He was wrong, as you see. Of course, when my uncle invented a new form of gunpowder that made firing a cannon easier and safer on ship, he was hailed as a hero of the family."

"It is certainly not a hobby for the weak-minded person. I am impressed by yer dedication to the science, though I hope ye are not currently looking for a new recipe for gunpowder."

"Not yet," she said absently, her focus on the contents of the bottle over her makeshift fire. It was hardly the rousing reassurance he had wished to hear. "I am doing experiments in luminescence. In this regard, it is helpful to work in the dark to see if I can find something that glows."

He watched her for a moment, impressed by whatever she was doing, measuring this, adding that, until a whoosh of blue flame blasted from the plate, sparking the thatched roof and popping into a cloud of black smoke.

"Oh dear," said Harriet, and dissolved into a fit of coughing.

Thornton pulled Harriet out of the way then grabbed a stick and batted at the burning embers on the thatch roof until they were all out.

"I'm so sorry. It hardly ever does that," said Harriet weakly.

Hardly ever? Thornton gathered together his raw nerves. Everything he worked for was in this compound; a fire would be devastating for him. Even worse was the thought of Harriet being hurt. "Miss Redgrave," he turned to her. "About these experiments—"

"You want me not to set your property on fire."

"Aye, I would appreciate it." He walked toward her and held her hands the way she had done to him. He liked holding her hands. "And more than that, I wish for ye to stay safe."

Harriet's cheeks turned pink. "I appreciate your concern." She softly squeezed his hands.

He stepped closer, his eyes focused on her rose-colored lips. She was just the right height. She was a *kissable* height. He leaned closer then caught himself and stepped back, dropping her hands. What could he be thinking?

"Oh look, the sun is rising!" Harriet sprang out of the building and bounded up the stairs to the walkway on the castle wall. The sun was emerging in the east, the orange rays warming the tops of the hills above them.

He followed her, moth to a flame. It was a crisp, fair morning and the sunrise painted the sky pink and orange. It was beautiful. Was it always so? He was often too busy to notice. He walked up the stone steps and watched the sunrise and Harriet in even measure. He was not sure which sight drew him more, the glory of the sun washing the world in color or the look of wonder on her face.

She leaned against the battlements, a slight smile on her face, her eyes wide. "I love this time of day.

Everything is new and fresh." She turned to him. "And I haven't messed it up yet."

Her slow smile haunted him. "I also enjoy a sunrise," he said. *And I enjoy ye more.*

"We are alone in this joy, I think."

He nodded. "Aye."

They stood witness as the orange glow crept closer until it suddenly burst over the castle wall and illuminated the grounds. And them.

She glowed in the sunlight. There was no other word for it. Her auburn hair turned to bright red under the sun's rays. She lifted her head and closed her eyes to embrace the warmth of the sun. He had a sudden urge to embrace her too.

"Beautiful," he said, looking only at her.

"But you are not even looking at the sunrise."

"Beautiful just the same."

She leaned forward and crinkled her brow at him. "Are you still drunk? Maybe left over from last night? You English drink quite a bit."

"I am a Highlander," he reminded.

"Is that better or worse?"

"Worse. Far worse."

"That explains it."

"Despite my birth, I shall claim sobriety at this moment and say with certainty that ye are a bonnie lass in the morn."

She blinked at him. For once it appeared she had nothing to say. She closed her eyes tight and opened them again with a wide smile. "I am going to remember this moment for the rest of my life. The moment a real Highlander called me a 'bonnie lass.'"

He drew closer to her; he could not help himself. He managed to keep his arms at his sides, but he leaned too close. She stepped even closer and put her hands upon his chest. Her green eyes revealed confusion—and something else. It was a heady, smoldering look, one he had never seen in any woman's eye. And this was for him.

He leaned forward and kissed one soft cheek then the other, lingering too long. Alarm bells finally decided to ring.

He backed up, away from temptation. "I hope ye shall have a verra nice day." He spoke softly, hoping his plain words could convey all he could not say.

Her lips parted, and he had to force himself not to step forward and claim them for his own. He must get away. Without another word, he bowed and ran down the steps, away from temptation, away from that fey creature, away from his Harriet.

Seventeen

"THORNTON!"

Thornton turned and paused while Marchford strode up to him in the hallway where all of the men were staying.

"I've got a favor to ask of you, old friend."

"Oh no. I know when ye evoke the length of our friendship ye truly have an onerous task before me," said Thornton.

"I am having another meeting this morning, one that I wish to occur without disruption."

Memories of Miss Redgrave standing on a chair flooded Thornton's mind. "I believe Miss Redgrave has taken ill."

Marchford raised an eyebrow. "I believe my grandmother circulated that rumor to explain her peculiar behavior yesterday. I have no confidence such trivial considerations as her reputation would convince Miss Redgrave to stay away from my proceedings."

"What would you have me do? Block the door?"

"Distract her. Ask her to go for a walk or a ride. Take

her to the library. Show her the castle. I don't know, just keep her out of sight of the rest of the guests."

Mixed emotions flooded through Thornton. On one hand there was nothing he wanted more than to spend more time alone with Harriet. On the other hand, his desire made Harriet the one person from whom he should stay away. "I shall do my best, old friend. But please do remember that charming women was always Grant's job, not mine."

"Time to take on a new hobby and learn to entertain ladies."

"She does not appear to be easily distracted from her object," said Thornton.

Marchford shrugged. "Or lock her in her room. Just keep her away from my meeting. It is a matter of critical importance to the Empire."

Thornton obligingly took up residence outside the door. He was determined to keep Harriet away from the meeting, but also himself away from her. It would not do at all to draw too near her. Such familiarity may make a lady expect a declaration, and proposing marriage was the one thing he could not do.

As Marchford had predicted, Harriet marched determinedly to the door where the aristocratic military leaders were holding their meetings. She had changed into a sensible muslin frock and twisted her hair into a plain knot. Gone was the fey creature of this morning, yet as she approached, Thornton could see the fire in her eyes.

"Good morning, Miss Redgrave," greeted Thornton.

"Are you now the door guard?" Harriet asked accusingly.

"Aye. It fits my skill and talents to stand here and do and say nothing."

"Self-deprecating humor will hardly raise my opinion of you."

"Then ye will only give me more reason to doubt myself."

"You are difficult when you don't fight back," Harriet accused. "I am accustomed to sparring with my brothers. I do not know what to do with easy victory."

"Alas! I had no siblings. I do not know how to play this game."

"Never? Did you never have siblings?"

"Nay. My parents were not the best of friends. Once an heir was produced, they felt no further need to spend a moment in each other's company." It was diplomatically stated. In truth, his parents loathed each other.

Harriet blinked at him and was uncharacteristically quiet for a moment. "My parents are forever in each other's company, always laughing, always by each other's side. I could not imagine growing up without them or my big, boisterous brothers. How quiet your home must have been." It was as if she was trying to find something kind to say.

"Aye. Like a crypt."

"I am sorry. But perhaps there can be benefits to being quiet. There is no one to steal your things or break your toys. No one to interrupt you when you are talking and snitch on you whenever you even think of doing something naughty. No one to make you laugh at the dinner table until your drink comes out your nose and you are sent to eat in the nursery for behavior unbecoming a lady."

Thornton tried to resist a smile but failed. "Sounds terrible having so many siblings."

"Truly awful." But she smiled when she said it. "My brothers are a pain in my backside. And oh, how I miss them. I just hope they have gotten the letter that I am all right. They must be terribly worried about me."

"I have a second cousin. I doubt he would be concerned for my welfare though, since the last time I saw him he informed me that if I was to die, he would inherit."

"How dreadful!"

"He was only eight at the time."

"A poor excuse."

"I have always thought so."

They stood in the hall, at a loss what to say next. The rumbling sound of men's voices could be heard from the room behind the door.

"So am I to wrestle you out of the way?" asked Harriet.

A horrible impulse to tell her to try her best swept over him. Somehow the unconventional Miss Harriet brought out impulses he did not even know he had. "I fear I might enjoy that," he said with too much candor. "But I wondered if I could show ye something first."

"I will not be dissuaded." She raised her chin.

"Have you heard of Monsieur Lavoisier?"

"Antoine Lavoisier? Of course! He is a giant in the field of chemistry." Harriet gave him her full attention.

"Then ye have read his work *The Elementary Treatise of Chemistry*?"

"I have heard of it. It is truly remarkable by all accounts."

"Were ye aware that it was translated by a Scotsman, Robert Kerr?"

"A Scotsman? No, I was not."

"I do like to support a fellow Scot when I can."

Much to his surprise, Harriet grabbed his sleeve. "Do you have a copy? Do you?"

"Aye, 'tis in the library—"

Harriet did not wait for him to finish but grabbed his hand and ran down the hall to the library. It was dark in the room, but she flung open the curtains and opened a window to let in the sunlight and the cool breeze. "Where? Where is it?"

Thornton went to a top shelf and pulled down the large volume, placing it on the table.

"Oh!" She tried not to squeal and jump up and down but failed.

"I had no idea ye would be quite so pleased." He was mesmerized at her reaction, so raw, so honest.

"I had no idea you had this book or I would have been living in this room."

"I shall not force ye to remain a prisoner. Take the book back to yer room and read it at yer leisure."

"Thank you. Thank you!"

Harriet opened the book with a loving touch and Thornton found he could not look away from her. He was a fair man, and he recognized there would be few who would consider her a great beauty, yet when her eyes gleamed with true pleasure, she was the most lovely creature he had ever beheld. It made him want to do more to see such raw joy.

"You were sent to get rid of me. Were you not?" Harriet sat down at the table without looking up from the book.

"Aye. Do ye mind?"

"No. I understand they do not wish me to interrupt. I do appreciate your honesty."

Thornton sat down across from her. "I shall always be honest with ye."

"Will you? If you would, it would be novel at least."

"People are no' truthful with ye?"

"People say one thing to my face and another behind my back. Sometimes they do not always make sure I'm out of earshot." Harriet trailed her finger down the page of the book like a caress. The thoughts it inspired in Thornton made him shift in his chair.

"Society can be cruel without cause."

Harriet looked up. "I fear I do give them cause. I interrupt meetings with generals and read books on chemistry. If that is not cause for being labeled as odd, I cannot think of what would be."

Thornton smiled. "Remember, we are loved for our uniqueness."

"Perhaps some are more unique than others," muttered Harriet.

"Did not Paul say in first Corinthians 12 that we are all made different but parts of the same body? '*But now God has set the members, each one of them, in the body, just as He pleased.*'"

"I cannot imagine what part of the body I would be. Something unattractive, without purpose."

"Ye be too harsh on yerself. Besides, in Romans

12 Paul writes, '*Having then gifts differing according to the grace that is given to us, let us use them.*'"

Harriet rolled her eyes. "I do not see chemistry being considered one of the spiritual gifts. At least no one in society would think so."

"Is this something ye aspire to? Would ye like to be prominent in society?"

"Oh no. I'd rather read my books and do experiments. But I would like the gossip to stop. I cannot imagine so much interest over my dowry." Harriet returned to her book.

"Get married," said Thornton bluntly.

"I beg your pardon?" Harriet looked up at him with wide eyes.

"The gossip seems focused on yer potential marital partner. If ye wed, there would be naught left to talk about. Or at least," he amended because he did promise to be honest, "there would be less."

She cocked her head to one side and narrowed her eyes. "Are you working now for the duchess and Penelope? Or perhaps my grandfather? They are all trying to get me to wed as soon as may be. Apparently, a wedding will make me more acceptable."

Thornton shook him head. "I am merely stating the facts, not recommending the institution. I have no personal experience, nor am I likely to, so I cannot recommend it one way or the other. Have ye ever thought o' matrimony?" He was edging around a dangerous topic.

"I suppose, but it does not seem likely. Besides, I have the benefit of having enough resources to meet my needs. If I wed, whatever income I enjoy would go directly to my husband—advantageous for him, not as great for me."

"Not if ye had my mother's solicitor," muttered Thornton. His mother retained control of most of her dowry, thanks to some careful negotiations in the marriage agreements.

"I beg your pardon?"

"What ye need is not to avoid marriage, but to get yerself a good attorney."

"I suppose so. It is not as if any credible offers have come my way, so it is a moot point. My father would never accept anyone he thought was a fortune hunter, nor would I."

"Nor should ye. But perhaps ye could find a man with a love for chemistry." On this count he felt safe. He knew no one who dabbled in chemistry.

Harriet's eyes gleamed with that same internal fire. "That would be a dream. Did you know that Lavoisier's wife was instrumental in his work?"

"I was not aware."

"She made sketches of his work and kept meticulous records. I would love to marry a scientist."

For some reason, Thornton was not pleased with the idea. "Or perhaps ye could share yer passion with a gentleman and win over his interest."

Harriet disappointed him by shaking her head. "No, it cannot be done. I've never met a man interested in chemistry unless he came that way from the start."

"There you are!" Miss Rose entered the room, her hands on her hips. "You were very adroit at sneaking away."

"Have you been looking for me?" asked Harriet, her attempt to look innocent marred by a guilty grin.

"Yes. I see you have found a book—"

"*Elementary Treatise of Chemistry* by Lavoisier!" exclaimed Harriet.

"Yes, yes, very nice," placated Miss Rose. "But Her Grace and I are trying to restore your reputation, which will not be improved by spending time alone with a man." She looked accusingly at Thornton.

"I confess I am guilty of the charges before me," conceded Thornton. "I shall leave the field in shame. Good day to ye both."

"Thank you, Lord Duncan!" Harriet's voice was warm.

Though she mangled his title, he liked it from her lips. "If I have pleased ye, I am happy, though I ken not how I did so."

"The book!" Harriet hefted the large volume as if it was obvious, which in retrospect he supposed it was.

Thornton bowed and quit the library. Miss Rose was right; he should be more circumspect with respect to Miss Redgrave. He should not be alone with her or any female save his own mother, and the less of that the better. He would not wish to encourage hopes of matrimony, which could not be. Of course, it appeared she had no interest in him in that regard, which was good.

Thornton sighed and his shoulders sagged. Very good indeed.

Eighteen

IT WAS GOING TO BE A LONG EVENING WITHOUT MISS Redgrave to liven up the atmosphere. It was strange how after spending time with her, everyone else seemed false, pretentious, and dull. Thornton would have attempted to avoid the evening, but his mother had decided he had not been present enough for his duties as host, which he must admit was most likely true.

"I want you to be especially attentive to Miss Crawley tonight," his mother said in a low whisper. She was adorned in jewel tones, a vision of silk and feathers. He supposed he might concede she looked well in it if he was not so busy counting the cost of her regalia.

"Why Miss Crawley in particular?" he whispered in return, wary of his mother's interference.

She smoothed her skirts and got that aloof look in her eye she wore whenever she knew she was in the wrong. "I had some trouble and General Crawley assisted me greatly. We came to an understanding."

"This understanding best not have anything to do with his daughter," warned Thornton.

"And why should it not," hissed Lady Thornton.

"Priscilla is an exquisitely handsome girl from a well-established family. The only thing they do not have in abundance is a title, and General Crawley is set on having his only daughter a countess. It is just our luck they are willing to settle on you."

"I have told ye before, Mother, I will not marry anyone for money, even if I am lucky enough to have them be 'willing to settle' on me."

"Foolish child!" Lady Thornton spoke louder than she intended and a few heads turned her way as people milled about waiting to be called in to the table. "You are always riding too fast," she said with a smile until people went back to their own conversations.

"You should know"—her voiced dropped once again into a harsh whisper—"General Crawley now owns most of my debt. If I cannot pay him back within a fortnight, Thornton Hall will be his."

"What?" Thornton had a meeting set with his steward tomorrow to discover the full extent of the difficulties with the estate. He had not thought the need quite so pressing. "Mother how much—"

"Mrs. Crawley!" exclaimed his mother, walking toward her new friend. "How lovely you look tonight. And your daughter is stunning as always. Does not Miss Crawley look stunning, Duncan?" His mother gave him a look that could blister paint.

"Aye." Thornton bowed to the Crawley family. "Verra well indeed," he said because he was an honest man. Miss Crawley was a lovely sight with black hair, porcelain skin, and a red rose mouth.

"Capital, capital!" declared General Crawley. "But then who could not think my little Priscilla an angel?"

Priscilla gave Thornton a coy look, as if to say there was more to this angel than met the eye.

"They make such a lovely couple," said Mrs. Crawley in a dreamy voice. "Their children shall all have such beautiful dark hair."

"Mama, please, you should not say such things," said Priscilla with a sweet smile.

Indeed she should not. Thornton wished to run for the hills. He was a Highlander; he could live out the rest of his days in a cave if need be. One look at the scheming Crawley family told him the need might be.

"Forgive me, must see to my guests." Thornton bowed and fled to the other side of the room.

Mr. Neville fortunately engaged General Crawley and his daughter in conversation, giving Thornton an opportunity to disengage himself. Neville appeared quite animated in the discussion, which was all the better distraction.

❧

"I hope you are feeling better tonight." The dowager duchess swept into Lord Langley's room with Penelope following behind. Langley and Harriet were playing cards and had been all night. Langley had a little more of his color, but Harriet was looking wan. Anyone seeing her would believe her unwell.

"Antonia, please forgive me for not standing for you," said Langley.

"Do not think of troubling yourself," said the duchess. "I do hope you are feeling better."

"I am on the mend."

"I hope I can be on the mend too," said Harriet.

"Getting tired of playing piquet with your grand-father?" asked Lord Langley.

"Oh no, I adore playing for hours," said Harriet unconvincingly. "At least I enjoy getting to know you better."

"Now that Her Grace and Miss Rose have come, we can have a game of whist," said Langley.

"That would be lovely," said Antonia, surprising herself. She generally went to sleep after a long evening, but when Lord Langley called her by her first name, as he had done so many years ago, she felt revived.

Penelope shot her a glance, one eyebrow raised, but Antonia ignored it. Penelope was young; she could stay awake awhile longer. "I will get some chairs for us," said Penelope.

They sat around a little table beside Langley's bed and he dealt. He would be her partner, naturally, and Penelope and Harriet would lose, naturally. In all the years she had played parlor games, Antonia had never met someone who played as well as Lord Langley.

After three games, Penelope could barely keep her eyes open and Harriet took to open mouthed yawning. "Why don't you girls turn in for the night," said Antonia. "I shall play one more game with Lord Langley."

The girls rose from their chairs with some relief. "Should I leave you alone in a man's room?" asked Penelope with a half smile.

Antonia smiled in return. "I think my reputation can survive attending a man on his sickbed."

"Ah, now you have wounded my manly pride," declared Langley. "'Tis no worse insult to a man than to be considered harmless."

The girls curtsied their good-byes and left the room.

"Good," said Langley when they were gone. "I was hoping I would have a chance to speak to you alone. How goes the progress of finding Harriet a husband?"

"Slow considering her current banishment."

"How long shall she be sick?"

"I believe she may return for supper tomorrow, assuming she can learn to behave. You have a very wild granddaughter."

"I know it. I wish she had been raised here, but I will do what I can to help her achieve her true place in society as my granddaughter."

"I am not sure she wishes to find a place in society."

Lord Langley sighed and leaned back on his pillows, absently shuffling the cards. "Being ill has given me time to reflect on a great many things. I do want Harriet to stay here, very much. But she needs to be happy. Tell Madame X that Harriet must be made to fall in love."

"A little late for such considerations," said Antonia. After all these years it still hurt. More than the embarrassment, the shame, the betrayal, was the horrible loss of her friend, the person she loved. Langley had broken her heart. Over the years she decided the experience was good, for it had made her tough, and she needed to be tough. She had buried her husband, her son, and even her grandson—three successive Dukes of Marchford. She had been dealt a difficult hand in life, yet she survived.

"Piquet?" asked Langley, concentrating on dealing the cards.

"That will be fine," said the duchess.

"I know it is too late to make amends for all the mistakes I have made," said Langley softly. "But I realize I have more years behind me than ahead, and I would like to live the rest of my life as I wish I had lived my whole life."

"Admirable," said Antonia, playing a card.

Lord Langley cleared his throat. "I wish to let you know how deeply sorry I am for my actions so long ago. I was wrong. I knew it was wrong when I did it, but I allowed myself to be cowed by my parents. In that regard, my daughter was so much stronger than myself."

"There is no need to bring up the past," said Antonia, though she was gratified to hear him say it.

"As you wish," said Langley, playing another card.

"I am only humoring you until you have returned to health, you understand."

"I am not forgiven. I understand that all too well."

Nineteen

"YE'RE AWAKE EARLY AGAIN," SAID THORNTON through the window of her stone laboratory.

"Yes, I have much I would like to accomplish today," said Harriet, even though all she had been doing for the past fifteen minutes was picking up bottles and putting them down again, wondering if Lord Thornton was going to arrive. "Besides, the only time I can come up here is before anyone is awake, even Penelope. I am still on my sickbed you see."

"Ye look remarkably well for a lady so ill."

"I thank you, sir," said Harriet with a little curtsy. She had been inundated with advice on how to behave from Penelope and the dowager duchess, and she was trying her best to act like a lady.

"I shan't disturb yer work. May ye have a pleasant day."

"Oh, you are not disturbing me. Not in the least. I mean I am busy, but you could never be a disruption." Harriet's smile wavered a bit. She was not sure she was coming across as the sophisticated lady she was trying to portray.

"I am glad of it."

"Are you going for a ride?" she asked, noting his boots and riding crop.

"Aye, every morning at dawn."

Good to know. She now knew exactly where she would be at dawn. "Why are you up here if the stables are down by the house?"

Thornton was still a moment and shrugged. "Saw yer light. Thought to check on ye."

"Oh. Thanks." He was checking on her. That was nice. Very nice.

An awkward silence fell and Harriet searched for something to say. "It is good to be awake before anyone else."

"Aye, they dinna ken what they are missing."

Harriet cocked her head to one side. "Dinna ken?"

"Och, sorry, lass. I tend to pick up the dialect more when I am in the Highlands. My mother would be so disappointed. She sent me to school in England to try to pry the accent out o' me, but it still finds me."

"I like the way you talk. It sounds nice," said Harriet, wishing she had phrased that sentiment more articulately. Something about standing in the presence of a handsome man made her speak as if she were still in the nursery.

"Ye are too American to ken that my speech brands me an outsider."

"I am too American to care if you are an outsider."

"Ah, verra good!" Thornton smiled, and his eyes gleamed at her. She liked the way his eyes smiled. His eyes didn't always smile when his mouth did, but they did this morning.

"I should love to go for a ride," blurted Harriet before she could remember not to be so blunt.

"Then ye must join me sometime."

"Yes, well, I do not mean to impose myself, only to say it is a beautiful morning for a ride with the mist low in the valley and the sun just creeping over the mountain. This land is beautiful."

Thornton's eyes grew serious but soft. He leaned on the window ledge and talked to her through the window opening. "The wildness of the country is not appreciated by everyone."

A rush of something warm flooded through her. He liked the same things she enjoyed. Perhaps, maybe, possibly, he even liked her. "Good. I am glad." And now she had no idea what to say next.

"I would enjoy taking you for a ride, this morning even, but I see you are not in a riding habit. Perhaps tomorrow we could arrange it if ye are allowed to leave yer sick room."

"Riding habit?" Harriet sat on the window opening and swung herself through. "You Brits have too many changes of clothes if you ask me. I have been riding in this many times." Her simple muslin gown was out of fashion for London society but was sturdy and sensible. "Besides, if we do not go now, I will never get the chance to sneak out of the house later in the morning. It is so dreadfully dull being shut up in my room all day."

A slow smile grew on Thornton's face. "Then I must invite ye to join me. Give me a few minutes to saddle the horses and convince a groom to come with us."

"A groom?"

"Propriety, my dear."

He called her dear! Harriet stifled an immature giggle. "That's another thing you Brits do too much of, propriety."

"I shall be bold and ask him not to follow too close."

"You are very bold indeed, but if a groom comes along and it should somehow get back to Penelope that I have been sneaking out in the morning, I'll be in for it."

A wrinkle appeared on his brow as if he was wrestling with an inner conflict. "I canna abandon a lass in distress. I suppose no one will see us if we have a quick ride."

"You are my true hero!" said Harriet with feeling.

Thornton asked her to remain and disappeared into the mist, returning a short time later with two saddled horses. Soon they were both mounted and riding down a road behind the ruined castle out of sight from Thornton Hall.

"Did ye ride often in America?" asked Thornton.

"Yes, quite often. Traveling by coach is difficult. The roads are not as developed as they are here. The mud in the spring is quite something. That is why I was traveling by ship down the coast. It is much faster by water than by land."

"I am still amazed at all ye have survived. It must o' been harrowing to have the ship seized."

"Seized and sunk." Harriet shook her head at the memory. "I know it was a bit drastic to confront the military men the way I did, and it has led to my current banishment, but I had to do something in the face of such injustice. Not for myself, but for every sailor who may be at risk for impressment into the British Navy."

"I do understand yer concerns. I wish ye to know that ye have got the men talking. There was anger and denial at first, but now I have been approached by some who wish to know more about what happened to ye."

"I am glad to know I might have made a difference! I still wonder about the fate of Captain Wentworth. I hope he is safe and has been able to tell my parents what happened."

"We shall hope for the best," said Thornton with a smile.

"Indeed. I have had to force myself to do so, else I would have worried myself sick. No purpose in that."

"None whatsoever. Allow me to help keep yer mind occupied."

"Yes, that would be appreciated."

He turned off the main road to a path and cantered through the trees at a sedate pace. The wildness of the Highlands was different from that of America, where she was accustomed to tall, thick forest. Here the land was filled with dense, short trees and rocks. The land seemed to be growing rocks. The mist was thicker here and it swallowed them whole.

"Is this the pace you usually keep in the mornings?" Harriet called.

Another slow smile lit his face. "'Tis the same path but on occasion I take a more vigorous pace."

"Let's to it then!" cried Harriet.

This won her a wide grin. Thornton turned back, kicked his mount, and was off. Harriet nudged hers

as well and followed. She had to keep close with the
thick mist. They raced through the forest, then across
a valley, covered with low hanging clouds. Though
she could still hear him ahead of her, Harriet lost sight
of Thornton in the thick mist. Her mount seemed
to know which way to go, so she trusted the horse's
instincts and let the beast run. It was an exhilarating
feeling, plunging headlong into the white abyss.

Suddenly, she was back in the forest again, dodging
trees until she came to a worn path that led upward.
Finally, she could see Thornton ahead of her as he
led them up the side of a large hill. Up and up they
climbed until the horses were breathing hard and they
suddenly emerged from the thick mist.

Bright sunlight blinded her. They had climbed
above the low clouds just as the sun's rays were
creeping over the horizon. She urged her mount
forward until she was on the top of a cliff next to
Thornton. Below was a sea of white where the low
fog had not yet been chased away by the sun.

"It is beautiful," breathed Harriet.

"Aye." Thornton turned toward the rising sun, his
face bathed in its orange light. The light caught strands
of ginger in his hair, giving him an unearthly glow. He
was a solid man. His back was straight in his saddle, his
shoulders square to the rising sun. He was the master
of his domain. Here was the Lord of Thornton.

Harriet also turned to the sun and watched in
silence as the rays crept over the horizon and flooded
the heights with its golden bath. Soon they were
completely engulfed in the full force of the sun. The
fog and mist began to creep away where the sun's rays

touched it. The forest came alive with the sunlight, the birds chattering to each other, some chirping happily, others squawking noisily.

"I cannot imagine London can have anything to compare to this," said Harriet.

"Nay, I suppose the good Lord knows how to make the best show in town."

"I would agree. Sunrises for me always came up over the ocean. We have a home close to the shore. The sun would turn the whole ocean red or orange, though usually that meant a storm was brewing."

"I should like to see it someday," said Thornton softly.

"Truly? You would like to go to America?"

Thornton frowned, as if not aware of what he had just said. Then he shrugged. "Perhaps a long way to see a sunrise, but it would be an adventure."

"The crossing is not too bad—only make sure you are not set upon by pirates or British warships."

"Aye, that I can do without." He turned to her with disappointment. "I suppose I should see to getting ye back before they discover ye are gone."

Harriet had to admit he was right.

Thornton clicked and urged his mount to return down the steep path back into the valley. The sun was rising now, chasing away the mist and giving Harriet a clear view of what before was only a white blanket around her. The field was bathed in purple heather, alive and swaying in the breeze. They crossed it and entered into forest. Harriet caught her breath. The trees, the ground, the rocks were covered by bright-green moss, making it look like little green people huddled about the forest floor.

·"What is this place?" she asked.

"They call it the faerie glen. Folks say the faeries come to play here. We shall have to keep watch on St. John's Eve to make sure the fey creatures dinna creep out into our world."

"I should like to meet a faerie."

"They would most likely cause ye mischief. Best to keep yer distance."

Harriet could not help herself. She slid out of the saddle and touched the bright-green, springy moss. "Do you believe in faeries?"

Thornton also dismounted and stood beside her. "Only the ones that are real, lassie."

"But you are not afraid to ride through the faerie realm at dawn?"

"Nay, they leave me be. Now on St. John's Eve, that will be another story. I'll be keeping to my bonfire like a good laddie."

"What is St. John's Eve?" Harriet took a few steps into the forest, marveling at the numerous different shades of green illuminated by shafts of sunlight filtering down through the trees.

"'Tis been celebrated for centuries, and even after it was discouraged, it was still practiced in the Highlands. Legend has it the faeries and other fey creatures come out to play on Midsummer's Night Eve. So for centuries people have been building bonfires to keep away unwanted spirits intent on causing mischief."

"Like Shakespeare's *A Midsummer Night's Dream*?"

"Precisely. Best to keep out of the forest lest that mischievous sprite Puck give ye a love potion."

"Disastrous! I shall stay away!" She wondered how she could arrange a meeting with this Puck. Might be useful to have a love potion.

Thornton smiled. "Aye, beware the faeries."

If he knew what she was thinking he would do well to beware of her. With some reluctance, she realized she must get back, lest her clandestine meeting be discovered. They walked back to their horses and Harriet realized that even with her height, there was no way to mount her horse with any shred of dignity.

Thornton kneeled beside the horse and held out his hands. The gesture got her thinking of something else and her heart pounded in response. *He is just helping me mount this horse, not proposing.*

Trying to remain calm, she put her foot in his hands and he tossed her into the saddle with ease. He made her feel feminine and almost delicate, a remarkable feat in itself.

"Time to go home," he said, easily jumping into the saddle himself.

Home. For the first time, the word was paired with an unhappy realization. Her home was not his. Going home meant leaving Scotland and Thornton. She may have grown to enjoy his company above all others, but there was a problem the size of the Atlantic Ocean separating them from any future together.

"Yes," said Harriet with regret. "Let us go home."

❦

A young lady crept silently up the stairs to the hall where the gentlemen were residing. She hesitated outside Thornton's door then softly opened it. The room was empty and sparsely furnished. She glanced around and stole quietly to the bed, her skirts brushing against the floor. She pulled up a corner of the mattress and slid a bundle of papers underneath. She blew it a kiss and covered the mattress once more so that none would notice it. With a smile, she slinked away.

Twenty

"COME NOW," BARKED THE DOWAGER SHARPLY. "WE must go down to tea now or we will be late."

Penelope looked up from her dressing table in surprise. She was struggling into a spencer coat so skintight it was difficult to pull on. "Late? Since when have you cared for that? Have you not always told me tea will begin when you arrive?"

Antonia waved off the comment. "Perhaps I am hungry. Have you no compassion such that you would make me wait?"

"Is something the matter?" Penelope knew the dowager well enough by now to know when she was out of sorts.

"It's all Lord Langley's fault. He emerged from his sickroom today and wished to play cards. So the Comtesse de Marseille, Sir Antony, and I obliged him."

"Lost, did you?"

The dowager's face scrunched, making her look old, for once. "Lost my pearls to Langley. Pearls that had been in my family for years. They had been my mother's and had sentimental value."

"Whatever made you bet them on a card game?"

The dowager cast upon Penelope a look that could spoil milk. "The cards were good. I should not have lost! I blame Langley. Or perhaps the comtesse cheated when she dealt."

"Of her, I would believe anything," agreed Penelope. The comtesse may have been one of the dowager's closest friends, but to those she deemed socially inferior, which was most people, she could be vicious. A noted gossip with a wicked sense of humor, the comtesse was dangerous, yet everyone accepted her opinion on music, art, and fashion as authoritative.

"I shall be forced to wear the rubies tonight," said the dowager with a sigh as she opened her jewelry box. "Oh no! Oh goodness no!"

"What is it?" Penelope rushed to her side. "Has something been stolen?"

"Paste! Oh, I'm ruined!" The dowager sat down hard on a chair.

"Paste? What is wrong?" Penelope asked.

"I was getting the necklace and I remembered." Antonia closed her eyes and shook her head. "I had forgotten about the pearls. How could I have forgot?"

"What about the pearls?" Penelope was lost in the conversation.

The dowager sighed again, long and mournful. "Several months ago, after Marchford had cut off my funds and before we had been blessed by Madame X and the matchmaking scheme, I needed sustenance to survive."

"You needed sustenance?" asked Penelope doubtfully. The dowager certainly never lacked for any basic need or comfort that she saw.

"There was a bonnet so divine, I had to claim it."

"I see." What Penelope saw was that the dowager's opinion of sustenance fell under a very different definition than hers.

"I could not go to Marchford, clearly, so I devised a scheme to pawn the pearls and have fake ones made so no one would know. Marchford found out. The idiot pawnbroker sent a receipt to the house and James went and collected the pearls." The dowager shook her head. "If Lord Langley finds out I have given him fake pearls, I shall be utterly ruined."

"Surely it is not so bad as that," soothed Penelope. "You have been on friendly terms with him lately. Why not go to him and explain what happened and offer the real pearls?"

"No! No, he must never know. If he discovers I needed to pawn my pearls for money, I shall die of mortification. I have been embarrassed enough because of him. To admit such a thing? No, no, life would be unbearable."

Penelope sat on a chair next to the dowager. She had to concede that this situation would indeed cast the dowager in an unfavorable light. Society could be cruel, often celebrating a person one day and ridiculing them the next. Passing off fake pearls as real ones in a card game would be seen as a breach of the societal codes of conduct, to which all members were rigorously held. The dowager was indeed in a difficult situation, and as her companion, Penelope felt the duty to help make it right.

"Where are the real pearls?" asked Penelope.

"I believe James has them. I asked him to bring

them with us so I could wear the real ones, not the fakes. I meant to get the real string from him this morning, but I forgot."

"So let us ask Marchford—"

"No! He must not know either. He would be furious if he found out I had lost the pearls. He attempted to give me a lecture when he found out I had pawned them in the first place. As if he had any right to comment on my conduct."

"Fine. You go down to tea and say I have a megrim. I will find the pearls in the duke's room and then replace them with the fake ones in Langley's room." It was not her best plan, but if everyone was at tea, Penelope should be able to set the situation to rights within a few minutes and then it would be over.

Antonia sat straighter and the light in her blue eyes danced once more. "Thank you, Penelope. I knew you would know what to do. I shall come back up to the room directly if they are not both in the tearoom. If I do not return, then please proceed. You are such a dear."

Penelope gave her a half smile. "You must promise me to send up tea and cakes. And if I get caught, I expect you to intercede on my behalf."

Penelope waited a while to ensure that the dowager was not going to return to inform her that one of her targets was not at tea. Fortune was on her side it seemed, for both the Duke of Marchford and Lord Langley were making England proud by participating in a proper tea. Penelope slipped out the door and walked down the hallway to the stairs to where the men had their rooms. She resisted the urge to tiptoe.

Going to retrieve the necklace sounded sensible when she was talking to the dowager, but now when it came to act, her confidence lagged. She feared she would run into someone. She felt guilty already and thus far she had done nothing more than walk down a hall. She balled her fists at her sides and commanded her courage to proceed. This is what comes of being raised by a straightforward clergyman—an overactive sense of guilt.

Fortunately for the cause, Penelope also possessed a strong sense of duty and continued on to help protect her patroness's reputation. It would not take more than a few minutes and it would be done, she reassured herself.

The gentlemen were housed on one of the top floors of the manor house. As she walked up the stairs she found herself walking back in time. The bottom floors had been remolded in a modern style, but on the top floors, she found stone walls and solid oak doors, most likely original to the manor house built during Queen Elizabeth's reign. The long hallway of oak doors stretched out before her. A problem. Which one was Marchford's?

"Can I help ye, miss?"

Penelope swirled around to find a maid holding a mop.

"I—I was looking at the architecture," said Penelope in a rush.

The maid raised an eyebrow and nodded. "Aye, the architecture is verra fine, t'be sure. There be many young ladies who've been appreciating the architecture. Particularly in the Duke o' Marchford's room there." She pointed to the second door on the right.

"Thank you, but I believe I've seen enough."
Penelope turned to walk down the stairs while the
maid disappeared into the servant's passage.

When the maid was out of sight, Penelope slipped
back up the stairs and into Marchford's room, shutting
the door softly behind her. She needed to find those
pearls and fast, before someone found her, or her heart
would explode from pounding so hard.

Marchford's room was neat, with nothing out of
place. In fact, nothing was out at all. She wondered
if the maid had been having fun with her and had
directed her to the wrong room, for this one had
no evidence anyone was staying in it. She walked to
the wardrobe and opened the ornately carved doors.
Marchford's clothes were arranged neatly. These were
his jackets; she knew them by sight. She knew them
by smell. Marchford's clothes were neat, orderly,
pressed to perfection, dignified, well built, strong...

Penelope shook her head to get back at the task
at hand. She needed to find the pearls and escape.
She rummaged quickly through the wardrobe but
did not find anything. She opened a chest at the foot
of the bed. She was surprised by a stack of neatly
folded unmentionables. She paused for a moment,
wondering what to do. Could she possibly touch a
man's undergarments?

She took a deep breath and put her hand on the
top of the neatly folded underthings. They were soft.
She ran her hand across them and caught herself. She
had entered a single man's room and was stroking his
unmentionables. Very wrong.

She quickly moved the stack to the floor and

searched through the trunk, being careful to remember how it had been packed. Toward the bottom, she found an old box that had clearly been used often and showed the marks of age. She opened the box and found the string of pearls. Yes! This had not been too bad. She took the pearls from the box and placed the string in her pocket. As she began to place the items back into the trunk she heard male voices.

Her heart leaped into her throat and pounded so loud she feared they would hear her. There could be no recovery, no plausible excuse for being found in Marchford's bedchamber. She hoped they were going into a different room. Forcing herself to concentrate, she worked at returning the trunk to its original form even as the voices got louder. *Do not come in!*

She was almost done, but the door began to swing open. There was no time to finish. She closed the lid and dove under the bed a heartbeat before Marchford entered the room.

"Your Grace, I must insist that you allow me to guard these plans," said a male voice Penelope recognized as Mr. Neville. "I swear I would protect them with my life."

"How very gallant of you, Mr. Neville, but I fear I have no plans for you to hold, and before you go about pestering my friends for the same, I would ask that you refrain. Think of it as a personal favor to me."

"Your Grace, surely I do not need to remind you of the very real danger of spies in our midst."

Penelope lay flat against the floor, praying she would not be found. She could see only a few inches of each man's boots from under the dust ruffle around the bed. On the floor, stacked neatly on the far side of the trunk, were the duke's unmentionables.

Twenty-one

"You must be aware of the danger. You must. I would like to work with you, not against." Mr. Neville sounded earnest.

Marchford sighed. The short man in a tragic coat with too much shoulder padding was something akin to a pebble in Marchford's shoe, but he did have a way of being right about things. Regarding spies, no one could doubt Mr. Neville's dedication to duty. He was tireless in his pursuit of traitors and had even killed in the line of duty, something Marchford appreciated, particularly since the traitor Neville killed was attempting to kill Marchford's best friend at the time.

"I do understand, Mr. Neville, and I will keep you informed. I agree with you in principle that we need to work together, not against one another, if we are to draw out traitors and protect information."

"James!" The Dowager Duchess of Marchford burst through the door, gasping for breath.

"What is wrong?" Marchford was immediately at his grandmother's side.

"I… I wanted to know why you left tea so soon." The duchess scanned the room with a nervous eye.

"I had things to discuss. You walked up all those stairs to inquire after my teatime habits?" Something was not right. His grandmother would hardly run up stairs to meet the queen let alone himself.

"Thank you, Mr. Neville," Marchford said to the government agent. He wanted to talk to his grandmother without an audience. She was up to something, and he did not wish the British Foreign Office to know about it.

Mr. Neville bowed to them both and left. His grandmother sank into a chair. He handed her a handkerchief and she used it to blot her forehead.

"What is all this about?" asked Marchford. "Why a sudden interest in my teatime habits?"

"You left early and I know you are partial to a light repast. I wanted to make sure you were in adequate health," said the dowager.

"I am in good health."

"Good! Well!" The dowager stood and took another quick glance around the room. "I see you are not in need of me, so I shall leave you."

He considered calling her back and demanding he know what was wrong, but he knew from experience, vast experience, that it would be a pointless excursion. He closed his door and walked back inside toward the window. Out of the corner of his eye he noted the small stack of his unmentionables by the chest. Someone had been in his room, and if his grandmother's presence was any indication, he knew exactly who. He drew his small pistol from his jacket, just in case he was wrong.

"Penelope Rose," he called. "Come out now!"

Nothing stirred. Still, he had a feeling he was not alone, and he always listened to his gut. It kept him alive when he was working missions in Cadiz. He trusted it to keep him alive now.

"Miss Rose, I would appreciate it if you would come out. It would save me the trouble of coming after you and potentially ruining my clothes."

A scrape and a scuffle came from under the bed and slowly Penelope emerged into the light of the room. She did not meet his eye but focused instead on smoothing her skirts.

"Good afternoon, Your Grace," said Penelope as if they had met in the tearoom and she had not just crawled out from under his bed.

"Miss Rose, I fear I am going to have to demand an explanation."

"Yes, yes, by all means, you have every right to demand one."

"And am I to hear this explanation?"

"Of course, just as soon as I think of one you will be the first to know."

"Miss Rose." The words came out low. He wanted answers. "Why were you rummaging through my chest?"

"How did you know it was me?" Penelope looked up with large brown eyes.

"I am remarkable. Now answer my question."

"Or you plan to shoot me?"

Marchford pocketed the gun. It had been bad form to have it still in hand. "I hope it will not come to that."

"I see." Penelope sat down on a wooden chair and folded her hands in her lap. She looked much too comfortable to have just been found under his bed. What on earth she was doing here? He knew better than to assume she was interested in him. This eminently efficient person had no interest in him or any man. Of that he was certain. Why he needed to remind himself of this fact was less clear.

"This would be the time to tell me why you were under the bed, Miss Rose."

"I can only agree with you."

Marchford waited again, but Penelope sat still, prim, and proper.

"Miss Rose," he said with a growl.

"Nothing would be easier than to tell you why I was, or shall I say am, in your room, but I am not at liberty to say."

"Because of my grandmother?"

"Yes."

"Naturally I need to ask if there is any other reason why you are here. These are dangerous times, Miss Rose."

"The only reason I am here is to run an errand for your grandmother."

"Under my bed."

Penelope at least had the good sense to shift in her chair. He assumed she was less comfortable than she appeared.

"That was not exactly part of the plan," she admitted.

"And what was the plan?"

"I am not at liberty to say."

Marchford pulled a chair from the other side of the

room and sat down in it across from her, so close their knees almost touched. She said nothing but her eyes grew wider. Good. He wanted her off balance, unsure. He wanted to know what was going on here. And she was going to tell him.

"An explanation if you please," he said.

"Perhaps I was looking at the architecture." Penelope glanced around the room as if noting it for the first time. "The maid said many young ladies seemed fascinated by this room and had asked directions to it. I can only assume there is some architectural interest here."

She was attempting to divert the question, but he was not going to rise to the bait. "And you thought the best vantage point to appreciate the architecture would be from under the bed."

Penelope's lips twitched up and she clenched her jaw as if to avoid smiling. "Yes, quite."

"Penelope, I can stay here all day, all *night* if I have to."

"Perhaps I have fallen prey to whatever afflicted those other women who invaded your privacy."

"I did not realize I should count you among my admirers, Miss Rose."

Penelope's cheeks flushed a pretty pink. "And what if I was?"

Her answer surprised him. Mousy young things should run and hide if he said anything suggestive. "Perhaps this is why you were rifling through my undergarments?"

Her eyes flashed and her cheeks grew pinker. "The undergarments were incidental to my plan—an unexpected pleasure."

Pleasure? Had she called touching his unmentionables a pleasure? Now his cheeks were growing warm. This was not how it was supposed to happen. He intended to flirt with her to keep her off guard. Now it was he who was scrambling to put her back in her place, or at least figure out which place she belonged. "I did not realize you held such a *tendre* for me, Miss Rose."

"Neither did I," murmured Penelope. Was she speaking the truth?

He looked at her, really looked. He had to admit her appearance had undergone a radical improvement of late. He understood his grandmother had replaced all her clothes with ones in the latest mode. His grandmother may have many deficits, but a lack of fashion sense did not rank among them. Penelope now appeared much more to her best advantage and Marchford would be lying if he said he had not noticed. It was amazing how clothes that actually fit properly revealed her figure. A strikingly good one he must admit.

He was too close. Much too close. He jumped out of the chair and opened the chest, forcing himself to focus back on his investigation. He rifled through the contents until he found the pearl box. It was empty. "The pearls, Miss Rose?"

"In my pocket," admitted Penelope with surprising poise.

"And this was why your mistress sent you?"

"The reason I am here is to run an errand for your grandmother."

"Then I should speak with her." Marchford shook his head. "She had best not be gambling."

"You would have to ask her, naturally," said Penelope.

"She is not the one I found under the bed. There is also the matter of what I was speaking about to Mr. Neville."

"I am familiar with Mr. Neville and his nervous nature."

"I wish it was just needless worry, but I fear Mr. Neville may have the right of it. There is most likely a traitor in our midst."

"I am very sorry to hear it."

"This is not a game, Miss Rose. I need to know whose side you are on." Marchford began to pace like one of the caged lions they kept at the Tower of London. "The stakes are too high. I cannot possibly allow access to sensitive information by anyone working for Napoleon. The war does not go well. We know the emperor is looking to England as practically the only country in Europe he has not yet conquered. He is coming; I feel it. It is only a matter of time."

"That much I have read in the papers."

"Read the papers, do you? Odd sort of habit for a lady."

"I am an odd sort of lady," retorted Penelope.

"No," said Marchford slowly. "I think you quite normal. You have lived in society for years and yet managed to keep yourself the same as when you entered it. You are not swayed by a pretty compliment or a pretty gown. In that, I find you extraordinary."

"A compliment?"

"No, simply stating the facts."

Penelope raised an eyebrow and a slight upturn in the corner of the right side of her mouth was the only evidence that he had amused her. Her reaction, muted as it was, pleased him.

He sat on the trunk and ran his fingers through his hair. "I hate this job. Always wondering whom you can trust." He spoke more to himself than to her.

"I came to retrieve an item for your grandmother that belongs to her," said Penelope with a reassuring calm. "I am not a spy or a traitor or a foreign agent. I am simply the companion to your grandmother. Despite being found under your bed, I hope you know you can trust me. I would be very sad indeed to think you did not feel you could rely on me. I hope you know I would tell you if I felt any of this had anything to do with a traitor to the Crown."

He did know and did trust her. He only hoped that trust was not misplaced. "I do trust you, Miss Rose." He spoke the words before he remembered this could be a fatal admission. He shook his head. Either he was going daft from being on missions too long, or he was growing soft from coming back home. Betwixt and between was not a good place for an agent. One always needed to know where he was and what he was about. With Penelope, things were different.

Penelope held out the pearls. "Would you like these returned?"

Marchford handed her the box instead. "These belong to my grandmother and her mother before her. She may do with them as she will."

Twenty-two

HARRIET PAUSED BEFORE KNOCKING ON THE DOOR OF
the Duchess of Marchford and Miss Rose. Raised
voices could be heard from inside.

"Did he catch you?" asked the dowager.

"Yes, of course he caught me," said Penelope with
more than a little exasperation. "It is Marchford after
all. He knows about the pearls—oh not everything,
but he can guess."

"How could you let him find you?"

"Find me? You were supposed to keep him at tea!"

"What can I do if he decides to leave the room?
Were you able to switch the strands?"

"No. And I do not wish to try. If I get caught in
Lord Langley's room I cannot think of what I could
say to explain myself."

"What shall I do?" wailed the dowager.

"You are going to have to talk to him directly."

"I would rather be buried alive," declared the dowager.

Penelope said something in a low tone that Harriet
could not hear. She wondered what the trouble was
about and if she should return later.

"Eavesdropping on people's conversations?" asked Priscilla Crawley from behind her.

Harriet jumped back and turned to face her accuser. "No, I was just coming up to meet them. I did not mean to, that is to say…"

"Oh, do not bother to explain. I understand your American customs are so much different than our own. I cannot expect you to know proper behavior. If you ever need some tips on polite society, I should be glad to assist," said Priscilla in a smooth voice.

"What is this?" asked Penelope, who decided to open the door at that moment.

"I was just helping Miss Redgrave understand some of our customs, such as not eavesdropping. Good evening, Miss Rose, Miss Redgrave." Priscilla gave them an angelic smile and continued down the hall.

"You were listening at the door?" asked Penelope.

"No!" Harriet hung her head. "Yes. I am sorry, I did not mean to."

"Time to go downstairs," said the dowager. Both ladies gave Harriet that pained, disappointed look she was getting so accustomed to seeing. It hurt worse this time.

Dinner was long, and afterward, when the ladies withdrew to allow the men time for their cigars, it was painful. No one spoke to her. No one acknowledged her. At least before, Penelope and the dowager were there to provide conversation. Even if they were instructing her on what to do or not to do, at least she was not ignored. Now, thanks to her carelessness and Priscilla's "help" she had no one.

It was enough. Harriet knew she did not fit in; they

did not need to make it so obvious. "I think I will go lie down," she told Penelope.

Harriet walked out of the drawing room to the hall without waiting for a reply.

"Are you ill?" asked Penelope, who followed her out.

"No. Simply tired," said Harriet. Tired of being so rejected.

"I do hope you are not taking ill. Sorry if I was not as conversational tonight. Perhaps you heard I had a little disagreement with Her Grace."

"Yes, and I am so sorry. I did not mean—"

"Of course you didn't." Penelope walked closer and lowered her voice. "Do be careful around Miss Crawley. I do not believe Priscilla is a friend of yours."

"Yes. That I know all too well." Harriet smiled. Priscilla may not be a friend, but Penelope was. She felt better already.

Harriet walked down the corridor and out into the main entryway to go up the stairs just as the men were leaving the dining room to rejoin the ladies.

"Miss Redgrave!"

"Good evening, Miss Redgrave."

"I do hope you are well, Miss Redgrave."

Harriet was immediately swarmed with men. She had a sudden impulse to bat them away like flies. "I am sorry, gentlemen. I feel the need to retire."

"I am so sorry."

"I hope it is not serious."

"Is there anything I can do?"

"Please, gentlemen, allow Miss Redgrave to rest," said Thornton, and stood between her and them until they all left to find the ladies.

"Thank you," breathed Harriet. "I am not feeling strong enough to fend them off tonight."

"I hope you are not actually taking ill."

"No, no, a little tired maybe. I would be revived greatly, however, if I could count on another ride in the morning."

Thornton bowed and came up smiling. "It would be my pleasure. But before ye find yer bed, I did speak to a gentleman ye may wish to talk to."

"I have had enough of gentlemen for one night."

"This particular gentleman is a retired general. He was in the room when ye made yer unorthodox proclamation and would like to hear more o' yer story. I believe he shares yer concern with the impressment of American sailors."

"Oh yes! Yes, I would love to speak to him."

"Perhaps you should go to the library and I will bring him to meet wi' ye. That way ye may speak in private."

"Yes, that would be perfect. You have thought of everything."

They did as Thornton suggested and Harriet met Sir Antony Roberts. The gentleman proved to be amiable, with silver whiskers and kind blue eyes. He was a good listener, allowing Harriet to tell the entire story. In the retelling Harriet surprised herself at the emotion that surged forth. She had been terrified, but until now had buried it deep within. Speaking about it became almost cathartic, even to the point of requiring Thornton's handkerchief when a few tears were spilled.

"Thank you for telling me your story," said Sir Antony. "I understand it is difficult to share some of these details and I appreciate your courage in doing so."

Harriet sat up a little taller and smiled at the gentleman. "You are very kind. I only hope my story can be used to help protect sailors in the future."

"I will most certainly begin a dialogue about this practice. I am disturbed in the extreme to hear it is being conducted. I can only offer my heartfelt apology for all you have been through."

"Thank you, Sir Antony."

"Thank you for bringing it to our attention. It took courage to do so, my dear," said Sir Antony with a kindly smile. "I shall return to cards now, still have money in my pocket to lose—ho ho!"

"I know you must have spoken to him," said Harriet to Thornton after Sir Antony left. "Thank you. You cannot know what it means to me to share this with someone who might be able to stop this horrible practice."

"I only said a few words. I agree with Sir Antony. It was yer courage that began this process." Thornton sat beside her on the settee.

Harriet gave Thornton a wobbly smile. It was an affirmation she needed to hear. Without meaning to and without even knowing how it happened she found her hand in his. It seemed natural. His hand was warm with the calluses of a workingman, perhaps from riding. Holding hands with Thornton alone in the library may have been all kinds of wrong in the eyes of society, but it felt all kinds of right. Despite her better judgment, her affection for him grew, and now it seemed the feeling was reciprocated.

Voices were heard outside the room and they both jumped to their feet. She should not be this close to him.

"I hope ye are feeling better," said Thornton with a formal bow.

"Yes, yes, of course." She felt silly now to have read so much into the simple gesture. He was simply comforting her after the pain of telling her ordeal. He was a kind sort of man. Nothing more. She curtsied and fled to her room.

Twenty-three

DESPITE AN ODD FEELING OF BEING OFF-BALANCE whenever Lord Thornton was near, Harriet was looking forward to the promised horseback ride. She also had a growing suspicion that something peculiar was happening at the supposedly unlivable castle. Workmen passed her makeshift chemistry laboratory, but where they went and why they were there she could not say. Something was amiss at the castle and she was going to find out what.

"Where are the horses?" Harriet asked Thornton when he emerged from the morning mist in the castle courtyard as she expected.

"Horses?" asked Thornton innocently, as if unfamiliar with the concept. "Good morning, Miss Redgrave. I thought we would meet down in the stables for our ride."

"Odd," commented Harriet. "It smells like the stables are right here."

"Must be the wind."

Harriet shook her head. "Wind is coming from the east, not from below. There must be horses nearby."

Thornton scratched the back of his neck. "Sometimes the crofters stable their horses here. There may be some in the keep." Thornton spoke casually, as if the subject could be of no importance. "The horses here coud'na interest ye. Let us go to the stables."

"Nonsense! I wish to see these beasts with which I share the castle. I have smelled them, sometimes even heard them, but never seen them." She wanted to know what Thornton was hiding in the castle.

Thornton began to walk toward the stables below, but Harriet proceeded to the wooden door of the castle keep instead. He turned and hustled to catch up with her.

"I confess I have been interested to see what was locked in here. Do you have a key? Oh, of course you do, since you were on your way there anyway," said Harriet. She ignored the voices of her mum, Penelope, and the dowager who were all chastising her for being unladylike. This was no time for propriety. This was a mystery!

He stood before the padlocked door, his mouth a thin line. He surveyed her closely as if weighing her worth. With a sigh, he pulled a key from his pocket and turned the lock. He unfastened the door and swung it open without a word.

They stepped inside and Harriet was amazed at the sight before her. The keep had been transformed into stables in four neat rows of stalls. The horses in the stalls were thoroughbreds, the finest of the species she had ever seen. The stables themselves had been built recently, with quality in mind. Each stall had a name carved in wood on the outside of the door. Nearby, a handful of stable lads were grooming horses, mucking out stalls, or putting up hay.

These were not a few old nags owned by crofters—this was a highly skilled operation. She walked up to the first stall to a chestnut brown horse aptly named Charger. He was a fine piece, muscular and lean. He swished his tail and his skin twitched over his rippling muscles. He was quite fine indeed. All the horses were spectacular.

She swirled to face him. "Crofter's horses?"

He had the decency to look sheepish.

"Do you want to tell me what is going on here?"

"Nay." He was honest at least.

"I assume since you had this locked that you do not wish anyone to know about this." She gestured to rows of thoroughbreds before her.

"Ye're familiar with horses?" he asked tentatively, as if measuring his response based on what she could see.

"Familiar enough to know you have quite an operation here."

"Would ye believe these are horses from the village?" He scratched the back of his neck again and didn't look too hopeful.

"Only if it was a village of racehorses."

"I was rather hoping ye woud'na notice," mumbled Thornton.

"Sorry to be so observant."

"I raise racehorses," said Thornton.

"That is rather clear."

"I do not wish this information to be widely known."

"That also is clear. But why?"

"Come riding with me and I will tell you all." His

eyes glinted with a mischief she had never seen in him before. She would follow him anywhere.

Harriet smiled slowly until she realized it was her turn to speak. "I would enjoy that very much."

Thornton motioned to a stable hand to saddle two horses and gave Harriet a short tour. He paused by a stall with a mother and gleaming black colt.

"This fine lad was born only a few nights ago. Named him Lazarus because he gave us a scare wi' his birth."

"Hello, Lazzy." Harriet stroked the colt's soft velvet fur. "This is an amazing place here."

"Thank ye."

"But how do you move the horses in and out and how did all these workers get here? I have been watching the keep, and I never saw anyone come or go out the door."

"'Tis not the only door. We are in a castle after all."

The two horses were saddled and brought to them. Thornton's stallion was quite a fine specimen, with a custom saddle and special shoes. They were both atop their mounts in the old keep before she could offer much more comment on his surprising secret stables.

"But how are we going to get out?"

"Follow me." Thornton guided his mount, a shimmering horse of midnight black, around the stall to one corner of the converted keep. Fresh beams had been put up to stabilize a passageway. Thornton entered the passageway and the ground immediately sloped down.

"Is this a secret passage?" She had always wanted to explore a secret passageway.

"Aye, this was used for escape if it came to it. We expanded it for our use, but from the outside it is difficult to find unless ye ken for what ye seek."

They rode their horses through the tunnel, which was lit by the occasional torch.

"Where are we now?" She could not hide her exuberance, but she did manage to prevent herself from squealing with joy. She was sure the dowager would definitely not approve of anything resembling a squeal for any reason.

"We are underneath the courtyard. We should be coming out soon."

As if to heed his command, the tunnel began to lighten before them and soon they both walked out from behind a large bush into the sun. Harriet blinked into the sun. The clouds had run away, leaving a lovely, sun-filled day. They had come out behind the castle wall, where no one from the manor house would be able to see the exit.

He was secretly raising horses. But why? She turned to ask him questions but rethought it. He said he would tell her all; best to let him choose his timing. Patience was a little-used virtue she was attempting to cultivate within herself, at least on occasion.

"Where shall we go?" she asked him instead.

"Follow me," he said with a smile. He nudged his mount and the horse responded instantly. She followed him and instantly fell in love with the ginger horse she rode. Her mount was smooth and easy, yet responsive and fast. They rode slowly down the hill with many rocks and boulders until they came to a large field, where they let the horses have their heads.

They flew across the field at an impressive pace and up another hill of heather until they crested a large hill overlooking a bright-blue loch.

"Beautiful," Harriet murmured, taking it all in. She had missed her home ever since she had been forced to come to the British Isles. But now, somehow, she felt like she was home.

Thornton dismounted and helped her dismount as well. She placed a gloved hand on his shoulder and he put his hands around her waist, almost encircling her to lift her to the ground. Her heart beat so loudly she hoped he would not notice.

She had always been direct and straightforward in her communications, but now she longed for subtlety and safe distance. She knew he was not one for romance, so she did not wish to misinterpret his actions for anything other than friendliness. Most of all, she did not want him to know how mutinously her body responded every time he was near. And when he touched her... she could hardly keep her heart in her chest. Or her hands to herself. She removed her hand from his shoulder. She was safely on the ground and her hand had lingered too long.

Tall grasses and heather rippled and flowed around her, brushing against her skirts. The wind teased tendrils of her hair that had escaped her bun. It was a glorious day, bright and warm and clear. Several large boulders with flat tops were at the top of the hill and Thornton motioned for Harriet to sit beside him on one. The stone was smooth and warm, and she had to resist the urge to lie out on one like a giant lizard.

"I warrant ye wish to know what I am about wi'

the horses," began Thornton, looking not at her but out over the clear, still waters.

"If you would like to tell me," said Harriet politely, which she certainly hoped he did, or she might perish from curiosity.

"I told ye o' the financial problems wi' my family."

"Yes, your mother spends far more money than she has."

He turned sharply and Harriet realized she had spoken too bluntly.

"Aye, 'tis true enough," Thornton conceded. "I found a way to raise our fortune by breeding horses. The best horses, naturally, o' the British Isles."

"Naturally."

"Unfortunately, my mother has difficulty wi' not—"

"Plundering?" Harriet supplied.

Thornton smiled. "Aye, I suppose ye have the right of it. If she knew we had racehorses in our stables, she would either sell them or use them as collateral for something. Either way, they would be lost to me."

"So you made the stables in your castle."

"Aye, 'tis generally not difficult to keep her from here, since she enjoys Town living most o' the time. But with the house party here, it makes things a wee more difficult."

"How long do you think you can hide it from her?"

"I am in the middle of several sales, sales that could change everything. At least I hope so. I am meeting with my steward today to go over exact numbers and my mother's latest embarrassments. Once those are completed…" He paused and looked once more over the blue-green loch.

"You still won't tell her."

Thornton turned toward her, his eyebrows raised. "Aye, ye have the right of it again. Not because of the financial reasons, but because these horses have become more valuable to me than their price tag. I want them to have a happy life. I do not wish to see them sold to someone I do not know."

"But can't you rein in your mother? How can she be so irresponsible? Forgive me, I know I speak of things I should not."

"Most of the money is hers. She is the daughter of a wealthy merchant with aspirations. My father married her purely for the money, I fear. Her father was aware of this and made several rather ironclad provisions regarding her dowry. Except for a large sum to pay for my father's embarrassments, and a small monthly allowance, her money remained hers. Between the two of us, she has decidedly more income than I. Unfortunately, she runs through it much faster."

"That must put you in an awkward position."

"Aye, it does."

"I wonder why your father would agree to such terms."

"He was in a vast amount of debt at the time. He made the decision he did to save the estate. However, it was not long after his wedding that he regretted his decision." Thornton stood and leaned against a tall boulder. "Before he passed, he impressed upon me the importance o' never marrying for material concerns."

"And now your mother wishes you to do just the same as your father did."

"Aye. But in that she will be disappointed. I plan to wed a lass wi'out fortune at all."

"I see." It was Harriet's turn to look out over the blue waters. She supposed it was his way of reducing any chance she might have pictured him in a matrimonial light. He was a friend, and one she was lucky to have. She should not be ungrateful. Or disappointed. But she was. Nothing could acquit her of the sin of being desperately rich.

They were quiet a moment, watching the birds circle over the loch, changing direction at once like some aerial display for their benefit. It was indeed a beautiful day, but Harriet was still chewing on Thornton's words.

"Do you have someone picked out?" she asked.

"I beg yer pardon?"

"Do you have your penniless lass chosen yet, the one you will wed?"

"Nay, nay." Thornton shook his head and leaned away from her, as if the mere thought of marriage might prove contagious.

"You ought to," declared Harriet. "You encouraged me to find a marriage partner to avoid fortune hunters, now I will give you the same advice. You should pick a wife as soon as may be. That way your mother will stop pestering you with wealthy marriage partners."

"Wealthy and well placed in society," Thornton amended. "She has never forgotten her birth, nor have many of society ever forgiven her for being the rich daughter of a merchant. She wishes to raise her position in society through my marriage to the daughter of a well-respected family."

An unhappy vision of Miss Crawley floated through

her head. "Even more reason to find the lady of your dreams soon."

Thornton shrugged. "Ye may have a point. My mother will not stop until she sees me wed."

"So you should be wed with all haste."

"I canna deny yer logic, Miss Redgrave, but I fear marrying to avoid my mother's interference may be an even worse motivation than marrying for money."

Harriet laughed. "I suppose. I was only trying to help. Would that I could make myself as poor as a church mouse, I would wed you before dinner to save you the trouble of having to dance with another round of rich debutantes."

Thornton joined her laughter. "If ye ever cared to lose yer fortune, my mother can help in this regard. I would hate to wish poverty on anyone, but if ye could manage it, I would be most grateful."

"I shall turn my fortune over to her hands when I see her for tea."

"Then you shall be impoverished and we shall be wed by supper." He smiled and walked over to where she sat. She leaned closer.

"Greetings, my soon to be husband of convenience." Harriet respectfully bobbed her head. "I think we shall start a new convention of people who wed not for financial concerns but to avoid an awkward conversation."

"Aye, I should be glad to start the trend with ye."

"To a long future of leading society." Harriet held out her hand.

"Ah, but I can do one better." He took her offered hand and pulled her closer to kiss her cheek. He kissed her left cheek then turned to kiss the other, but Harriet mistook the gesture and turned her face so that their lips met. And stayed together. One second. Two. Three.

He pulled away. "I apologize." His eyes were wide, his lips parted. It was not so much a kiss as an accident. One she hoped to repeat in the near future.

"My fault entirely," said Harriet, looking down. "I am graceless as always."

"Nay, this is my fault." He reached for her, his eyes fierce with desire. She slid off the rock toward him, landing in his arms. He held her tight and their lips met, not just warm but searing hot. She feared she would burn yet pressed closer. Though she had only known him a short time, she felt she had been waiting her whole life for this moment.

He broke the kiss and bowed his head, touching his forehead to hers. He was breathing hard, as was she.

"Forgive me. I should no' have…" He turned and stepped away toward the blue loch. The magic of the moment was gone.

With a slice of fatal awareness, she realized she would give it all, her fortune, everything, to be with this man. The realization flooded her with fear. What of her parents? She needed to return home. How could she be so careless as to lose her heart to a Highlander?

"We should get back to the house." Thornton spoke without looking at her. His formal, taciturn style had returned. "I would ask that ye keep what ye learned today to yer own counsel."

"Yes, of course," said Harriet. "You can trust me." And she meant it.

"I know. 'Tis why I showed ye." And he meant it.

When Harriet returned to the manor house, Penelope and the Duchess of Marchford were waiting for her. They wished her to meet someone.

The Duc d'Argon.

Twenty-four

"WHAT THE DUC D'ARGON LACKS IN APPEARANCE HE more than makes up for in charm," Penelope commented to the dowager. Penelope pulled a shawl around her shoulders as they descended to tea, ignoring the exasperated look from the duchess, who did not appreciate the shawls that covered Penelope's new wardrobe.

"For fifty thousand pounds, he has a great deal of inducement to be charming," replied the dowager. "Now let's see if we can guide this romance along its proper course."

"I should hope he would not marry her only for the money."

"You have met our dear Miss Redgrave. I should be happy if anyone should wish to wed her for any reason."

"Not anyone," reminded Penelope. "He must have a title after all."

"Naturally." The duchess glided regally down the stairs for tea.

Penelope had meant it as sarcasm, a sentiment utterly lost on the more pecuniarily minded duchess. The Duc d'Argon was a recent entry into the marriage mart games at this house party and was welcomed by many in the tearoom with some interest. He was in possession of a medium build, which was dressed to perfection.

Penelope may not have esteemed fashion, but she knew quality when she saw it, and the duc certainly was in possession of an enviable tailor. The cut of his coat and the gleam of his boots were underscored by his own personal polish, which outshone every man in the room.

In truth, the duc's visage was hardly notable, with a long, hooked nose and a weak chin. On him, however, he made it appear rather regal. He was quick to notice those of importance and made conversation with those most notable in the room, including the comtesse, whom he complimented profusely in French. If Penelope's ears did not fail her, he criticized others in the room with such wicked humor that he made the comtesse laugh out loud, a rare occurrence in itself.

Penelope took a cup of tea to the dowager, where she sat watching the events from one corner of the room. "But how can we have any assurance he would take an interest in Harriet?" asked Penelope in a quiet voice.

"He is a refugee in England, living off of the kindness of English nobles who feel some affinity for French aristocracy displaced by the Revolution. He has not a farthing to call his own, however, and more than anything, he is in need of a rich wife."

The duchess lowered her voice even further. "And I have it from Leclair that he arrived traveling post without a valet of his own and had to be assigned one of the footmen. Marchford also had to settle his bill with the grocer to whom the duc had promised to pay a crown for a ride to Thornton Hall. His debts are extensive and pressing. If he cannot raise funds soon, he must return to the continent. And that, for him, would prove fatal."

"I do see your point, but why should Harriet be inclined to wed?"

"He is a French duke. He has all the charm and polish she lacks. I would see it as an advantageous match on both counts. Now all I have to do is plant the seed."

"Please tell me you are not going to tell him her worth."

"As you wish, my dear." Antonia rose from her chair, smoothed her perfectly coiffed white hair, and glided over to the duc, who was standing among a throng of admirers. Penelope had no doubt he would soon be in possession of a certain number. Fifty thousand pounds. The amount any man willing to wed Miss Redgrave would instantly take into possession. It was enough to turn the head of even the bluest of bloods.

From the smile that lit his face, she could already see his head turn.

❧

"May I present the Duc d'Argon?"

Harriet curtsied and came up slowly with a half smile, the one she was trying to perfect—pleasant but not overly encouraging. She glanced at Penelope, who gave her a supportive nod.

"Miss Redgrave, it is indeed a pleasure to meet

you." The duc spoke with a French accent that made even his most banal words sound seductive.

"Yes, it is a pleasure, Your Grace." Harriet glanced at Penelope again and had a strong suspicion that matchmaking motivations were at play. If there was to be any matchmaking, she was more inclined to an earl than a duke. What she wished to do now was to have some time to think about what had happened between herself and Thornton.

"I understand you have recently arrived from America," continued the duc. "I should very much like to hear of it."

"Truly?" Harriet was surprised. Most of those she had met treated her American birth as something needing to be hushed up.

"I should think you would be getting many of the requests to talk of your homeland."

"No, not at all. I believe most people think it an embarrassment for me."

"Ah, but we French, we look at it with the different eye, no? We helped with your defeat of the British."

"Yes. And were quite instrumental in that regard, or so my father tells me," agreed Harriet.

"I should like very much to hear more of this." He smiled at her and she smiled in return. Perhaps he was only charming her to get her money, but he did it better than most.

"Perhaps tonight we can talk. I should like to hear of France and the terrible things that have happened there of late," said Harriet.

"Ah yes, they are terrible indeed." He paused, only for a moment, but the emotion still appeared raw.

"I would not wish to bring up difficult memories," Harriet hastily added.

"Not at all, not at all." The duc graced her with a pleasant smile. "Tonight we shall talk of our homelands and how we come to this. Until then." The duc gently took her hand and kissed the back of it. Usually she found such affectations rather ostentatious, but he did it with such an air, she could only find him charming.

❧

"Ye're sure o' the numbers?" asked Thornton, desperate for something, anything to make what he was hearing somehow different. The amount they owed was shocking, their assets plundered. His plan to save the estate by selling racehorses now seemed futile in the face of such mounting debts.

"I am certain," said his steward with regret. "I have been over these numbers many times since I received this most recent contract from Lady Thornton."

"How is it that she entered into such an arrangement?"

"It was entirely without my knowledge," defended the steward. "I would never have—"

Thornton held up his hands to stop the man. "I know ye woud'na have advised this." Thornton sighed. "I don't know what to do."

"I shall submit my resignation, my lord," said the steward quietly.

"No, no I dinna wish for that."

"Truth is, sir, ye dinna have the money to pay me. To be blunt, I hav'na been paid in over three months."

Thornton stared at him and swallowed convulsively. "How is that? I put the funds in the account myself."

"Lady Thornton hired an attorney to find the funds we had sequestered. Without my knowledge, the accounts were drained. At first I thought we had been robbed, but inquiries led to the realization that the money had gone into the account of General Crawley on the authorization of Lady Thornton."

"Ye were right in the first place. We were robbed."

Thornton rode home at a slow pace. What was he to do? Without a sudden influx of capital, he was in serious trouble. No longer was he simply going to lose Thornton Hall; he might be forced to flee to the continent.

He did not know how General Crawley had manipulated his mother, but it was clear Crawley meant him to marry Priscilla. If Thornton was going to marry an heiress, it would not be Miss Crawley. The memory of Harriet's lips on his returned to mind. He wanted more. It had taken everything he had to pull away.

He had never met anyone like Harriet Redgrave. She was smart and honest and kind, and mysterious, and more than a little touched in the head. And her fifty thousand pounds would fix everything.

Thornton pulled up so short his horse whinnied in complaint. What was he thinking? He had sworn he would never marry for money. Never! He must stay firm. If he married an heiress now, he would never know if he was attracted to her character or her money. Harriet deserved better than that.

He dug in his heels and urged his mount to a gallop. He knew what he must do.

Her face hurt from smiling too much. Or perhaps it was the falseness of the smile that hurt. She was trying, valiantly, to fit in, to not make a scene, to appear smaller and frailer than she was, and to not speak of anything of which she had actual knowledge. It was exhausting.

After dinner, the ladies retreated to the drawing room where polite feminine arts and conversation were to ensue. Instead, at least to Harriet's mind, the young women discussed the young men with as much a critical eye as one would choose a bonnet. The men were examined for their manner, their appearance, and their pocketbook. The mothers were no better, adding to the conversation such important facts as the man's connections and the location and condition of his estate. Potential bridegrooms were evaluated on a variety of scores—namely appearance, rank, wealth, and whether their estates were advantageously situated.

No one spoke of common interests or any real affection. The interests of these young women seemed fleeting, bestowed lavishly on one gentleman one day and then another gentleman the next. Foremost in the conversation was how to get the gentleman to propose: whether he would, when he would, and what could be done to increase the likelihood that he would.

Of these conversations, Harriet had no part. She was tolerated only as a necessary evil. An American among them. Uncouth but rich. At times there was open discussion of whether one gentleman or another would be tempted to offer for Harriet's hand due to his financial constraints. No one considered her prospects as anything other than a marriage of convenience, and these conversations occurred with only the poorest attempts to shield her from the embarrassment of overhearing.

The dowager and Penelope were supportive once more, but they could not stand by her side at every moment, and so she was often forced to read a book in a corner while pretending not to hear anyone. Harriet was not sure if the ladies assigned a sentry, but there was always a call that the men were coming, so that inappropriate conversations could be stilled, books and needlework could be raised, and everything could appear proper when the men arrived.

Harriet wished to run away to her room again, but she was not a coward. She was determined to stay a respectable amount of time in the drawing room. The cry came that the men were coming and Harriet tensed in response.

This was the worst part of the evening, for Harriet was swarmed by men of all ages who flattered her without thought. They were the fortune hunters, of whom Penelope had warned her. The advice in this case was unnecessary. Harriet could see quite clearly their interest lay squarely in her bank account.

One gentleman even had the audacity to compliment her "golden curls" when her auburn hair was pulled back into a simple knot. He had his eye on a beauty with flaxen ringlets across the room.

Harriet gave him a painful smile and patted her hair. "Thank you, sir, I have often thought my blonde hair to be one of my great beauties."

"Yes, yes, quite right," said the man, who clearly heard nothing she said.

"Would you care for a drink?" asked another man, who noted a raven-haired beauty had walked to the refreshment table.

"No, no I will get her a glass," demanded another, with an eye on a similar prize.

"You young cubs, go. I will keep our dear Miss Redgrave company," said an older gentleman with a bushy moustache and fingers stained yellow from smoking cheroots. "I'm sure she has some charming anecdotes that can amuse us all."

Enough. She had enough of this. "Why thank you. Perhaps you would like to know a little something of America?"

The men looked at her blankly if they looked at all.

"We have some different customs regarding marriage and dowries." Harriet quickly began to twist together a convincing story.

All heads turned to her. She was speaking of money and she now had a captive audience.

"Did you know that the age of majority in America is much older than here? Why, a girl has to be at least thirty before she can see a penny of her inheritance."

The men looked at her blankly. Their smiles had vanished. Her own smile didn't hurt so much anymore.

"And how old are you?" asked a young buck with painful bluntness. A few gentlemen winced at the directness of the question, but all leaned in to hear the answer.

"Oh, I won't see thirty for many years. Also, were you aware of a new law passed in America that the dowry must only be allocated in America? I do hope my future groom will be willing to move to Massachusetts; otherwise, I shall forfeit my entire inheritance."

Her swarm of suitors all appeared slightly pale and very disappointed. She smiled again. And this time it didn't hurt at all.

Twenty-five

ONCE SHE HAD DIVESTED HERSELF OF HER UNWANTED suitors, Harriet felt moderately better, but she was still in a drawing room filled with people who found her mere presence an inconvenience. She needed escape. She needed to talk to Thornton. Ever since their kiss earlier that day, she had thought of him, dreamed of him, wanted to spend more time with him. She saw him in the drawing room, making polite conversation, looking, if anything, more formal and reserved than usual.

He glanced her way once then turned away, never to look in her direction again. It was frustrating and lonely. Now that her suitors were gone, she was obliged to sit by herself as the rest of the drawing room thronged with vitality, people talking, people laughing, a young lady on the pianoforte exhibiting her considerable skill. A few young people even got up to dance as she played a reel. It was quite the diverting sight—if only she had been invited.

Harriet quietly left the drawing room to have a little break. The hall was cooler than the room, a relief after so much pressure and heat. She wandered to the library again, in search of a good book, or at least privacy. She had read through her chemistry book while she was "ill" and was ready for more.

In America, she was considered a bit of an oddity for her interest in alchemy, but her family was well-known, and she was always welcome in gatherings to talk and laugh, play and dance. She never entirely fit in, but she never considered herself an outsider before now.

Though her back was to the door, she knew the moment Thornton entered the library. The door squeaked, and footsteps fell on the floor behind her. His boots. His steps.

"Good evening, Lord Thornton," she said without turning around.

He walked around her chair and sat in one across from her. "How did ye ken who it was?"

She smiled at his drab attire and his somber face. "I know your step."

The fact did not appear to please him. "Miss Redgrave, I noted ye came here and I felt I needed to talk with ye about what occurred this afternoon."

No. Don't. "I do not see that we need to—"

He held up his hand to stop her. "I cannot rest easy with my conduct. It was too forward. I should not have taken ye riding unchaperoned. The nature of my conversation was not appropriate, and my actions I can only look upon with regret. I do apologize for the discomfort I have exposed ye to then and now. Please do forgive me." He stood. Bowed. And left the room.

Her book slid from her hand and dropped to the floor. It was over then. She had lost her only friend.

Harriet rushed out of the library and away from the company of guests as far as she could, emerging on the top of a turret, without quite knowing how she got there. She could not return to the drawing room, could not stay in the library, and could not go to her room. She wanted to be where no one could find her. She wanted to go home.

Always a practical girl, Harriet rarely cried, but the tears ran down her face without a thought to sensibility. She missed her mother, her father, and even her brothers. She missed home, where she was accepted and where she belonged.

In the still of the summer night, truth crept in on soft paws. If she was honest, truly honest, she did not fit in at home either. People were kinder to her, and her family made sure she did not hear most of the gossip, but little bits managed to slip through the cracks.

What kind of heiress did experiments in her garden shed and spoke of minerals with the passion that most young women reserved for Byron? She was different. Where other ladies her age were married with children, she remained awkward in social situations. She had no credible suitors; her father or brothers ran off anyone who smelled of fortune hunting, which meant there was no one left to show interest.

Truth was, she was an outsider even before coming to the British Isles.

She wiped away more tears and blew her nose on a handkerchief. She leaned on one of the parapets and put her cheek down on the cool stones. Maybe if she closed her eyes and wished very hard she could wake up in a different world where science was considered fashionable and a woman was judged not by her external beauty but by her knowledge of basic elements. She smiled in spite of her situation and tried to imagine a world in which she would be the leader of society and everyone would be envious of her collection of acids and bases.

"*Bonsoir, mademoiselle.*"

Startled, Harriet opened her eyes to find the impeccably dressed d'Argon. "Oh. It's you. Hello." She could not even muster enough energy to be polite. She had not hiked up several flights of stairs to be accosted by another fortune hunter, even if he was French.

"I can see I am disturbing you. A thousand pardons, *mademoiselle*, I merely wished to take in something of the view. It is very nice, no?"

"It's dark. Can't see a thing."

"Ah but the stars, they are very beautiful."

Harriet glanced up and was slightly surprised by just how many stars hung low in the sky. They twinkled brightly, clustered in a wide band that crossed the sky. To the north, Harriet was surprised by dancing lights of green and blue. "My word, what is that?"

"It is what I hoped to see. The northern lights. Aurora borealis. I have heard of it, but never before have I been at such a northern latitude to see it."

The lights flickered and danced before her eyes. It was startling. How could she not have noticed it before? The tears must have clouded her vision. She stood a little taller and took a deep breath of the cool, clean air.

"Thank you for showing them to me," murmured Harriet.

"I thought it was why you were here."

Harriet shook her head. "I needed to be alone."

"I am disturbing you then. I shall leave you."

"No, no, it is all right. I am sorry to be such poor company. Stay and watch the show. I could not deny you the opportunity to see it."

"I thank you."

They watched in silence until d'Argon commented, "No one knows what causes it. Perhaps the gods, they are angry."

"I believe science will explain it. Perhaps it is related to magnetic fields as Benjamin Franklin proposed. I should like to discover its cause someday."

The duc turned to her, one eyebrow raised. "You should like to be a scientist?"

Harriet bristled at the jab at a fresh wound. "Yes, I should like to be one very much. In truth, I study chemistry. I like to do experiments as my uncle did before me." She met his surprised look eye for eye, her chin raised. She was tired of pretending to be someone she was not.

The duc paused for a moment, clearly surprised. "Why, this is marvelous. I should like to hear more of it. One does not often meet a young lady with such a passion for alchemy."

Was he merely flattering her? He could not possibly be interested, could he? "You need not feign interest to be polite. I understand it is a topic few find as interesting as I."

"I cannot claim to possess such an expertise as you

have, but I am always willing to better myself. Now tell me, for I am interested, what is Mr. Franklin's theory on the aurora borealis?"

So Harriet described the theory to him. He listened intently, and even asked questions that showed her he was actually paying attention. Best of all, she did not feel she needed to feign disinterest or lack of knowledge. She could simply be herself.

"Fascinating," declared d'Argon. "I am so glad you were here to describe it to me."

"I am glad you were here to point it out to me."

"May I ask, or perhaps I am too bold, may I ask why you came to here, to be alone?"

Harriet sighed. "I am a newcomer here. I often feel a bit out of step with the rest of the company."

The duc nodded. "I have understanding of what you say. I also am come from afar. It is often I feel a longing to be back in the country of my birth."

"Yes, I know how you feel. I miss my parents awfully."

"I also miss my parents. They died in the horror. The guillotine."

"I am so sorry for your loss." A lump formed in Harriet's throat. She was lonesome for a home she could still return to. But the duc, he had lost everything. He could not return.

He turned and faced the green lights, softly swaying, his face a picture of noble suffering. "I like to remember them as it used to be." He turned back to her. "But I must live here and now. Even though I am, as you say, an outsider, I still choose to move forward. One cannot change the past, but one can choose the future."

"Yes, you are right." She felt better now. Stronger. She would not let narrow-minded people tell her who she was. "I should not let others make me feel small."

"No, indeed you should not. Were you feeling the smallness?"

Harriet smiled at the way he phrased things. "Yes, the smallness I was certainly feeling."

"Is that why you created the story of not inheriting your dowry and having to live in America to claim it?"

Harriet smiled. "Did you see through that ruse? You would be the only one. I simply wished people to want to speak to me because they enjoyed my company, not because they coveted my inheritance."

"A worthy cause. Many a mistruth was spoken for far less a noble purpose."

"I appreciate your understanding. I hope you will not reveal this deception to the world."

"No, indeed, I shall not. I shall keep your secret, on that you can rely." The duc took a step closer to her, his voice low and throaty.

"I should go," said Harriet. For the first time, she realized she was on a tower quite unchaperoned with a man.

"No, do not be so hasty. I should like to hear more of your stories of your homeland."

"Perhaps tomorrow." Harriet took a step toward the exit.

The duc took another step blocking her. "No, I insist you stay to speak. There is much we can learn from each other, *n'est-ce pas*?"

In her mind Harriet had a flash of fortune hunters who were known to compromise a young lady, thus forcing a marriage. Was he trying to compromise her, or did he simply wish to be friendly? If he thought he was going to put pressure on her to stay one moment more than she wished, he had no idea he was speaking to the daughter of Captain Redgrave, scourge of the sea.

"Very kind of you but must dash." Harriet stepped up to him and vigorously shook his hand. "Have a nice sleep." She stepped forward and shouldered past him, more than brushing by him. "So sorry, good night."

The surprise on his face was evident, and he stepped back instantly, making her feel poorly for attributing to him such dastardly motivations. "*Bonsoir, mademoiselle.* I hope you will have a pleasant sleep."

Sleep? Harriet flew down the stairs all the way down to her room. It had been a long, emotional day, but one that was illuminating. New facts had come to light. New variables had been introduced. If her life were a science experiment, it was about to get interesting.

Twenty-six

HARRIET STARED OUT HER WINDOW AT THE CASTLE ruins above, barely visible in the early dawn. She had gone to her castle laboratory every morning—but not today. She did not wish to see him today. She had to remind herself not to be disappointed. Thornton had been honest with her from the start. He said he would not marry her nor any other lady, and he had kept his word, so why should she be upset?

She was not upset. And she did not care. At all. Not in the least. She wasn't even thinking about it.

Harriet paced in her bedroom until she could take it no longer and strode out behind the house in the opposite direction from the castle. Someone had made a halfhearted attempt at taming the wild bushes and trees, particularly those that could be seen from the house. But once she got beyond a few yards, the gardens turned wild. They matched her mood. She brushed past unkempt bushes and sprinted past overgrown trees. It was good to get some fresh air, to be out in nature again.

She decided it was time for a brisk constitutional

up and down the overgrown paths and into fields of heather. The grasses brushed her skirts, most likely leaving stains, but she continued without a care. Her social credit could not be made much lower if she walked about with stains or even entered the ballroom as naked as when she was born. Of course, then she might be locked up for lunacy.

She breathed deeply. She could get used to living here. It was wild and the air was fresh and sweet. It brought to mind her family once more and she hoped they had received her letter telling of her safe arrival.

If her parents could be reassured, she would enjoy spending more time in Great Britain. Not in society, of course, but this was the hub of scientific exploration. Many scientists had moved from France to avoid the Terror and had organized communities of people with like-minded interests. Naturally, she would be banned from these meetings. No single female would be allowed. It just was not done.

A married lady might have a chance, as Lavoisier's wife had been accepted due to her marriage to a noted scientist. If only she could find a man interested enough in chemistry to support her by gaining entry for both of them into scientific meetings. Maybe she could even write a treatise about her results and publish under his name. She smiled at her happy dream.

Harriet reached the top of a rise and sat on a fallen tree to enjoy the view. The top of Thornton Hall was visible through the trees below her. Farther away, the old castle ruins rose majestically in the distance. It was a lovely view and she remained there until the sun rose over the hills. She was calmer and refreshed from the exercise.

In the distance, a man on horseback rode along a country road below her. She stood to see who it was and the Duc d'Argon came into view. He noted her as he got closer and stopped to wave up at her. She waved back. He dismounted and began to walk up the hill to see her, and she obligingly ran down to meet him.

"Miss Redgrave! It is a surprise to see you."

"I went for a walk." Harriet caught her breath from her run. Perhaps, she realized too late, skipping down the hills of heather might be seen as quite unsophisticated and unladylike, but d'Argon, if a trifle surprised, only smiled at her. A welcome change from the almost constant barrage of criticism.

"And a healthy walk it must have been. You are far from the house."

"Am I? Such a beautiful day, so I kept going. It is lovely here."

"Ah yes, I have also been enjoying the countryside. It is a lovely but wild place, no?"

They walked back to the road and d'Argon walked beside her, leading his horse down the narrow lane, which eventually led back to the house.

"I did not know you enjoyed riding. Is this your mount?" asked Harriet.

"No, I cannot claim it. I borrowed the horse from our gracious host to see if my equipment had arrived. I sent it separately to the nearest town to Thornton Hall."

"Equipment?"

"It is nothing much, only some things to help me make some observations."

"Observations?" The man had certainly caught her interest.

"*Oui*. But maybe you would be interested. When I had received an invitation to Thornton Hall, I hoped the northern latitude would allow me to witness what I had heretofore only read of in books, the aurora borealis. It is so pleasant to have this wish gratified and to have shared this first night with you. I have sent myself my telescopes, through which I hope to observe this phenomenon further and perhaps even present my observations at the Royal Academy of Science. But I should not bore you with such things."

"Oh, I am far from bored. Have you been to some of the meetings of the Royal Academy?"

"*Oui*. I can tell you it was the greatest honor of my life. I have endured many unfortunate occurrences. I survived the Terror, yes, unlike my parents, but though I was safe, I was far from home. I have been lost. Then a friend invited me to a lecture, and a new world opened for me. I began to take interest in things; I began to see that my life could have purpose once more."

"You must have endured much," said Harriet with feeling.

The duc only gave her a wistful smile. "Many things I would change, but I cannot. This is my life. I must play the hand I am dealt. I must do what I must to survive."

"I am glad you have found solace in scientific inquiry. I have always found it to be a comfort."

"In what way, *mademoiselle*?"

Harriet smiled involuntarily. Something about

being called *mademoiselle* in a sultry French accent sent shivers down her spine. "Science is constant. It does not judge; it has no bias; it simply is. The secrets of the world are available to all with the patience and temperament to unlock them. It is a great equalizer. Your upbringing, your pedigree, mean nothing; only what you can do with your mind matters. It is open to all thinking people without prejudice."

"I feel in myself the same. It is a comfort to connect with absolute truth, not something of relative opinion. I enjoy facts."

"Yes! Me also!" cried Harriet. "I cannot tell you what a pleasure it is to have found someone so like-minded."

"I cannot express how much it pleases me to have been able to give you pleasure." His voice dropped lower and the smile in his eyes heated.

Harriet turned away and tried not to blush. Of all the stupid telltale signs, blushing was the one she wished she could ban from her life forever. She had thought herself safe speaking of science, but somehow it had turned into something else. Once again she realized, too late, that she most likely should not be walking by herself with a man. And yet they were never out of sight of the house. Surely there could be no real harm.

"Did you know that Lord Thornton has a copy of one of Lavoisier's works in his library?" d'Argon changed the subject. "Someone has borrowed it for now, but I hope it will be soon returned so I may read it."

"What a remarkable coincidence! I am reading that book!" declared Harriet.

"You are? Well, of course, you told me so your own self that you have an interest in chemistry."

"I shall lend it to you immediately."

"No, no, you must keep your book." D'Argon held up his hand to silence protest. "No, and I insist on that. However, I would not be opposed if you would tell me a thing or two of what you have learned."

"I would be delighted to. But I must allow you some reading time as well."

"Perhaps we can do this. We can share the book; you spend some time reading then myself, and we can discuss what we have read together."

"Yes, I would love that!" Harriet clapped her hands in excitement, in a manner not at all consistent with a lady.

"I am glad the plan meets with your approval."

"I am glad we met. You are so different than any of the other men I have been introduced to. I cannot imagine speaking of scientific theories to anyone within the *haut ton*. It is rare to find anyone who shares my interest even remotely."

"You should enjoy attending scientific meetings then, to be with a room of like-minded individuals and listen to investigations."

"I should love that above all else, but as an unmarried female, I would be barred."

"I would gladly serve as your escort, but no, as we are both unmarried it would not do."

"No, unfortunately not."

"We shall devise some plan," said the duc. "Perhaps as a married lady, you could attend with your husband."

"Yes." Why must she always need a husband to

do what she wanted to do? And where could she find one quick?

"And we are returned to Thornton Hall," said the duc as they arrived at the house. "It has been so refreshing to speak with you. I hope to have this repeated many times in the future." He bowed and walked off toward the stables, his gray horse following behind.

He enjoyed science. He was unmarried. He did not appear to be horrified by her presence.

Perhaps it was time for a new plan?

Twenty-seven

"I THINK WE SHOULD HAVE TEA ALFRESCO."

It was all the Duchess of Marchford needed to say to convince the other guests to try a meal outdoors. A lovely site on the green in between the manor house and the ruined castle was selected, and an army of servants was recruited to carry up chairs, tables, table-cloths, dishes, and even large canopies—everything one could want for tea, only with much more fuss and bother for the Thornton staff.

The duchess was insistent that everyone come up for tea. No excuses. So everyone came, although the young people were more difficult to tether and immediately went scurrying about exploring the castle above them or the wilderness surrounding them. It was not proper, and everyone enjoyed it.

"You have made the suggestion of the season," commented Penelope.

"I only hope they can be successful," said the dowager.

"They? Who is they?"

"You are right, not 'them.' Perhaps I should say he or she. I think the handwriting was more feminine."

"As always, I have not the slightest idea what you are talking about." Penelope sat next to the duchess at the table but wondered if she could sit on a blanket on the grass instead. It looked as though the young people were enjoying themselves.

"I received a missive this morning, put under my door. It said if I could get the guests and the people out of the house for a while, the pearls could be switched."

"I beg your pardon?" Penelope instantly turned her thoughts away from sunlight and crickets to attend to what the dowager was saying.

"All I had to do was leave out the pearls and wait for them to be switched."

"But who is this from? Can we trust this person?"

"I do not know, nor do I care. If this problem can be resolved, so much the better. Of course, I would not have been brought to this had you not refused to help."

"Refused?" hissed Penelope. "I was caught under Marchford's bed."

"A minor mishap."

"Not to me. But do you think it wise to trust this situation with someone we do not know?"

"What do I have to lose?"

Penelope pressed her lips together. There was a lot to lose, potentially. She went off in search of Marchford. He should know what was happening.

"May I speak to you?" Penelope asked Marchford, but he did not respond. Of course, he was surrounded by a gaggle of gawking young women. He caught her eye and held it. Though he spoke nothing, she felt his silent plea. *Help me.*

"Your Grace," she spoke louder.

"Yes, Miss Rose," he answered, despite the furious glares he received from a few of the ladies surrounding him.

"I do believe there is an important post for you," she fabricated.

"Thank you. I shall come at once." And he did.

They were almost back to Thornton Hall before Penelope deemed it safe enough to talk about the situation. "Your grandmother received a note from an anonymous 'friend' offering to help out with the situation with the pearls."

"Exactly what is the situation with the pearls?"

"I am not at liberty to say."

"Penelope!"

Penelope stopped and looked up at him. It was the first time he had used her first name. And it was said with a growl.

He took a breath and amended himself. "Miss Rose. What is this about? I need answers."

"You said to let you know if anything happened I found suspicious. Well…" She considered what to say. She did not wish to expose the dowager, but she had a strong suspicion something was not right. "Your grandmother lost the pearls to Lord Langley."

"Cards?"

"Yes, but that is not the important part. What is relevant is that she put up the fakes by mistake. I was in your room to get the real ones so I could exchange them for her and no one would be the wiser. You caught me, and I decided not to attempt entering Langley's room."

"Good girl."

"This morning, the duchess received a missive from an anonymous 'friend' saying they could help her if the dowager got everyone out of the house, hence the alfresco tea."

"My room, now."

They ran up four flights of stairs, Marchford easily outstriding Penelope. Of course, she appeased herself with the consideration that she was at least a foot shorter and wearing a gown, which made running not quite as easy as it was for Marchford. When Penelope entered the room, Marchford was examining his wardrobe.

"Something of interest?" asked Penelope.

"Someone has rifled through the papers I kept under some shirts."

"A spy?"

"Undoubtedly."

"Did they get much information?"

"Nothing they would not already know. I do not keep secret documents where they can be found."

"Where do you keep secret documents?"

He turned to her and raised an eyebrow.

"I withdraw the question. What now?"

"Somewhere here, there is a spy. Now we just need to find out who. Where was this 'friend' going to get the pearls?"

"The duchess left them out on her dressing table."

"Stay here, I'll check."

It was a pointless command, one Penelope had no intention of following. She ran after Marchford, who strode down the stairs to the room of the duchess. When they arrived, the pearls were gone.

"Do you think they replaced the fake ones for the real?" asked Penelope.

"More likely they filched these and moved on."

"Oh dear."

"The real question is who is our thief."

"Do you think the person might still be in the house?"

"Possibly, but this is a large home, with numerous rooms and places to hide. We could search for the rest of the day and not see all of the house."

"True, but we could at least see who is at the tea to know who we can rule out," suggested Penelope.

A smile spread onto his face. "Quite right, good thinking. Let's go back to the party."

"Or we could look from the tower. It would be faster and we should be able to see everyone."

"Perfect!" Marchford grabbed her hand and kissed the back of it before turning to run down the hall and up the stairs to the tower. Penelope followed along behind, her hand tingling from the unexpected attention.

Marchford was already leaning on the battlements and squinting to see as far as possible.

"Who is there?" asked Penelope. "Or more importantly, who is not there?"

"I do not see our new French noble. All the military seem to be accounted for. Grandmother is talking to the comtesse; Sir Antony is speaking with Thornton's mother."

Penelope tried squinting to see what she could. "Most everyone is accounted for. I do not see Lord Thornton or Mr. Neville."

"I do not see Miss Redgrave, either," said Marchford.

"Surely she cannot be involved."

"I never rule out a suspect."

"Suspect? Are we at the point where we need to assign people the label of suspect?" asked Penelope.

"I find it helpful to call things as they are. Tell me, who was in that card game? Who might know Grandmother had passed the fakes?"

"She was playing with the comtesse, Sir Antony, and Lord Thornton."

"I can see all three of them."

"I believe they were playing in the drawing room. Anyone with a clever eye might have seen the game and noted the fakes."

"This does not help us narrow our suspects."

"Do you think the spy would be looking for information?"

"Without a doubt."

"I must go." Penelope spun and flew down the stairs, as fast as her gown would allow.

Marchford was following her easily. "What is this about?"

"Nothing of importance, truly. I just want to make sure a certain book I have is still where it ought to be." Penelope walked as fast as she could, but she could not shake Marchford in the least. When she arrived at her room, she tried to tell him good day, but he was in the room searching it for the mystery spy.

Penelope went into her room and checked under the mattress. To her relief, the book was still there.

"What is this?" Marchford strolled into the room, making the small space altogether tiny.

"I simply wished to ensure that my book was here."

"What book?"

"A copy of the *Peerage*, nothing of any consequence."

"Miss Rose." Marchford's voice was low with warning. "I have ignored whatever schemes you have hatched with my grandmother, but now I need you to be honest and tell me what you two are doing and how this book is of such importance you hid it under your mattress."

Penelope sighed. She knew it would someday come to this. "The book is one that my sisters and I used when choosing a spouse. The *Peerage* has a list and description of all the peers of the realm, and we augmented the list, particularly in regard to men in want of a wife. We made certain notations regarding their temperament, their holdings, their habits—anything of interest to a future spouse." She tried to keep the book from him, but he snatched it from her hand and began to read.

"I see if there was a bachelor without a title, you made an entry for him. How enterprising."

"I can see you are disapproving."

"Not at all. I bask in the glory of your brilliance. Now tell me what these abbreviations stand for by the potential victim's name."

"Perhaps you would like to flip to your own entry and I will enlighten you," said Penelope with a voice so sweet it almost made her choke.

"Brilliant," said Marchford, and turned to his entry.

"The *A* and *P* by your name is an assessment of your character—arrogant and proud."

"Very true, how kind of you to notice. But what of these other initials?"

Penelope smiled until it hurt. "The letters *PP* stand

for 'plump in the pocket.' I think you get the general idea." She attempted to retrieve the book to no avail.

"Not at all. What does *QA* stand for?"

"Perhaps we should go down and watch for people as they return."

"Perhaps you could answer my question."

"Quite attractive."

A slow smile spread on Marchford's face. "You find me attractive."

"I do not think you are so; I am merely documenting what is plain fact."

Marchford's smile did not dim. "You find me attractive."

"These are merely notes to aid in finding you a wife," said Penelope, nettled into speaking more than she should.

"You are Madame X, matchmaker to London society." He spoke with complete confidence.

Penelope paused and said something cowardly. "It was your grandmother's idea."

"I do not doubt it. Let me see if I have this correct. When I cut off the additional funds to my grandmother, you both decided to set up shop instead and peddle your wares as a matchmaking service, fleecing your friends and relations. Have I got that about right?"

Penelope was saved from having to respond by the sound of a door closing. Marchford was instantly in action, slipping out the door to discover the culprit, Penelope's book still in his hand. Marchford ran after the potential spy; Penelope ran after her book.

The hall was a long corridor of closed doors. Was the spy behind one? Which one? Perhaps it was merely a maid or one of the guests returning. Marchford walked slowly down the hall, listening for a sound in any room. At one door he stopped and listened closely. Penelope listened too and could hear the telltale sounds of movement. Someone was in there.

"Whose room?" Marchford mouthed to her.

Penelope shrugged.

He knocked on the door, but nobody answered. He motioned to her to stand back, which she did. He burst open the door to the shriek of the comtesse.

"Marchford! How dare you invade my privacy?" she snarled.

"A thousand pardons," said Marchford. "I thought this was a different room."

Penelope flattened herself on the wall outside the room, out of sight.

"Go take your rutting needs and your filthy self out of my room and go straight to hell!"

Marchford took her advice, at least insofar as leaving the room. He walked with Penelope down the hallway to the stairs.

"She seemed a bit put out," commented Penelope mildly.

"Just a bit," agreed Marchford.

"You are going to be the talk of the evening I fear. You and your rutting needs."

"Do let me know how that goes. Apparently I am on a journey to Hades."

"I hear it's warm there."

"Bit hot here too."

Penelope couldn't help but smile, which earned her an upward twitch in Marchford's scowl. His eyes softened and gleamed.

"James, my dear!" The dowager approached them once they reached the entryway, with a throng of people following.

"Where have you been? Did you receive your package? What could be so important you had to leave the tea?"

"Yes, I received what I needed." Marchford shifted the book from one hand to the other and held it close. "I do apologize for missing the amusements, but sometimes duty calls. Now I need to put this somewhere safe. You will excuse me." He strode off in full view of the assembly, with Penelope trailing along behind. He still had her book.

He retreated to a small parlor on the second floor in the older part of the manor house. The room was not one that had been renovated and still held much of its Renaissance charm, which some might consider plain old. The large stone fireplace and heavy wood furniture matched the somber expression on Marchford's face.

"What was that about?" asked Penelope when they were out of earshot and the door was safely shut. "Everyone will think my copy of the *Peerage* is some sort of government document."

"Precisely the point." Marchford's scowl relaxed into an air of self-satisfaction. "Word will spread to the spy that I have received this book, an important book, one that he will want to see."

"You are using my book as bait!"

"Very good."

"But I need that book."

"Miss Rose, please do not tell me that you place the

needs of finding a matrimonial partner above the needs of the Crown to defend ourselves from foreign agents who wish only to destroy our way of life, conquer and invade our country—"

Penelope held up a hand to stop him. "Fine, keep the book for the moment, but please stop trying to convince me before you break out into a rousing chorus of 'God Save the King.'"

"I am an accomplished singer, you know."

"I did not know. I would make a notation in your file, but I suppose you would like to cancel your request now."

"Certainly not! I still need a bride. And you, Penelope Rose, are going to find me one."

Twenty-eight

IT WAS A LOVELY DAY FOR TEA OUTSIDE. THE OLDER members of the party sat on the provided chairs, while some of the younger members went a little wild and sat on large blankets stretched out on the ground. Harriet was accustomed to the idea of a picnic and felt herself more at home in the sunshine than in the formal drawing room. While most young ladies shielded their faces from the sun, Harriet turned to allow the sun to kiss her cheeks. It was warm and comfortable, and for once, she felt peaceful in the presence of society's finest.

"What does she think she is doing?" came a whisper from behind her.

"She will burn herself putting her face in the sun like that."

"I hope she does; maybe then she won't make us suffer her presence."

"If she had any sense, she would leave the house. How can she not understand she does not belong here?"

"Inferior blood. You can see it on her vacant expression and hear it in every single word she utters."

"I have seen her talking to Lord Thornton, and it makes me so mad I could spit. Who does she think she is? He will never marry a chit like that. Besides, my parents have arranged a deal with his mother. We are practically engaged. All that is left to be done is sign the papers."

"Is that so?" asked Thornton.

Harriet turned around. Behind her was the group of young ladies who had been tearing apart her character, and behind them stood Lord Thornton. He was somber in an olive-green coat and polished Hessians. He looked down disapprovingly at the group of ladies, with an air that had nothing to do with his considerable height.

"Lord Thornton, I did not mean... that is to say..." stammered Priscilla Crawley, who had boasted of her engagement.

"Yes, I quite understand ye did not intend for me to hear ye, but I am glad I did for it allows me the opportunity to clarify any misunderstanding. I am not privy to the machinations between my mother and yer parents, but let me make something quite clear. No state of engagement between us exists nor will there ever." Miss Crawley could only gasp in indignation. "Miss Redgrave, there is a pleasant view yonder. I wonder if you might be persuaded to join me."

"I would be delighted." Harriet jumped up and strolled past Miss Crawley, who was glaring at her so hard that Harriet was surprised her own head didn't spontaneously combust. Harriet could not resist a smile, but she did refrain from sticking out her tongue, even though she was sorely tempted.

"Thank you," breathed Harriet when they were out of hearing from the rest of the party. "You are my knight in shining armor today, though I rather thought you were no longer speaking to me."

"I ought not to if I had any sense. I heard what they said and it made my blood boil," growled Thornton.

Harriet glanced at him to make sure it was the same Thornton. He appeared the same on the surface. She would not have guessed that he would abandon propriety and come to her passionate defense.

"I do apologize for their behavior," said Thornton, his reserve returning.

"Oh no, do not offer any apology. Their behavior is entirely their own. They are not my dearest friends as you can see."

"I hope I did not make things worse for ye."

"I cannot imagine they could hate me any more than they do. I just hope they will let me be and move on to other targets. Is it true the Crawley family is trying to arrange an engagement with you?"

"Aye, 'tis true. I fear things are even worse financially than I thought."

"Are things quite so bad?"

"Aye. But dinna tease yer head over it. I shall manage."

A light breeze blew just enough to cool the warm sun into a very pleasant day. They walked aimlessly up to the castle and toward her laboratory. She had missed going that morning for several reasons, chiefly the man walking beside her.

"Ye did no' work this morn," said Thornton softly.

"I wanted to come this morning, but I decided to stay away so as not to see you," began Harriet. She paused, realizing she should be more circumspect, less blunt in her communications. Yet Harriet longed to tell a friend how she was feeling. Since one was not readily available, Thornton would have to do. "You have been one of the few here who is kind to me. I hate the thought of losing our friendship, all because of... one kiss." One wonderful, unbelievable kiss.

Thornton shook his head. "I dinna wish to hurt ye. I felt I needed to make very clear my intentions, which did not match my actions."

"I understand it was simply a case of my perpetual lack of grace."

"Nay." Thornton stopped walking and took her by the hand. They had traveled out the back gate of the ruined castle and were well out of sight of the others. "I shall no' have ye blame yerself. It was no mistake. I kissed ye, Harriet. The fault and the pleasure were all mine."

Harriet could not think of anything to say. His eyes blazed, drawing her closer. He leaned toward her. She leaned toward him.

Suddenly he turned away and stepped back. "Sorry. I dinna ken what I am about. That is the trouble. Truth is the estate is in a bad way. Verra bad. I want to kiss ye, but how can I know if it is due to true affection or a desperate desire to use yer dowry to avoid losing Thornton Hall? I would never know if my interest was true or financially motivated, and ye are worth so much more than that."

Harriet smiled shyly at him. All she heard was that he wanted to kiss her. "I should like to kiss you too," she breathed, hardly making a sound.

"Truly?" His voice was raw.

Harriet nodded and gazed over the fields of heather. She could not meet his eye and feared her cheeks were burning. "Trouble is, I cannot offer my dowry. I do apologize, but I need to return to America and soon. I cannot think of leaving my mother and father."

Thornton nodded slowly. "I understand. Actually it does help to know ye're unavailable. It spares me the fear o' misleading ye."

"So we can be friends again?" asked Harriet.

"Aye." Thornton gave her a rueful smile. "Perhaps if things go as badly as I fear, I will join ye on yer voyage back to America… as a cabin boy."

"I fear you are too old for that occupation," said Harriet honestly.

Thornton threw up his hands in mock surrender. "There goes my plan of a life at sea."

Harriet smiled and surveyed the panorama before her—the gray stones of the castle, the purple flowing heather, the scraggly trees buffeted by wind and weather. "This is where you belong."

"But I fear it will not be where I stay. Especially not after how I embarrassed Miss Crawley. Ought not to, I suppose, but I cannot, will not allow anyone to insult ye."

Harriet had never been the subject of anyone's passionate defense and had no immediate response except, "Shall we say hello to the horses?"

"Aye, 'tis a fine idea."

They walked a bit further to the secret entrance to the keep, hidden by bushes. The passage was dark, and after they had stopped a few times, Thornton took her arm and led her to the main keep.

"How can you see?"

"I canna see a thing, but I've done it many a time and I know my way."

Harriet held on to him and tried to ignore the heat coursing through her with every touch. They emerged from the tunnel into the dim light of the main keep-turned-stables. High above them, the wood ceiling had multiple cracks and holes, some intentional to let out the smoke from what used to be the central hearth, others created over hundreds of years of neglect. Pale light slanted down in beams, casting patches of sunlight on the ground. All was quiet in the stable and none of the stable lads or grooms could be found.

"Where is everyone?" asked Harriet.

"I warrant they have all been pulled to help with this outdoor tea as requested by the duchess."

"So we have the place to ourselves." In a flash, Harriet realized two things. First, she should not be alone with this man in a stable. Second, she was going to make the most of this opportunity. The stables themselves were neatly organized. The horses were lined up in an orderly fashion in their respective stalls, and a large pile of hay was kept in a corner of the stable.

"This reminds me of being at home with my brothers," said Harriet. The large pile of golden hay was at least twenty feet wide and almost as tall as she was. Did she have the courage to do it?

"How so?" asked Thornton.

"We used to love the hay."

Thornton looked at the hay and back at her, confusion on his face. "Why hay?"

"This! Hiiiyeee!" Harriet ran and jumped with abandon into the pile of hay. She landed with a floosh in a soft pile, hay strands falling on top of her.

"What are ye doing?" His face was confusion.

Harriet sat up. "Jumping in hay. Do not try to tell me you have never done it."

"Nay. Never." Thornton crossed his arms.

"No, please tell me your childhood has not been so neglected. Every person needs to jump in hay at least once."

Thornton shook his head. "I suppose I have been neglected. My grandmother woud'na allow such behavior."

Harriet paused. There was much she did not know about his background. "So what did you do for entertainment?"

Thornton's face hardened. "I was not allowed amusements."

"Come now, that cannot be possible. No one would raise a child in such a manner."

"My parents' marriage was a farce. Once the money changed hands, there was naught left for them but to loathe each other. My mother spent most o' her time in London, my father hunting and gambling. I was raised by my paternal grandmother, who feared the inferior blood introduced by my mother's merchant relations would cause me to go wild. Thus, I was not allowed any toys or amusements for fear it would ruin my character."

"You had no toys?" Harriet was incredulous.

"None. When I was finally sent to Eton, it was like going on holiday."

Harriet shook her head, having a difficult time believing anyone's childhood could be so grim. "But your mother? Surely she gave you some amusements."

"My mother and her mother-in-law did not get on. In truth, they could not abide to live under the same roof. My grandmother never approved of my mother and never let her forget it. Even on her wedding day, my grandmother refused to allow my mother to wear the traditional silver crown, called Maid Marion's crown. It has been worn by generations of Maclachlan brides, but not my mother." Thornton shrugged. "My mother stayed away and left the child rearing to my grandmother."

"Unfathomable." Harriet's heart broke for him. Somewhere about his eyes she could see the small child he used to be, neglected and unloved. No wonder he was so stiff and reserved. It strengthened her resolve to show him some of the amusements he had been missing in his life.

"My grandmother did what she thought best."

"Well, granny is not here now. So come on!" Harriet grabbed his arm to encourage the jumping to commence, but he held back.

"I will get hay on me."

"Yes, and it brushes right off. Don't be such a ninny. I dare you!"

"Dare? Ye impugn my honor by calling me a ninny and then issue a dare?" His words were harsh, but his eyes danced and he removed his jacket as he spoke. "Never let it be said that a Highlander did not respond to a dare."

"Go on then. Jump!"

"Nay, if ye are going to instigate, ye are coming too.". He held her hand and grinned. "One, two, three!" They ran together and jumped in, rolling together in the soft pile of hay. Harriet started to laugh and Thornton joined in, an unusual sound for he laughed but rarely.

Harriet lay next to him and he rolled on his side to look at her, his arm naturally going around her. It felt so normal, so right, Harriet hardly recognized she was treading onto dangerous ground. She moved closer to him and wrapped her arm around his shoulder. It was wrong, but in the dim corner of the stable, she did not possess the will to stop. Indeed, the only thing she feared was that it would not continue.

"I suppose I should say we shoud'na do this and we should go back to the tea," said Thornton with resignation.

"I am sure you are right. But I'd rather not hear that right now."

"What do ye wish to hear?" he whispered.

"A kiss." She was almost as surprised as he was at what she had said.

He raised an eyebrow. "Does a kiss make noise?"

"Let us do a scientific experiment and find out," suggested Harriet.

"Well, normally I would say it would be inappropriate, but if it is for science…" He pressed his lips against hers and retreated. "No sound."

"Not much of a kiss."

"I concur. Let us try again." He brought his lips to hers again and a warmth radiated through her everywhere he touched. She melted into him, holding him close as he deepened the kiss. It was strange and wet, and involved more than simply lips. It was even more than their previous encounter. So much more. She realized she had never known a kiss before this moment. When their lips finally parted, she was breathing hard and her heart was pounding.

"I cannot hear anything. Let us try again," said Harriet without opening her eyes.

"I thought I heard some smacking sounds."

"I'm not sure. The most important thing in science is to replicate results."

"I must agree." And so he rolled her onto her back and kissed her again. And then she rolled over and kissed him. Then they rolled back and kissed each other. The more they kissed, the more she felt a yearning, a tugging for something. She wanted something, needed something that only he could give her.

Suddenly, Thornton broke the kiss and laid back, his eyes closed. "I should stop. I need to stop now before I can no longer stop."

"I don't want you to stop," said Harriet sulkily. He said nothing in response. "Lord Thornton... Duncan, I don't want to stop. This is for science."

"I must or I will no' be able to."

"So... what if we did not stop?"

"Wait... what? Not stop? There are consequences to such things." Thornton propped himself up on his elbow, his silver eyes gleaming. He may appear restrained on the outside, but there was a fire inside.

Harriet's heart pounded in her chest. She would risk anything just to keep him next to her. "This is our one chance. I know you cannot marry me, and you know I plan to return to America, so what we have between us isn't about money or marriage, or trying to get something from the other. I am here for… for the science!"

"The science," Thornton sounded skeptical. "If I was thinking clearly, I would say that sounded like a rationalization to continue to kiss a bonnie lass."

"I am sure you are right," said Harriet, beaming that he had called her "bonnie." "But dedicating oneself to science sounds better."

"Aye, it does."

"Beside, while I confess I am not terribly knowledgeable in these matters, I believe one may kiss without the risk of impregnation, which is the primary concern."

"True. There is much that can be done without that particular risk."

"Truly?" Harriet's interest was piqued. She twirled a stray strand of hair around her finger in a nervous gesture. She feared proceeding might be a poor choice, but she could not fathom letting him go now. "One of the most important aspects of new discovery is scientific curiosity."

"For science." He leaned to her and kissed her again, deeper, harder.

"I love science," she murmured.

"In truth, my affection lies more with ye than with academics. I confess that my thoughts toward ye are no' what they should be as a gentleman."

"I fear my thoughts have also gone astray for I am glad to hear it."

He went to kiss her again then stopped. "Here, if ye change yer mind lass and I dinna seem to listen to ye, give me a poke wi' this." He slid a knife from his boot and jabbed it into the hay next to her.

"I do apologize I have no such weapon to give to you, so you can defend yourself against me."

"I'll take my chances."

Harriet smiled a little because she was happy and a little because she was nervous. "I've never kissed a man before you."

"If I have ever kissed anyone but ye, I have forgot." He leaned close and kissed her again, not just on her lips but her jaw and down her neck. She arched to allow him free access to her throat, feeling at once dangerous and vulnerable. He continued working his way down until he kissed along the edge of her bodice. She immediately knew his progression must not be hindered by something as inconsequential as her gown and stays, and worked to try to untie them from the back. She required some assistance, but soon the front of her dress was loosed and he was able to continue his progression, opening a new world of sensation. She arched her back and gave herself to it, enjoying every moment.

At the same time, he worked his hand up her gown, caressing her thigh, working his way higher and higher until she gasped out loud.

"I should stop?" he asked.

"Don't you dare!" she answered with a feral growl she did not recognize as her own.

He continued his work, whether out of enjoyment or fear she did not care. One look at his face, his eyes heavy with desire, told her she was not the only one who was experiencing a powerful effect.

"I think I am experiencing some sort of chemical reaction," she gasped. "Shall I explode?"

"Aye, I fear I will too." His words were low and heavy.

She reached for him, understanding just enough of what occurs between a man and a woman to know something in his breeches must be set free.

"Nay, lass," he pushed back her hand with grim determination. "That would be too far." He began to kiss her again and she held on to him as he began working his hand again, building up a sensation in her she feared may be the end of her.

"I never knew... don't stop... oh my word," panted Harriet.

Some sort of reaction was building inside her and she had a momentary worry the hay might actually combust, for it certainly felt as if she would explode.

"Is it... safe?" she gasped. He did not answer but kissed her again, and she knew he would not let her come to harm.

An all-consuming need drove her to this precipice, but far from avoiding it, she reached for it, straining, yearning, gasping, until something within her unleashed with wave after wave of pleasure. She closed her eyes and drifted into beautiful unconsciousness.

"Harriet?"

"I am not here."

"We should return to the party." His voice was mournful.

"I do not wish to return."

"Are ye... well?"

Harriet opened her eyes. "I am fine. No, that can't

be right. I am beyond that. I have no words for it. And you?"

He lay back with his arms over his head as if surrendering. "I never knew how much I love science. My only disappointment is the experiment ended too soon."

Harriet was about to comfort him and tell him not to worry, since they had years of experimenting ahead of them. In a flash, she realized none of that could be. He would not ask for her hand. She would not stay. They would be apart forever.

She busied herself in getting dressed. Perhaps if no one else could see it, she would be all right again. But how could she ever be content knowing what she had lost?

He helped her with the enclosures in the back. She stood on wobbly legs.

"Do I look all right?" she asked.

He reached toward her and pulled several strands of hay from her hair. "Ye are beautiful."

Harriet shook her head. "I know I am not."

"Aye, but ye are. Ye are to me." The plain truth of the statement was in his eyes.

Harriet looked away and blinked the tears from her eyes. He was everything she wanted. And nothing she could have.

Twenty-nine

By the time Thornton and Harriet returned to the picnic, most people had already returned to Thornton Hall. They had stayed too long. Thornton's stomach dropped at the realization.

"We should go down separately," he said, though he did not wish to leave her.

"I suppose you are right," she replied.

Despite her sturdy frame, she appeared vulnerable, and he wished he could spare her all harm, though he feared since they had publicly strolled away together and did not return until late, he had done the very thing he wished to avoid.

"Good afternoon, Miss Redgrave," he said, though he wished to kiss her instead.

"Good afternoon, Lord Thornton."

She walked down the main path, and he ran around a different way and approached the house from behind the stables. He entered the house from the side, just as she was walking in through the main door. Most of the guests were still milling about. He sneaked through a servants' entrance and ducked inside a parlor, cracking the door so he could hear the reception she received.

"Why, Miss Redgrave," said Miss Crawley in a voice so sweet it could rot her teeth, "I saw you leave in the company of Lord Thornton. Are you just now returning?"

"I went for a walk," said Harriet.

"A 'walk'—is that what you call it in America? We call it something different here," said Priscilla. The young ladies around her began to titter.

"I have no idea what you are talking about," said Harriet. Her voice was tired.

"Do you not?" said Priscilla in a sly voice. "Too bad about those stains on the back of your gown. However did you get them?"

Thornton wanted to jump in to rescue her but held back, knowing if he did so it would only make the rumors worse.

"I'm sure we all have stains from sitting on the grass," said Penelope with a carefree voice. "Let's get dressed for dinner." She linked arms with Harriet and walked upstairs.

"Little tart," hissed Priscilla when Harriet was barely out of sight. "I've never seen such a large girl. I suppose she knows she cannot hope to find a husband without lifting her skirts."

"I do believe she declared she was not inclined toward marriage," said the Comtesse de Marseille. "Perhaps she is interested in a different occupation."

Priscilla and her friends laughed with malicious enjoyment. "With that face *she* would have to pay the men to be seen with her."

"That must explain why Lord Thornton, with his pockets to let, is often seen in her company," said the comtesse.

The girls laughed again.

Thornton felt sick.

He slipped away from his vitriolic guests and dragged himself upstairs. He wanted peace. He needed to be alone. He was apprehended by his butler before he could reach his room.

"Lady Thornton awaits you in the map room," said the butler with an odd look.

"The map room?" Thornton asked. It was a room in a little-used part of the house. It contained his father's collection of maps and was one of the few rooms his mother had not renovated.

"Is everything well, my lord?" asked the butler in a hesitant voice.

Thornton opened his mouth to reassure the man, but realized he could not offer such reassurances. If the house was sold, the staff may also be replaced. Thornton sighed. He had not even thought of what would happen to his staff and his tenants if Thornton Hall changed hands. His butler, his back curved ever so slightly with age, awaited Thornton's reply. It would not be well for him.

"I will speak to my mother," said Thornton. He found his mother in the map room, but she was not alone. General Crawley was present, with a particularly nasty look on his red face. In a chair next to him was a sight so unexpected he stopped short. His mother, ever the fighter, was in tears. "Mother, what is the matter?"

She turned her face from his and said nothing.

"Lady Thornton has been informed that she may be spending some time in debtors' prison," said General Crawley with a snarl.

"O' course she will not. Mother, please dinna give this man a second thought. Go upstairs, I will deal with him." Thornton's hands clenched. Once he had no witnesses, he was going to wring this man's neck. How dare he threaten his mother?

"Why could ye no' marry Miss Crawley?" wailed his mother. "Why did ye need to insult her?"

"Because I will not marry for money, and I would never marry Miss Crawley under any circumstances. She is a vicious little thing without compassion or remorse."

"You will pay for your insults," raged General Crawley. "I will see you both in debtors' prison!"

"I do not know how ye managed to gain such access to my mother's accounts, but I can see now it was calculated. If you are angry, it is with me alone. Ye will not threaten Lady Thornton. Ever." Thornton spoke with quiet authority. He had fought with his mother, been furious with his mother, and at times wished her far from him, but nobody threatened her. Nobody.

"Do not underestimate my power, boy," sneered Crawley. "If I want to see your mother in jail, I shall surely do it!"

"I say!" Sir Antony Roberts stood at the doorway, his snuffbox in hand. "Forgive the intrusion, but I feel that you are not quite acting the gentleman to our hostess."

"This is none of your affair. Get out!" demanded Crawley.

"It is certainly not my affair, that we can agree upon. But I cannot see a lady in distress, refuse to help, and still call myself a gentleman." Sir Antony snapped his snuffbox closed and strolled into the room as if entering a garden party.

"Thank you, sir," said Lady Thornton, drying her eyes on a handkerchief.

"Here are my cheaters." Sir Antony held up a pair of glasses from the table. "I have been greatly enjoying your maps, Lady Thornton."

"They were my late husband's," said Lady Thornton.

"Shall we adjourn to the parlor?" Sir Antony held out his arm and she took it.

"Thank you," mouthed Thornton as Sir Antony escorted her away.

"This is not over, boy," growled Crawley.

"I believe it is. I shall speak to my solicitor about repaying the debts. We may need to sell Thornton Hall, but before ye start picking out the draperies, please know that I have no intention of selling to ye."

"You don't have a choice. Once you forfeit the loan I granted your mother, Thornton Hall is mine."

"But I do not intend to forfeit the loan," said Thornton mildly. "I have some assets yet." He hoped if he sold every horse he owned, he could raise the blunt. It would be painful to sell everything he had worked for, but so be it. "Until then, I believe our solicitors should do our talking." He turned and walked toward the door. "You can have nothing to say to Lady Thornton," he said over his shoulder. "Do not inconvenience her again."

"Should I ask what happened?" asked Penelope when she had safely returned Harriet to her room.

Harriet shook her head.

"Are you well?"

"I will be fine, but I will never be accepted here."

"You may not ever claim Miss Crawley as a friend," conceded Penelope.

"I should return to America as soon as possible."

"I am sorry this house party has been a disappointment." Penelope turned to go but paused, trying to find the right words. "If there is anything I can do…"

"No. Thank you." Harriet was not her normal self. She seemed smaller. Sadder.

Penelope was not certain what had made her so sad. She had left Harriet sitting happily on a blanket with a tea sandwich in one hand and a biscuit in the other. What could have happened?

Penelope left Harriet with some reluctance and returned to her room, where the Dowager Duchess of Marchford was smiling.

"The pearls are gone," said Antonia. "They must have been replaced for the fakes with Lord Langley. See, I told you it would all work out well."

"Or someone stole your pearls and Langley is still in possession of the fakes," said Penelope brutally.

"No! No, that could not be."

"Truly? It could not be that a thief could have written that note to get everyone out of the house so he could steal the pearls and possibly some military plans on the side?"

"Whatever are you talking about?"

"Someone rifled through Marchford's things. He suspects a spy."

"That boy is overly concerned," muttered Antonia.

"And you are altogether too trusting," retorted Penelope. "Somehow we need to determine if the real pearls found their way to Lord Langley."

A note arrived at that moment saying that Lord Langley was desirous of an audience in the yellow drawing room.

"What happened out there?" demanded Lord Langley when Penelope and the dowager entered the drawing room. "You are supposed to act as chaperones. Why am I hearing disrespectful talk about my granddaughter?" He paced the room as the duchess and Penelope found seats around the tea service that had kindly been set. It was a cheerful room, yellow as the name would suggest, and much in contrast to his demeanor at present.

"I believe Miss Redgrave took a walk," said Penelope. "Unfortunately, there are some young ladies here who have caused some unpleasantness, as can happen. I hope we can refute or ignore false rumors."

"Why is she not married yet?" Lord Langley demanded.

"Lord Langley, surely you realize we have not been long at Thornton Hall," said the dowager mildly, but she clanked her spoon against her china cup as she stirred with uncharacteristic vigor.

"What of it? I was promised that this Madame X was a matchmaker extraordinaire."

"Extraordinary, not miraculous," said Penelope.

"For what I'm paying, I damn well expect miracles."

"Watch your language and drink your tea," commanded the dowager.

Lord Langley stopped pacing the room and sat down with a harrumph. With a grumble, he picked up his cup and sipped. "Still don't know what's taking so long."

"These things take time. Affection must grow. Arrangements must be made," said the dowager vaguely.

"Time? Doesn't take time to fall in love. Takes an instant."

Antonia looked up from her cup. "Does it?"

"Take my daughter. Met some American on the road, and within the week she was running away with him."

"So you think your daughter fell in love with this American in an instant?"

"Well, how else do you explain it? And if she weren't happy, she'd come home, now would she not? She's not come back, thus she must love him."

Antonia frowned at him. "Your powers of logic astound me."

"It stands to reason. You know I am not romantic."

"Yes, I am well aware of that fact."

"But others let their emotions dictate their actions, like my daughter. She fell in love, so she followed him. Can't explain it any other way. Why, I was like her once myself. Fell in love and proposed to you."

Antonia's teacup smacked down on the saucer. "You declare that you loved me?"

"How else would you explain why I proposed to you? You had no money, no connections, you were a most unsuitable choice."

"I lived this once. I very much doubt after all these years I need to be subjected to a litany of all the reasons your mama found me unsuitable." Antonia held herself with rigid hauteur.

"Not trying to offend."

"Is that so?" Antonia raised a silver eyebrow. "Perhaps then you should try to offend and you might then avoid it."

"What I am trying to say, if you would cease these interruptions, is that I fell in love with you in an instant. My daughter fell for her husband in an instant, and I expect my granddaughter would be afflicted with the same constitution. Find the man she is in love with and make him marry her. As long as the man has a title," Lord Langley added.

"You have laid it out so simply, I do not know why we did not think of it before," said Antonia with an arch look. "However, with Miss Redgrave, we are taking a more measured approach. We do not need to wait for fickle affection to grow; we can help her arrange a union that will be beneficial to both parties. She has a considerable dowry, so I believe we can entice one of these titled young men to make an offer."

"No, no, I do not want her to marry a fortune hunter."

"My dear Lord Langley, you never specified we could not entertain the offers of a fortune hunter, only that the fortune hunter needed to have a title," said Antonia.

"No! I do not wish that for my granddaughter."

"You did contract with a matchmaker, did you not? Are you backing out now?"

"No! I do want my Harriet to marry, but I want her to marry for love and I want the man she falls in love with to have a title. Why else would I let her come here? The guest list is so packed with members of the peerage you can hardly walk down the hall without tripping over an earl or a baronet."

"Even Madame X cannot control with whom Miss Redgrave falls in love," said Penelope.

Lord Langley sat back in his chair and shook his head. "I know," he said softly. "I wish it were not true. At least it would be much easier if it was not true."

"Why this concern about love? You are not a romantic man, remember?" accused Antonia.

"I remember. I remember I did my duty to my family. I married whom they wished to fulfill my obligations. I did not marry for love or happiness, and I found none." His voice was low and rumbled like gravel. "I would wish for better for my granddaughter. I would not wish her to suffer as I have."

"Bah!" exclaimed the duchess. "What do you know of suffering?"

Langley sighed. "I did not realize how these emotions, once formed, are not likely to dissipate."

"Even you would not suggest that you still harbor a *tendre* for me." The dowager cast aside the notion as nonsense.

"Not suggesting. Telling. My feelings for you are unchanged, more's the pity. What good does it do me now?"

Antonia shook her head. "I believe you have drifted into the land of the absurd."

He took a biscuit and bit slowly, looking up to the

corner of the room in a considering sort of way. "Does Madame X help people to fall out of love?"

"Now you are mocking me."

"I am in earnest. I still have these feelings for you. Can't shake them. Not doing me any good, are they?"

"Lord Langley, I believe you are having some sort of mischief with me. Your words are nonsense," retorted Antonia.

"Perhaps we can let Madame X decide," said Penelope. Both Antonia and Langley looked a bit startled, as if they had forgotten she was in the room. "Lord Langley, the duchess recently lost a pearl necklace to you. It had sentimental value. It was her mother's. For the return of the necklace, we shall ask Madame X if she can assist in your request." Penelope saw an opportunity to reclaim the pearls and snapped at it.

Langley shrugged. "If you wish for the pearls, you may have them. Though you should not bet things you care not to lose."

"The cards were good!" defended Antonia as Langley walked out of the room. "I do not know what that man is playing at," she added as soon as he left.

"You don't suppose he may be telling the truth?" asked Penelope.

"Absurd. Ridiculous! Have you ever heard such fribble in your life?"

"I admit it would be unlikely that he had carried a torch for you so long, but it would be quite romantic."

"It would be quite impossible. This is the man who abandoned me on my wedding day."

"Perhaps he is sorry."

"I could not care less whatever he is. That chapter in my life was closed long ago. The less we see of him the better. Once we have retrieved the pearls, we can be done with him forever."

Penelope folded her hands in her lap and said nothing. It was good, when dealing with a duchess, to know when to keep her mouth shut.

Langley returned, his mouth a thin line. "The pearls are gone."

"Stolen?" exclaimed the duchess.

"It must be. The box I kept them in was there but the pearls were gone."

"How very strange," said Penelope, now convinced they had fallen victim to a thief. At least now the duchess could not be exposed for fraud.

"Yes, especially considering they were worth very little," said Langley.

Antonia froze. Penelope did not dare to say anything at all.

"You knew," said Antonia, rising from her chair and stepping toward him. "You knew the pearls were fake."

"Course I knew. I can spot the real from the fake from across a crowded room—least I could when my eyes were better. The fake are smooth and perfect; the real have imperfections. You need to look for the flaws to see if they are real."

"If you knew, why let me wager them? Why not expose me at once?"

"Have you not been attending to what I have been saying, woman? I would no more wish to hurt you than to cut off my right arm."

Antonia's mouth opened but no words emerged.

"I want to be cured of this affliction. Costing me much, don't you see? Get your Madame X and fix me!" He turned to leave but then turned back and picked up another biscuit. "Quite good, these." He bowed and quit the room, the two ladies staring mutely after him.

Thirty

HARRIET WAS SO TIRED SHE ASKED IF SHE COULD FORGO the evening's dining and entertainment, but the duchess would have none of it.

"You must go," declared the duchess. "To avoid it would be to confirm the rumors. You must go and look happier than ever."

Harriet did not feel happy, and she did not want to meet with the cruel Miss Crawley. And what could she say? Much of what Miss Crawley was accusing her of was true. The pain came not from the memory of what she and Thornton had shared, but of the realization that they could never share it again.

The evening wore on like sand grinding in one's bathing costume. Harriet pasted on a smile. If there was talk, she did not hear it, but there were looks. Guests that were indifferent to her before were now downright hostile. Her would-be suitors had all abandoned her, and now the only person left speaking to her beyond her immediate circle was the Duc d'Argon.

Of Thornton she saw nothing at all. Every once

in a while she glimpsed him across the room, but he ignored her entirely. She knew he was trying to help her. If he gave her any special attention, the rumors would be confirmed. Still, it hurt.

After the men rejoined the ladies, Thornton was the last to walk into the room. He glanced over at Harriet, made a sign as if he were reading a book, then walked off. Harriet doubted anyone had noticed, but she knew what he wanted.

After a few minutes she excused herself and made a secret detour to the library. The room was comforting the way only a room full of books could be. All that knowledge, all that promise. It was all there. She sat down on the settee and breathed in the aroma of books.

"I am sorry," whispered Thornton as he sat next to her.

Harriet shook her head and kept her eyes closed. She did not wish for apologies.

"Would ye reconsider yer plans o' going back to America?" he asked softly.

Harriet shook her head again. "I am sorry, but America is where I belong. That is where I need to be."

"In that case, we should stay apart. The gossip has gotten vicious. We should not add to it."

Harriet forced herself to open her eyes. He was more handsome than ever, solemn in gleaming black. She knew what she must do. "Good-bye, Lord Duncan."

"Good-bye, Harriet."

She closed her eyes again and listened as he softly left the room. Tears did come then. She tried to keep them in check, knowing any sign of weakness would be exploited, but they kept coming and she cried until her throat burned and her heart broke.

"*Bonsoir!*" said the Duc d'Argon in a cheerful voice as he walked into the library. Harriet searched for a handkerchief and came up short. In desperation, she used the edge of her sleeve to wipe her tears.

"What... what are you doing here?" Harriet tried to compose herself but was woefully unequal to the task.

"I thought we had arranged to meet to discuss the book? I found the next chapter very enlightening. But perhaps I come at a time inconvenient for you?"

"Yes. No. Sorry, I am not quite myself. Perhaps discussing chemistry will do me some good."

D'Argon held out his handkerchief, for indeed she was in need of one again. She wiped her eyes and blew her nose. She attempted to return the maligned cloth, but he politely refused.

"Forgive me. I can see that I trespass upon you at a time of sorrow. I should leave you, but I do not wish to abandon you in time of need. Forgive me for pressing into your affairs most private, but I believe I can hazard a guess at what has upset you. Indeed, I was most grieved by the slanderous gossip I was unfortunate to hear. I cannot fathom the lack of decency and good breeding that would lead to such filth to be spoken from pretty lips."

He spoke of Miss Crawley, of course. Harriet dabbed her eyes and said nothing. She was only part of her troubles, but it was an acceptable reason to be found snuffling in the library.

"Miss Redgrave, I cannot tell you how distressed I am to see you suffer the injury of their barbs. I wish to provide you some comfort. I wish to…" Here the chevalier stood and began to pace in the room. His distress at her discomfort surprised her. Perhaps she had underestimated the depth of his regard. She remained silent, as she was unsure what he was about, and felt certain he would get to it faster without her help.

"I had not thought to speak of this until I had known you longer, but now I see I must speak out. I cannot tolerate you being so abused by such a creature. You must permit me to say how much I have grown to admire you." He paused to gauge her response.

Harriet was surprised at his declaration but made no reply. He considered this sufficient encouragement and continued.

"From the first day we met, I knew you were different from any other lady. I can say unequivocally that you are the most intelligent woman of my acquaintance, and even among the gentlemen scientists I have been honored to meet, you should not come ill-equipped to the conversation. I would like to offer you a partnership, one that I believe would be mutually advantageous to both. We could work together. You could assist my investigations and be allowed to witness the scientific meetings which I know we should both enjoy. I shall not make you uncomfortable by declaring a love, which I know you would find immature. Instead, I offer a partnership. With marriage, you can leave the world of simpering debutantes and enter into an alliance of scientific investigation. You could have entry into the scientific academy as my wife."

Harriet swallowed hard. Despite being lauded as

more intelligent than most women and almost as smart as most men, she felt the need to confirm what he was saying. "Are you proposing marriage to me?"

D'Argon sat beside her on the settee and took her hand. "I will not insult your intelligence by declaring any romantic foolishness, but I will say that I believe we can be happier together than apart. We have similar interests and goals. We can help each other. Truly, I can think of no other lady to stand beside me as my bride."

"I am honored by your proposal, but I plan to return to America. I could not entertain a future in which I never saw my parents again."

"Nor should you. If I had the opportunity to see again my loving parents…" The Duc d'Argon closed his eyes for a moment and shook his head. When he looked up again there were tears in his eyes. "I could never stand in the way of you seeing your parents again. I suggest we travel to America and begin a new life there."

"You would live in America?"

"I can never return to my homeland, my country. Thus, I am free to begin again. America is the land of opportunity, no? I should like to continue my studies in science, and I believe I can do that there."

Married. Harriet squeezed his hand and reclaimed her hands for her own. He was offering everything she had thought she wanted. And none of that romantic folly which so far had only led to heartbreak. Perhaps it was for the best. This was a good offer. A man who valued her for her brain, not her money. Or at least he presented a very convincing case.

"It is a goodly offer," said Harriet. "I shall think on it carefully."

"Yes, but you must. I shall think of nothing but you. I wish you peaceful dreams."

He bowed and quit the room. Harriet let out a long sigh. She had no doubt her dreams would be anything but peaceful.

Thirty-one

HARRIET HAD STILL NOT RETURNED. THORNTON DID another rotation through the room, stopping to greet his guests, being the polite host, all the while scanning the room for Harriet. She had definitely not returned. The Duc d'Argon was also not there, leading to some disagreeable conclusions as to where she was and whom she was with. Naturally, he was not at liberty to care about such things. He was unaccustomed to wanting to do damage to any of his guests, but in the span of one short evening, he not only wished to do harm to a certain general, but he also wished a particular French duke to disappear, preferably somewhere near Botany Bay.

With a sigh, Thornton recognized he was not the sort of man to actually do such a thing; until recently, he was not aware that he was the type of man to actually think of doing such a thing. But when it came to protecting Harriet or his mother, he was ready to do about anything. Why he felt Harriet needed to be protected from the duc was less clear. He could only say he knew it with confidence.

He had not the slightest doubt that d'Argon's interest in Harriet was entirely materialistic. He was certainly playing a good game, but fifty thousand was enough to get a man to do almost anything. He struggled with the prospect of informing Harriet of his suspicions, but realized that other than a gut feeling, he had very little actual evidence. He considered telling her of how d'Argon had laughed at Miss Crawley's jokes at her expense, but rejected it as cruel.

No, there was no way to communicate the truth directly, which led him back to the plan of having d'Argon kidnapped and sold to a press gang on a ship heading to China. Of course, none of this was going to be effective if d'Argon was currently convincing her to do goodness only knew what.

No, he wasn't going to let this happen. If anyone was going to marry Harriet for her money, it was going to be him!

Thornton's shoulders slumped as he recognized the direction his thoughts had taken him.

"Why so glum, my friend?" asked Marchford.

They were surrounded by guests, happily talking and dancing without a care, unlike the two men now watching the festivities. "I realize I am not the man I thought I was," said Thornton.

"Congratulations."

"It is not a happy realization."

"And what sort of man have you become?"

"One who would do anything to put a bit o' blunt in his pocket. I thought myself immune to the seduction of wealth, but I find myself verra much at risk."

Marchford raised an eyebrow. "Would you care

to enlighten me as to what this guilt-laden tirade is about?"

Thornton shook his head. "Nay, the only difference between myself and those I condemn is that I am better at weaving justifications. I would do better to be honest about what I have become. A mercenary, up for the highest bidder."

Marchford frowned. "Come now, tell me what this is about."

Thornton was spared from answering by the sudden appearance of Miss Redgrave. Thornton spotted her walking into the room on the arm of d'Argon. Something inside him tightened and he had the insane notion to give the Frenchman a facer and lay him out. He took a deep breath, imagining his mother's look of horror if he carried out the mad scheme. "Must dash," he said without taking his eyes off Harriet. He was not going to let her go.

Thornton walked in a straight line toward Harriet and the annoying Frenchman. If anyone attempted conversation with him as he crossed the drawing room, or even if anyone was trying to dance, he saw none of it in his straight progression toward Harriet. The duc was smiling. She was smiling in return. Could she not see he was a snake?

"Good evening," Thornton interrupted their conversation. "I trust ye are enjoying yerself?"

"Yes, delightful entertainment. I do enjoy country life," said d'Argon. "I find I am always learning new customs, such as the technique for walking through dancing couples. I would never be so bold, but you are at this a master, no?"

It was an insult, but Thornton preferred it. The gloves were coming off and they were going to settle this. "Aye, d'Argon, I am the master of this house." His voice was low. If the words were laced with warning, so be it. His temper was uncertain this evening. The tremor of threat was sincere.

The duc's face hardened. Harriet's eyes opened wide. Perhaps he was being less than subtle, but Thornton did not care.

"I wonder, d'Argon, if I could interest you in a game of billiards." It was not a suggestion.

"I fear I know nothing of the game," said d'Argon evenly, though his eyes glittered.

"Then I must insist on teaching ye." Thornton forced a smile. Whatever he needed to do to keep d'Argon out of Harriet's company, he would do. If Thornton couldn't be with her, he would make sure that d'Argon was also feeling the same misery.

"I think perhaps I would like to dance," d'Argon turned to Harriet, but Thornton put an arm on the wall between them, turning his back on Harriet and blocking her from the conversation and from d'Argon.

"Oh, but I insist." Thornton put his arm around d'Argon's shoulders and, in a move that hopefully appeared friendly, he muscled the Frenchman out of the drawing room. They walked across the entryway as bosom friends to all who saw them, until they reached the privacy of the billiard room.

"And to what do I owe the honor of this insult?" sneered d'Argon, breaking free of Thornton's grip.

"Perhaps I wish to spend some time with ye." Thornton set up the billiard table. He might as well do something enjoyable since he had decided to be d'Argon's jailor for the evening. Besides, the oak billiard cue felt weighty in his hands. Almost like a quarterstaff. A man could do some damage with this cue.

It appeared d'Argon did not appreciate the malicious glint in Thornton's eye, for he also picked up a billiard cue, perhaps more for defense than out of any great desire to learn to play the game. "You wish me away from Miss Redgrave. It is the jealousy. If you wish to win her heart, go talk to her yourself. Do not let me stop you."

"Since you are a novice, I shall break," said Thornton.

"But no, you do not wish to win Miss Redgrave for yourself. You merely wish to prevent anyone else from claiming her money."

"Miss Redgrave is not a prize to be claimed," Thornton growled.

"Ah, but she is." The Frenchman gave a slippery smile. "She is a juicy fruit ripe for the plucking if the master is skilled. She craves attention. She needs to be understood. Say two kind words and she is mine for the taking."

"You shall not take her anywhere."

"And who are you to stop me? I have spoken with Langley. He is most interested in having Harriet marry, soon, and to a title. I have all these requirements."

"You would be merely marrying her for her money! You are not in love with her!"

"Ah, yes, you are correct. My heart has not been touched by her charms, if you could call them that. But there I have been honest with her. I have not promised love, but merely a partnership."

"I will speak plainly. If you do not break off this pursuit, I shall reveal your nature to her."

"You must do as you think right. Go ahead and reveal me. But what would you say? You could say I am poor, but she knows that. She does not care for financial restrictions and bristles at the thought of being told whom she can marry based on their fortune. You could tell her I enjoy the company of women, but I am French, so I doubt that would come as a surprise. You could even tell her I do not love her, but I have made no such claim. Our relationship is based on science, the logic of the mind. Not petty emotional states. No, dear friend, I shall invite you to tell her all these things."

"You are a wretched man," said Thornton, except he was the one feeling wretched.

"Ah, the insults. I have learned the Englishman, he learns to curse when he knows he has been beat."

"It is not over. If ye think I shall stand aside and let ye ruin her life—"

"But that is exactly what I expect you to do. You have no other choice but to kill me, and you are not the type. I have learned to tell the difference between those who merely wish to kill me and those who will actually do the deed. You, dear host, are not the type to murder a man who has come to you for hospitality."

"Aye, ye would be the type to need to have such knowledge, perhaps because of your career as a gambler."

"Yes, I am a gambler. And this may be my highest hand yet. But if anyone would be the one to stop me, it would not be you." The duc made one more shot, sinking the ball in the far right pocket.

"This is not yer first game o' billiards," said Thornton.

"No, not at all. But it is the first time you have tried to scare away a potential rival for a woman's hand. I have been confronted by many watchful parents. I fear your performance is not equal with the task."

"I am sorry to disappoint."

"Not at all. I despise competition."

"And in me, you see none."

"None at all. Pity too, because she used to think of you so very highly. Here is irony for you. I do believe you had a chance to capture her heart. It was yours for the taking, but you refused her. You wish to protect her from heartbreak, yet it was you who crushed her tender feelings. In fact, I should thank you for leaving her so vulnerable. With her emotions raw and sensitive, she was ready for the idea to marry for sensible reasons, not affection. Oh no, you yourself have turned her heart from love."

Thornton said nothing. He hated d'Argon. Even more, he hated the truth he spoke.

"You had your chance, and you rejected her. Her broken heart is precisely what I need to wed her. And make no mistake, she will be my bride. Good night, Lord Thornton."

The Duc d'Argon strode from the room, leaving Thornton exhausted. His anger, initially focused on the wrongs done by d'Argon, was now focused on himself. He himself had put Harriet into the arms of a fortune hunter.

Thirty-two

THE NEXT MORNING, THORNTON WAS AWAKE EVEN earlier than normal. Sleep, and the blissful escape from consciousness, had evaded him. He planned a hard ride to match his mood. A glow emanating from the library caught his attention.

"Miss Redgrave?" Thornton's heart stilled upon finding her in the library.

Harriet jumped. "What are you doing here? I thought everyone would be in their beds."

"I thought ye would be too. 'Tis the middle o' the night."

Harriet shook her head. "Couldn't sleep. Besides, it is almost morning."

"Are ye doing experiments here again?" It was a pointless question given the scientific equipment sprawled over the table.

"No! I, well, yes, but you see I couldn't do it in the castle because I needed pure darkness for some of the experiments."

"And why would ye need that, lass? Or a better question, why here?"

"The castle has so many open windows, there is no way to prevent some light from getting through. Even now the moon is so bright I can see my own shadow. Here, you have those." Harriet pointed to thick burgundy drapes. "No light gets through."

"I see." What he saw was Harriet focusing on her experiments and ignoring anything that may have occurred between them.

"Truly?"

"Nay. I would only caution ye that this is my library. I dinna wish to see it go up in smoke." He could ignore his feelings too.

"Oh, I am not doing any experiment that requires open flame. Well... right now at least. This desk is all the surface I need." She kept her eyes on her powders and glass tubes. "Why are you awake so early?"

Because I cannot stop thinking of you. "Need to run the horses," Thornton said instead. "Saw the light, so I came in. Which begs the question, if ye need to have complete darkness, why the lantern?"

"I am setting up the experiment now. I will turn off the light when I am ready. Would you like to see it? I am trying to make light."

"Light?"

"Yes. I am trying to find a chemical compound or reaction that can produce light. I have been experimenting with phosphorous." She busied herself with the experiment and Thornton drew nearer. She was in her element. He remained quiet, watching her, not wishing to disturb her concentration. She may appear awkward in society, but here, she was the sophisticate, and he the country bumpkin.

All the criticism of her rang in his ears; he wondered if it rang in hers too. She had chosen another game to play, one of science, not flirtation. But he knew there was more to her—a vast desire to love and be loved. It would be a waste to throw it away.

"I wish the others could see how skilled ye are," he murmured his thoughts out loud.

She shrugged but did not look up. "I thought, especially when I first started, if only I could show people how fascinating chemistry was, they would join me in my pursuit of science. It never worked. First, no one wanted to see. And second, they never appreciated it when they did. I would do a brilliant experiment and they would talk of how I had stained my gloves. It was a pointless exercise."

"So you stopped trying."

"Naturally. I believe in using scientific principles in my approach to life. If the experiment does not work, change a variable, try it again, but at a certain point, one must give up even cherished hypotheses and make new ones in the pursuit of truth."

"So what have ye given up?" He was almost afraid to ask.

Harriet slowly looked up at him. "Some elements do not mix, and if they do, a disastrous explosion can occur."

"Some explosions can be good." He rather liked her explosions.

"Explosions can cause damage and pain." She focused back on her work, refusing to even glance at him. Her tone was matter of fact. "In science, we make no value judgments regarding the outcome of experiments. Facts are facts. Some elements do not belong together and there is nothing more to be said."

He wanted to refute her findings, but he could not. What could he say? Harriet wished to return to America. It would be easy to promise her he would leave everything behind and live there too, but he could not. Goodness only knew what would happen to his people, his tenants, his own mother if he left. He must stay. She must leave.

"All of yer experiments may not have worked out the way ye wish, but ye have used yer time wisely. Ye have invested in the pursuit of knowledge."

Harriet met his eyes. "Thank you," she said softly. "This is what I will focus on for the rest of my life. I will dedicate my life to science." The resignation in her voice was unmistakable.

"Do not give up on finding happiness in marriage entirely," blurted Thornton, not wishing her to be susceptible to the lures of d'Argon.

"All I need is a husband to gain access to the scientific community. If I had been born a man, it would have been different. I could have joined a scientific society and learned from colleagues, and my scientific pursuits would have been met with interest, not derision. Unfortunately, I am in need of a husband to continue my work."

Thornton struggled with how to respond. He felt her slipping away and yet knew he could not pull her back. "Show me yer experiment, for though I can hardly excuse the misogynistic tendencies of my entire gender, I can make it up to you by being an appreciative audience now."

Harriet nodded, did a few more preparations, and doused the light, casting them into complete darkness. In the inky blackness he could not see what she did, but all of a sudden an eerie green light began to glow on the desk.

"It's working!" she exclaimed.

"Good heavens," he said. It was working. In the green glow, he could see her wide smile. At least something had made her happy, and it certainly wasn't him. "It is amazing." And it was.

"What a find! I replicated some results, but changed a few things and it works even better. I would love to present this at the academy."

She was back to talking about a marriage of convenience again and it made Thornton cringe. "Do not rush into a union unadvisedly."

"If two people have a clear understanding of the arrangement, what does it matter?" She threw him a hardened look in the unearthly green glow.

"I do not trust d'Argon."

"He told me you would say that." She dismissed his concern.

"I warrant he would," muttered Thornton. He heard noises from outside in the hall. "The servants are awake earlier than usual to prepare for St. John's Eve."

"Is that tonight?"

"Aye, and we will have a bonfire and a feast to celebrate."

"I shall be on my guard for faeries." In the green glow with her hair down, she could easily be mistaken for one of the fair folk herself.

More noises came from outside and he knew it

would be dangerous to be caught with her alone. "I should go. Will ye be all right?"

"I shall be fine. I will simply clean up a bit. I wonder how long this will glow."

He could not wait to find out and slipped out the door.

❧

"I believe the proposal from d'Argon is sincere. He shall marry her, his financial difficulties will be over, and so also will ours," said Antonia.

"She is prepared to enter a marriage of convenience, but has some doubts as to his sincerity," said Penelope. "And, truth be told, so do I."

Antonia frowned. "Whyever so?"

"Something Thornton said to her. She thinks him interested in her money."

"Well of course he is interested in her money. It would be an odd thing if he was ambivalent. And if Thornton isn't interested in making an offer, he should clear the field."

"Harriet says she will marry for science. I have no idea what that means."

"Always an odd girl."

"A trifle unusual perhaps." At the dowager's raised eyebrow Penelope was forced to concede the point. "Quite unusual I grant you. But I fear she is not marrying for the right reasons."

"Right reasons? Bah!" The dowager stood and shook out her skirts as if rejecting the offensive notion. "I suppose you are going to start talking to me about romance and love and other nonsense like Langley.

I blame novels. Too many romantic notions being bandied about. Dangerous I say."

"No doubt," said Penelope. "But we must find some way to prove to her and to ourselves that the Duc d'Argon is interested in more than just her inheritance."

"How would you do this?"

"I have an idea…"

❧

It was time for her performance. Penelope took a deep breath, grasped the folded piece of paper in her hand, and walked into the parlor where Miss Crawley and many young ladies were spending a respectable afternoon with their diligent chaperones. Penelope chose a chair in the middle of the room, within sight of many of the young ladies. She opened her missive and pretended to read.

"Oh no!" she exclaimed, staring at the paper. "Her entire fortune gone?" She stood for effect.

"What is the matter, Miss Rose?" asked Miss Crawley.

"Oh, nothing, nothing at all." Penelope clutched the paper to her chest, as if hiding it from prying eyes. "Forgive me, but I must speak with Miss Redgrave immediately."

Well now, thought Penelope as she walked back to her room, *that bit of gossip should be spread like wildfire.*

"Is it done?" asked Harriet, who was waiting for Penelope's return.

"Yes. The rumors will be flying."

"What should I say if anyone asks?"

"I doubt anyone would. It would be highly impertinent. If anyone broaches the subject, you should give them a setdown."

"I wouldn't even know how to begin." Harriet shook her head.

"Ignore them and walk away."

"Would that not be rude?"

"Of course it would be rude; that is the point."

"Oh, of course." Harriet slumped back in a chair and Penelope didn't have the energy to correct her.

"If the Duc d'Argon passes this test, are you sure you would like to marry him?"

"A marriage with him makes a good deal of sense. There are things I cannot do, doors to scientific societies that are permanently barred because I am unmarried. I could never publish a paper or attend a scientific meeting without being escorted by my husband. The duc is charming and personable, all the things I am not. He can take care of our position in society while I can be free to focus on my work. Beyond that, he is willing to live in America so I can be near my parents."

"Very sensible."

"Thank you."

"But do you love him?" asked Penelope.

"No," said Harriet simply.

"Harriet, I don't mean to pry, and please do not answer if it makes you uncomfortable, but is there anyone else for whom you have feelings?"

Harriet stood and smoothed her dress. "Whatever are you talking about?"

"You appear to me to have developed a friendship with Lord Thornton."

"Yes, the rumors of that are endless. However, Lord Thornton has sworn never to get married, especially not to somebody with a fortune. He is a very nice sort of man, but he has not misled me in his intentions. In addition, I wish to return to America. Thus, I have no cause to be unhappy about him." Harriet raised her chin and looked away.

"Very sensible," said Penelope again, this time with sympathy.

"Yes. Thank you. If the Duc d'Argon is who he claims to be, I think we shall be quite happy together," said Harriet without conviction.

"I am sure you will," Penelope agreed with the same lack of confidence. She was not sure now whether she hoped the duc would prove worthy or not. Either way, it was certain to get interesting at Thornton Hall.

⤐

The spy slipped into the room of Lord Thornton while everyone was at tea. He gave the room a contemptuous cast of his eye then went directly to the bed. Underneath the mattress, he found the documents he expected. After a quick perusal, he placed the plans in a satchel and slipped unseen from the room. He needed to get those papers posted to London before sundown.

Thirty-three

IT WAS MIDSUMMER'S EVE AND THE HOUSE WAS ALIVE with excitement. The wood for the bonfire had been carried up to the base of the castle, since the fire had to be lit on a high place, at least so the legend went. The populace had to be protected from faeries. But of course the tradition was little more than an excuse for a party to be held late at night and outdoors. The possibility for mischief put a spring in the step of many of the young people, and put a note of caution and extra resolve on the faces of their parents and chaperons.

Most of the guests were in the holiday spirit. The weather was fair, the wine was flowing, and the musicians were tuned and ready to play. After a meal of several courses, the guests retired back to their respective bedrooms to change into their costumes. To add to the amusements, the Midsummer's Night Eve celebration would be a masque. Perhaps this way the faeries would pass unrecognized among the guests.

"I heard ye give my mother the idea for a masque," Thornton accused Marchford as they walked down the steps from the men's wing.

"Yes, I did. This way no one will know it is me, which will be helpful for our little trap and also allow me to pass this evening unmolested," said Marchford.

"Ye fear for yer virtue?"

"Thornton, you have no idea the lengths these women will go to ruin me. I live in fear that I will be discovered alone with one and she will cry that I have made violent love to her. I have found women in my bed, under my bed, in my wardrobe, hiding in the billiard room, even stashed in the liquor closet, which is not an easy feat. I fear females may jump out at me at night or drop upon me from the trees. I am glad to be avoiding the celebrations tonight, for I suspect I would be no match for their cunning."

"So ye are going through with yer plan?"

"Yes. This is the perfect night to do so. You understand what to do?"

"Aye, 'tis simple enough. I will walk up to the bonfire wi' yer valet so everyone believes it is ye."

"I only feel sorry for my valet."

"I shall try to keep an eye out for him." Despite his words, Thornton appeared distracted.

Marchford paused on the stair, concerned for his friend. "How goes it with you? You have been in a strange humor all day."

Thornton shrugged. "I will manage."

"If there was something wrong, you would tell me."

Thornton shook his head, leaving Marchford to wonder. "It is my problem. I shall solve it somehow. Trouble is, I ken how right now. But I will. I must."

"If you are in need of some money—"

"Nay!" Thornton shouted. "Sorry, old friend. But nay, I shall no' be borrowing money from my friends. I'd rather buy a set of colors and see the world."

"Before you join the Regulars, please do talk to me first. I am certain you would be an asset to the army, but I need friends I can trust more than you can imagine."

"Thank ye, but some problems are my own to solve."

Marchford could only watch as his friend walked away.

❦

Despite her unequivocal success with her phosphorous experiment, Harriet was restless and disappointed, though she could hardly say why. Everything was going as planned. She should be thrilled. Instead, she felt sadly flat.

There was a knock on the door and Penelope stuck in her head. "Why, Harriet, you are not even dressed."

"I do not have anything suitable for such an occasion," said Harriet. She honestly could not care less, but she grabbed on to the first excuse that came to mind.

"Well, why didn't you say something earlier? I'm sure I have something that will do nicely." Penelope took her by the hand and led her to her dressing room, where the duchess was waiting. "Her Grace took it upon herself to buy me new clothes, and despite the fact that I did not wish for them, I must say she has good taste."

"Oh no," said Harriet. "I am much bigger than you. Your gowns would not fit."

"Leclair may be able to fix it. It might be a trifle short."

They found Leclair and asked if there was any hope. Leclair sniffed the air, her head held high. "I once dressed the Comtesse de Chauvé to perfection with nothing more than draperies and the bed clothes."

"Did she not die at the hands of the revolution-aries?" asked Penelope.

"*Oui*," said Leclair with a shrug. "But she looked divine."

It was not long before Leclair was able to lengthen the skirt and Harriet found herself tied into an emerald silk gown that was sheer perfection. It was a trifle snug, and as a result the gown hugged her curves and her décolletage spilled out the top.

"I don't think my father would approve," said Harriet, looking at herself in the glass.

"You look lovely," declared the duchess. "My, but I do have good taste."

"I look like a harlot," complained Harriet.

"An expensive one at least," said Penelope, grab-bing a shawl to conceal her own cleavage.

"Wait now. For what purpose do you wrap up in a shawl? I would like one too!"

"No, you look very well," appeased Penelope. "I merely look silly."

Harriet put her hands on her hips and the dowager crossed her arms.

"Fine," muttered Penelope and removed the shawl.

At the duchess's request, Leclair condescended to do the young ladies' hair. The result was stunning. With cascading curls, skintight gowns, and salacious curves, Harriet and Penelope hardly resembled their former selves.

The duchess grinned with delight. "I am sure the men will be throwing themselves at your feet."

"Sounds like a lot of bother," said Penelope.

"We might trip over them," finished Harriet.

"Hopeless, the lot of you," muttered the dowager. "Put on your half-masks, we shall see what this evening brings."

They donned their masks and walked down the grand staircase together, receiving more than a second look from the guests assembled in the marble entryway.

"They must think we are someone else," whispered Harriet.

"That is all the fun of a masque," replied Penelope. "Oh no, he would not do that!"

Harriet was surprised by Penelope's sudden change in topic and watched as Penelope marched up to a tall man holding a copy of Debrett's *Peerage of England*. Penelope pointed to the book and seemed quite unhappy, though why the book would cause distress was beyond Harriet.

Harriet felt a momentary discomfort at being abandoned by Penelope, until she realized that with the mask, no one knew who she was. With her emerald silk gown and styled hair, no one would likely guess either. She could be anyone—except she was six inches taller than most women.

The happy revelers were encouraged in their appreciation of St. John's Eve by a round of hot toddies, which were passed out on trays in order to facilitate the walk up the path to the bonfire at the castle. Some of the elder members of the party, the dowager and Langley among them, decided to forgo the walk and have their own celebrations in a more moderate, although hardly temperate, manner. They played cards and drank wine until midnight, when they all switched to whiskey, neat.

The younger members, or those still interested in adventure, took to climbing the hill. Not wishing anyone to feel the least uncomfortable from the short hike, way stations were arranged along the path offering more hot drinks, such as rum punch or wassail, and a nibble of biscuit or sandwich was offered as well. Once revelers reached the courtyard of the old castle, they were greeted by more generous libations and musicians playing all the country-dances. In the middle of the courtyard, a large bonfire raged, casting everything in an orange hue. The seasoned wood cracked and sparked, shooting fiery bursts high in the air, giving the arrangement a dangerous tone.

It was Midsummer's Night Eve, and mischief was in the air.

"*Bonsoir, mademoiselle,*" said d'Argon with an accent that could only be his. "Such celebrations, they are quite amusing, no?"

"Good evening, *monsieur,*" replied Harriet, adjusting her mask. She could hide her face but not her height.

"I must say you look stunning tonight. So different from your usual self I would not have known you. Would you care to dance?" He swept her a bow so polished there would not have been a lady in all of Britain who would have denied him. Of course, she was an American.

"I would be delighted." Apparently some things worked just as well on Americans as on the English. Despite the barb about her "usual" appearance, she followed him to where the other dancers were assembling. She did wish to know his reaction to the rumor of her poverty if he had heard it yet. Apparently, he had taken a ride that afternoon.

He led her to the dance area, which in this case was the grass of the courtyard. They joined a line of couples for a country-dance. It was familiar to Harriet, yet outside in the dark with the bonfire, the dance had never seemed so vibrant and alive.

After the set, Harriet was breathless, and the mask was uncomfortable. "I need to catch my breath," declared Harriet.

"Allow me the pleasure of escorting you," said d'Argon. He led her away from the others to a dark corner on the side of the castle. They were perhaps not as alone as one might think, since many couples were engaged in a private *tête-à-tête* in the dark recesses of the castle courtyard.

Harriet removed her mask and was relieved by the coolness of the night air on her face.

"You are very beautiful tonight," said d'Argon in a low voice.

"I borrowed the gown from Miss Rose."

"You should do so more often. With the masque, you look quite the picture."

Did he mean she looked better with her face hidden? She decided to change the subject. "It is a beautiful night."

"*Oui.* Perhaps we should walk behind the castle. I believe there are some hidden treats for the guests there, or so I have heard a few say."

"That sounds amusing." Harriet was always interested in fun diversions.

They walked around the back of the castle until the sounds of music were muted and the darkness surrounded them. In the corners, out of sight, Harriet

noted the soft sounds of people together, whispering…
kissing. When they reached the far side of the castle,
they were greeted only with darkness. She suspected
there would be no surprise other than what may be
found on the arm of the duc d'Argon.

"I do not believe there is any secret here to be
found," said Harriet.

"Do you not think so?" His voice was low and
seductive.

"But I can show you something remarkable."
Harriet grabbed his hand and dragged him to the old
kitchens where her laboratory was. She knew this area
well from climbing in the dark, so the lack of light did
not alarm her. "Wait here," she said and left him at the
door. She did not want him bungling about making a
mess of things.

"Miss Redgrave, what is this you wish to show
me?" His tone could not hide his annoyance.

"See, look. I was doing some experiments with
luminescence and, well, see for yourself." She held up
the bottle of the strange powder and it glowed in her
hand. "It is very odd. I cannot wait to complete more
experiments on this."

"Interesting," said the duc in the manner of people
who did not find it interesting in the least.

"'Tis verra interesting," said a voice that could only
be Thornton's.

Thirty-four

"No. I will not allow you to use this book as bait," Penelope whispered, following Marchford as he greeted guests and was altogether too friendly while holding her annotated copy of *Debrett's*. "What are you thinking of walking around the entryway so that everyone can see it?"

"I can only concur with Miss Rose," added Mr. Neville, coming up behind them. "If this book is of a sensitive nature, it should not be where anyone can see it."

"But who would think anything unusual? It is merely a book which many of the peerage have in their possession," said Marchford.

"But they don't carry it about," chastised Penelope. "I will put it away safely."

"No! I should be the one to do that!" declared Neville.

"Here." Marchford handed the book to Neville. "Wait for me in the library, I will be along shortly."

"What are you doing?" hissed Penelope as she watched her precious volume walk away.

"If Neville thinks it is a sensitive document, so will the traitor," Marchford whispered in return.

Marchford greeted guests awhile longer and then strolled to the library, where Neville was sitting on the settee. He slapped the book closed when they entered.

"I need not tell you to keep that volume safe," warned Neville.

"No, you need not," agreed Marchford, extending his hand for the book.

Neville handed it over and stalked off.

"I do not wish my book to be used in such a manner," said Penelope when they were alone.

"The demands of King and country, my dear." The room was well lit by several lanterns blazing and Marchford quickly checked them. "I want this room as bright as the noonday sun."

"The book represents years of work," Penelope tried to explain.

"Listing the worth of men to be judged and sold to enterprising young women? I could suggest that I would be doing mankind a service by removing this text from your possession."

Penelope gasped. "You would not be so cruel!"

"At this moment, I only wish to use the book to catch a spy. You may have it when the mission is complete." Marchford placed the book carefully on the table. He stepped back to the curtains, surveyed his perspective of the book, and appeared satisfied.

"Can you assure me that it will be safely returned?" Penelope resisted the urge to snatch the book from the table.

"No," replied Marchford, for he was an honest man. "But you shall have the supreme comfort of knowing that your precious object was used in the service of your country to protect England from foreign invaders. What more could anyone ask?"

"But—"

"Enough. I do not wish to displease you, but I must use this. I will be here, waiting for the spy. When it is taken, I will grab him. It is very simple. But you must leave, and now. The trap is about to be set."

"Your Grace?" called the butler. "You are needed at the bonfire, sir."

"I'm on my way," called Marchford. He opened the door to the library. "Go!" he hissed.

Penelope folded her arms across her chest and shook her head.

Marchford's valet walked in and the men quickly exchanged coats. Marchford handed him the mask and the valet walked off.

"Go now," mouthed Marchford.

But Penelope retreated out of reach and Marchford had no choice but to swing the door shut, with her still inside. He motioned for her to leave and ducked behind the drapes, between the wall and the curtain. Penelope followed.

"Leave!" he whispered in an irritated tone.

"I'm going to stay with my book," she whispered back.

"There's no room."

"I am small enough." She pressed herself against him behind the curtain. She was immediately hit with a wave of heat.

"Penelope," he growled in a whisper. "You need to leave. Now!"

"As long as my book is here, I am here."

"You are compromising an investigation."

"You are compromising the work of many years."

"If you get any closer," he hissed in her ear, "I will be compromising you!"

Another wave of heat flashed through her. If he was attempting to get her to leave, this was not the best tactic. She put her hands on his chest in order to move closer. He glared down at her in a decidedly unfriendly manner. He may have been unhappy, but there was nothing he could do about it. He needed to remain still and silent in order to lure in the thief. If the spy would even take the bait.

Consigning himself to wait, he leaned against the wall. She leaned against him. He sighed and put his arms around her. It felt good. It felt better than good. Utterly inappropriate thoughts flashed through her head.

Here she was, concealed with one of the greatest catches in all of marital history. The opportunities were endless. True, he didn't want her here. And true, she knew he had many more tempting offers if he wished for a discreet liaison. But she was here now, and he was, if not hers for the taking, at least in a position to do very little to fight off her advances.

She raised her head off of his chest, unsure of when she had actually laid it on him. She must stop these thoughts. First of all, she was a respectable lady, and in a position where she needed to keep that respectability intact. She was not a married woman with deep societal ties. She could not bandy about her reputation without a care. Her social status, her credibility, her very living as a companion all depended on her keeping her reputation untarnished. She had not the face nor the fortune for anything else.

"You should go," Marchford whispered again, but he held her tighter instead.

She struggled against the urge to melt into him. She must focus her attention on something else. "I have some marital prospects to review with you," she whispered. The library was large and the curtained window was far from the door, so that no one could hear them whisper.

"Now?" His face was incredulous.

"I have your attention." And she needed to get her mind off of his physique, which was flawless by her estimation. "First of all, there is Miss Maria Cornwall."

"No."

"But I have not even begun to tell you her finer qualities," protested Penelope.

"I am sure they are lovely indeed, but I went to school with her brothers. Twins. Would rather jump in the Thames than have those hellions for brothers-in-law. I would go broke just paying their debts."

"Fine. There is Lady Evangeline, daughter of the Earl of Braxton."

"No."

"I put a good deal of thought into these choices and even wrote up short descriptions of each. The least you could do is listen to the entire presentation. Besides, what could be wrong with Lady Evangeline?"

"Nothing is wrong with her. Lovely girl. Now her mother on the other hand is a horror and currently not on speaking terms with my grandmother, who despises her. Evangeline will not do."

"I don't suppose you would consider Miss Crawley. She is an attractive girl."

"And vicious. I do not wish to marry anyone who scares me."

"Coward," accused Penelope.

"Quite so."

They were quiet for a moment, and Penelope found she was enjoying his masculine scent. It was quite intoxicating. She struggled against doing something horribly embarrassing and searched for some topic of conversation to focus her mind on something other than the strong man before her.

"How did you get into this business anyway?" she whispered. She looked up and realized he was peeking out of a hole in the drapes he had previously made. Clever.

"Since my half brother was intended to be the next duke, my job as the younger brother from a second marriage was to find respectable work as far away from home as possible. Besides, my grandmother complained I made her teeth grind."

"You still do make her teeth grind."

"She would say I am too much like my mother, a more heinous insult she could not imagine."

"Naughty boy."

"Very true."

"So how did you end up in Cadiz? It is far away and under a constant state of war with the French and their allies."

"Precisely so. It was the perfect place for me. I met the diplomat through the normal channels. There is a work program for second sons of the aristocracy. We must be farmed out to do something respectable, such as politics, military, or the clergy. We must stay out of the way and marry rich so as not to put too many demands on our elder brothers who will inherit."

"I wonder that younger sons are not simply drowned at birth," commented Penelope.

"It would be efficient, and I grant you there may be some who would agree with you, but you are forgetting the primary reason for being a second son."

"And what would that be?"

"Why to serve as a spare to inherit in case the elder sibling dies or is not able to spawn young."

"And that is what happened to you."

Marchford leaned the back of his head against the wall and looked up at nothing. "I was angry at Fredrick for dying. I know that cannot make sense since it was hardly his fault."

"I understand. I was mad at everyone when my parents died. Them. God. My sisters. The doctor."

Marchford nodded. "I was so displeased, I returned to Cadiz. Of course I did have work to do there. But also, I wanted to avoid returning and taking the title that belonged to my brother. Fredrick was…"

He paused for a long time. The minutes dragged on and Penelope listened to the clock tick away the seconds. It was eternity but she would not interrupt his story for the world. He never spoke of Fredrick. Never.

"I begged him not to die." Marchford's voice was flat. "But he was always doing things his own way. He was a remarkably strong man for having such a weak body. It was the fever early in life, you understand; he never fully recovered. Maybe because his body was weak he learned to be strong inside. I wish you could have met him."

"I would have liked that." Despite hearing little from him about his brother, Penelope knew Marchford looked up to him and protected him. His wishing her to meet him was an honor. Truly.

Marchford took a deep breath as if to clear away the painful memories. "It was just me and my grand-mother then. She could not look at me without grinding what was left of her teeth. It was a hard time for all of us. First my father and then my brother had acted as a buffer between us, but then it was just too painful to be together."

"So you continue to work for the Foreign Office."

"Yes. I catch spies. It is an odd line of work for a duke, I grant you, but I still wish to protect my country."

"I am sure your father would have been proud of you."

"I would like to think so." Marchford's tone was somber.

"How old were you when he passed away?"

"I was ten. He died in a fire at his hunting box."

"I am so sorry for your loss." Penelope meant it. She could see the pain on his face, even after so many years. She searched for something to get his mind off the painful subject.

"So tell me, since you have rejected my leading candidates to be your wife, what exactly are you looking for in a partner?"

"I have already told you the qualifications."

"Tell me again." Penelope's voice sounded husky, even to herself.

Marchford looked up at the ceiling in thought. "She needs to come from a good family, one that has no members who are currently at war with my grandmother."

"That rules out half of the families in England."

"Second, she must have a brain in her head."

"That rules out the other half," muttered Penelope.

"And third, as to appearance…" He glanced down at her, his arms still around her. "I thought I asked you to cover your cleavage."

"Your grandmother strikes again."

"Then I will be bold and say I would wish for a lady whose décolletage resembled yours in form, shape, and plumpness."

"Your Grace!" Heat scorched up the back of her neck.

"I am holding my hands around you to try to avoid touching them."

"You are jesting with me."

"I most certainly am not. I am only human. And a male human at that. I have had to avoid all feminine company lest I fall prey to a scheming female. I cannot tell you how badly I wish to touch you, Penelope."

"You should not say such things." Mostly because it made her want to loosen her stays and let him have his way.

"I did ask you not to be here. I cannot take this torture much longer. You smell too nice."

"I am sorry. You smell nice too."

"It would be inappropriate to say or do any more since you are in the employment of my grandmother."

"I may be resigning soon if we can raise enough capital through our efforts as Madame X."

"Visit me when you are no longer in her employment."

"What would you do if I was no longer your grandmother's companion?" She shifted closer.

Marchford gazed down at her, his eyes black in the dim light. "I might do this." He ran a finger along her skin at the edge of her bodice. She sucked in air. No one had ever touched her like that. No one had ever wanted to touch her like that.

"Or I might do this." He leaned down and kissed her chastely on the lips.

"Could you review that?" asked Penelope, breathless. "I want to make certain I understand."

Marchford kissed her again, real and soft and wet. It was her first kiss and it sent tingles clear down her spine to her toes and then up to a place she hardly knew existed.

"My goodness," she whispered when their lips finally parted. "I can see how inappropriate that would be."

"You see why I could not do anything like that."

"Yes, quite so. My, it is hot here. Why is this thief taking so long?"

"Could be any time or not at all."

Outside the door, a commotion could be heard.

"What is it?" whispered Penelope.

But Marchford didn't respond. He was listening intently.

The commotion grew louder until a voice shouted through the hall, "Fire! Fire in the castle!"

Thirty-five

"HELLO!" SAID HARRIET, HAPPIER TO HEAR THORNTON than she ought to be. She was with the Duc d'Argon, though she would rather be with another. She pushed such thoughts aside. "I am glad there are so many people who take an interest in chemistry. It is not a common interest."

"Nay, I would think not," said Thornton softly. His mask was black and in his dark cloak he was nearly invisible even in the pale moonlight. "Ye seem to have strayed from the bonfire. I should encourage ye to walk back. 'Tis a night of mischief, this Midsummer's Eve."

"I shall escort Miss Redgrave," said d'Argon.

"Let us all walk back together," said Harriet, linking arms between Thornton and d'Argon. "Tell me, Lord Thornton, what kind of mischief is afoot on Midsummer's Eve?"

"They say 'tis time for the fair folk to walk freely. Who knows what confusion they may give us for their own amusements."

"How quaint are your provincial customs, Lord Thornton," said d'Argon with stiff politeness.

"I think it would be lovely to meet a faerie," sighed Harriet.

"I dinna ken ye were a believer in the fair folk," said Thornton.

"I am not, so alas I doubt I shall ever see one." She laughed at her own circular logic. None of the gentlemen joined her. They were too stiff, both of them.

"Too much of this nonsense, it atrophies the senses," said d'Argon with more disdain than she had heard from him before.

"I suddenly remember that Miss Crawley had inquired into yer whereabouts," said Thornton carelessly.

Even in the dim light, she could see d'Argon flinch. She could not fathom why, except that if Miss Crawley was looking for her, she would flinch too.

"I would not even know how to recognize her," said d'Argon. "Let us return to the fire."

"I shall escort Miss Redgrave," said Thornton with a ring of authority she rarely heard.

The Duc d'Argon had been dismissed, and he could do nothing now but demand a duel or leave the field. "It has been a pleasure," he said, though his tone told another story. He bowed and walked away into the night.

"I may be slow when it comes to society," said Harriet, "but I believe you were actually trying to get rid of d'Argon."

Thornton shrugged. "Never belittle the fair folk. They have a way of getting a laugh at yer expense."

"So you are a believer?"

"On Midsummer's Eve, it would be unwise not to be."

"Then I shall believe as well. Shall we return to the dancing?"

Thornton glared in the direction d'Argon had gone. "Nay, nay, let us tarry here a while longer." Thornton removed his mask and rubbed his eyes.

"Are you feeling well?" asked Harriet. She was trying to convince herself it would be better to walk away from Thornton—goodness only knew what people would say if they saw them together. But she could not leave him unwell.

Thornton nodded his head. "I am well, though perhaps a wee bit tired."

"Perhaps you should go back to the house. I also have been tired of late."

Harriet began to walk toward the courtyard, but Thornton held her arm.

"I do not wish anyone to see us and begin more talk. Let us go back to the house by the back way." Thornton stood tall, his eyes glittering in the soft moonlight.

Harriet paused. She should not go with him. It was one of those easy questions to be honest. Should an unmarried lady go unescorted with a Scottish earl into the dark of night on Midsummer's Night Eve? No. Of course not.

Was she going to go with him?

Of course she was.

"I am an idiot," she muttered and linked arms with him so he could lead the way. "If I end up in a bog, I deserve no less."

"No bogs on this route."

It was hardly a reassurance. They walked a ways into the dark, Harriet's eyes adjusting to the pale light of the moon. Thornton walked steadily on, and although he did not waver, she hoped he was not so overcome by fatigue so as to get them lost.

Suddenly things around them began to look familiar. "I know where we are." She stopped and turned around in a circle. "We are in the faerie glen."

Thornton muttered under his breath something that did not sound like a young maiden should hear. "Shoud'na have come this way. Must have rocks in my head. I confess I was mainly thinking o' separating ye from d'Argon."

"Were you? Why?"

Lord Thornton cast her a look so desirous, so full of lust, even she could not pretend not to understand his meaning. "We should leave." He turned to go.

"No." Her heart pounded. Now it was her turn to try to keep him for herself. It was so wrong, but she could not say good-bye. "Let us tarry a little. Maybe we shall see a faerie." Harriet began to look about, as if to glimpse something otherworldly, yet her focus was entirely on the man before her.

"Nothing good can come from straying into a faerie glen on Midsummer's Eve. Mark my words." His words were soft, yet the warning stung.

"Whatever could happen?" Harriet stepped closer, her breath coming in quick pants, her excitement and her tight gown conspiring against taking a deep breath.

Thornton stepped closer, his hands trembling at his sides. "We must leave this place."

"If this is an enchantment, I do not wish to break it," whispered Harriet.

"What fey creature are ye that ye have so bewitched

me?" With one stride he was before her and pulled her into his arms. His kiss was urgent, demanding, passionate, unlike anything they had yet shared. Despite the alarm bells ringing in her head, she melted into him and kissed him in return.

He finally broke the kiss and immediately let her go, stepping back as if a mere touch would burn him. "I am sorry."

"No, you are not." Harriet's only regret at the moment was that he stopped. Later… later would come later.

"Ye're right. I'm not. More's the pity."

"Duncan, I have been thinking," which was a gross falsehood since she had stopped thinking the moment he greeted her this evening. "I understand you do not wish to marry someone for money and I need to return home. Thus, soon we shall be apart."

"Aye. If I could stop thinking about it, maybe I could sleep," mumbled Thornton.

"If we look at this logically," began Harriet, which was another falsehood since all logical faculties were silent and all she had left was pounding desire, "since we obviously have some attraction for each other and we cannot actually marry perhaps you might wish to… to…" Her courage chose that moment to give out.

"To what?" He gave her his full attention.

"I do not know what I am about." Harriet began to pace around the faerie circle. "When I am with you, I want to do more experimenting of the kind we did in the stables. When I remember we shall not be together, I wish to avoid romance forever and live for my work."

"My advice to you at present would be highly suspect."

"What advice would that be?"

"I want you. I want you here and now." Duncan's voice was raw and it struck within her a chord so deep it vibrated through her soul.

"Duncan…" She took a step toward him and stopped.

"We should leave this faerie circle," said Duncan without a trace of humor. "We may be truly bewitched."

In the light of day, Harriet would have dismissed the notion, but under the pale moonlight she felt a desire, a *need* to be close to him. "What can we do?"

"Submit to temptation or…"

"Or?"

"I dinna ken. I be stuck on submitting to temptation."

This time it was Harriet who closed the gap and kissed him with all the power of the raging emotions within her.

"This gown…" Duncan traced a finger along the edge of her exposed bosom.

"It belongs to Penelope."

"I will buy it from her. It will be yours forever. Ye should always wear such things. But only for me." He removed his cloak and spread it over a patch of moss. He pulled her down beside him and nestled his face into her cleavage, kissing her along the line of the gown. It did not take much to release her from the tight bodice.

The combination of the cool night air and Duncan's warm mouth made her tremble with anticipation. This time he would not escape untouched. She reached for his breeches and he did not stop her. Somewhere in the back of her mind, she knew there was a price to pay for this action. She would be ruined. Blame it on faerie dust, but when his hand slid up her thigh, she could not bring herself to care.

He was hers tonight. They would soon be parted. This was her last chance, her only chance to be with the man she loved.

She loved him. The realization slammed into her, painful and giddy.

He covered her and she understood that this was what she had been waiting for her whole life. She belonged to him. She needed him. With a flash of pain, she was joined with him.

"Have I hurt ye?" he asked, and she realized she must have winced.

"Was that it?" She must confess the ending was a bit anticlimactic.

"Nay, there is more, if ye wish."

"Oh, yes, lots of wishing here."

He began to kiss her again, and she pulled up his shirt until she could feel his smooth skin beneath her fingers. Somehow feeling his skin close to her made it better. She needed him close. She pulled him closer and everything moved, him, her, something coiling within her. He moved back and she pulled him forward again. This time was better and the coiling deep within her rumbled and seemed to take over any rational thought. She struggled against the rising heat and pain and friction and irrationality even as she lunged into it.

A war was raging within her, even as the movement between them heightened. She fought against it and struggled to claim it, all the while wondering what she was trying to achieve, until even that thought was robbed from her and she hurtled toward something she feared might consume her and destroy her. She fought against it until she could no longer resist the pull and fell into the abyss.

Waves of pleasure coursed through her even as Thornton removed himself and spilled his seed beside her. He rolled next to her and draped his arm protectively over her. She snuggled closer, trembling with emotion and aftershocks of their joining. She would never be the same.

"I fear I may love you," she whispered.

He froze then slowly pulled her closer. "I wish I could blame it on the faeries, but I ken I cannot. I adore ye. I need ye." He paused and leaned his forehead against hers. "I love ye."

This was the price.

She had made a grave mistake, for the chemical bond forged by their love was permanent. They were forever bonded, forever united.

And forever apart.

Thirty-six

Both Marchford and Penelope turned to look out the window. A red haze of flame and smoke funneled from the castle above. Penelope's stomach sank. Maclachlan Castle was on fire.

"Thornton!" shouted Marchford. He did not take the time to go back out through the house. Instead, he opened the window and jumped out into the garden and ran for the path up the hill, with Penelope right behind.

Guests were running down, away from the fire. People were screaming, ladies were crying—it was a disturbing scene.

They ran until they were out of breath. Penelope's sides were screaming in pain, but she kept running up the hill. Gasping, she entered the castle gates, her lungs stinging with acrid smoke. People were running about, shouting, screaming. She stopped to try to make sense of the scene before her.

One of the outbuildings, which Penelope suspected Harriet was using as a workspace, was completely engulfed in flames, shooting blasts of fire fifty feet into the air. The flames had spread to the thatched roofs of the surrounding buildings, and the old wooden roof of the main keep was beginning to burn.

For one dreadful moment, she was paralyzed. Harriet. Thornton. Were they all right? What could possibly be done? Marchford! Where was he? She ran forward to find him. Smoke hurt her eyes, but she stumbled forward until she saw his silhouette against the orange flames. He was standing frozen before the blaze.

"Marchford?"

He was staring at the flames without expression.

"Marchford?" She touched his arm. "James? What do we do?"

Her questions seemed to revive him. He shook his head. "We cannot stop this. If anyone was in this building, they are gone."

"I am sure no one was in it," reassured Penelope, mostly to try to convince herself.

Marchford gave a quick nod. "We need to put out the blaze before it spreads to the house."

"Yes, of course. But how?"

"Water!" He pointed at the castle well. "Let us hope it still functions." He swept off some glasses from a table with his arm and stood on it. "Ladies and gentlemen. We have a situation that requires immediate action. If the ladies will calmly make their way down to Thornton Hall, the gentlemen and staff members can assist me. We must douse the flames to prevent this fire from spreading."

At his authoritative words, people stopped panicking and followed his directions. Penelope ran to the well and started turning the wheel to raise the bucket. The water was cold and pure and a welcome relief from the hot, acrid smoke billowing around her. Marchford brought another bucket, and she poured the water in it. Several men ran to help and they began to form a line.

"Keep going!" Marchford grabbed a bucket full of water and ran to the fire. He splashed it onto the base of the fire to no effect.

"This will never work," said Penelope as she grabbed another bucket.

"It must," said Marchford grimly. "Where is Thornton?"

❧

Thornton wrapped his arms around her. "I must ask ye something."

Harriet's attention was drawn by some strange noises. "What is that?" she asked absently.

"I ken yer desire to return to America, but I'd rather ye stay here. With me. I know I said I would never propose marriage to an heiress, but—"

"Wait. Do you hear that?" Harriet adjusted herself to be more decent and sat up. "It sounds like shouting."

"Harriet. What I am trying to say is—"

"Duncan, listen. I think something is wrong." Harriet stood up and was shocked by the orange haze and rising smoke she saw. "Fire!"

Thornton was up in a flash, dressed and running. "The castle!"

Harriet followed him up the hill to the fire. The monster grew before her eyes. When they reached the castle, the sight made her stomach drop. Smoke and flame billowed from the windows of her laboratory. It was all gone. Everything was gone. In desperation, she ran to the ancient kitchen, hoping that she could rescue her equipment. Someone grabbed her hand and yanked her back.

She smacked into Thornton's chest. She tried to pull free but he held her fast.

"I must get my equipment!" she shouted, even as a whoosh of heat blasted them.

Thornton spun her out of harm's way and half carried, half dragged her back as the laboratory burst into a fireball. The roof blazed and roared with flames in the whirling winds. Sparks flew to neighboring trees and higher.

"Thornton!" She pointed up to the roof of the keep. A little patch of fire burned and smoked.

"The horses!" Thornton shouted. "Get to the house and stay there!" He ran for the secret entrance and she followed. If he thought she would simply walk away, he was mad. Her projects were gone, but she could still be of help.

People were organizing against the blaze, with Marchford leading the charge. They were going to try to save the keep, but it might already be too late.

Harriet glanced again at the roof before ducking into the tunnel. The fire spread fast on the old brittle wood. They did not have much time. Thornton outpaced her, but she kept running through the dark. She tripped once and landed hard on her knee. She cursed as only a sailor's daughter could, got up, and continued to run.

She burst into the keep, which was lit with an awful

orange glow. Sparks and embers floated down from the wooden roof above. It was only a matter of time before the whole thing caved in. Grooms and stable hands joined them and began to run outside with the horses. The main doors were already ablaze; the only way out was the tunnel.

"Get them out of here!" yelled Thornton as he worked to open the stables.

The horses whinnied and shrieked, sensing danger. The freed horses ran around the stable keep, spooked and unsure where to go. They would need to be led to safety.

Harriet found the mare she had ridden before. The horse bucked in her stall, making Harriet jump out of the way. She approached the horse again, forcing herself to be calm and gentle.

"That's all right, everything is going to be all right," she crooned. She grabbed a bridle, slipped it over the horse's head, and buckled it in place. More embers were falling from the burning ceiling above. She did not have the time for a saddle. She climbed the stall planks and onto the horse's back, hiking up the skirts of her gown that was not in the least made for riding.

Horses were running through the stables with stable hands trying to chase them out. She held on tight and kicked her mount into action. A group of five horses was running in circles, led by a bay horse with wild eyes. If she could turn this horse, the rest would follow. She swung around in the opposite direction to head them off. She galloped past the stalls, keeping one eye on the horses and the other watching for Thornton. Where was he? She spotted him for an instant pulling a horse from a stall, before she had to turn her attention back to the horses.

She galloped toward the leader at an angle, blocking his path. The horse swung left and out of the tunnel, the other horses following it. Stable hands and grooms ran to the tunnel, leading multiple horses.

"Come, miss!" Shouted a groom. "The roof will no' hold much longer. Get out!" He ran past her leading several horses.

The stable had grown unbearably hot and was filled with smoke. She coughed and searched for Thornton. Almost all of the horses were out now. A burning ember fell on her head and she brushed it off quickly, slapping her hair to make sure it did not ignite.

She spied Thornton in one corner trying to lead a frightened mare out with a young colt. It was Lazarus, the baby who had just been born. She kicked her mount toward him, but the animal shied and shrieked, not wanting to go further into the burning room. She kicked the mount harder and got her moving again, galloping to Thornton.

"Duncan!" she screamed.

He turned, his face red with the heat. "Harriet! Get out o' here now!"

"You must come. The roof is about to fall!"

"Take the mare!" he shouted, thrusting the reins in her hands. "She winna leave her baby."

The colt was lying on the ground, bleating terribly.

"His leg was trampled in the confusion. Now go!" Thornton smacked her mount hard on the backside and her horse took off for the tunnel at a gallop. Harriet managed to look behind her to see Thornton lift the colt and put it on his shoulders before beginning for the tunnel.

Harriet galloped out of the burning stable, holding tight to the mare and dragging her along with them. She emerged into the cool night, taking a large breath of air. The grooms were trying to collect as many horses as possible, but many had run into the hills. Around the castle, servants and guests alike were beating out fire from bushes and shrubs with large sacks. Lines had been formed with buckets of water from the old well to douse the burning outbuildings.

The fire completely engulfed the roof of the keep, sending flames shooting into the night sky. Never had she seen anything so terrifying in her life. With a large crash, the roof fell in, sending a fiery wave out of the tunnel. Everyone stopped.

Where was Thornton?

Did he get out? She asked a stable lad but he could only stare at the destruction in mute horror. Flames leaped into the air, fueled by the hay and stables. Still there was no Thornton.

Where was he? She watched the entrance to the tunnel, waiting, willing.

"Lord, please let him get out," she whispered. "Please don't let him die."

She dismounted slowly, handing the reins to one of the stable hands. Thick black smoke was gushing out of the tunnel. She walked toward it then ran. He was in there, somewhere, and she was going to find him. She ran to the tunnel entrance, putting up her hands against the hot stinging smoke. Suddenly someone grabbed her arm and yanked her back.

"Let me go!" She whirled around to face…

"Duncan!" His face was so black with soot she could barely recognize him. But the colt was still on his shoulders. She could not speak words but embraced him, colt and all.

He coughed and set the colt down. Little Lazarus stood on three legs and leaned against him, shaking. She knew how the colt felt; she was shaking too.

"I am so sorry." The flames around the castle had mostly been contained, but within the keep, there was nothing to do but let it burn itself out. All was lost.

Thornton squinted at the billowing smoke and shook his head. He handed the colt to a groom with hoarse instructions to care for the leg. He walked to the front of the castle and she followed. What else could she do? She would follow him anywhere.

The guests had gathered around the front. Many had helped to put out the flames, leaving them sweaty and disheveled, without coats or cravats. Sensing the worst was over, some had wandered back to the castle to witness the carnage.

"Thornton!" greeted Marchford, who was standing in shirtsleeves, holding a sack for beating out flames. Penelope, water bucket in hand, stood at his side. "Good to see you, old chap. The fire has been contained, but we could not save the keep."

"Aye," said Thornton in a low voice. "Thank ye, all o' ye for yer help tonight. The fire may have spread even to Thornton Hall without yer help. I canna say how the bonfire got out of control, but because of yer assistance, I know how the fire ended."

"Forgive me, Lord Thornton," said Miss Crawley, looking radiant in a spotless lavender gown. "But

I know exactly who started this fire. It was not the bonfire at all. You can see it is still contained."

All eyes turned to the prepared bonfire. It indeed appeared contained. The worst of the damage was elsewhere, not around the bonfire.

"How did it start?" asked someone in the crowd.

"There she is!" accused Miss Crawley, pointing at Harriet. "It was Miss Redgrave whose unholy experiments have been putting us all at risk. This fire was no accident. It started in her secret laboratory!"

"That is untrue!" exclaimed Harriet. "I mean, I have been doing experiments here, but none tonight."

"I will apologize for her actions, *mes amis*," said the Duc d'Argon. "I was to announce tonight that she has made me happy by consenting to be my wife, but now all I can do is to apologize for the harm she has done and to assure you all that I will ensure that her hobbies will in no way endanger anyone again."

Thornton turned to her, his eyes large and filled with betrayal. Something in Harriet's heart snapped. She put her hand to her chest. It hurt—it actually physically hurt. Surrounding her were eyes of accusation. Thornton had always protected her, always shielded her from the derision of people's disdain. Tonight, he slowly walked away.

"No!" called Harriet. "No, I did not cause this!"

Harriet followed Thornton with her eyes until he disappeared into the darkness. How could d'Argon believe such horrible things about her? And why did he think they were engaged?

"I did not do this! And I have not given you my answer," she insisted to d'Argon, but he was not listening. Instead, he was apologizing again, as if he was her parent and she had been a naughty girl. She wanted to scream.

People began to talk, glancing at her sideways and hushing their voices so she could not hear.

Miss Crawley had no such compunction. "I do not know why he would want to marry her," she declared. "Now that all her money is gone."

"What is this?" the duc d'Argon dropped a conversation he was having and immediately questioned Harriet.

"I thought you had heard about the money," said Harriet.

"No, no, indeed I had not."

"But you said what was important was the work, the science."

The duc d'Argon stuttered for a moment. "Yes, yes, of course."

"Come now, my dear friends. We need to return to the house." Marchford raised his hands to usher the guests back down to the Hall. "Thornton has graciously offered to put out a nourishing wine punch which will be good for the soul." Marchford and Penelope led the way down the hill.

Harriet watched as the guests, including d'Argon, turned their backs on her and left. Her knees shook and she fought against falling to the ground. She had lost everything. Everything.

She tried to take a deep breath but coughed on the smoke. She considered having a nervous attack or collapsing from grief, but instead, she walked back to her former laboratory, careful to stay out of the way of the servants attending what was left of the blaze.

The stone building was nothing more than a charred husk, but she inspected it inside and out. Was it possible something she was working on had gone awry? Or perhaps someone had tampered, intentionally or accidentally, with her equipment?

She inspected more, trying to determine the cause of the fire, but nothing inside appeared to be the culprit. Instead, she found a line of scorch marks on the outside wall, as if someone had poured lamp oil down the wall. This was no accident.

This fire was intentionally set.

Thirty-seven

PENELOPE WALKED BACK DOWN TO THE HOUSE WITH Marchford, leading people away from the scene to a safer area. The worst of the fire was over. Now they needed to soothe the nerves of the frightened guests.

"See to the guests," said Marchford. "I will check on the book."

The book! In all the excitement she had forgotten. She wanted to run to the library herself, but she doubted her legs would carry her.

In the entryway of the house, she quickly arranged for wine punch to be available to take the sting out of the sad night. The guests began to request hot water to bathe and other amenities, which kept the house busy and led to a bit of confusion.

The duchess, Langley, Sir Antony, and Lady Thornton emerged from their intense game of whist, so focused they had not heard the warning cries. They were immediately concerned and were quickly informed of the unfortunate events.

Last to arrive was Harriet. A more bedraggled

creature one could not imagine. Her dress was ripped and stained, her face covered with soot.

"Come with me." Penelope took Harriet's hand and led her through the glaring crowd and up to her bedroom. "You need sleep."

"We need to speak," whispered Harriet.

Penelope nodded and ushered her up to her room. Whatever she wanted to talk about, it would certainly not be for the ears of the assembly.

"The fire was intentionally set," said Harriet when they were alone in her room. "This was no accident."

"How do you know?" asked Penelope.

"Scorch marks on the outside of the building, leading up to where the roof was."

"But could that not happen during the fire?"

"Forgive me, but I have had my share of setting minor fires, accidentally of course, and I have some experience in noting the patterns. This fire did not begin in my laboratory. It was intentionally set from outside. What I cannot understand is why. Who would do such a thing?"

"I think I know why," said Penelope. "But who remains the question."

"Why?"

"I shall call for some water for you," said Penelope, standing to leave and attempting to divert Harriet's attention. "Please get some rest." She needed to tell Marchford this news.

Harriet caught her hand. "Please tell me why. I have a sense I am caught up in some larger game, and since someone seems to have taken pains to implicate me, I want to know what is amiss."

Penelope sighed. It was only fair. "You know Marchford has been holding meetings to discuss strategy for the war. He suspects a spy or traitor among us. He attempted to set a trap tonight. I would conjecture that the fire was a diversion."

Harriet took a moment, digesting the new development. "How do we catch this spy?" She sat straight, her eyes clear and bright. She may have appeared ragged, but she was far from defeated.

"Let me talk to Marchford and see what our next move will be."

Harriet stood. "I will come too."

"No, please stay here. Lock the door. I will let you know what he says."

"Promise me." Harriet once again took her hand in her steady grip. "I do not know why I was involved in this, but it has done more damage than you can know and to someone…" She paused and swallowed back emotion. "To someone very special."

"Thornton." Penelope did not have to guess.

"Yes. I cannot stand idly by and see him hurt. I want to find whoever did this." Harriet's eyes burned with an intensity that made Penelope take a step back.

"I will let you know. But rest now. You will need your strength."

❧

Penelope found Marchford in the library. He had washed the soot from his hands and face and put on his coat, but when she walked nearer, he still held the telltale aroma of smoke. He acknowledged her with a brief nod, his face gray.

"Is the book gone?" she asked, but she already knew the answer.

Marchford gave another short nod. "I have searched the place looking for clues. I have found none. I do apologize about the book."

"I expected it. I believe the fire was set purposefully as a diversion." Nothing else could be said about her book. It was gone.

Marchford gave her his full attention. "Continue."

"I spoke with Miss Redgrave who said she found scorch marks on the outside of the wall of the building. She says this means the fire was set from outside. Someone set it intentionally."

Marchford frowned. "It is as I suspected."

"You do not believe it was caused by one of Miss Redgrave's unholy experiments?" Penelope had expected more of a fight on this point.

Marchford shook his head. "Too coincidental. The castle bursts into flame at the same time I attempt to catch the spy—this was no accident. No, it was the spy. But who?"

"Who knew you would be hiding in here? Why would the thief not just take the book, thinking you were outside?"

"Must have been suspicious. No one but you knew I was here."

"Did Lord Thornton know you had set a trap?"

"Yes, but he would not have told anyone."

"Forgive me, you are not going to like what I have to say, but have you considered the possibility that Thornton himself might be responsible?"

"Thornton a French spy? Don't be absurd." He waved a hand at her to dismiss the comment.

Penelope sat across from him, her back straight, her hands folded neatly over her soiled dress. It was time to give bad news, and she found it was best to get it over with quickly. "Here are the facts. When we searched for the thief of the pearls, Thornton was not accounted for outside. He has been getting up early for some unknown reason. I often see him coming back into the house, his boots muddy, when I have just come down for breakfast, and I am one of the first to rise. Tonight, he was the only one who knew you were in the study, waiting."

"Stop." Marchford's voice was gruff. "Thornton is a friend and one I would trust with my life. Besides, he would hardly set his own castle ablaze with all his livestock inside."

"I do not know the particulars regarding what was in the keep, but maybe there was a reason he wanted it destroyed. And you cannot deny that his financial situation would make him an easy target."

"A target yes, but easy, never."

Penelope raised her hands to surrender. "Just think about it. I sincerely hope it is a false accusation, but we need to look at all the information we have."

"Enough. Thornton is a good man." But the seed of doubt had been planted.

❧

By morning, Thornton felt like hell. Truth was he had felt that way since the fire. His throat burned, his head pounded. He spent most of the night running after his horses and trying to find neighbors and townspeople willing to house them. He could not even begin to think of the financial impact this was going to have. The keep was nothing more than a burned shell. All his hard work, all his money—it was all gone. Gone. Just like Harriet was gone.

How could she have seduced him all while she was engaged to d'Argon? She was false. And everything he thought he knew about her was false too. He pushed away the thought that perhaps he had been the one to seduce her. Or perhaps they seduced each other. Or maybe it was the faeries at work. In any event, she was engaged to another, to that bastard d'Argon.

Thornton dragged himself back to the house in the gray light of morning. He wanted to toss out every houseguest, turn the keys over to Crawley, and curl up in some hole. Instead, he stumbled up the stairs to his room and collapsed on his bed.

"It was not her, you know." Marchford walked into his room and sat down across from him. Marchford handed him a glass of cold water. It felt good.

"What do ye mean?"

"Miss Redgrave. It was not she who set the fire."

Something inside him burned at the sound of her name. "How would ye know?"

"The fire was started as a diversion to get me out of the room and get the book we set as bait."

"The spy! Did ye catch him?"

"No. I put out a fire. The book was left and we lost it."

"Ye lost it?"

"Stolen. By the person who set the fire."

"I know it was not Miss Redgrave who started the fire," said Thornton. He did not say he knew it because he had been with her the whole time. "She is getting married now, so it hardly matters what I think."

"I doubt it."

Thornton rubbed his temples. "You doubt what?"

"I doubt she will marry d'Argon. First, she declared that she had never agreed to any such union, and then, when he discovered that her fortune is lost, he disappeared."

"Wait, what?" Thornton's world was spinning. Harriet had lost her money? The duc was gone?

"Yes," said Marchford slowly, as if to help Thornton's tired brain understand. "Apparently, if the rumors are to be believed, Miss Redgrave's fortune has been lost. She is poverty stricken, or at least that is the gossip over eggs this morning. Langley denies it, of course, but my grandmother and Miss Rose are strangely quiet on the subject, adding fuel to the rumor. The duc has not been seen since last night."

"Gone," murmured Thornton.

"That's not all that is gone," said Harriet, standing in the open doorway.

The men turned to her and Thornton attempted to struggle to his feet. So many emotions pulsed through him at the sight of her he could not discern one from the other. All he knew was she made his head hurt and his knees weak.

"Please do not get up," Harriet said to Thornton.

"Forgive me for the intrusion," said Penelope, who appeared at her side. "But we have been looking for you both. This morning several ladies were complaining of missing jewelry."

"They blamed me," said Harriet with a smile that was not at all amused.

Marchford frowned. "I received some complaints of missing watch fobs and misplaced snuff cases. I had thought in the confusion of last night some articles may have been misplaced. Perhaps it is more."

"It appears our French friend has chosen to take leave just as a thief has struck," commented Thornton.

"Too bad d'Argon has got away from us," said Marchford.

"Let us go after him," said Thornton, managing to stand. He splashed water on his hands and face.

"In all this wilderness?" asked Marchford. "He is long gone by now."

Thornton shook his head. "This is my land, my people. It may not mean much to some, but he would be hard pressed to go anywhere without my people knowing."

"Perhaps, but I have not found your people forthcoming when it comes to information."

Thornton had to smile. "Forgive me, but to many, ye will always be naught but a *Sassenach*. They will not tell ye, but they will tell me."

Marchford lifted an eyebrow. "Lead on, my friend. Lead on!"

"We shall come too," demanded Harriet.

"No!" said Thornton and Marchford together.

"It is my reputation this traitor has attacked," argued Harriet. "I am being blamed for everything from petty theft to arson. If the crops fail, I should not be surprised if I was burned at the stake as a witch."

"I will clear yer reputation, Miss Redgrave. I owe

ye that much at least," said Thornton. With a chill, he realized he would do anything for her. Anything.

The men bowed to the ladies and quit the room.

"I suppose we shall have to wait for them to return," sighed Penelope.

But Harriet shook her head. "I have no intention of letting him run off into goodness only knows what without me."

"They shall not take us, so how can we follow them?"

Harriet smiled. "I'm an American. I can track."

Thirty-eight

THE FRENCHMAN HAD COVERED HIS TRACKS WELL. HE bribed the locals, threatened townsfolk, and even cut across country, which, considering his genteel upbringing, showed an athleticism Thornton would not have thought possible. At one point, the Frenchman attempted to steal one of Thornton's horses. The crofter described with some detail the number of times d'Argon had attempted to ride bareback and was thrown from the horse. Eventually, he had taken the crofter's packhorse at the point of a pistol, which was not an animal known for speed.

"He must be getting desperate to go to such measures," commented Marchford as they remounted to continue the search.

"He does not believe anyone will follow him," returned Thornton.

"It is comforting to be so underestimated."

They continued down the road until they came to the next township. It was small, but there was a lodging house.

"I warrant he would be tired from riding on that pack mule," said Thornton.

"I would think so."

Inquiries within the inn brought wide eyes and quick shakes of the head. These were people unknown to Thornton; they had no loyalty to him. He switched tactics and asked the questions again in Gaelic. This time the answers were forthcoming.

"And what language are you speaking?" asked Marchford, as they stepped out of the common room.

"Gaelic."

"How was it I never knew you spoke such a tongue?"

"My mother wished us to be English."

"But still, I should have known. You have depths, man, that I have yet to fathom."

"I wish ye would no' fathom my depths if ye please."

Marchford smiled. "What did the good inn-keeper say?"

"He reported an irate Frenchman is upstairs, first door on the right. Our man has threatened rather unspeakable harm to the innkeeper's daughter if he ever revealed his presence."

"I believe it is time to pay a social call," said Marchford, straightening his jacket.

"If that is a polite euphemism for drowning him in the loch, then count me in. Do ye believe him to be yer spy?"

Marchford shrugged. "I would not have thought the aristocracy to be in league with Napoleon, but anything is possible. It would be rather convenient too, so let us hope."

After some discussion, the innkeeper knocked on

d'Argon's door and said he had brought a wine punch. At Marchford's direction, the innkeeper scuttled back down the stairs, leaving Marchford and Thornton to face the duc.

The door unlocked and opened a crack. Both Marchford and Thornton put their shoulders to it and banged the door open, sprawling the Frenchman to the floor, a pistol in his hand. Thornton jumped in, again knocking d'Argon to the floor as he tried to rise and retrieve the pistol. Marchford walked in, pocketed the pistol, and shut the door behind him.

"My dear duc d'Argon," said Marchford in a mild tone. "What an unusual place to find you. We have had such an adventure following your trail."

"What do you want?" The Frenchman stood tall, his hand on the back of a chair.

Thornton walked over to his trunk and dumped it onto the floor.

"What are you doing?"

"Merely helping you pack for your journey," said Marchford. "You are going on a journey, are you not?"

"I am the Duc d'Argon. I demand you stop this insult at once!"

Thornton rifled through the trunk, caring not how he handled the man's belongings. If he was rough, d'Argon should be grateful Thornton did not have his hands on him.

"Sit down, d'Argon," ordered Marchford. "You are in no position to demand anything."

Finding nothing, Thornton moved to the room, tugging the blankets off the bed, then the sheets, looking for the stolen items. If they couldn't find them, they would have some explaining to do.

"Stop this immediately or I will call for the magistrate!" yelled the chevalier.

"Be my guest," said Thornton, picking up the mattress itself and searching through and under it.

"My dear d'Argon, I would be interested to know why you left in such haste?" asked Marchford.

"Am I your prisoner? I owe no answers to you!"

"Perhaps, but to Miss Redgrave you most certainly do. Did you not woo her and declare your intent to marry her?" asked Marchford.

"No, I never intended marriage," hedged the duc.

"My memory can be faulty, but I believe it was just last night that you declared to all the company that you were engaged to Miss Redgrave," drawled Marchford.

"It was a mistake," stated d'Argon.

"The only mistake," said Thornton, jumping into the conversation, "is that when ye discovered her money was gone, ye pinched what ye could and stole away in the night, like the snake and coward that ye are."

"I am insulted. I demand satisfaction!" cried d'Argon.

Thornton crossed the room in two large steps and struck the surprised man on the jaw, knocking him to the ground. "Consider yerself satisfied."

The duc put his hand to his jaw and said nothing, standing up slowly.

"Gentlemen, such display is unseemly," said Marchford with an aloof tone. "*Monsieur*, we have come for the pearls and other items."

"What pearls?"

"The pearls ye stole, ye rat," said Thornton, moving on to the wardrobe. "And if ye want satisfaction for that I'll be happy to oblige ye."

Marchford raised an eyebrow at Thornton. "I am seeing you in an entirely new light, my friend. I do not believe I have ever seen you so angry in the twenty years we have been friends."

In true caveman fashion, Thornton grunted in reply.

"Now d'Argon," said Marchford. "I suggest you tell us everything you know before my friend, who has apparently regressed into some sort of primitive man, turns from tearing apart the room to tearing apart you."

"I know nothing about no pearls," said the duc.

"Careful, your accent is slipping," cautioned Marchford. "Time for a true confession. Remember, Thornton is one of those Highlanders. Oh, he looks domesticated from the outside, but I am fast learning what passions course through his blood."

"If he wanted the chit, he should have made an offer."

"I would advise caution," said Marchford.

"No, he is right," admitted Thornton. "If I had proposed to Miss Redgrave, there may not have been an opportunity for a fortune hunter like him to prey on her good nature."

"Good nature?" d'Argon snorted and Marchford had to step in to prevent Thornton from ill-advised violence.

"Where are they? Where are the jewels?" demanded Thornton.

"I have taken nothing. I demand you leave. I will be calling the magistrate to make you answer for your crimes." The duc lunged for the door, opened it, and called for the landlord to rouse the magistrate before Marchford dragged him back into the room and shut the door.

"We are not done with our visit," said Marchford mildly. "Though I confess we may overstay our welcome if need be."

"You have damaged my property and accosted my person. You will answer for this!" challenged d'Argon.

"You have abandoned your fiancée," accused Marchford.

"I debate that term. If she thought that, then she was confused."

"You are a liar and a thief!" Thornton experienced an odd new feeling. He was out of control. He wanted to rip this man limb from limb. He had never experienced anything like it before. He was always the one pulling his friends back from the brink of disaster, keeping them safe, being the voice of reason. But now all sense of reason had gone, or at least it had shut up and was watching something feral take its place. Marchford turned to him again, with a raised eyebrow and an expression somewhere between surprise and worry. If Thornton lost control, who would pull him back from the edge?

Thornton wanted to reclaim rationality, but it was elusive. Maybe he was wrong, maybe the duc was only a fortune hunter who was slipping away, not a jewel thief. Then he would have grounds for a complaint against him and Marchford. He had to find those jewels or there would be consequences, and he was going to have enough of those in the coming weeks. Perhaps the items were on the Frenchman himself.

Thornton went to the man's coat, rummaging through it, even pulling out the lining, the seams ripping.

The duc yelled in protest again, but somehow the ripping sound was cathartic. Thornton liked causing destruction. He moved toward the Frenchman, but Marchford intercepted.

"Allow me to search his person," said Marchford. "I would hate to have to visit you in prison for killing the man."

Killing the man? Not an all-bad idea. Thornton shook his head. What was wrong with him? He was allowing this man to control his emotions and turn him into someone other than himself. He sat down on the mangled bed and took a deep breath. This was not like him. He was angry at d'Argon, but he would not let the man control him.

"He does not appear to have the jewels on him," said Marchford.

Thornton felt a prick of desperation. He needed to find them. A tiny rapping at the door caught their attention. He and Marchford exchanged a glance and Marchford opened the door. The innkeeper stood outside, a worried expression on his face. Another man in a bright-blue cloak stood behind him.

"I heard raised voices and such a crashing, then someone called for the magistrate," said the innkeeper. He motioned to the magistrate, who proceeded into the room with an air of confidence Thornton did not share. How were they going to explain their behavior without proof?

"What seems to be the matter here?" asked the magistrate.

"Good day, sir," said Marchford, taking on a business like tone. "I am the Duke of Marchford. I believe you are acquainted with Lord Thornton, and this man is the duc d'Argon. Until this morning he was a guest at Thornton Hall. He left unexpectedly early this morning and we followed due to our suspicions."

"And what suspicions are those?" asked the magistrate.

"We believe he has been stealing from the guests at Thornton Hall," said Marchford.

"This is untrue!" demanded d'Argon. "They are jealous because I won the heart of a lady Lord Thornton desired. He has created this fabrication!"

The magistrate surveyed the room quietly. "It seems you were thorough in your search of the room. Looks to me the work of an angry man. I've never known ye to loose yer temper before, Lord Thornton."

"There! You see, he is enraged over this lady," declared d'Argon.

"A lady involved, eh?" asked the magistrate. "Never knew Lord Thornton to be much of a skirt chaser either. Who is this lady?"

"Her name cannot be important," said Thornton.

"I understand. Well, sir," said the magistrate looking at the duc, "if ye won the heart of this maiden, what was the outcome? She rebuffed ye?"

"No! She wished to marry me!" The Frenchman's pride got the better of him.

"But ye dinna want her, is that the lay? Ye run off from Thornton Hall to avoid her?"

"Slightly more sinister than that," said Marchford. "He proposed marriage then ran away when he found she did not have quite as plump a dowry as he needed to pay off his debts."

"Ah! What say ye to that, sir?" the magistrate asked d'Argon. While the Frenchman was searching for an answer the magistrate continued, "I canna like such an unscrupulous man, no sir, I canna like it one bit. But more to the point, do ye have proof this man has been stealing?"

There was the rub. Thornton and Marchford glanced at each other again. If they had no proof, this was not going to go well for them.

"We have yet to find where he hid them," said Thornton.

"I have stolen nothing!" growled the duc. "I have been accosted by these two gentlemen without cause. I demand they both be arrested!"

"Well now," said the magistrate slowly. He glanced between Thornton and Marchford. "If ye have any other evidence, my lads, tell me now. Otherwise, I must side with the Frenchman here."

Thornton's stomach sank. What if they were wrong? He did not like d'Argon, but he could not say he knew for sure if he was a thief. One thing was certain: things were going to go poorly if he could not find proof of the man's guilt in the next few seconds.

Thirty-nine

HARRIET AND PENELOPE MANAGED TO TALK THE STABLE master into saddling two horses for them to take a ride. It helped they now had more horses than stalls, so an offer to exercise two was a welcome one.

At first it was relatively easy. A casual question regarding the direction the men had taken led them down the lane to the west. After that, Harriet began to track.

"How do you know what you are doing?" asked Penelope from horseback as Harriet inspected the ground.

"It is actually not difficult," said Harriet. "Thornton's horse is a fine one and wears a particular shoe, one I noted before when we went riding. The ground is soft and the shoe makes a distinct indentation, see?" She pointed out the track to Penelope.

"Oh. I do see, actually. But how did you learn to do this?"

Harriet shrugged. "I have four older brothers. We live outside town with the ocean on one side and the great woods on the other. Dinner often meant shooting it oneself. What you English do for sport, we do for supper. I accompanied my brothers many times."

They followed the trail until they found the men's horses in a stable next to an inn. They entered the common room and were about to ask for assistance when the raised voice of the duc could be heard.

"I do believe we will find the men upstairs," said Penelope.

Harriet led the way, and they paused just outside the open door. Inside they could hear the duc, Marchford, Thornton, and an unknown man. It was clear Marchford and Thornton were in trouble if they could not find evidence to the duc's guilt.

"Good afternoon, gentlemen." Harriet strolled into the room with admirable confidence, as if she was entering a drawing room.

The men were notably surprised and took their bows. Harriet and Penelope curtsied in return. Thornton glared at her, his jaw set. He was not pleased to see her. At all.

"My dear ladies," said Marchford in a tone that implied anything but endearment. "Please go to the common room and wait for us so we may escort you home."

Harriet surveyed the room. They needed proof and she needed to help. She knew d'Argon was guilty; she simply knew it to be true. She felt the duc's eyes on her but refused to look at him. He had made a fool of her. A memory she could easily do without.

"The common room is too stuffy, too… common," said Penelope. She was hedging for time, but Harriet knew they would soon be expelled from the room. They must do something, and fast.

Harriet visually searched the room, which appeared to have been torn apart. The mattress was tossed in a heap, the trunk stood on end, the duc's clothes were strewn about. The trunk, at this angle, looked a little odd. Harriet stepped further into the room and found the bottom of the inside of the trunk was higher than the outside.

"This trunk is oddly shaped, do you not think?" she asked.

Thornton glared at her then glanced at the trunk, paused, then walked around it to get a good look. "Aye, verra suspicious." Thornton placed the trunk on the bed and drew a long knife from his boot. He held the knife menacingly over the trunk and leveled a glare at the duc. "Anything ye care to say?"

Harriet had the satisfaction of seeing the duc squirm. Thornton stabbed at the bottom of the trunk a few times, then a few times more than he had to for good measure.

He tore open the splintered wood and found a leather bag. He held it up and dumped it without ceremony on the bed. The pearls slid out, along with a ruby necklace, several watch fobs, and a diamond encrusted snuffbox. Never had Harriet been so glad to see something sparkle. From the looks of relief on the faces of Thornton and Marchford, she knew they were appreciative as well.

"Well now," said the unknown man in a blue cloak, who must have represented the law here in the Highlands. "How would ye like to explain this?" he asked d'Argon.

The duc folded his arms across his chest. "I have no idea. I can only say that someone has placed those items there without my knowledge."

"Tell me how you knew about the pearls!" demanded Marchford. "Someone must have told you. You had not even arrived when my grandmother lost them."

"Lost the fake ones you mean," said d'Argon with a sneer. "Fake ones that she presented as real. You have the pearls now. Let me be or else I will be required to tell the whole story of what she did. She will be ruined and you know it!"

Marchford lunged at the man, and Thornton again stopped him. "Dinna let him win," he said in a low voice. "The likes o' him is no' worth it."

Marchford took a deep breath, straightened his cravat, and pulled down his waistcoat. "Yes. Thank you."

"Gentlemen," said the magistrate. "Let me remind ye that we are in the presence of ladies." He once again bowed to Harriet and Penelope. "Thank ye, ladies, for yer service here. I've seen enough. I've got me many a trunk, but none what's got a false bottom like that. Only thieves would need such a thing if ye ask me. And now we have these jewels, which ye admit are not yers and were found in a place in yer trunk only ye would know. I am hereby placing ye under arrest for theft."

"No! They just do not want you to know about the pearls. Call this off or I'll tell him about the pearls!" screeched the duc.

"No more o' yer nonsense. Ye are coming wi' me," said the magistrate.

"Still have the pit for thieves?" asked Thornton.

"Aye, but we shoud'na put quality in the pit," objected the magistrate.

"He is hardly that," stated Marchford.

"Well then, the pit it is!"

"No! Not the pit!" The Frenchman's eyes were wide.

"Have ye anything to tell us? Anything about who helped ye?" asked Thornton.

"If I tell you, will you let me go?"

"No, but I'll try to convince my friend not to throw ye in the pit," said Thornton.

"*Oui*, I will tell you."

Thornton asked politely if the innkeeper could provide the magistrate and the ladies with a light repast while he and Marchford interviewed the suspect. The magistrate was more than willing; the ladies, however, refused to leave.

"I have been accused of everything this man is guilty of doing," said Harriet. "I deserve to know the truth." She folded her arms across her chest, determined to leave only if forcibly removed. In the end, the innkeeper left with the magistrate and the door was closed, leaving the four of them to interview the suspect.

"Now," said Marchford. "Time to tell all."

"I do not know much," said d'Argon, sitting on a chair.

"Ye best hope ye ken something," commented Thornton, standing at the window. "Where ye sleep tonight depends on it."

The Duc d'Argon took a deep breath. "I had barely arrived at the house when I received a note, written in a neat hand in fluent French. The missive said I had a friend who understood my financial woes. The note asked me to do a few small things in return for great reward."

"Who wrote you?" asked Marchford.

"I do not know. Truly, I do not."

"So you thought you would join a traitor?" Marchford asked.

"I have no political leanings. The only thing concerning me is my debt. I cannot return to France. It would be fatal for me. At first it was easy. I received a message that told me there would be pearls lying out in Her Grace's room."

"But why did you take the others from Langley's room as well?"

The duc shrugged. "You never know when it could become useful."

"You planned blackmail!" accused Penelope.

The duc merely shrugged.

"Tell me what else these mysterious messages told you to do." Marchford's voice was calm, but his fists were balled at his sides.

"All I was supposed to do was transport some papers."

"Papers? What papers?" Marchford's eyes narrowed.

"It appeared to be talk of military plans, invasions, and such."

Marchford shook his head. "I asked specifically that no one take any notes regarding our planning meetings. Someone did not listen. Where did these plans go?"

"I took them to town. I was supposed to send them special delivery to the French embassy, but it was cheaper to send them by post."

"When did you send these things?" asked Marchford.

"I sent the first a few days ago, and the second I sent yesterday. Although the mail does not leave every day from the town, so small, so provincial it is here, so I think both packets left this morning."

"And who gave ye these papers?" asked Thornton.

The Duc d'Argon gave a slippery smile. "You did."

❧

Harriet, Thornton, Marchford, and Penelope rode back to Thornton Hall in silence, d'Argon's accusation still ringing in their ears. The Frenchman claimed he had taken the papers from Thornton's own room, stashed under his mattress. Harriet did not know why he would claim the papers were there, but she knew Thornton could not be at fault. As to the fire, the Frenchman denied all knowledge.

"I dinna ken anything about the papers," Thornton finally said.

"Of course not," said Marchford, but he did not look at him. The poison of doubt had seeped into the fabric of their friendship, building walls and barriers between them.

The trail narrowed, allowing only two horses to ride across. Marchford and Penelope took the lead with Harriet and Thornton trailing behind.

"You were right about d'Argon," said Harriet when they were far enough behind to be out of earshot. "I should have listened to you."

Thornton shook his head. "Even I woud'na have predicted he was a thief and a traitor. I had no' thought it possible for me to think less o' him." Thornton was speaking to her, but in his reserved manner, his eyes on the road ahead.

"We were never engaged." It was important to Harriet to correct any misunderstanding about this. "He had asked me to form an alliance based on science. He promised to gain entry for me at the Royal Academy of Science. He said he would move with me to America." She tried to make him understand.

"He would have promised anything for the fifty thousand he thought he would receive."

"Yes, you are quite right. I feel rather foolish now to be so taken in. If he had sworn his undying affection, I would have seen what he was. But he appealed to my love for science."

"Slippery fellow."

"I never had any feelings for him," Harriet added.

Thornton slowed his mount even more and she did the same. Marchford and Penelope were still in sight, but well out of hearing range. "I fear this is my fault for causing ye grief. I take the blame."

"Nonsense! Had I taken your advice, I would not have gotten so close to him. And you have never caused me a moment's grief. Except," she amended to be honest, "when we have been apart."

"I am truly sorry for ever causing ye pain." The mournful truth in Thornton's gray eyes was almost painful to see. This was the truth. Their time together was swiftly coming to an end. They would be apart forever.

"I am so sorry for your loss in the fire," whispered Harriet, reaching out to him. "Please know that it was not my equipment that started it."

He reached out and grasped her hand, warm even through the gloves they both wore. "Nay, o' course not. I also am sorry for the loss of yer equipment."

"Thank you," murmured Harriet, relieved to find he did not blame her.

Thornton gently squeezed her hand. "I want ye to know I regret nothing in our time together, except anything that has caused ye pain. Ye have shown me a kindness, an affection, and a playful joy I have never known. I will remember ye always."

"You will always be in my heart." Harriet blinked back tears.

"Miss Redgrave?" called Penelope, shocking Harriet out of the trance of Thornton's gaze. Harriet realized they had brought their mounts to a stop and were holding hands in the middle of the road. They dropped their hands.

Harriet and Thornton urged their mounts forward to catch up with Marchford and Penelope.

"We have work to do," said Marchford, his face grim.

"Work?" asked Harriet.

"We have a spy to catch."

Forty

THEY WERE EXHAUSTED BY THE TIME THEY RETURNED. Not having slept the night before and very little the night before that, Thornton harbored hopes of finding his bedchamber, preferably with Harriet. His sleep-deprived brain had no sense of reason or propriety.

A small group of discontented matrons in the foyer put an end to this line of thought.

"I wish to leave this place tonight!" demanded Mrs. Crawley. "I cannot stand to spend one more night with that arsonist!" She glared at Harriet.

"You should make her leave," said another matron. "How can we sleep at night with her running free?" She pointed at Harriet in a rude manner.

The guests who had gathered in the drawing room before dinner began to pour into the entryway, hearing that Thornton and Marchford had returned.

"I have never been so scared in all my life," said a thin matron. "First the fire, then the thefts. I am afraid we shall be murdered in our beds!"

"I understand your concerns," said Marchford with

authority. "And I assure you we are doing all we can to protect your safety and find the culprit."

"But we already know who is to blame," said Priscilla. "It was that Harriet creature who set the fire and then stole from us all after she lost her fortune. Why she is still allowed to stay under the roof is beyond me."

The crowd tittered their agreement in a manner that made Thornton's skin crawl. How quick they were to condemn. Harriet stood tall before the crowd, taking their insults with a calm he could only respect.

"Miss Redgrave is no' responsible for the fire," said Thornton. "Ye would please me all by not bandying about false accusations."

"We have good news. The thief has been discovered," said Marchford. "It was the duc d'Argon who confessed to the thefts."

"That is a scandalous thing to say," said the Comtesse de Marseille.

"I fear it is the truth. And if I am no' mistaken, these are yer rubies." Thornton opened the pouch and pulled out the rubies to the gasps of the crowd. "Sir Antony, I believe this is your snuffbox."

"Why indeed it is. Good show!"

Thornton returned the items but still wondered what to say about the fire. They had solved one mystery, but the spy was still someone among the crowd. But who?

"My dear friends." Lady Thornton appeared on the stairs dressed in exquisite blue silk and a silver tiara. His mother looked stunning and happy, which considering the circumstances was a surprise. "I am so pleased we have a resolution to that unpleasantness. Tonight is Midsummer's Night and we have arranged for a ball!"

The crowd, angry and scared only a moment before, now chattered to each other in a happy tone.

"A wonderful idea," cried Sir Antony. "I shall be bold and claim the first dance with our hostess!"

Lady Thornton blushed. Blushed. Thornton rubbed his eyes. He had been awake too long. Must be affecting his vision. He looked more carefully at his mother and realized she was not wearing a silver tiara but a crown.

"Mother," he asked quietly. "Are ye wearing the crown o' Maid Marion?"

His mother smiled in a manner most unusual. "I thought it time I wear it." She flitted off to converse with her friends in a most cheerful manner.

Thornton was too tired to make sense of it. He nodded to Harriet, and she and Penelope quietly made their way upstairs to change for dinner. He dared not do anything more.

The majority of the guests were appeased, but Mr. Neville approached them before they could make their escape. "I have serious concerns regarding your conduct, Your Grace." He spoke the title with contempt. "I understand the book of codes has gone missing. Who knows what the enemy will do with them. You assured me it would be safe. I fear this must go into my report to the Home Office."

"Yes, of course, you must do what you think best," said Marchford with complete calm.

Mr. Neville stalked off. Marchford nodded to Thornton, and they walked into the library.

"Your mother is in good spirits," said Marchford, reaching for a sip of something.

"Surprising for a woman who has just lost her home. Maybe she finally cracked." Thornton lay out on the settee, too tired to even sit up.

"Whatever her motivations, she did help us out of a tight spot."

"What o' Neville?" asked Thornton.

"He will make as much trouble as he can. And when he finds out about the plans that were smuggled out, it will be worse. I only wish we could intercede the post. If it left today, there may still be a chance to beat it to the French embassy, but none of my horses could do the job."

Thornton sat up with a start. "But mine could."

"Surely they could not make it all the way to London."

"No, but I have sold horses across the country, to Langley, to Sir Antony, and others. If we strung them together…"

"Yes! Let's do it."

"I shall write a letter for the messenger," said Thornton, jumping up.

"No, let me do that," said Marchford, sitting down at the writing desk.

"Are ye no' sure ye can trust me?" asked Thornton quietly.

"I trust no one."

"I am sorry."

"Do not be. If you could choose a horse and a messenger, I would be grateful."

Thornton gave a bow and left the room. There was

nothing he could do to clear his name... except find the true traitor.

❦

"Such excitement," said Harriet as she and Penelope walked into her room.

"At least we have found the thief," said Penelope.

"But we still have not found the spy, and I am still being blamed for the fire." Though now that Harriet was convinced Thornton did not hold her responsible, she felt immensely better.

"We do still need to find our arsonist," agreed Penelope.

"Yes, though I do not look forward to attending a ball. I do not think I would be well received."

"Perhaps not. No one would blame you if you stayed in your room. Though I can tell you the duchess would say you would only give credence to the rumors."

"Maybe I will ask him what to do," murmured Harriet.

"Your grandfather?" asked Penelope.

"No, Thornton," said Harriet without thinking.

Penelope gave Harriet a half smile. "Interesting you should seek his opinion."

Harriet realized she had spoken too candidly. She flopped down on the bed. "It does not matter what I might feel for him. It will not change the fact that his life is here and my parents are in America. I could never leave them."

"Is that not what your mother did when she eloped with an American sea captain?" asked Penelope.

Harriet opened her mouth for a retort, but then

closed it again. Penelope was right. Insight suddenly dawned on her and she sat up suddenly. Her mother had left everything to be with the man she loved. Surely she would understand if Harriet did the same.

"You are right, she did marry for love." A smile flashed on Harriet's face but disappeared just as quickly. "But after everything that has happened, he must be consumed with saving his estate."

"Forgive me, but you are in a position to help him with that."

Harriet shook her head. "He would never accept it. Never. As long as I have this dowry, Lord Thornton will never propose."

Penelope shrugged. "Rumor has it you lost your dowry." Before Harriet could reply, Penelope continued, "Let us dress for dinner—that is, if you are coming."

Harriet stood tall. "Yes, of course. I am going to catch this spy for Thornton. I may not be able to solve all his problems, but at least I can help him do that much."

Harriet and Penelope quickly dressed and walked down the side staircase to avoid some of the more malicious comments from the guests. They found Marchford in the library, writing letters by the light of a single candle.

"Good evening," said Marchford, standing as they entered.

"Please continue what you were doing," said Penelope.

Marchford did so, mumbling about losing the light.

"The horse and rider are ready," said Thornton,

walking in the room with a thin messenger. He spoke to Marchford but was looking at Harriet.

Marchford gave the letters and the instructions to the messenger, who left at once. Marchford sat back down at the table as the candle guttered out, throwing the room into darkness.

"I'll get a light," said Thornton, feeling his way out of the room.

"Good heavens," exclaimed Penelope. "What is that?" The table emanated a greenish glow.

"Oh. Sorry," said Harriet. As if things weren't bad enough, now everyone was going to know she was conducting experiments in the library. "I was doing some experiments in luminescence. I fear I may have left some traces of the phosphorous behind."

"My goodness, you really do have some interesting experiments," said Penelope. "Would everything that touched the table be glowing too?"

"Most likely."

"Good to know my poor book is somewhere glowing for me," sighed Penelope.

"What book?" asked Harriet.

"I had it here. It was stolen. We think by the person who also set the fires."

"Even I am glowing," said Marchford, looking at the sleeves of his jacket that had touched the table.

"As would be the thief," said Harriet.

Everyone was quiet.

"Here we are," said Thornton, walking back into the room with a lantern.

"Forgive me, my friend. But where is the coat you were wearing yesterday?" asked Marchford.

"Still wearing it," said Thornton. "Long day."

"Douse the light," said Marchford.

"What?"

"Douse the light!"

Thornton did as he was requested.

"You are not glowing!" cried Harriet. "I knew you would not be glowing."

"Why would I be glowing?" asked Thornton, puzzled.

"Could you get a light now?" asked Penelope.

"First lit then out, now lit again," muttered Thornton and he went out to light the lantern again. "Now tell me what this is about," he said, coming back in the room.

"The book that was stolen was on the desk. You remember my experiment?" asked Harriet.

"The green glow?"

"Exactly! It is still glowing. So the thief would also be glowing."

"I imagine he would have changed clothes, unlike me."

"Not the gloves," said Harriet. "If the thief was wearing gloves, as most people were last night."

"I have a plan." Thornton looked at the assembled conspirators and smiled.

Forty-one

HARRIET PLASTERED A SMILE ON HER FACE AS SHE entered the ballroom. The faces that stared back were not nearly as friendly. She had a job to do though, and she would do it. Someone in the candlelit ballroom was a traitor. But who?

The ballroom itself had been transformed into the likeness of a faerie glen. In honor of the solstice, the chandeliers above them remained unlit, but were decorated with branches and flowers instead. The only light came from along the walls, with numerous lit lanterns.

Thornton walked up to her in a royal-blue coat of glistening superfine. He said not a word, and nothing could be discerned from his taciturn demeanor. He was the same Lord Thornton she had met only a few weeks before. Solemn. Strong. Handsome.

"It is time," he whispered.

She nodded in response. She knew what to do. She nervously stood by one of the lanterns, waiting for the signal while trying to appear casual. When the musicians began the first notes for the third set, she blew out the lantern, as did Penelope to hers, and the servants to theirs, casting the ballroom into sudden darkness.

A woman screamed. Men shouted. But Harriet was scanning the room for the familiar glow. She saw it for a moment, a flash then gone, then back again. It was moving.

"Over here!" she cried and ran toward the light. She knocked into someone, throwing them to the floor but kept going, keeping her eyes on the glow.

"Where?" shouted Marchford.

"Here!" said Harriet, and without a thought, tackled the person attached to that glow. She landed hard on top of him and was rewarded with a foul curse. "I have him!" She was struck hard and fell back with a cry.

"I got him!" Thornton roared. "Dinna move or I shall rip yer arm clean off."

"Lights!" called Marchford.

The servants ran in with candles and Harriet turned to face the thief.

"Mr. Neville!"

"What is the meaning of this?" demanded Neville. "Unhand me at once!"

Thornton dragged him to his feet, holding his arm twisted painfully behind his back.

"Mr. Neville." Marchford's face was stormy. "You took the book. Explain yourself. Now!"

"I did no such thing. I only wanted to protect the book," defended Neville.

"Now I know where the leak was coming from in the Foreign Office. It was you!" accused Marchford.

"I say, that is quite an accusation," said Sir Antony. "Can you prove it?"

"Certainly," said Marchford. "Mr. Neville fell prey to a trap. I put a particular book out as bait, suggesting that it was a book used by spies, and Mr. Neville took it. The evidence of this is in his glowing clothes. Miss Redgrave, perhaps you can best explain the history of this."

"Yes, of course," said Harriet, slightly flustered by being put in the center of attention. "The study of the luminescent properties of phosphorus started with Hennig Brand, who, in his attempt to create the philosopher's stone, used putrefied urine to create—"

"Not that much history," whispered Penelope.

"I beg your pardon," amended Harriet. "I did experiments with stuff that glows in the dark. I left some of the substance on the table and the book, so that anyone who tried to take it would glow in the dark too."

"If you would please douse the lights," said Marchford.

The lights were removed as requested and the entire gathering did a collective gasp as Mr. Neville's gloves began to glow. With a very ungentlemanly curse, Neville bolted, followed by Marchford, Thornton, and several footmen. He might possibly have gotten away had Harriet not been in the way to trip him, sending him sprawling to the floor. Finally, years of finding ways to stand her ground against her older brothers paid off.

"You can take me, but you'll never get us all! England will fall. Napoleon will rule, not your madman king!" shouted Neville as he was dragged out of the room by two large footmen.

The lights were brought back into the ballroom and people began to talk in the most animated manner about what had just occurred.

"Ladies and gentlemen," said Marchford. "I am pleased to announce that you need not fear anymore, for the traitor has been apprehended," said Marchford. "Neville set the fire to create a diversion so he could steal what he believed to be a sensitive document."

"And now that the culprit has been apprehended," added Thornton, "we can share wi' ye all the verra great service Miss Redgrave has done for us. It was only through her expertise in alchemy that this dangerous spy was apprehended. I am sure ye will all wish to thank her for her invaluable service as I do now."

Emotion swelled in Harriet and brought tears to her eyes. She stared at Thornton though her vision swam. In a few sentences he had turned her from social pariah to national hero. She blinked again with a wide smile.

A slow smile graced his face in return.

"We will now search Mr. Neville's room for the list of people who have been providing him aid," said Penelope. "If he has deceived you in his capacity as an agent for the Foreign Office, please see us now or you will be considered as much a traitor as he."

Priscilla Crawley let out a terrified squeak.

Harriet exchanged a glance with Penelope. Clearly, Penelope thought there were more people involved and now they both suspected who.

"Please do continue to dance," entreated Thornton and signaled the musicians to play. Marchford,

Thornton, Harriet, and Penelope, retreated to the library.

"Mr. Neville a spy. I would not have guessed." Penelope shook her head.

"Nor would I," said Thornton. "I have seen him kill his own kind in the line of duty. Why would he do that?"

"To prevent any spy from being captured alive. They know too much," said Marchford. "I appreciate everyone's help catching this traitor, but we have more business to attend to."

With a knock, the Crawley family was escorted into the room by the same burly footmen who had dealt with Neville. They were invited, forcefully, into the library to discuss the situation.

Harriet knew it was wrong to triumph at anyone's expense, but she could still hear all of the cruel comments Priscilla had made and could not help but feel a bit pleased at her current difficulty. Miss Crawley, however, would not be defeated so easily and sat defiant next to her mother on the settee.

"Tell us about your involvement with Mr. Neville," demanded Marchford.

"She had nothing to do with it," defended General Crawley.

"Mr. Neville was a sly one. He almost convinced me into conspiring with him," said Penelope in an understanding voice. "Naturally, since he was a government agent, you would have believed him."

"He said I was doing it for England!" cried Priscilla. "He said I was doing it for you!" She pointed at Thornton.

"For me? In what way?" asked Thornton.

"I gave the papers to you," said Priscilla.

Everyone turned to Thornton. "What papers?"

"The papers you wanted. The notes Papa took at the meetings. I took them and put them under your mattress."

"General Crawley." Marchford's tone was deadly. "Perhaps you would like to explain why you were taking notes regarding our meetings after it was expressly forbidden."

General Crawley turned ashen. "Mr. Neville requested it. Said it was my duty to King and country. I never intended anyone to see those notes."

"Miss Crawley," said Thornton. "Let me understand this. Mr. Neville asked ye to take yer father's notes and put them under my mattress?"

"He said it was the right thing to do!" she defended.

"And then d'Argon was paid to take the notes and send them to spies in London," said Marchford, his voice cold.

"I did not know that." Priscilla was pale.

"Now, Miss Crawley," said Thornton. "Tell me about yer involvement in the fire."

Priscilla's eyes grew large but she shook her head. "I was not involved in the fire."

"I remember ye told the guests that Harriet's laboratory was to blame," said Thornton.

"I thought it was!"

"But the fact that Harriet was working on experiments in the castle ruins was not publicly known. Who told ye?"

Priscilla jumped up. "I do not know why you are

questioning me. Everyone knows Miss Redgrave is to blame."

"The fire was set from the outside," said Harriet. She stood to face her accuser. "It was you. Admit it."

"I certainly did not. You have no proof of any of this. You are speaking a dreadful slander against me."

Harriet kept her emotions in check and considered the problem logically. "I would imagine it would be difficult to pour lamp oil down the wall without leaving any trace. I warrant if I analyze the bottom of your skirt from the dress you wore that night, we would find traces of lamp oil where your skirts brushed against the wall."

Marchford gave a short nod. "Impressive deduction, Miss Redgrave. Let us send for the gown."

"No!" Priscilla burst into tears. "Neville said I needed to help him because the stuff she had was dangerous. I only meant to burn down her building, not the entire castle. I am so sorry." She buried her head into her mother's shoulder. Both women were crying.

"I would guess Neville had already doused the area with lamp oil so as to make sure the keep did catch fire," said Marchford. "He needed someone else to set the blaze so he could steal the book. It does not change the significant material damage to both Miss Redgrave and Lord Thornton that you have caused."

"She did not mean any harm," said General Crawley in a voice much quieter than normal.

"There is also the matter of aiding and abetting the enemy," added Marchford.

Priscilla began to cry louder.

Marchford looked to Thornton, and Thornton

looked to Harriet. They wanted to know what she wanted to do. It was a perfect moment for revenge. Priscilla had destroyed all her equipment, all her work, and had been horrid to her. To see her handed over to the magistrate would be sweet justice.

"Miss Crawley," Harriet asked, "I would like to know why you took such an instant dislike to me."

"Because you were different," she snuffed. It was all the explanation Harriet was going to get. She was different from the other ladies.

She turned to Thornton to tell him to send for the magistrate. Surely there was room in the pit for another prisoner. Instead, Thornton's words of acceptance floated back to her. Everyone, even people one did not like, were part of the same body. God made people different but loved them all. Perhaps Priscilla was a painful rear end, but she was still part of the body. If Harriet could belong, then so could Priscilla.

"I do not believe we should be judged by our worst days, but by our best," said Harriet, turning back to Priscilla with a small smile.

Priscilla stopped crying a moment and looked up at her, hiccupping.

"You were tricked regarding the true nature of Mr. Neville, as were we all," continued Harriet.

"Why are you being nice to me?" whispered Priscilla.

Harriet shrugged. "You made a mistake. I make mistakes all the time, so I know what it's like."

"I was beastly to you," said Priscilla softly. "I am sorry."

"I forgive you." The weight of anger and bitterness fell from Harriet's shoulders and she breathed deep and free.

"There are few people who could show such grace," praised Penelope. "Forgive me for ever wanting to change you, Harriet. You have employed your time in developing qualities that are much more important than anything I was attempting to teach."

"Aye," said Thornton, stepping forward. "But there is still the matter of the cost of the damage done." He leveled General Crawley a piercing glare. "I believe the amount of the damage should roughly equal the amount of the debt owed."

"Yes, yes quite," said Crawley in a shaky voice. "I shall contact my attorney."

"Nay, my solicitor shall draw up the papers," said Thornton with a small smile.

Marchford gave some more directions and the Crawley family sought their rooms for the night. Tomorrow they would leave.

The music was still playing and the guests were continuing to dance at the ball. "I believe I shall ask you to dance, Miss Rose," said Marchford.

Penelope smiled. "I would be delighted, Your Grace."

They all walked out of the library, and Thornton offered his arm to Harriet. "Thank ye. Well done."

"You as well," praised Harriet. "I hope this helps to relieve some of the financial burden."

Thornton gave her a smile, bright and true. "Aye, it does, lassie. Thanks to ye. Now all that is left is to claim a dance."

Harriet accepted and she walked into the ballroom on the arm of Lord Thornton. Her knight. Her Duncan. This time when she passed, people gave her small smiles and a friendly gaze. It was better. Much better.

Duncan bowed as the music began to play and held out his hand. They would dance. She smiled, for although she was clumsy with many things, she was a good dancer. And so was he. They danced together and all the troubles of the past week faded away. All the malicious glares, all the snide comments, all the awkward moments slid into nothingness, and all that was left was him and her and the dance.

Harriet flowed with the music, glided and twirled. Duncan never spoke a word, but his touch was gentle, at times a caress. She could not say how he danced differently than any other man, but the emotion was expressed in his touch.

The dance ended too soon and reality slipped back into her consciousness. They were in the middle of the dance floor, but Duncan did not walk her back to the side. She looked up at him, expectant, but he said nothing, his eyes glittering in the candlelight.

He took her hands in his. "Good evening, Miss Harriet."

"Good evening." She glanced around the ballroom; people were staring. Even the musicians had paused before beginning the next set, waiting to see what they would do.

"Tonight is a night of revelations," said Duncan, and he reached out to hold her hands in his. "We spoke before of how the Lord makes each one of us different for a purpose. Ye have certainly showed how important yer gifts were in helping us apprehend a dangerous traitor. Perhaps our respective gifts could complement each other, to help each other, love, and support each other. I am a better man wi' ye than wi'out. I had no idea what I was missing in my life until I met ye. I know ye plan to return to America, and I would never wish to separate ye from yer family, but I must ask ye." He gently squeezed her hands and dropped to one knee. "Harriet Redgrave, would ye consent to be my wife?"

"Yes, yes, a thousand times yes!" Lord Langley ran up to the couple, beaming with excitement.

"I am sorry, Grandfather, but I must make my own answer," said Harriet. She turned back to Duncan. "I have enjoyed our friendship more than I can express, but you must know about my dowry."

"I care not," declared Duncan, rising but not releasing her hands.

"Truly? You would accept me rich or poor?"

"I never wished to wed for anything less than love. And so I am asking ye, beyond all practicality or reason, will ye be my wife?"

She paused a moment, waiting for the anguish of gut-wrenching indecision, which never came. She knew exactly what she wanted, what her parents would want for her. "My answer is yes."

"I understand, but I needed to…" He stopped for a moment, the meaning of her words beginning to dawn on him. "Did ye say yes?"

Harriet nodded with a wide grin.

"She said yes!" Lord Langley crushed them with a large hug.

"She said yes," said the dowager duchess with a self-satisfied smile. "My solicitor will contact you."

"Not yet!" demanded Langley. "They need to be wed first. And I have the paper to do it!" He produced a special license with a flourish.

"You knew I would marry Lord Thornton?" gasped Harriet.

"I had them leave the groom's name blank," admitted Langley.

"How much do you think he had to bribe the clerk to do that?" muttered Penelope.

"Is this really what you want?" Harriet asked Duncan.

"I will meet ye at the kirk tomorrow," declared Duncan with a gleaming smile.

"Duncan!" Lady Thornton walked to them and Harriet's heart sank. Duncan's mother had not been supportive of her when she first arrived and everyone knew Lady Thornton wished her son to marry Miss Crawley.

"Mother, I hope ye will wish us happy," said Thornton, the reserve in his voice returning.

Harriet held her breath, waiting for the final verdict.

"I will indeed wish for ye all the happiness in the world if ye will do the same for me. Sir Antony has proposed," announced Lady Thornton.

"What?" Duncan gasped.

"She said yes!" exclaimed Sir Antony standing next to Lady Thornton with a smile that belonged on a much younger man.

"Mother, I had no idea," said Duncan.

"Sons are never much aware of their mothers," said Lady Thornton, but she smiled when she said it. "I also was not aware of your true feelings for Miss Redgrave."

"She is my choice, Mother," said Duncan, as if warding off disapproval.

"And no doubt better than my choice for you,"

Lady Thornton whispered to her son, referring to Miss Crawley.

"Thank ye," said Duncan, relaxing again. "I wish ye and Sir Antony a happy marriage."

"My dear Harriet," Lady Thornton said, giving Harriet a kiss on the cheek. "Welcome to the family."

"Thank you," said Harriet, and could not help but smile.

"Do me the honor of wearing this on your wedding day." Lady Thornton removed her intricately woven delicate silver crown and gave it to Harriet. "They say this was worn by Maid Marion herself when she wed Robin Hood. I cannot say if that is true, but it has been worn by generations of Maclachlan brides."

Harriet understood the magnitude of this acceptance. "Thank you, Lady Thornton," she whispered in a voice suddenly choked with emotion.

"You shall bear that title now," said Duncan's mother. "It never suited me, but I think it will fit you much better."

"Are you certain you wish to be wed tomorrow?" Harriet looked up at Duncan.

"Aye, lassie." And he sealed the proposal with a kiss.

And another.

And another.

Until even Lord Langley was forced to separate the two of them. "Save it for tomorrow night!"

Forty-two

"Not too late to make a run for it," said Marchford in a low voice as he stood next to Thornton at the front of the chapel, waiting for the bride to arrive.

"Too late for me," said Thornton. "She's stolen my heart."

"Doubt the magistrate will take that case. You're on your own."

"Aye, but no' for long."

"Incorrigible," muttered Marchford. "It is as if you wanted to be leg-shackled."

"Aye, I do. And someday I hope it happens to ye too."

Thornton heard the guests who had filled the village kirk rise, and he knew Harriet had entered the chapel. He had initially been concerned that his guests might not come, considering some of the rumors that had circulated about Harriet, but he need not have worried. With the same passion with which they had decried her as dangerous, they now lauded her as a hero.

Following tradition, Thornton faced the altar and could not look to see his bride approach, though he was sorely tempted. When she finally reached the altar, he turned to her and his breath caught. She was tall as a statue and just as shapely, dressed in a simple white gown with a baby-blue sash under the bust line. Her dark red hair fell in ringlets and was framed with the silver woven band, the crown of Maid Marion. She was going to be his wife. All the pain, all the trouble they had been through came down to this moment.

"Dearly beloved," began the minister.

"Stop!" The doors banged open and a man wearing a brace of pistols and a cutlass strode inside.

Thornton immediately pulled Harriet behind him and he and Marchford acted as a human shield against this unknown threat. For all the world, the man looked like a pirate, his dark hair was slashed with silver and he had a wicked scar across his cheek.

"Where is my daughter?" demanded the large man. "Where is she?" He was followed by four younger men, all tall, grim-faced, and armed.

"Ye can have no business here," warned Thornton. "Ye will leave at once!"

"They told us at the house you had come here, and I'm not leaving without my daughter!" demanded the man.

Harriet wiggled around Thornton. "Papa?"

"Harriet, my pumpkin!" Captain Redgrave opened his arms and Harriet ran to him.

"This is yer father?" Thornton could only stare in amazement. What kind of man was this?

Harriet hugged the man with delight. "I am so

happy to see you! And all my brothers too!" Harriet gave hugs to all the men now crowding the space between the altar and the pews. "Papa, this is Lord Thornton. Lord Thornton, may I present my brothers, Matthew, Mark, Luke, and John. But how did you find me all the way in Scotland?"

"Captain Wentworth was able to make it back to shore and send notice to us of what happened," said Captain Redgrave. "I gathered the boys and we left the next day. Took a bit to track you down in London. Had a talk with that Captain Beake and finally we found where you had gone and traveled to get you. Did you ever think for a moment that I would not come for you?"

"I did not know if Wentworth would make it to shore. I am relieved to hear he did," said Harriet.

"That was quite an entrance, my dear," said a dignified lady joining the party.

Lord Langley stood, his mouth agape. "Beatrice?"

"Hello, Father."

No one spoke. It was the return of Lord Langley's insane daughter, who looked remarkably self-composed for a madwoman.

Langley moved to the aisle before her. "Beatrice," he said again and took a step toward her, but stopped as if unsure how to bridge the gap between them.

No one moved. It was utterly silent in the chapel. Langley held out his hands to his daughter. "Forgive me, Bea. I have been an unmitigated ass."

Lady Beatrice smiled and strode to him, hugging her father and kissing him on the cheek. "You have no idea how long I have waited to hear you say that."

"Too long. My fault entirely," admitted Langley.

"These are your grandsons," said Beatrice, "and my husband, Captain Redgrave."

Again everyone again held their breath as Lord Langley confronted the American who had stolen away his daughter. Captain Redgrave was a large, muscular man, and even if he had not been wearing a brace of pistols with a cutlass stuck in his belt, he would still have appeared rather dangerous.

"He looks like a hero from all those romance books I told you not to read," muttered Langley, shaking his head.

Lady Beatrice smiled. "Yes, he does."

"Lord Langley, I'm Captain Redgrave. Nice to meet you." Captain Redgrave held out his hand.

Lord Langley surveyed Captain Redgrave with displeasure. "Captain Redgrave," he said and shook the captain's hand with an obvious reluctance. He may be reconciled to his daughter but decidedly not to the man who stole her away.

Thornton was at a loss for what to do. Now that her parents had arrived, would she like to visit with them before the wedding? Would she call off the wedding entirely?

"Harriet," he said quietly. "Perhaps we should stop and spend time wi' yer parents."

"Do you not want to get married?" Her eyes were wide.

"Aye, o' course I wish to marry ye. But do ye wish to speak first wi' yer parents?"

"Yes, yes, she does!" demanded Captain Redgrave. "Exactly who do you think you are, trying to marry my daughter?" Captain Redgrave gave him a furious glare, flanked by four younger copies of himself with equal animosity.

"Papa, this is Duncan Maclachlan, he is the Earl of Thornton," said Harriet.

"Don't care. You're not marrying him."

"Papa!"

"No. Never going to happen! I won't have you running off with some man I've never met to some strange country far away from me."

"Is that not exactly how we were wed?" asked his wife with a crooked smile.

"No, we were… it was completely different…" Redgrave stuttered and blustered until his shoulders sagged. "Oh hell and bother."

"Watch your language, you're in a church," chastised Lady Beatrice.

"Lord Langley," said Redgrave with his head bowed. "I never knew till this moment. I am so, so sorry."

Langley's lips twitched up. "Horrible, I know."

"How did you survive it?"

"Bourbon. I'll pour you a glass when we are done here."

Lady Beatrice glided to her daughter and held both her hands. "You look lovely as always. I am so relieved to find you so well."

"Thank you." Harriet hugged her mother. "I was mostly concerned that you would be worried about me."

"I could not call myself a mother if I did not worry about you. But you are well?" she asked with a hint of anxiety.

"Very well."

"And you wish to marry Lord Thornton?"

Harriet met Duncan's eyes. "Yes. I love him."

Those simple words melted away any fear or doubt Duncan had harbored. If Harriet loved him, all would be well.

"I wish you every happiness in the world," said Lady Beatrice to her daughter.

"I only hope to be as happy as you and Papa," said Harriet.

"Sit down, boys," said Lady Beatrice to her sons.

"But, Mother, you can't expect us to let our sister get married to some bloke we don't know," argued the tallest Redgrave son.

"Yes, that is exactly what I expect you to do."

"But—"

"Sit!" commanded Lady Beatrice in a tone only a peer of the realm could muster.

They sat.

"I cannot allow this to continue." Captain Redgrave had turned sullen.

"You must trust," said his wife.

"I have never even met this man. How can I trust him?"

"You must learn to trust your daughter," said Beatrice.

Captain Redgrave was silent for a moment. "I hate it when you're right."

"I thought you would be accustomed to it by now," murmured Beatrice.

"I will allow this to continue on one condition," demanded Captain Redgrave. "If she is getting married, I am going to walk her down the aisle!"

So the bride, deciding it was good form to humor her well-armed father, walked down the aisle once more, this time on the arm of a snarling pirate. With one raise of her eyebrow, Lady Beatrice snapped her husband's behavior back into good regulation.

"Are ye certain ye wish to be wed today?" whispered Duncan when Harriet was once again standing by his side.

"I do," whispered Harriet in return. "My family can be overwhelming. Do you still wish to marry me?"

"I do."

Forty-three

SHE WAS A MARRIED LADY. MARRIED! HARRIET SMILED broadly as people greeted her and Thornton in the receiving line.

"Your wedding will be talked about forever, Lady Thornton," said one lady. "It was so... exciting!"

"Yes, it was unlike any I have ever seen, Lady Thornton," said one young lady. "And your brothers are all so handsome!"

Lady Thornton. It took Harriet a while before she stopped looking around for Duncan's mother and realized they were talking about her. She smiled at Duncan. He smiled back. All was right in her world.

She greeted everyone in the line as they went into the dining room. Last in line was her father, hands folded across his chest, a furious frown on his face. Her mother was by his side, looking radiant.

"Thought of something," said Captain Redgrave with a growl. "We need to complete the marriage settlements for Harriet's dowry."

"I have had papers drawn up that states that

whatever Harriet brings to the marriage will remain within her control, for her and her children," said Thornton.

Harriet's parents glanced at each other and then at her.

"Duncan says he does not care at all about financial concerns," said Harriet, wishing she had a moment alone with him to break the news about her dowry. She gave her parents a tight smile and willed them not to say anything to give away her little secret before she could tell him in her own way… preferably after their first child was born.

"Well then. Very good," said her father, his face relaxing into a smile. "Can't raise a complaint about those terms."

"No, indeed," said her mother with a little crease between her eyebrows that told Harriet she suspected something was amiss. Harriet knew her mother would not betray her suspicions, but her father was not known for delicacy.

"Glad to hear you are not one of those impoverished peers looking to marry an heiress to set your course to rights." Captain Redgrave slapped Thornton hard on the back and put his arm around him with a jovial smile.

"Perhaps we should go in to dinner," said Harriet, desperate to change the subject. "I think they are waiting for us."

"Yes, of course," said her mother smoothly, guiding her husband to the door.

"Hullo there!" Harriet's four brothers ran into the room. To be fair, they were actually walking, but they were so large and moved so quickly, they gave the impression of a run.

"Not too late for the receiving line I trust," said Matthew, shaking Thornton's hand.

"Got a good girl here in Harriet," said Mark.

"You are aware she likes to blow things up?" asked Luke.

"Nothing to worry about," said John. "That fifty-thousand-pound dowry will pay for a lot of singed draperies, eh?"

Lord Thornton said not a word, but Harriet could sense every muscle in his body tighten. He turned to her with a cold stare. "Let us go in to dinner."

❧

Harriet wanted to strangle her brothers. She wished so many times to see her brothers again, and yet now that they were here, she wished they would go back to America. Preferably tonight. It was not that they were loud and large and ate too much and laughed too loud; it was their repeated jokes about the size of her dowry and Thornton's good fortune.

Since Thornton had been particularly sensitive to not marrying a girl of good fortune, and indeed had thought he was marrying one with none at all, Harriet was sure her brother's merciless jabs about the size of her "assets" were not received with good humor.

She tried unsuccessfully to get them to stop. They were a force of nature and railing against them was as effective as rebuking the waves. Her four older brothers ran free until Harriet pleaded with her mother to stop them. Lady Beatrice, though dwarfed by her sons, managed to rein them in with effectiveness, if not with ease.

Thornton was unreadable. He was pleasant and solemn. Not good. After dinner, the women whisked her away to prepare for her wedding night with the idea that Thornton would join her shortly. She had been given what she suspected had been Lady Thornton's bedroom, and after some preparatory primping and discussing of the night before her, both of which she found rather embarrassing, she was left to wait for her lord alone.

Trouble was, he did not appear.

Harriet paced the room and even tried rereading a chapter of Lavoisier's book on chemistry but nothing helped. He had not arrived and she doubted he ever would. Time to take matters into her own hands.

She slipped down the hall to the master bedroom. She tested his latch and it was unlocked. She took a deep breath. Was she really going to do this? She pulled on the latch and the door swung open. Duncan was sitting at a writing desk. He had removed his cravat and his shirt hung open. He stood when he saw her, saying nothing.

She stepped into the room, closing the door behind her. She felt powerful; she could find him; she could take what she wanted. And right now what she wanted was him.

"I was waiting for you," she said.

"I have written a letter for ye. Would you care to read it?" He held out a paper before her.

"You can tell me yourself."

"It would be easier if ye read it."

"I am not here to make things easy for you." No, indeed, she was here to make things hard.

Duncan cleared his throat. "Considering yer parents are here now, and considering yer *assets* of which I heretofore had no prior knowledge—"

"I am going to kill my brothers."

"I could suggest some methods. But be that as it may, I think it best if we quietly annul this misguided marriage and allow ye to return home."

"Duncan, I know nothing can forgive the iniquity of being rich—"

"*Obscenely* rich."

"Yes, yes, all right, you needn't make it worse than it is. As I was saying, I know it was wrong of me not to clarify your misunderstanding about my dowry, but you did say you did not care about the money."

"That was when I thought ye were poor," exclaimed Duncan.

"But since you wanted to marry me then, couldn't you find it in your heart to stay married to me now?"

"But yer brothers—"

"Are going to meet a most horrible demise if you allow those fools to destroy this marriage." She was surprised at how sincere she was.

"I would hate to be the cause of anyone's demise. Though for yer brothers, I might be willing to make an exception," he added in a mutter.

"They were beastly."

"They were saying what everyone else will say, that I married ye for the money. It is the one thing I was determined to avoid in my life. The one promise I made to my father."

"No one who knows you could think this of you. Everyone, including you, believed the rumor that I had lost my fortune. It was meant as a test for d'Argon, you see."

Thornton shook his head. "However it happened, the fact remains that I was not given all the relevant facts before the nuptials. I would not cast ye out, but since yer parents arrived, I will take it as a sign—"

"That what?" interrupted Harriet. "My parents came because they were worried about me, not to break up the marriage." She took a step toward him.

"I swore I would never do this."

"I see." Harriet took a deep breath. It was time to be bold. "I am sorry to have to do this, but you leave me no choice. I shall have to seduce you."

"Seduce?" Thornton's eyebrows disappeared into his hairline.

"Yes. You are being so illogical, I am forced to trap you into remaining in this marriage."

"How?" Duncan seemed reluctantly interested.

"I will seduce you into making love to me and then manipulate your honorable instincts to force you to remain with me. Unfortunately, I have a small problem with my plan."

"Yer sense o' decency winna let ye go through wi' it?" he asked.

"No, I'd do it if I knew how. Alas, I have spent too much time reading chemistry books and not enough time learning how to properly seduce."

Duncan stared at her. "I'm trying to decide whether to be flattered or horrified."

Harriet opened her dressing gown and let it drop

to the floor. She was wearing a sensible nightgown. All she owned were sensible nightgowns. In a flash of belated insight, she wished she had thought to wear nothing under the dressing gown. But of course, she did not wish to catch a draft.

She loosed the tie and opened the front of her nightgown, revealing more of her chest. She noticed that he watched intently what her fingers were doing, so she let them wander, trailing, circling, pinching, squeezing. If she was embarrassed, she forgot it when she realized how riveted he was to her one-woman show.

He whipped off his shirt, revealing a muscular chest. "Ye should leave."

His actions and his words were so much in discord, she knew she must ignore one of them. She chose to disregard his words, which honestly made everything easier.

She pulled the pins from her hair and let it fall down in a tussled mess.

"I do not want ye here," he said while stripping off his boots and breeches. Standing before her in short clothes, the falseness of this statement was blatantly obvious.

She marched over to the bed and crawled on it, having to hoist herself up onto the high mattress. She hiked up her nightgown to get up onto the mattress then realized it might also be an opportunity, so pulled it up even further as she scrambled up the mattress.

Behind her, Duncan began to swear in some unknown language. At least she thought it was swearing because it sounded loud and excited. He caught her from behind and hiked her nightgown up even more. She tried to move forward, but he held her fast. His hands on her backside left no doubt as to his interest or intent.

"Och, lass, ye win," conceded Duncan.

"I haven't yet." Harriet turned around and divested herself of the nightgown entirely. Then, feeling a little naked, she retreated under the covers, but not before Duncan got a good look. In his eyes she saw only admiration and frank lust.

Duncan sighed and joined her under the covers. "I have been an ass."

Harriet snuggled beside him. "Yes, you have, dear." She patted his chest in sympathy. "But we all make mistakes. I suppose my plan to trap you into marriage was not the best."

"Well now, I woud'na go so far. In fact, I believe it has merit."

"You wish to be trapped in this marriage?"

"Aye, wi' all my heart. I canna fathom a life wi'out ye."

A smile spread across her face and she felt it radiate through her down to her toes. "Fortunately, you don't have to."

"Good, now ye promised to seduce me, so I do believe ye have some work left to do tonight." He smiled at her. She smiled in return.

"I do not know quite how to seduce you, but I am willing to learn."

"And I am willing to be seduced. Ye see what an amiable husband I shall be?"

"Thank you," she whispered, and to her alarm, tears sprung to her eyes.

"What is it? How have I hurt ye?"

"No, you have not hurt me. I am simply happy. I feared I would lose you."

"Forgive me. I swear to ye I shall never act like a fool." He paused and corrected himself. "I am not certain I can quite swear to that, but I do swear that I am yers forever." He kissed her once. "That is to show ye I mean what I say." He kissed her twice. "That is because I love ye." Then he kissed her again and did not stop kissing her.

Finally she gasped for air. "What is that one for?"

"Dinna ken. Need ye," he growled and resumed the kiss, this time his hands feeling, stroking, caressing, making her body come alive.

She craved his touch, pulling herself closer, needing to feel him cover her, needing him to touch her. His hand worked its way up her leg to her thigh, to that place that throbbed with need. She reached for him and explored with her own fingers, finding the things that made him gasp. He pressed closer and she relaxed into him. She belonged to him. She needed him.

"Och, I do love ye, lass." He joined with her and she held on tight, leaving no doubt as to her own feelings on the matter.

She ran her fingers up and down his back, enjoying the way it made him shudder, until his own movements released something raw within her. Her entire being was focused on the building desire and raw passion they created. She held him tighter, never wanting to be parted. This was right; they were together. Husband and wife, united forever. This was her true desire.

Pleasure blasted through her, burning her inside with the heat of pure bliss. Aftershocks of joy pulsed through her. She gasped for breath, wondering if this was pleasure or death, and deciding that even if it was the end, it had been worth it. She went from feeling light and weightless to heavy and was certain she could never move again. She closed her eyes and drifted away.

"Ye belong to me," his voice was guttural, primal.

"I love you too."

~∞~

"It appears Madame X has been successful," said Marchford, motioning to his grandmother and Lord Langley as they argued on the other side of the drawing room over the amount of remuneration for services rendered.

"They have been arguing about this all day," sighed Penelope. "I would just concede the point so I could cease a tiring conversation."

"I think the point is they do not wish to stop the conversation," said Marchford, taking another careful look at the dowager duchess and Langley.

"Best be careful lest you acquire a new grandfather-in-law," said Penelope, sitting perfectly straight, perched on the edge of her chair.

Marchford waved off the comment and relaxed back in the upholstered chair. "People my grandmother's age do not get married. However, people my age do. I believe I also contracted with Madame X, and I have not reaped the rewards of this investment."

"Investment?"

Marchford leaned forward in his chair and whispered to her. "Where is the list of my potential brides?"

"Been a little busy. Besides, you rejected the potential ladies I reviewed with you." Penelope said no more because the memory of their kiss stole away all rational thought.

"When you have presented me with the right lady, I will let you know. Until then, I expect you to work tirelessly on the project."

"Unfortunately, the primary tool of my trade was stolen by a traitor," said Penelope, still disappointed regarding the loss of her matchmaker book.

"Ah yes, I nearly forgot." He reached under the tablecloth of a small side table and pulled out her Debrett's *Peerage*.

"You found it!" It was only a book, but it was dear to her, and she was beyond happy to have it returned.

"It was in Neville's room. I even cleaned off the chemicals, so it should be ready to use."

"I shall do my utmost, Your Grace, to find you a suitable wife," said Penelope. "It would be helpful if you would endeavor not to be so particular in your choice of brides."

The Duke of Marchford raised one aristocratic eyebrow. "I anticipate you will find me a suitable bride. If you cannot present anyone worthy, I shall expect you to perform the office yourself. Good night, Miss Rose."

Penelope watched as Marchford strolled away, self-confident as always. He must have been jesting when he said he would marry her.

He was joking... wasn't he?

Epilogue

Thornton Hall, 1817

HARRIET HAD TO YELL TO MAKE HERSELF HEARD OVER the din of the twins. Two sets. One set of boys, one of girls. The girls were louder.

"Happy Christmas!" shouted Harriet to her mother-in-law, who arrived for Christmas Eve dinner on the arm of Sir Antony Roberts, who hardly could be seen for the number of parcels he carried.

"Happy Christmas, my love," said Lady Roberts and swept past her to embrace her grandchildren. All four at once if possible. The children embraced her savagely, hugging and kissing with abandon, and pulled her into the parlor to play games.

"We did some shopping for the children," said Sir Antony, handing the butler a stack of packages. "How are you, my dear?"

"Very well, thank you. I do hope you did not put yourself out for the children's sake." Harriet was occasionally worried, when she had the time, that her mother-in-law would beggar her new husband with the gifts she brought.

"No, no, not at all. She has more blunt than she can

spend now that she has given up gambling. She was such a horrible gambler." He shook his head. "I don't think she even liked it. More to get back at her first husband if you ask me."

"I am so glad she is happy."

"We are happy and I benefit more than anyone. Why she would marry an old goat like myself is beyond me. But she did, and I hope she doesn't realize her mistake until I'm dead and gone!"

"One thing I know is that your wife adores you."

"You know a good deal more than that," countered Sir Antony. "Saw your latest chemistry article from 'Harry Maclachlan.' Well done! Could not understand most of it, so I know it must have been good."

Harriet smiled in response. She was a little proud of her paper too.

"Now where's that husband of yours?" asked Sir Antony with a smile.

"In the parlor, playing some sort of game with the children. Most likely something messy and loud."

"My favorite!" His eyes twinkled. "The young people are coming."

The young people turned out to be Sir Antony's nephew, Dr. Roberts; his wife, Lady Louisa; and their four children. They arrived, all smiles, the children quietly standing in the entryway like perfect angels until they were given leave to join the other children. Then they tore into the parlor like beasts.

Thornton stumbled out of the parlor laughing, his jacket off, his head wet and water dripping down his shirt.

"Duncan! Are you playing with the children again?"

"Aye!" he said with sheepish grin. "They dared me to get two apples at once."

"But that's not possible."

"Well, I know that, dear, but it was a dare. I coud'na back down now, could I?"

"Duncan, you are a poor influence on our children. I am trying to teach them not to take foolish dares."

He shrugged. "I know ye are right. I just need more practice with this child-raising thing. I'll get the right of it. I promise ye."

"I should hope so. Perhaps you will do better with the next one."

"Aye… wait—the next?"

Harriet smiled. "Yes, the next." She patted her midsection with a smile.

"Och, five bairns. They shall be the death o' me."

"Unless we have twins again."

"Six! Nay, 'tis too many bairns we have here."

"Shall I tell the housekeeper we have finally decided to be respectable and sleep in separate rooms? You know she has been hinting at it since the second set of twins."

Thornton wrapped his arms around her and graced her with a Christmas kiss. "Nay. I do believe we shall go for an even dozen."

They walked, hand in hand, into the parlor, which was crawling with children. Some were playing bob for apples, others were playing on the pianoforte and dancing, while still others had paper dolls in one corner and stick horses in another, and they were all talking at once in a happy cacophony of noise.

"Happy Christmas, my love," said Thornton.

"A Merry Christmas to you too."

Author's Note

Although the situation in which Harriet Redgrave found herself when her American ship was attacked by an English frigate may seem far-fetched, it actually has a basis in fact. During the Napoleonic Wars, the Royal Navy routinely turned to impressments, the taking of sailors by force to serve in the navy, in order to man their six-hundred-ship fleet. Press gangs could operate both on land and at sea. By British law, any officer of the Royal Navy could, if the need arose, stop another seagoing vessel and press eligible men into service of the navy. British frigates often stationed themselves outside U.S. harbors in order to search American vessels for contraband or men they considered eligible for impressments. Since Britain did not recognize American naturalized citizenship, they considered anyone of British descent to be fair game for impressments. In 1807, the American frigate, the USS *Chesapeake*, was attacked and boarded by a British warship and four sailors taken as deserters, one later put to death. These incidents outraged Americans and became one of the reasons America declared war on Britain during the war of 1812.

Acknowledgments

I greatly appreciate all the support and encouragement I have received from my family, friends, and other authors who make me feel slightly less crazy. Thanks to my editor, Deb Werksman, and my agent, Barbara Poelle, who encouraged me to go where the story led. A huge debt of gratitude to my beta reader, Laurie Maus, whose insights and edits are invaluable. And of course, to my husband, who picked up the slack so I could follow this dream.

About the Author

Amanda Forester holds a PhD in psychology and worked for many years in academia before discovering that writing historical romance was decidedly more fun. Whether in the rugged Highlands of medieval Scotland or the decadent ballrooms of Regency England, her novels offer fast-paced adventures filled with wit, intrigue, and romance. Amanda lives with her family in the Pacific Northwest. You can visit her at www.amandaforester.com.